GW00391365

Print and e-books books by Wolf.

Non-Fiction

Land of the Sleaze and Home of the Slave

(available now at both Barnes and Noble and Amazon online)

Fiction Series

The Chronicler of Deeds Novels

The Chronicles of Jayden

Volume I	The Gifted
Volume II	Monster and Saviour*
Volume III	Dark Secrets*
Volume IV	Two Hearts*
Volume V	Master of Mayhem**
Volume VI	Orra's Grace**
Volume VII	Blood of the Three**
Volume VIII	Let It Burn**
Volume IX	Theogony**
Volume X	Full Measure of Devotion**

The Brotherhood Chronicles

Volume I	Hatred Grows**

*Currently in re-edit   **In complete manuscript form

Thank you for beginning this journey with me. The original book, The Gifted, was released a decade ago when I was unprepared to bring you this remarkable series of books. I was attempting to tell a story as an old bard. I failed. Since then, a lot has happened in my life, and I have had the opportunity to become a better storyteller.

The Gifted is Volume I in the Dekalogy of The Chronicles of Jayden. However, these books are part of a much larger compendium. I appreciate that I can now republish these Chronicles as part of this much larger family of tales that allow for the telling of the most beautiful story ever told.

I thank you for allowing me this opportunity to bring you a compendium of interconnected stories collectively known as The Chronicler of Deeds Novels. These stories will ignite the passion of love and open your eyes to burning hatred. You will feel the cold pain of loss and suffering in the electrifying euphoria of the one thing we all desire to have…hope.

I want to thank the original publisher, who, sadly, is now out of business. They gave me a chance to bring these Chronicles to printed life. I am forever grateful to them. I also want to thank some extraordinary people who helped me keep these books safe during the darkest days of my life. (read Land of the Sleaze and Home of the Slave for a full accounting of those darkest days.)

There is one that I want to especially thank. You know who you are. You are the one who kept my animals safe and happy during my dark days. I will not embarrass you by putting your name out to the world, but I will for all eternity be in your debt.

I now present to you a story shared with me in the most unique of ways. As recalled from the memories of Sanura, the original Chronicler of Deeds, I present to you, my dear readers, the beginning of hope.

The Chronicles of Jayden

Volume I

The Gifted

A Chronicler of Deeds Novel

By Wolf

Table of Contents

Prologue

Dear Reader,

Allow me the humble honor of being your translator. I am Sanura, a simple historical writer. I try to bring history to life so that the past will not be forgotten, no matter how distant or current.

The original languages of these Chronicles are so harsh to the ear that you could not listen. Each of the various races on Jayden uses a common root language. However, each race's dialect is heavily laced with its own guttural intonations. This makes it challenging to listen to and, at worst, nearly impossible to speak. These Chronicles are a compilation of memories, journals, recordings, and personal interviews. I hope you will read with diligence as the information can save your species, your planet, and your very way of life.

Please do not put this book down. It has been carefully translated into many languages throughout the universe, from a language you would never comprehend without decades of learning. But their life stories must be told. These collective Chronicles of Deeds are also a warning. They tell of beings so despicable, so vile, that all who read these Chronicles will understand the capability of this horrid species. Be forewarned; *THEY* are here. ~ Sanura.

Chapter 1

The Forest

Mari Semineu waited silently in the clearing, pouting at the circumstances. The area was not large, perhaps sixty paces across. The vixen did not want to be here, but sometimes what she wanted was not in the best interest of her fellow Mitdonians. Softly she growled at the role that he had placed her in. It was his fault that the citizens loved her. Being at the forefront of the war was his fault. Again, she softly growled at her predicament. With the casual ease of a veteran of countless battles, the thin female fox turned in a small circle. The long shadow of her five-foot six-inch frame only wavered as she took in the peaceful surroundings. However, she was not sightseeing; her keen senses searched for a very familiar scent. It was his fault she was here.

She sighed the resigned sigh of someone trying to deceive themselves. Zenti Semineu was not to blame for her lot in the escalating war. The war was the war. It had raged in one form or another throughout the entire history of Mitd. *THEY* had always raided the island continent of Mitd. However, Zenti was to blame for her capture and imprisonment. Again, she growled, this time with a hint of anger at the memory of her betrayal at his paws. Kicking the toe of her combat boots into the fresh spouts of spring grass, the vixen debated the wisdom of seeking a meeting with him after thirteen months. Trying to calm her emotions, Mari let the mating band drop from her left paw back into her thigh pocket. Slowly she zipped the opening closed.

With hints of brown and spotted with tufts of

white, her red fur softly glowed in the late afternoon sunlight. Sniffing at the air, Mari attempted to pick up a trace of Zenti Semineu's musk. The vixen's keen senses tuned into the surroundings. The air stood still at her paw pads while the top of the tall tree branches gently fluttered and swayed in the light breeze. Thick limbs of the blossoming grove of hearty trees drooped heavily with an abundance of fresh leaves. Sunlight filtered down into the clearing, bathing her in comforting warmth. Again, she scanned the area searching for the slightest hint of Zenti's musk. Strangely, there was none. Thirteen months ago, he abandoned her; yet she knew the white wolf well. It was unlike her former mate to be late.

If it were not for Zenti Semineu she was meeting, this clearing would be a beautiful spot for a picnic. If you excluded the ever-present danger from the invaders and those that served *THEM*, today was a perfect spring day. *THEM*, what funny name the citizens had concocted. However, it was centuries old. No one knew *THEIR* name or species. With their nearly furless skin, they were not Jaydonian. For a moment, she wondered if *THEY* were also on the continent of U'thar. Half a world away, U'thar was as much a mystery to her as it was to almost all other Mitdonians. Turning her muzzle skyward, she watched as light and shadow danced along the tree line. Azure skies stretched in all directions as clouds dotted the horizon. Subtle hints of new growth brought a sad smile to her muzzle. As if the war were not bad enough, she had to deal with him again. At that thought, the smile faded. The warmth of the sun brought little comfort, knowing she needed her former mate's help.

"What am I doing here? He is not going to listen to me. He never listened to me," Mari softly whined. She kicked at the new grass again, knowing that it was a lie. Her former mate always listened to her, even when the vixen complained. Slipping her left paw back into her pocket, Mari felt the coolness of the golden mating band. They were still mates. She had never found the time to sever their bonds officially. It was a formality, one she intended to complete when the opportunity presented itself.

Pulling a knife out of her thigh sheath, she looked at it silently for a long moment. A heavy sigh escaped her muzzle as she caressed the words etched in the pearl white handle. They were just a lie. "*For Ever And a Day*; how gullible I was back when," whispered the vixen.

Putting the knife back in its sheath, Mari fiddled with the gun's holster flap. Absentmindedly the vixen released the snap. She was restless. Drawing her pistol from its hip holster, she examined it as she held it in her paw. Smiling, she thought how she liked this gun... no, she loved this gun. Countless times, when **THEY** had attacked, it had saved her life. Those bittersweet memories ran through her mind, distracting her from the frustratingly long wait. She wondered just how many more times it would save her life when a twig snapped, breaking her thoughts. Wheeling around, she brought the gun up in a ready-to-fire stance, claw firmly on the trigger. The vixen's digitigrade[1] legs were poised wide in a combat

---

[1] A digitigrade is a form of walking where the life form stands or walks

stance. Her paws were steady as she leveled her favorite gun. Diligently she sniffed the air; there was no trace of his musk.

~   ~   ~   ~

The silver-white wolf stood in the shadows of the fading daylight beneath the cover of the thick-branched trees watching every move the little fox made. Thirteen months had brought small changes to her attitude. She was still a temperamental kit, and it was his fault. Watching her in the sun, a thin smile crossed his muzzle. She was no kit, though she acted like one at times. However, he remembered a time when not only did she excite him, but she stirred a bit of fear with her unpredictable nature. Little he thought, how deceiving that description was. Yes, her height was small, at only five and a half feet tall. Her frame was thin but more muscular than the last time he saw her. However, it was hard to tell through the worn Faction uniform. She wore the blouse and loosely pleated skirt that females in the Factions favored. He noted she had removed all vestiges of her rank or Faction. She could be one of any number of fighters who defended Mitd. However, there was only one Mari Semineu, Miss Mari, to all. She was unmistakably unique among Jaydonians. Of course, he was biased; he still loved her.

Mari Semineu was fast and a bit hotheaded. Recalling their past, a smile crossed Zenti Semineu's scarred muzzle. No, she was a lot hotheaded. Fighting

---

on its digits or toes (the balls of their foot). The "backward" knee is actually an ankle. Many life forms in the universe have digitigrade legs.

with her was like fighting **THEM,** though he knew she could be much more dangerous. He watched as she played with her knife for a moment, finding himself longing for a time lost. She could be so immature for her age, though he had to accept some responsibility for that. He had never denied her anything and, in doing so, had never helped her grow.

She turned her thigh to return the knife to its sheath. A slit in the Faction Fighters pleated skirt allowed access to a pair of mid-thigh shorts she preferred. She had not really changed that much in the past, what, thirteen months or so? Zenti shook his head in disgust at himself for having lost track of time. It was easy to do when fighting a technologically superior invader. The war consumed his life daily. For an unknown reason, the frequency of the invader's raids increased fourfold. Still, watching her fluid movement reminded him that she was a dangerous opponent.

The vixen's fur was as still a soft, ruddy red with tufts of white and brown here and there. Mari's ears twitched back and forth, revealing their black tips with a faint cream color. Her tail slowly swished back and forth in frustration when she was not in control of a situation, like now. The vixen had a kit-like temper that she still had not learned to control. With years of experience from when they were together, Zenti Semineu knew if he did not remain calm, she would be impossible. The sunlight caressed the ruddy red color revealing the glimmering umber of her fur, losing its dull winter tones.

Those ears and tail never stopped twitching. Some

things never change, Zenti thought. That is what kept the vixen and her command alive. Mari was a professional when the moment demanded.

He remembered how he used to stroke those ears for the longest time when she was flustered or hurting. Mari played with the gun like a toy, and he thought that she must have developed one of her kit-like attachments to it. Losing himself in the past for a moment, the silvery-white wolf stepped on a branch, and it snapped. Instantly Mari brought the barrel of her gun up to chest height as she spun to face him some thirty paces away. She had a steady, determined look on her muzzle. Her blinding fast reaction time is why she is dangerous, he thought. Mari Semineu had a kit-like temper with the training of a seasoned warrior.

Looking Mari over, Zenti noted that her clothing choice had not changed much since their last time together. Her plain clothing was utilitarian, though a bit more of the civilian cut than the Faction's military style. Nonetheless, it was attractive.

"You are late," Mari said lightly through scowling eyes as she backed up. She allowed the white wolf into the clearing and maintained the distance from one another. They each matched the other's pace, step for step, as Zenti moved into the clearing. It made her sick with apprehension to see him again. Memories trickled from the recesses of her thoughts. Memories of one of the few times in her life that she had actually cried. It was a time when something in her still loved him.

She reached up and wiped a tear away from her right eye. She felt the shallow row of the long thin scar down her muzzle. The blade that had caused this wound almost cut into her right eye. Had her reflexes been a second slower, the combat knife would have sliced her eye. Instead, it cut through her eyebrow and crossed the length of her muzzle, ending just before the tip of her left nostril. Remnant memories of a night when they had both been foolish enough almost to be killed crept into her thoughts.

"I am not late," the silvery-white wolf said in a low growl, "I just wanted to make sure that this was a conversation and not an execution." Zenti could sense the disgust emanating from her. How Mari could believe he had abandoned her was unfathomable. Yet, here they were, speaking for the first time in thirteen months. That alone attested to the fact she did think he abandoned her.

Zenti Semineu's ears twitched back and forth as if listening for the very voice of the woods around them. The air had become still with a bit of a crisp nip on this fading spring afternoon. It felt too silent, and he thought of calling on his Gift but refrained.

"A peace offering, my dear fox," he said in the subdued tone of one chastised. Zenti let his voice linger as he opened and then slowly extended empty paws to her, showing her he was no threat. She mockingly slapped his paws away, continuing to keep the distance between them.

"I don't know why you came if you think that little of me," Mari Semineu said with a stout glare. Her gun rose, aimed at Zenti's head. Her ears were swiveling, one to face him, the other inspecting every other sound. She also felt it was too silent.

He looked at her with the cold gaze of a male scorned. However, Zenti's heart cried out to Mari. She abandoned him, leaving him to his fate. Yet, she was the one bitter and angry with him for the same perceived offense. Thirteen months had not calmed the vixen's temper at all. Why did it not surprise him that Mari would still be harboring misguided feelings? She had always possessed a quick temper, but she was also mostly level-headed. What had gotten her tail all in a knot?

"My name is Mari. I would expect you to remember; your enemies certainly do," she spat. Her words hateful and angry as the fur on the nape of her neck stood on end. She was not his dear fox.

Mari looked at him with bitter hatred. Focus, she told herself, do not lose control of your temper. Remember that you need his Gift, Mari reminded herself. You need Summoner Zenti Semineu for the war. Keep your anger in check and find out if the rumors are true about him. Those rumors were unbelievable. Zenti was a driven military commander. When it came to tactics, none were his equal.

However, Zenti had never been ruthlessly brutal with his enemies. The rumors of his savage acts over the past thirteen months could not be accurate. Mari knew the one thing Summoner Zenti Semineu loved more than she was Mitd. Her eyes narrowed, and her muzzle clenched at the thought that he might still love her.

"I try not to remember you at all, Mari," the white wolf lied, "and there was a time when me calling you 'dear fox' was not so offensive. Nevertheless, I will give you the point on our enemies. I am just not sure that I am ready to trust you just yet." That, too, was a lie. He trusted her with his very life.

Folding his arms across his chest, Zenti turned slightly away from her, looking the forest over. A gentle breeze picked up, softly kissing his fur. This was not turning out the way he had hoped. He could only guess why she had requested a meeting with him, but he was sure now it was not to listen to what his heart wanted to tell her. Some things do not change, he thought.

Mari snorted slightly and put her gun back into the hip holster. She needed him; no, Mitd needed him. Quickly she gained control of her temper.

"There was also a time that I laid down beside you. Obviously, that was a long time ago if you do not think you can trust me anymore. We need to trust each other, if not for our past, then for a common enemy and our species," Mari replied softly. The vixen crossed her arms before turning her head away from him. She refused to believe he was the monster of the rumors. Still, there was something different about him. He was even leaner than before. Looking at him, she confirmed one rumor; the silvery-white wolf had a multitude of new scars.

Memories of her capture and his abandonment of her flooded Mari's mind as she gazed upon the silvery-white wolf. Thirteen months had done little to quell the anger and hurt rising in the pit of her stomach. A voice in her head warned her to remain calm and not lose her temper. It was a tiny voice easily crushed.

She wanted to scream at him, curse him for being so cold and hateful to her. Her muscles knotted up, and tension hung in the air for what seemed like an eternity before he spoke again. The late-day sun shown down upon the two, and the warmth should have felt welcoming; it did not. Together, yet apart, they stood silently in the clearing wishing the heat of the sun would break the icy wall between them.

"Trust is a two-way path, Mari, one that you seem to tread very lightly with me as well," retorted the wolf, with a bit of sadness in his gruff, deep voice. Not all the scars we bare are on the outside, Zenti thought, looking at the thin, long scar on her muzzle. She still captivated him, and he knew it. Focus, you stupid wolf, he told himself mentally, get control of your feelings; she is not here for your heart. Mari turned back to Zenti, fire in her eyes, her brows coming together as her anger grew. She was on the verge of one of her famous temper tantrums.

"You were the one that left me there; you were the one that betrayed me to **THEM**. Don't you dare talk to me about trust, Zenti Semineu, because I am the one that stayed faithful," Mari growled.

Her tail curled around her, serving as a subconscious barrier between the two of them. At the vixen's raised voice, the birds scattered like light bouncing off the surface of a gently rolling stream. They darted off in all directions at the sound of her guttural growl. Darting in and out of the branches, the squawking birds looked for a safe place to roost.

Mari watched as Zenti slowly turned away from her and knelt down, picking at a blade of grass. He looked to the sky as if there were answers written in the clouds. Kneeling down stretched and separated the fur along his spine. The act exposed a scar that ran from the base of his skull to just above his hips. The vixen looked at the scar; it was two digits[2] wide and had formed a deep-knotted thick mound of furless flesh. Had he not been stretching, she was sure the fur would have covered it. She would need to be much closer to observe it otherwise. He was bare-chested, which was unlike him. In fact, she finally noticed that he wore nothing more than his favorite shorts. The unique design was loose-fitting. The shorts gave the appearance that he wore nothing more than a loincloth. She knew it was for the ease of movement.

"I guess you could call what happened 'betrayal,'" he said as he stood up and walked to the edge of the woods. "Perhaps this meeting was a mistake, one best remedied from a distance. I have an enemy to hunt, and the day is not getting any longer. I will leave you now."

She watched him go, noting that his sharp dress and

---

[2] Jaydonians do not call their digits fingers. Though they share similarities to human fingers, the range of motion that Jaydonian digits have is far greater than most other species in the universe. Also, all Jaydonians have retractable claws. Several species in the universe share this trait as well.

military manners had become but a memory. However, the finality in his voice had not changed. This conversation was over, and nothing she said would change his mind. Once Summoner Zenti Semineu made up his mind, nothing changed it. As he turned, she saw the leather belt with a few pouches attached hanging at his waist. It was beneath the flaps of the loincloth. She thought she saw a hunting knife tucked neatly away. He hated paw weapons, preferring unarmed combat or long guns. His fur was thicker than when she last saw him thirteen months ago; still, he kept it well. She watched as he stepped to the edge of the woods. His fur appeared to have a deeper silver tint than the white she remembered. It was not the graying silver of age but the color of silver metal.

Slowly Mari Semineu shook her head. Zenti was still handsome even though his body was lean, almost to the point of being gaunt, though toned. He had never been as large as the other wolves she knew. At only five and three-quarter feet in tall, he was only average in height. However, the vixen also knew that he did not need muscle mass that others relied upon for strength. He was a Summoner, a powerful Gifted. He was also a brilliant tactician. The best Unconventional Warfare Commander that graced Jayden had trained Zenti. Formerly graced Jayden, she thought. Her father, General Haverick Waxton, was dead, killed by *THEM.*

No, Zenti Semineu seemed much different, harder as if his body were hiding something. Still, he was handsome, she thought. Mari also thought she detected a few new facial scars, but it was not clear from this distance. It was hard to look at him and not remember what had been.

Running her fingers over the gun at her thigh, she watched him walk away. Her quick temper flashed.

"You always talked when you trained in my father's camp. You always made grand battle plans. You were a leader that everyone willingly followed because you were successful. Now I hear all you do is run!" she shouted in an angry growl. How could he walk away; she needed his talents and skill.

Quick as a flash, Mari drew the knife and threw it in his direction. As if guided, the tailored blade did not tumble through the air; it glided. Zenti had commissioned it as a gift for their first anniversary. You threw it side-armed or under pawed. He felt the knife speeding towards him through his Gift heightened senses more than he heard it. It lodged in the tree level with his head, vibrating briefly.

"I am one thing that you will never be able to run away from," Mari screamed. "I will chase you to the very pits of despair and back so that you will never forget the betrayal you have committed! There was a time I would have walked through the fires of Orra's wrath for you. I would have gladly given my life for you but you... you... you betraying coward!" The vixen stuttered in frustration, throwing her paws into the air and walking to the other side of the clearing. Deep in the recesses of her mind, the vixen acknowledged she had lost her temper when she should have swallowed her anger. However, knowing that did not sate her rage at his betrayal.

She pulled out her revolver and shot a hole through a

patch of trees, allowing her anger to explode with the round's expenditure. Again, the sound of beating wings erupted in the early evening air at her outburst as the sound of the gunshot rang out and faded.

"This was a mistake," Mari said softly. "Zenti will not hunt with me anymore. Mitd needs him, and I blew it."

A thread of sadness wove, barely visible through her voice as she stood there, holding herself. Her arms wrapped around her shoulders, the gun dangling in one paw as the vixen glared at the thicket. The leaves drifted to the ground like her hopes. She wrapped her tail around her legs while the tip twitched rapidly. This was a horrible idea. Why did she ever think Zenti would help, the coward that he was? All of those rumors of him not fighting with a faction must be true. What had changed this once strong leader into such a coward?

The silvery-white wolf stopped at the tree line and looked at the blade still quivering in the tree's bark. Zenti shook his head at her kit-like attitude. The gunshot's echo faded as the woods returned to their normal, tranquil state. It was too quiet and lacked all the scents that it should. However, his thoughts were too clouded to think clearly about what those deficiencies meant. Stopping in the shade of the tree, Zenti stood for a moment, trying to focus on the task at paw. Why did Mari want to meet with him if she did not want him back into her life? Perhaps it was curiosity; maybe it was because she needed his skills. Rolling his head back, looking to the treetops, he sighed heavily. He began to speak without turning around, allowing his Gift to carry his voice to her alone.

"Talk; yes, Mari, I now talk a lot when I am around others. Even now, being near others is a rare occasion. I prefer to hunt in solitude. In the time of our absence from each other, I have begun to talk a lot more, though no one listens. However, you know my temper and wrath. I would as soon burn a whole village to the ground to get one or two of," Zenti paused as he almost uttered the invader's species' name. Cautiously he continued. "I would simply hunt *THEM* as individuals. There was a time when my rage and anger worried you. My wrath scared you for the sake of the others who followed me. Why seek me out now?"

He grasped the knife from the tree and pulled it free. Looking at the iridescent pearl white pommel, he remembered the day he had the etching engraved into it. That it was still intact made him wonder. *For Ever And a Day,* it read. He had promised those words to her on their mating day. He had them etched into the pommel so that she would always have them to remember that promise. He turned to face her. She was watching him as always.

Forever, Zenti thought, his heart aching at the memory and loss. Mari deserved to know the truth, but the truth would alter her forever. She was not ready for it. Perhaps she would never be. That realization meant the doom of Jayden. Closing his eyes, he wrapped the knife in the presence of his Gift and felt it leave his paws. Through Gifted sight, he watched as Mari looked away.

"When I was your second in command, our soldiers listened to me talk about the detailed plans I made. They listened to me impart some of your father's teachings and wisdom to them. I talked and tried to encourage diplomacy, reason, and levelheaded thinking as opposed to fighting. That is what a good leader does. You have not forgotten your father's teachings, have you? However, things have changed. I have changed; I am no leader of rational thinkers. I simply act alone now. And whether or not you choose to believe, I still serve the King and our species," Zenti said, taking a deep, exhausted breath, trying to ease the frustration that was inside. "And I still serve you."

Anger was building within him, a rage she did not need to see. He heard her sweet voice carry across the distance between them, knowing the few paces was but a small paw step in the ever-widening ocean separating them.

"The time for reason and diplomacy has not passed. The only difference is that now I am not foolish enough to believe I am the reason you do not fight with our forces," Mari said. The vixen held up her paw and waited for the knife to return to her. She never failed to marvel at the control Zenti displayed over his Gift.

The Gift was just that, a gift from Orra, the Creator Mother of life. To a few, Orra's chosen, she blessed with the Gift. The Gift was the Summoner's power and control over the elements. The Gift was a Shaman's ability to heal or an Oracle's Visions of the future. Few could ever master their Gift; Zenti was not one of those few. He was a Summoner of great power with many Talents. Those Talents, facets of his Gift, had saved countless Mitdonians from death at the invader's paws if that is what they called them. Honestly, Mari did not care about the invaders as long as they died. She needed Zenti to hunt and kill the invaders alongside her Faction.

Slowly the knife drifted across the clearing to her. The blade glistened in the late day sun as it came to a stop in front of her. The blade hovered there, waiting for Mari to pluck it from the air. Zenti drew a deep breath and slowly exhaled again, allowing a little of the frustration, fatigue, and anguish to escape his body, leaving him emotionally drained. Controlling his anger was becoming more and more difficult. He feared it would overcome his iron will, and he would give in to his rage. When his iron-will finally failed, all of Jayden would suffer.

"No, my vixen, I do fight. What you hear of my talk is what I project to others. I do not fight with anyone by my side because" Zenti's words became heavy and labored as they drifted off. He looked down at his paws, staring deep into the palms as if looking for an answer. A silence filled the air, and even the breeze rustling through the leaves seemed to die down.

Taking the knife from its hovering place, Mari looked directly at Zenti. He seemed so lost. Never had she known that look of despair on his muzzle in all the years. What could have transpired that would have caused him to waver? Mari knew why she had never assigned a second in command, why she had never let someone take Zenti's place. He was the dangerous sort, the kind that made things happen. His plans worked, and his soldiers lived. No one could replace that kind of military skill and leadership. Why did it seem to waver now?

Mari had done well in his absence, thanks to her father's training. Zenti had done better, and he did it alone. Why was it now no one wanted to follow him? His own Faction would not fight beside him, yet he had to be the one planning all of their raids. Was it by choice, or had Zenti order his Faction to fight without him. No other Faction had been that successful. So why did they call him a monster? All she had were rumors about why, but no monster stood before her, a betrayer, yes, but not a monster. How could any of the tales be true with someone so apparently lost?

However, the wolf standing before her was not the nightmare that everyone had claimed he was. Zenti was just a coward who could not even talk to her. Deep inside, an emotion stirred, one she had been trying to destroy for a year now. He betrayed her, which was unforgivable; that helped Mari quickly suppress that lost feeling of love.

However, if the rumors were true, her species needed him. Before she could fight beside him, she had to put the hatred aside. There was an enormous hurt between them that would not be overcome easily, if ever. Mari did not want Zenti back in her life again after his betrayal. The vixen also did not intend to die anytime soon by fighting beside him if the rumors were true. She shook her head in a futile attempt to shake those thoughts away as she tucked her knife back into its place at her thigh.

The sun began to kiss the top of the trees on its trek into the evening sky, casting dancing shadows on the ground. The winds brushed by her fur gently as she watched the fading light embrace him. He stood silently facing the forest. In the dimming rays, the silvery-white wolf looked like a ghost, literally and figuratively. Zenti ears flattened in frustration.

Looking away, Mari sighed at the open sky and let the stress flee her body. This had to be one of the most intense meetings she had ever had. It was pressing on her. As she looked back up to Zenti, she saw perhaps for the first time in him a depth of horror on his muzzle: a look that said, 'I have committed the sins of a lifetime, and there are more to come.'

She had seen that look before when she was a young kit. When her father and mother were arguing one evening. They had sent her to bed, and she had snuck back out when the arguing started. Her mother was growling at her dad. Her father refused to talk about the mission he had just completed. Her mother was chewing her father out when he raised a paw to quiet her for a moment; it was then that she saw the same look she now saw on Zenti's muzzle. Her father was a great military leader. Mari knew the sins her father had committed during the war weighed heavily on his heart until the day **THEY** stilled it.

When Zenti looked back at her, she saw a fire and hatred within him she had never seen before. There was sadness yet raging determination that reminded her of years past. Those were stressful times when she feared what Zenti's rage would drive him to do. This brutal and senseless war began to take the calm reasoning of a good commander from him. However, he always seemed to retain control, never letting the war cloud his judgment. Now she was not sure that Zenti was still in control.

Something felt wrong when she looked at him. He looked lost. Something inside her shifted, and memories of their past seemingly took control of her.

"Zenti?" Mari's voice was soft, like it had been before, back when they had been close enough to know what worried and stressed the other. The vixen paced back towards him a few steps. Her steps were slow and calculated. She positioned herself so she could run if he did lose control, and the rumors were true.

"Come here," she commanded him just as she had done in the past when things had become tense between them. To her surprise, Zenti obeyed as he had done for the past nine years they were together. He walked towards her near the center of the clearing. Zenti detested yelling, preferring a soft growl to quell a potentially explosive situation. She had not mastered that habit; neither had her mother. In that respect, Zenti was like her father. Both detested shouting matches.

As he approached, the silver in his fur did look like metal. She could see more of the rumored scars. They were numerous, far more than she remembered. There was something different about his stride as if he was hesitant. That was also unlike him. The Zenti she remembered was confident yet moderately humble. He exuded an air of command without demanding respect due to a commander.

Reaching out, she touched the side of his muzzle, and she felt a roughness he did not have before he abandoned her. Then it hit her. He had no scent; he must be using a descenter. However, even that did not accurately describe the lack of his scent. Zenti felt warmer to the touch than he should.

"Yes, Mari?" He did not look up to her nor react to her touch. His voice trembled. He was straining to control his emotions, and for an instant, she hesitated. Something was decidedly wrong with a male who never hesitated.

Bringing her other paw under his chin, she forced him to look at her. His eyes blazed a brilliant, fire-hot white. He was holding on to his Gift. She opened her mouth to speak when a sound of branches rustling behind her snapped her back into the veteran soldier she was. Had Zenti betrayed her again? Turning, she pulled her gun when an echoing crack of a pistol's report broke the silence.

The gun flew out of the vixen's paw and landed some feet away as soldiers circled around them. Pain shot through her paw from the impact. It must be a rubber bullet as a welt began to form. Her heart flew to her throat. Were the soldiers here to capture her. Zenti had betrayed her again. She fought to force the thought down and focus on the situation before her as she rubbed her sore paw. There was two squads' worth of soldiers surrounding them, weapons drawn. Zenti's deep, low growl gave her pause. She knew him well; he was angry and surprised by the soldier's arrival. He was not involved, or he was acting for her benefit. This was unlike him.

"Down on your knees, now," barked a lanky hyena! The hyena wore the uniform of the King's Military Special Forces. What were they doing here, and why were they openly hostile towards them, Mari wondered?

The soldiers were at the edge of the clearing. The hyena leading the advance slowly approached the two of them. Mari looked at the uniform the hyena wore. There was no doubt he was one of the Crown's soldiers. This was confusing; why would the Crown want to arrest Zenti or her? Had the King issued directives that she was not made aware of?

From behind her, Zenti's angry howl flooded her memories, and the fur on the back of her neck stood on end. For a brief moment, she felt the air become as hot as a funeral pyre. Closing her eyes to the light and heat, she dropped to the ground and huddled safely beside Zenti's paw pads. It lasted only a few seconds, but in that time, it became hard to breathe as the air began to thin around her. Slowly the heat died away, and she dared to open her watering eyes. Thick stinging smoke rose from the ground. Her sight was hazy, and her eyes stung from the smoldering ground. The soil around her was melted into shards of black rock. The crackling of burning wood filled the air surrounding her with the sounds of hissing and popping.

Wiping away the tears, the vixen's vision cleared, and she could see the soldiers' smoking corpses, the charred ground, and smoldering trees around the clearing's edge. Many of the trees were scorched, while some resembled the white-hot coals of a fireplace. Looking around, she saw the forty dead soldiers lying on the ground. Some were charred as if meat cooked too long over an open fire. Most were dismembered, literally sundered limbs from the torso. The smoke hung in the still air as the clothing on the bodies smoldered. A glowing ember flared out here and there, with the stench of burning fur filling the air.

Immediately she turned back to look up at Zenti. Her eyes widened as she scurried away from him, tripping over the shattered body of the hyena, falling to it like a lover to a bed. The stench curled in her nose and nearly made her sick. It was one thing that she had never grown used to as she leaped away from the dead soldier. Zenti's Gift controlled the element of fire. However, what she witnessed here was a new expansion of his Gift.

Mari drew her knife, now believing that she was in real danger, as his face did not hide the extreme rage that must be consuming him from within. He could kill her if he wanted to. It was not that she had not already known this, but this was a different power. This was something that he had not possessed before. He had never been able to kill so many, so fast, destroying so much of the surrounding area in just one action.

Thoughts raced through her mind trying to recall when he had ever been able to do this much damage at one time, but nothing she had ever seen was like this. Before, it had been in the midst of a rage-induced battle, and even then, it was never to this scope and scale. This was something completely new. His Gift only had a range of a few feet. This was nearly two hundred feet in diameter. Blood dripped from the tip of his nose, a telltale sign that a Gifted was using their Gift. The use of the Gift caused the Gifted to bleed from their pores. Most bled around the nose and gums. She noted that Zenti was also bleeding from the corner of his eyes.

Rumors of Summoner Zenti Semimeu's battles over the past thirteen months could be true. The horrors that other soldiers had told of Zenti were no longer unimaginable. The nightmarish stories that her patrons told of Zenti's powers, shared around the campfire, raced through Mari's mind. Maybe not all of the rumors she had been hearing were as farfetched as they sounded. The vixen's mind raced for any explanation, finding only one.

"You went to her, didn't you," Mari said in an accusing tone?

She started to open her muzzle to continue when she noticed he was rubbing his temples the way he did when he was becoming exasperated. She thought better of saying anything for a moment, but her temper got the better of her.

"You bastard! How many souls did it require to gain the Oracle of Breest's favor? How many Mitdonians did it take before she would take you in? How many innocent citizens did you have to turn over to her? She isn't one to give her Gift for free," Mari screamed!

Everyone knew to gain the Oracle of Breest's favor, the price would be high. Zenti knew of only one Oracle powerful enough to see his future. She remembered the stories from those who had sought the Oracle of Breest out. Mari cursed under her breath because this particular Oracle would demand an exceedingly high price. Of all the Gifted, the Oracle of Breest demanded payment for the use of her Gift. Though other Gifted accepted tokens of gratitude, the mysterious Oracle of Breest Isle was a foul witch. How could Zenti have sought her out? What was the price he agreed to pay for her services?

The Oracle of Breest was a mysterious, shape-shifting creature that no one, except two, knew anything about. Neither spoke of the Oracle of Breest, except in disparaging tones. However, no one doubted the raw power she wielded. Her master of the Gift was legendary. She was rumored to have lived for thousands of years. However, in hushed circles, she was called the Bitch of Breest. Mari stared with hate-filled eyes at Zenti. He was staring at his paws with the look of a lost pup. Tilting his head back, she could see even more scars.

Again, Zenti looked at his paws then returned to rubbing his temples. He was growing tired of explaining himself and tired of the accusations of horrors for his personal gain. He thought this vixen would understand him and the motives for his actions. Shaking his head in disbelief, he sighed in regret of coming here to meet with her. Mari had not grown up in the past thirteen months, and her accusations were wearing on his last nerve. Closing his eyes, Zenti struggled to maintain what little control he had left.

"The price I have paid, some say, is too high, but in the end, it is me who will pay the ultimate price. This is why I talk to others, why I don't fight beside them," Zenti said, waving a paw at the destruction surrounding them.

The silvery-white wolf sank to the ground on his knees, exhausted. While long minutes passed, neither said

a word. Mari quietly knelt down and sat back on her tail.
She may be furious with him, but she knew him all too
well. He was on the verge of breaking. Looking around,
she swallowed hard at the sheer intensity of destruction.
Summoner Zenti Semineu might very well be the threat
that causes the King to send the Royal Assassin to
terminate him.

Mari watched as Zenti slowly rose to his paw pads
and counted the dead, thirty-nine in all. They were not
THEM. Searching the remains, he determined these
soldiers were not crown soldiers. However, there were
enough bits of invader technology to conclude these
soldiers were servants loyal to the invaders. Zenti's jaw
clenched at the realization that the invaders were recruiting
Crown Troops to fight. It was logical that **THEY** would
recruit from within the Mitd citizenry considering the
limited number of invaders.

An Island Monarchy, Mitd was divided into
Baronies. Each Baron had a free paw in their local
government yet paid homage and fidelity to the Crown. In
return, the Crown maintained a vast network of roads,
communications, and other civic duties.

The Baronies showed division on how to handle the
invaders. Several wanted to welcome the invaders. Their
logic was flawed. The Barons believed they could reason
with the invaders and offer a servitude level that would
placate **THEM.** They were misguided, yet the King
tolerated their position. The elder King would say it was
their choice. The freedom of choice made the Mitdonians
citizens free. However, Zenti was of a different opinion.

The King had acknowledged that difference of opinion. The Crown allowed Zenti a free paw in dealing with the invaders and those who chose to support them.

Mari watched in silence as the silver-white wolf methodically searched the dead. What was he looking for? Zenti was thorough in everything he did. Her father had instilled the skill of being meticulous in him while at the academy. She recalled the young male wolf when he first arrived.

He was seven, just four years from his Coming-of-Age date. Mari's heart ached at that memory; the invaders had slaughtered Zenti's family while they searched for him. Somehow, **THEY** knew Zenti Semineu was Gifted. He was five when that life-altering attack happened. That day was his Gifting day, the day a Jaydonian passed from being a kit or pup and began the six-year journey to become an adult.

Unlike the invader's pups, if that is what they were called, Jaydonian aged considerably faster. From observations, a Jaydonian reaching their Coming-of-Age date, at eleven years old, was the equivalent of a twenty-year-old invader. Of course, that was just a distant observation. No one had captured a living invader in recorded history. The technology the invaders possessed made it hard to capture or kill one. That changed when Zenti began using his Gift to hunt them.

When Zenti arrived to study Unconventional Warfare from her father, many scoffed. A seven-year-old was considered too young, even by Jaydonian standards.

Mari's father announced the young white wolf as Summoner Zenti Semineu, a Northwest Faction member of two years. That proclamation silenced everyone.

The Northwest Faction had become the most successful and brutal of the Factions. The Factions had grown from each of the Baron's militias formed centuries ago. Within a year of her father's tutelage, many considered Zenti, the foremost unconventional Warfare student. To many, it seemed as if his Gift fueled his learning. Mari watched intently as her former mate perform his duty with cold neutrality. Zenti was searching for something, and she wanted to know what it was.

The bodies littered the once beautiful clearing. Mari picked up the shards of black soil, now charred. It would take a long time before anything would grow here again, she decided as the black glass-like chips fell out of her open paw. Mari watched intently as Zenti walked about the dead and dismembered. Something caught his attention. She noticed one soldier on the outermost of the circle hung to life by a thread, a Timerian by the looks of him. The look on Zenti's face grew even colder and decidedly harder. She could understand why. A Timerian traitor was unheard of.

The Timerian breed of Jaydonian felines was fierce tiger warriors from the mountain region in Mitd's main island. As Zenti looked down up the dying Timerian, she wondered why a tribal warrior breed, who was fiercely loyal to the Crown, would want to serve *THEM*? She knew Zenti well enough to know what he was contemplating. He also wondered why the royal army was hunting the two of them. There was something not right here, but the vixen could see that Zenti's anger was clouding the clarity of his thoughts. The stress and exhaustion of the war were beginning to take their toll on the silvery-white wolf. Mari could see and feel the reason that Zenti's self-control was slipping from his grasp.

The vixen glared at him as Zenti counted the dead and knew what he meant by 'ultimate price.' She hated that it sent a little ache down into her heart. She wanted to continue hating him for abandoning her. Still, the fatigue on his muzzle told her he had paid the price already. Her father had told her mother once that the soldier's duty was to pay any price to ensure the Crown's safety. Zenti would die for Jayden, for her. That thought cooled the fire burning within her.

"I am assuming that you went to my sister," Mari finally said. She hoped that by acknowledging that perhaps Zenti had not visited the Oracle of Breest, it might help shift his souring mood. Her sister Rini Waxton was almost six years younger. She was also a Gifted Oracle. The young lioness was well respected in the Royal Circle, especially with the Queen. Mari's sister hated Zenti, blaming him for the death of their parents. However, if the Crown commanded Rini, the Royal Oracle, to assist Zenti, she would have.

Zenti tensed for a moment and then relaxed. Mari knew he saw through her pretense of shifting the subject from the Oracle of Breest to her sister. That he could see through her facade of an apology only irritated the vixen, and she snapped out at him again.

"Since it was Rini you went to and not the Oracle of Breest, I won't be able to get you out of whatever bargain you struck. Whom did you get to intercede for you? It must have been the King," Mari said while her heart climbed again to her throat. The King, for some unknown reason, seemed to favor Zenti above all others.

Mari's voice cracked with emotion for a second. She and her sister Rini had not spoken civilly since the date of her and Zenti's mating day. Why did she say, Rini? Why could she not have said another Oracles name? In the recesses of her mind, she knew why. Thirteen months of bottling up her emotions about being abandoned, the loss of her family a decade ago, and her only sibling rejecting her finally came crashing down. She lashed out at Zenti, though she knew he was not the cause of the rift between Rini and her. Still, the anger boiled out, and she let it all flow out at him.

"How stupid can you be? I told you! I told you! Orra, damn you, how can you be so stupid," Mari screamed? In an anger-driven fit, the vixen then stabbed the knife into the closest body, kicking another one as she took out her frustration.

Zenti watched as Mari threw another temper tantrum. Some things might not ever change, he thought. However, Zenti suspected Mari desperately needed this release. He always allowed her to vent, even though he hated the screaming. Within him, he found the wellspring that fed his iron will. Like cold well water, a peaceful wave washed over the white wolf, cooling the raging fire within. As always, Mari's tantrum quickly faded, leaving the vixen mentally spent.

"It has been a long time, Mari. I have met many on my travels," Zenti began, "It is not your sister; she hates me as much as you do. No, my fox, it is not her, but another, and how can I be so stupid?"

He stood up from the dying Timerian, turned, and walked to where she stood kicking the dead. He looked down at her face, waiting for her to let the pent-up anger out. No, she had not resolved her kit-like temperament.

Turning to face him, Mari had no regret in slapping him across his muzzle. Her hurt was showing, and she knew it, but there was no way to hide it right now. The vixen slapped Zenti again. She glared up at him, white-hot tears streaking down her shallow cheeks. She tried to deny them but could not stop crying, no matter how hard she tried.

"You were born stupid," Mari hissed.

He did not flinch away from her blows, nor did he try to stop them. The price he knew was high indeed. He saw the tears in her beautiful green eyes and remembered how she looked before the scar. She was still as magnificent as she was when he first met her. She was shaking, and he knew from their past that her anger was leaving her, and reason would soon return. Breathing in deeply, he held it a moment and then exhaled, letting a touch of his anger flee as well. Hesitating a moment, he looked at her, deciding what his next action would be.

Zenti reached out a clawed paw to Mari's muzzle. Only then did the vixen notice that his claws were no longer the ivory white they once used to be but were now an onyx black. He touched her with one powerful claw and ever so gently traced the long scar all the way down her muzzle. In that brief contact, she felt his Gift unlike she had ever felt it in the nine years they had known each other. Before, it had been like warm sand on her paw pads; now, it felt like a raging fire. It did not hurt her, but it radiated throughout her whole body. Again, fear crept into the back of her mind.

"No, Mari, not born stupid, but made stupid by the pain and hurt of my failure to save you from what *THEY* caused you to suffer through. It is when I failed that I cried to Orra for the ability to avenge you. When the chance came, no price was too high," Zenti said softly, looking deep in those beautiful green eyes.

"Zenti, I was not dead; vengeance was never needed," Mari said and pulled away to get her gun. The vixen's body still shivering as she moved. Jayden needs him, do not let your temper get the better of you, she told herself.

Zenti noticed another scar, one that led up her right thigh. It was nearly hidden on the outside of her leg, half under the thigh holster that held her knife.

A moan came from the Timerian to which Zenti turned away from Mari and coldly strolled over to the near-death tiger. Reaching in a pouch at his side, he pulled out a small, golden orb with a ruby set in one end. Kneeling, he put the sphere to the chest of the tiger, and it briefly glowed. The tiger violently lurched about and screamed in incredible pain briefly before becoming limp.

Mari watched in fascinated horror; Zenti had never tortured a captive. The wounded received treatment with respect and temperance. That was the Mitdonians way. There were the rare occasions that a captured enemy was treated with disdain, but that was not the way of the Zenti she remembered. Only one Mitdonian tortured an enemy. The Royal Assassin was the bane of all criminals, which she suspected was why crime against the Crown was rare. She watched as the small ruby pulsed. She had never witnessed a small item cause so much suffering. What was that device, that ruby with a little golden orb attached? The Timerian ceased to spasm and quickly expired. She did not understand. The tiger's wounds were terminal and should have killed him instantly. What was it that Zenti had done? Mari looked at him quizzically.

"You should leave now; his screams will have attracted more soldiers. That is if there are more," Zenti said.

Standing up, he turned to Mari and saw the confused, shocked look on her muzzle. He had never been cruel, but he could tell by the look on her muzzle, the brutal act he just committed turned her stomach. Mari's expression said she understood killing in the time of war was part of the war. Nevertheless, she believed what he had done was not a mercy killing; it was murder. That look should have concerned him, but he no longer cared what people thought of his acts. The war will end one way or the other. Lifting his nose higher, he sniffed the surrounding air for any new scent. Filtering out the burnt smell of flesh and fur was an easy task for him now.

"I have more hunting to do, and what better to aid me in attracting more soldiers than the cry of a wounded comrade? The rumors of my cruelty are not exaggerated. I have no mercy for our kind who helps **THEM**," he said and smiled a sad but wicked smile. Zenti noted Mari's shock and horror out of the corner of his eyes. The white wolf returned the orb to his pouch.

So, it was going to start; Mari would now believe all of the stories he had allowed to escape. Either it would make her hard, or it would seal the fate of Jayden. Jayden needed Mari Semineu to be hard. He did not need the Gift of an Oracle to know that Mari was the one that must collect the ultimate price he willingly would pay.

Walking toward the edge of the now smoldering tree line, Zenti spoke in a subdued tone that still resonated across the now silent battlefield without looking back at her. It reminded the vixen how he used to do on her father's military camp training grounds. His voice seemed to silence every sound. She knew it was an effect of his Gift. Zenti could do so many things with his Gift that other Gifted could only dream of doing.

"When I finally recovered from the wounds on my back, it was months after you and I had been attacked at the lake," he drew a heavy breath as sorrow filled his voice, "I was told you had died. It was then that I cried to the

Heavens and the Hells for a touch of Orra's rage and vengeance. That day the Zenti you knew died. It was at that very moment the monster you have heard so much about was raised."

Quietly he stepped into the forest, leaving the dead to the birds as the first stars of this spring twilight began to emerge from a blackening evening sky. The finality in the voice of Summoner Zenti Semineu, the vixen's former mate, held no room for discussion. His mind was made up, and only Orra about could unmake it. She shuddered at the thought of what his newly expanded Gift might be capable of accomplishing. Looking around the decimated clearing, with the dead still smoldering, she corrected her choice of words. It was not what his Gift might achieve, but the certainty of the destruction that her former mate would inflict upon all of Jayden. Zenti seemingly vanished within the stream of smoke that slowly wafted skyward.

~   ~   ~   ~

"You bastard," Mari whispered after him before covering her muzzle with both her paws. The vixen turned to leave the once beautiful clearing. However, Mari Semineu did not run from the charred battlefield; she meandered in a mindless stupor. Looking up, she noted the day was fleeing into the arms of night's dusk.

Occasionally looking to the stars, Mari felt that the evening air had grown colder. Aimlessly the vixen wandered throughout the woods that lead to her camp five miles away. She did not notice the walk or her surroundings. Her mind was lost in the acts of a Summoner about to lose control. The Gifted was to Jayden what air was to breathing. A Gifted that lost control was as devastating as suffocating.

Mari barely noticed the dusk of daylight give way to the loving embrace of night. Spring was a marvelous time on Mitd. The promise of life beginning again gave all those who were war-weary hope. Mitd was a war-weary land. Yet the citizens supported her Faction more than they supported any other. Was it because Zenti, as a powerful Gifted, was still her mate? Mari regretted losing her temper; Jayden needed Summoner Zenti Semineu. However, the Zenti she saw today was a Summoner about to lose control.

That was the greatest fear of a Gifted. The price of touching the Void was indeed extreme. The Void was the name the Gifted gave to the power of Orra. The Mother of all Life was an endless wellspring of cosmic energy, according to a Gifted. She did not fully understand the Gift. However, spending all the years in the presence of Zenti at her father's training camp had given her a brief understanding. Having lived with Zenti for nine years, Mari understood more. Her sister Rini was a developing Gifted Oracle. Though they had not spoken as family, she still loved her sister. Rini was an arrogant flake. But then again, those who touched the Void in seeing another's future tended to be flaky. That was a woefully inadequate description as the non-Gifted could never grasp the sheer chaos of the Void. However, Mari could only imagine what touching the face of Orra could do to someone's mind.

The vixen paused and looked over her shoulder. Her heart pounded in her chest at the thought of the price Zenti would pay. The vixen hated that feeling because she wanted Zenti out of her life. As she looked back at the darkness of the woods, she felt confused. What was Zenti becoming? Was he what Jayden needed? Why was the Crown sending Special Forces after him? Would the Crown's Royal Assassin be next to hunt Zenti? That foul enforcer of the King's will was as much feared as loved by the citizens. The looming yet unspoken threat of what that cruel enforcer had done to the enemies of the Crown was legendary. No matter the monarch, the Royal Assassin's paw work invoked obedience to the Crown's primary law. Treat others with the same respect you wanted for yourself.

Though other Gifted served Jayden, none possessed the power and military ability like Zenti, except perhaps the beloved Gifted Shaman Torit. The elder buzzard was as much a mystery as the Oracle of Breest. Torit was decidedly more friendly and accessible. However, the Zenti she saw today displayed a power that bordered on frightening. Taking a deep breath, she held it as she tried to regain her focus.

"Sometimes, Mari Semineu, you are a spoiled brat," the vixen whispered to herself. At the sound of her mated name, she snorted in disgust that she would address herself in the same breath as Zenti. Growling at her reminiscing, she returned to her homeward trek. Looking up to the stars, Mari looked for one in particular that would guide her relatively close to her Faction's main camp.

In the distant night, faded echoes of sporadic shots rang out. Mari paused but could not discern where they came from. Looking at her watch, she realized she had traveled only a mile or so in the past hour. She picked up the pace, deciding the sporadic gunfire was someone target practicing. It could not be a battle as there was no rapid echo of machinegun fire.

The walk was peaceful as she approached her Faction's outer rim camps. The guards were there; she knew it. However, they were not visible. One lone, run-down travel trailer seemingly sat abandoned near a stand of trees. It was a lure to attract the attention of anyone searching for easy victims. There were too many raiders that needed an attitude adjustment.

Her main camp was a little under two miles away. Apparently aimless in her movement, the vixen approached the abandoned travel trailer, then veered off suddenly and approached a clear patch of scrub-covered forest. Weaving her way around clumps of brush and undergrowth, the vixen suddenly stopped.

"Private Harmis, you will join the roaming patrol when they return this way in half an hour. You will then join the main camp supply detail until you learn to properly mask your rut musk. I picked you scent nearly forty paces back," said Mari as she stood in the rough patch of scrub.

"Yes, Miss Mari," replied an incorporeal voice at her booted paw pads.

"Good Private Harmis. You might want to avoid a certain female raccoon working in the laundry detail. She is in a bad state of heat, and you seem fond of frequently visiting her. Perhaps I should transfer her to another camp," mused Mari. The vixen suppressed a smile. Private Harmis and Penip Meresa were nearly inseparable, though neither had acted on their relationship's carnal nature.

"I would consider it a favor if you did not. Peni and I have been talking," came the unseen hound's reply. Mari again suppressed a smile. Even amidst a brutal war, love did find a way to bloom. Something tugged at her heart, a memory of Zenti and her a decade ago. Mari batted the memory away.

"I will have a female-to-female talk with her later. Do learn to mask your rut musk. It is rather, um, powerful," answered Mari before continuing on. She could not afford to have a Jaydonian supporter of the invaders tracking her scout's locations. Too many had died because of those traitors.

The vixen eased through the scout post and continued to ponder what she could do to try and establish another meeting with Zenti. Though the Crown forbid

Factions from working together against a single Barony, the rules for a combined Faction operation were vague. If the Northwest Faction would assist her Faction, they could sweep this region of traitors. However, she could not stop her mind from circling back to wanting to talk with Zenti again on a more personal level.

What if Zenti was just as much a victim as she was in their capture all those months ago. If he thought she was dead, then he would not have looked for her. The invaders collected certain Jaydonians for experimentation. *THEIR* purpose was all conjecture as no one had ever escaped once captured. Only the mutilated bodies of those Jaydonians gave a partial clue as to the invader's intentions. *THEY* were ruthlessly brutal.

The vixen's pace slowed. Mari never considered that Zenti might be a victim as well. However, that gave him no excuse to not contact her when he learned she was alive. The war between her heart and mind began again. It was ever-churning, and by the time she returned to her Faction's main camp, the vixen was in a foul mood.

Guards greeted Mari first but quickly withdrew at the first hints of her foul mood. Though they were rare, they were explosively violent. However, as she approached the inner camp, the sound of pups playing and the mundane work of everyday life temporarily lifted the vixen's spirits. These were her patrons, and they put their trust in her military decisions. The main camp housed nonmilitary personnel. Most all were displaced from the continual raids of the invaders and their traitor's minions.

Looking at her patrons, Mari became angrier that Zenti had not returned to lend his military skills. The thought of her Faction only fighting alone turned her mood instantly sour. Because of Zenti's cowardice, many of her patrols and Faction soldiers might die. She thought of his last comment about hunting, and her temper rose. He hunted solo while the Factions needed him. He was a coward, she muttered under her breath as the vixen approached the Factions inner camp.

She stomped into her camp, and the air filled with the small talk and greetings of her patrons. The camp was well organized and well out of the way of any town or city. However, that did not mean they were completely safe. Though temporary in design, the encampment felt like home. Patrons waved and greeted her with smiles of enthusiastic welcome. The look on several of the Civilian Elders told her more than words could have. She returned alone without the promised Faction leader for negotiations. The look said they knew why; she had lost her temper, and that might cost them their lives. The Civilian Elders did not know who she was meeting. However, Mari knew that Mitd needed Summoner Zenti Semineu, and she had failed to return with him.

Mari felt sick to her stomach that she had lost her temper. She wanted nothing more than to chase Zenti down, but what good would that do her? The vixen knew you could never unsay something once said. Her temper began to rise as she struggled to control it. The voices of her patrons, all who were loyal to her Faction, became decidedly subdued. They could sense her boiling anger. Mari took a deep breath and slowly exhaled.

"All I can say is he better not come and find me while I sleep," Mari snapped to herself quietly, knowing that was probably what was going to happen. Summoner Zenti Semineu was wholly random when employing the arts of war. However, when it came to her, he was entirely predictable. She hated that he still loved her. A small voice in the depths of her mind echoed the unspoken truth; she still loved him too. With an angry self retort, Mari Semineu silenced that inner voice.

There was more to her and Zenti's conversation, yet she had let it get off on the wrong paw, damn her stubbornness. If the rumors were as accurate as she witnessed, her species needed Zenti now more than ever. Entering her private four-person tent, she sank to her knees and allowed her heart and mind to rage in an argument for the first time in thirteen months. The last time she allowed this eternal war to rage inside, her mind won.

~   ~   ~   ~

Zenti, having slipped into the darkness of the smoldering trees, allowed the shadows to consume him. Calling on his Gift, he wrapped his body in its umber glow. Only another Gifted actively searching using the Gift's Talent would have been able to detect him. He allowed the Talent of Descenting to "burn" off any trace of scent or musk without looking back towards Mari. That Talent did not task his body the way other Talents of the Gift did. Through Gift's enhanced hearing, he heard Mari walk away. He briefly thought of chasing after her. Whatever it was she wanted of him needed to be discussed. However, he hesitated and ultimately decided to let her go.

Zenti knew Mari had the skill to get away unless he used his Gift. His heart urged him to pursue her, but rational thought knew she wanted nothing to do with him on a personal level. Mari Semineu was stubborn to a fault. Logic dictated he look at the situation with cold calculation. She had shut him out of her life and only wanted his Gift. With that thought, his heart lost the battle. He had hoped that this meeting would have gone better.

However, the white wolf knew the darkness within him grew stronger every day. His Gift was consuming him as the echoes of the Prophecy lingered in his thoughts. The Prophecy was specific about his future. He wondered just how much longer he could control the burning raging rising deep inside him. He was called a monster, but he knew the truth. He was becoming the Monster of the Orra Prophecy. Within him, his emotions and logic continued the eternal war. He sat down and leaned against the trunk of a shattered tree. The damage to the area was uncalled for yet effective.

"Focus, you stupid wolf," Zenti whispered and tried to remain calm as the evening grew darker. The better part of an hour later, he opened his eyes and breathed a focused breath. Still, he held out hope.

What did he hope for, though? Did he honestly think that Mari would just open her heart to him, that this meeting would have been a happy reunion and that they could just get back to the life they had? Only a fool would believe that someone as stubborn as Mari Semineu would return to him with open paws. His ears flickered as his Gift allowed him to pick up faint sounds.

Listening to that distant noise, he knew that it could only be more soldiers. Turning silently, he walked back into the clearing. He listened and knew they were a mile or so away. With an open paw, Zenti coaxed the smoldering embers back to life, burning the bodies to an unrecognizable mass of bones and charred flesh. Smoke rose skyward, adding unnatural darkness to the skyline. Glowing embers floated skyward above the treetops.

With his Gift, Zenti enhanced the ember's glow. To the unknowing, it would seem like the Zemu bug[3] dancing in the air. He knew from past experiences the scent of burning flesh would confuse the incoming soldiers. Surveying the scorched area and the sky above, Zenti felt comfortable that the intended message was sent to his Northern Faction.

However, the silvery-white wolf had hunting to do. This was a good a spot as any for an ambush. His Gift allowed him to manipulate fire. A summoned fire consumed everything in its path. Like tangible fire, the

---

[3] The Zemu bug is a distant relative of various species of bioluminescence beetles. The carnivorous Zemu bugs produce a natural chemical light in their abdomens for multiple reasons, including attracting a mate or potential prey.

proverbial fire of anger at the traitors stirred deep within the white wolf. He moved into the tree line with a casual purpose and then deftly climbed one of the few undamaged trees.

Less than half an hour passed when the first of what would be forty soldiers approached the clearing. Zenti pulled himself close to the tree trunk. He watched as the soldiers cautiously began to enter the burned clearing. They were checking what was left of the bodies. Several soldiers tried to sniff the air, but he could tell by their reactions that the odor of burning fur, flesh, and bone obfuscated his scent.

These were troops of the Royal Army, not Faction troops. The company of soldiers was acting oddly in an otherwise secure area. Was this company of soldiers looking for the Crown's Special Forces he just executed. Or was this another force searching for something else and diverted their search? What were so many troops doing in a secured area? Formulating possibilities as to their behavior, Zenti watched some soldiers begin to gather what was left of the bodies. Others went about searching the site.

Smoke still rose as they gathered identification bands from the dead when the Captain stepped into the clearing. Batts Uller was a lean hyena who graduated at the top of his academy class. The hyena had led many successful battles against **THEM.** Zenti shook his head at the civilian given name of the invaders. However, this was a prelude to a hunt, and it demanded his attention. Focusing his Gifted hearing on the conversation, Zenti listened to the discussion.

"Can you find traces of who was here? I need to know if she was here," the Captain asked, kicking a few of the dead and flipping them over.

"Sir, we cannot tell if she was here or not, but he was most definitely here," said a corporal, snapping to attention as he turned to face the Captain.

"Of course *he* was here, idiot. Get out of my sight," growled the hyena.

"Sergeant, we need to leave the area. Secure the identifications, and leave what is left of the bodies. We have another place to be, and we cannot afford to be late for our containment duties. Marshall the troops," said the hyena as he moved towards the edge of the clearing.

Zenti watched from his perch on the broad branch. The troops gathered in the clearing, preparing to move out. The moment the troops were in formation, the white wolf raced down the length of the thick branch. His weight sagged down the tree's limb as he approached its end. Zenti called on the Gifted Talent of Repulsion. With a spring-like leap aided by the sagging branch's rebound, the silvery-white wolf silently launched himself towards the formation's center. The Gifted Talent of Repulsion propelled him away from the tree branch in a high arc.

Two of Jayden's three moons illuminated the night sky with a pale light. A large shadow passed over the Captain as he reached the edge of the tree line. Looking up and behind him, the Captain turned just in time to see the silvery flash descending upon his troops. Not waiting for the outcome of what he knew was about to happen, Batts Uller turned and fled for his life. He could hear the screams of his troops; they spurred Batts Uller on faster.

Flame erupted from the air surrounding the soldiers as Zenti's rage burned inside him. Like a meteor falling to the ground, the silvery-white wolf landed on a fat raccoon sergeant. He drove his knife between the raccoon's shoulder blades, an act that severed the spinal cord just below the base of the male's skull. The heat generated by Zenti's Gift distorted the aim of his terrified targets.

The white wolf could feel his strength waning, yet his anger drove him onward. Soldiers were batting at their clothing, trying to put out the multitude of flames. His initial strike had only killed half of those there. Concentrating harder, he caused the fires to flair higher, sending the remaining soldiers into a screaming panic. Grabbing a pistol, he began to shoot each of the panicked soldiers in the head as they fought the flames. Exhaustion began to set in as he continued his coaxing of the fire higher. Zenti shot any soldier who attempted to draw their weapon. He did not bother reloading. Instead, he simply discarded one pistol when it was empty and took another off a dead or dying soldier.

It ended within a few minutes. The last soldier's head snapped forward as the bullet entered the back of his skull. Zenti watched as the stag hit the ground with a dull thud. Picking up a new pistol, the silvery-white wolf walked around the twice-charred clearing, shooting each of the burned soldiers in the head, ensuring that no one survived. These soldiers were hunting his Mari and perhaps him.

Gathering the identification bands, he noted the various regions of Mitd that the soldiers were from, none indicating a predominance of one area. Mitd was a multi-dialectal nation, though it was rooted in one common language. This was indeed perplexing as all of the army organization was formed on a regional basis. That regional organization ensured the varied dialects would not create complications in understanding orders.

None of the bodies was the Captain's, who was undoubtedly far away by now. He cursed himself for not moving faster as he searched the backpacks. Zenti found a few unburned ration packs. He was physically exhausted; the Gift consumed the Gifted's body with each use. With proper nutrition, a Gifted would perform limited Talents. Zenti took a deep breath, knowing that he rarely performed his Talents in any limited fashion. He stood for a moment on unsteady paw pads. His physical strength was fading from the lack of nutritional fuel. The newly dead, combined with the clearing's previously remains, continued to burn. Zenti just let the fire naturally burn out. He ate as much of the rations as he could find while searching the non-charred bodies for any clues or orders.

He was weak and needed more fat and protein than standard field rations held, but these would have to do for now. Zenti looked at the rations and wished they were sugary sweet. Sweets were instant fuel to feed his Gift, though ultimately it would leave him weaker. Zenti snorted at the thought that there was anything other than the ultimate price he would pay. The absurdity made him chuckle. The Orra Prophecy was clear, and he knew the price.

The evening twilight began to fade into the dark cloak of night as he was finishing his search. He found nothing of any value. If they had any orders on them, they were nothing more than ash. Shaking his head, he resolved to learn how to tailor the control of his Gift. Too many secrets were consumed in the fire of his rage. Taking a canteen of water, he drained it before opening another of the surviving ration packs and picking up another canteen. Looking around, he found that nothing more could be gained from further searching.

Zenti took a moment and sat down in the smoldering clearing, just listening as the night air began to cool off even more. He was too tired to hunt the hyena down. Three such Gift fueled attacks in one day were detrimental to his health. Again he shook his head at that thought. Mari needed to become the leader Jayden needed. She had a duty to fulfill, even if it was unclear to him exactly how she was to do that. Listening carefully, Zenti heard nothing that resembled an immediate threat. Waiting a few moments longer, he got to his paw pads.

Moving into the trees, Zenti began to follow the way that Mari had traveled. He knew there was more left to the conversation between them. She had called him here for a reason, and both had allowed the hurt between them to distract them from the real purpose. He needed to know what she wanted and needed. He needed to say goodbye one last time. If Mari could not fulfill her duty, then all was lost anyway. The plans he carefully wove would hopefully end this war. Zenti knew that if his strength held, it would be enough to carry those plans out, and then Mari would never need to fulfill her duty. He could carry the burden all by himself. He recalled the words of the Shaman who tended his wounds.

"Pup, the strength to change this war lies within you. All you have to do is call for it," Zenti whispered. Those were the Shaman Torit words, the male who had been the father he lost.

However, he found that he was fatigued, and the lack of proper food was currently a significant hindrance. Anger could only carry him so far, and the past four days, he had been in almost constant battles with just pilfered rations to eat. Opening another ration pack, he threw out the vegetables and went straight to the starch and meats. As he ate, he followed Mari's lingering scent. He thought of his mate, his Mari, his vixen. The emotional distance was great.

No, he needed to bring closure to Mari's hatred of him, if only so she could end the chapter of their relationship and move forward with her life. She was still a kit in so many ways. No matter how skilled and competent a beloved leader she was, she was still a kit. No, he needed to make a choice, and though she had always hated him making choices for her, they needed to be made. However, when she was having one of her kit-like moments, she needed a guiding paw.

Thinking about those choices, would they free the inhabitants of Jayden or kill them all? Would those choices he made, the price he paid, be enough to save the only life that mattered to him on this planet, even if it meant losing her forever?

Tears flowed across the silvery-white wolf's muzzle as he looked to the stars for answers he already knew were in his heart. The price was already indeed very high with still more to pay.

Chapter 2

Meeting

An unusual silence settled over Mari Semineu's Faction camp. Hundreds of soldiers and civilians normally busied themselves with the noisy tasks of the day. Though subdued by the necessity of the war, normal levels of conversation and laughter were typical. However, the camp was silent enough that the loudest noise was the rustling of the tree branches. Mari Semineu was usually interacting with her troops and patron. Tonight, she had stomped directly to her tent with but a few pleasantries. To her patrons, that meant she was on the verge of one of her famous temper tantrums. However, her tent was silent, except for the soft sobs of crying. Soldiers kept the paw pad traffic away. Miss Mari was hurting, and no one wanted to leave her alone. Her soldiers knew better; Mari needed a measure of solitude.

A long and tumultuous four hours had passed since Zenti left the vixen standing in that burned-out clearing. The walk back to her camp should have been one of delight this time of year. However, the several hours it took to return left Mari Semineu empty. Spring was in full bloom; however, she had noticed none of it. The shock of seeing Zenti again evoked hatred laced with confusion. Moreover, the frightening way in which he killed those soldiers numbed her to the beauty of spring.

Zenti Semineu was a professional soldier. Mari wiped away hours of tear and reminded herself of one cold fact. He was a professional soldier thirteen months ago. When had he become such a cold murderer? Could the rumors of Zenti's exploits really be true? Mari's paws trembled at the memory of his powerful touch. When had Summoner Zenti Semineu become that frighteningly powerful?

Mari continued to lie on her cot. She had not moved in two hours as the memories of her life with Zenti repeatedly replayed. Every little detail bubbled to the surface as her heart and her mind battled. Laced within those memories were the events of the past few hours. The violence Zenti displayed, the brutal way he murdered those soldiers, and the cold-hearted method in which he searched their bodies was not the Zenti she once knew.

Her heart begged to differ. It reminded her that Zenti was a Summoner of considerable power, even when he was young. Her mind rebuked her heart's argument, reminding it that the former Zenti would have never abused the laws of Mitd. It was not the Mitdonian way to brutally kill when a surrender was an option. The logic her mind presented was firm. All of Mitd knew of Summoner Zenti Semineu. Undoubtedly, the soldiers would have surrendered if presented with the choice.

Mari tried to clear her memory of those burning bodies. Death was not new to her, wars brought death, but this was a darkness in him. The Zenti she knew was not a monster. The wolf she met today was not her Zenti. Her Zenti, her heart echoed. Mari balled up tighter and continued to sob.

What he did today was on a scale that was beyond

what he had ever been able to do. Never had the vixen witnessed such destruction with so little emotion from him. Mari knew the Gift could, and most often was, fueled by emotional outbursts. Zenti's rage seemed passive today for the level of destruction he displayed. Thirteen months had not diminished her memory of his Gift. Before today it took a substantial rage-fueled outburst to cause a mere fraction of the damage he did today. However, Zenti Semineu had the rage to spare.

For more than ten years since her family's death, Mari had fought by Zenti's side. She knew of him several years before they mated. Her father, General Haverick Waxton, instructed Zenti in the Unconventional Arts of War. However, Zenti paid the vixen almost no attention. He was battle-hardened at seven years old. Mari thought of the invader's pups, or whatever **THEY** were called; she really did not care. At seven years old, **THEY** were no more developed than a two-year-old Jaydonian. This information was according to the limited intelligence the Mitd Royal Assassin's Corp had on them.

Mari recalled how seven-year-old Zenti would practice the control of his Gift on the drill grounds. He was intense, and his rage seemed unreal. However, the young white wolf displayed extraordinary control. The Gifted Shaman Torit would visit sporadically and offer pointers to the young Zenti. Mari always enjoyed the visits of the mysterious male buzzard. However, the greatest gift Zenti Semineu possessed was his ability to maintain control in any situation. All the other trainees were past their

Coming-of-Age Day. Despite the age differences, the trainees obeyed the pre-Coming-of-Age white wolf's ordered implicitly.

As Zenti grew, so did not only his Gift but also his power of command. By the time he reached his Coming-of-Age Day, Zenti was in command of most of the missions. There were times he was away with the Shaman Torit. During those times, the success of the missions significantly diminished unless her father planned them.

Zenti had returned from a visit to Torit's home shortly before the invaders attacked the training camp. Mari forced those memories of the night the invaders slaughtered her parents out of her mind. She was unprepared to relive them. However, some things cannot be forgotten. Mari should have been in the camp that night, but her temper had gotten the better of her.

On that fateful night, Zenti was by her side when her father passed to the stars. He carried her sister, who now hated him, to safety and medical help. The Zenti she remembered only killed when there was no other choice. Today, in that clearing, he was not the Zenti of the past. What had driven him to such cruelty? Was he losing to the madness of the Void, which was the bane of all the Gifted?

Even though her sister, Rini, held Zenti responsible for their parent's death, the vixen did not. Mari accepted his paw, and they mated a little more than a year after losing her family. She willingly shared his bed, bound his wounds, and cooked his meals. Together they laughed and cried. They fought together, bled together, and defended Mitd together. What had changed in him to make him such a monster? Mari thought back to any memory that should have betrayed his current nature. Was he hiding his true self all these years?

The first year after her family's death, Zenti trained her in the tactics her father had instilled in him. Teaching her how to be a good leader, Zenti shared the skill needed to motivate troops with positive command while maintaining order and discipline. It did not take long, she recalled, as the soldiers started obeying her orders as if he had given them.

When General Hetchon spoke with Zenti in private about combining and leading the two factions, the white wolf refused. It was in the following years that she found out why. Zenti had told the General that he, at some point, would become an ineffective leader. Though he was skilled at war, a civilian army needed a loved, respected, and trusted leader. He knew that would not be him one day. That confusing statement should have given everyone warning that Zenti knew the Void would one day claim him.

The Gifted avoided pushing their Gift. It was not an occasional avoidance but a full-time, active one. According to ancient journals, a Gifted who abused their Gift to the point where the Void claimed them was a terrifying ordeal to behold. No Gifted in the past few hundred years had dared push. With that one statement, she now realized that Zenti knew all along that he would push himself to the point where the Void would claim him. The vixen dried her tears on her pillowcase as she recalled the past. Getting off the cot, she moved over to her desk and mindlessly picked up a book.

Mari Semineu became the Eastern Faction leader when General Hetchon suggested Zenti for her second in command. Though Zenti was a Faction leader, it was an acceptable compromise to not combining the two Factions. Mari took that suggestion to heart and began several years of watching and learning from Zenti. He was a superb tactician being able to plan and implement many successful raids and battles. Zenti was an excellent teacher for the first four years. One day he quietly stepped aside, allowing Mari to take over entirely.

However, as time progressed, the war became more intense, and Zenti lost the desire to fight with others. He had left almost all of his Northern Faction's day-to-day operations to his second in command, only planning the attacks and raids. The white wolf stopped fighting with Mari's Faction, only making suggested modifications to her battle plans. He told her he preferred to fight, which he now referred to as hunting, as a solo act. He promised to stay near. She had accepted that as he was never far from her. Anytime things went wrong, he was there to alter the course of the battle. How could she have missed all the signs that he was losing himself to the Void?

"What was it that blinded you to all those signs," Mari asked aloud? It was not logic that answered, but her heart. It was but a silent feeling, but she knew its taste. It was love for Zenti that blinded her.

In the last year before he betrayed her, there had been more crying than laughing between them. He had become darker, more intense, and withdrawn to the point her troops and his troops began to fear him. However, they fought even more ferociously in hopes that he would not appear on the battlefield. Even in all of his rage, Zenti was not cruel. He followed the Mitdonian laws of surrender. He always obeyed the rules of war. Nonetheless, his ferocity should have been a warning to her. Her love for him blinded the not-so-subtle signs.

In the last two months before his betrayal, his rage could hardly be contained. His methods became anything but military. He hid those actions by hunting exclusively alone. He would make minimal suggestions to the vixen's battle plans, but the ones he did significantly reduced her Faction's risks. As the war continued, his rage seemed to burn brighter with each passing battle.

The white wolf became a bane of the enemy and a source of fear to the Crown's troops. Yet Zenti never allowed that rage to come into their private life. He would hold her at night, brushing her fur or stroking her ears, bringing a calming peace. That simple act brought a solace that she had not known since she was a young kit. Yet, even then, she could feel the mounting distance between them.

However, Zenti had never harmed her. No matter her temper tantrums, he had always been loving and kind. That is what confused her. What could have caused him to betray her? Again, the thought occurred to Mari that Zenti might have been a victim just like her. Instantly the vixen's temper flared. She was stubborn and refused to consider he might be a victim.

Cursing herself, she slammed the book down on her desk with both paws for allowing their conversation to degrade so fast. Where was her head? Damn, her species needed him, and she let her temper get the better of what needed to be a rational conversation. Growling loudly, she ran her claws through her hair.

"Thirteen months of unanswered questions because I am stubborn. Some leader I am. Mitd needs Zenti," Mari growled. Neither her heart nor mind commented. Again, she ran her claws through her hair, combing out the tear-drenched tangles. Slumping back into her chair, she pushed back from the desk. There she sat in dejected silence.

"Pardon me, Miss Mari, but there are those who need your guidance," said a lanky, young ferret.

He was well over six and a half feet tall but still only a few years past his Coming-of-Age date. As a favor to one of the vixen's late patrons, she took him in as one of her aids and personal guards. Mari needed no guard in all reality. A sniper could kill her just as efficiently as an assailant could. The position was for his protection until he reached the age of military eligibility at fifteen.

Heaving a deep sigh, she relented. Duty called, and though she needed to resolve the issue of Zenti Semineu, her patrons counted on her or, more correctly, leaned on her.

The next three hours became pure agony as her Faction members came to her tent, wanting an audience. The line forming grew longer and longer. Various civilian heads repeatedly brought matters of little to no importance before her. Usually, she would smile and help them through it, trying to teach them a little self-reliance along the way. That the patrons came to her seeking advice was Zenti's fault. Had he not established her as the civilian liaison, they would leave her alone. She had a war to fight, not decide who needed to perform specific civilian duties. Yet she willingly listened. The patrons required a leader.

Mari knew today was different. She had let that conversation with Zenti go down the wrong path. It infuriated her, and the vixen screamed inside at her lack of control. How had she let that hardheaded white wolf get under her fur? She departed for their meeting with a plan. However, the moment she arrived, she lost her temper. Her temper was a character flaw, one she needed to correct.

Mari was closing yet another boring meeting. This

one was with the civilian tailor. He was a portly ram who crafted some of the best clothing any soldier wore. They were sturdy, well-constructed, and very utilitarian. The ram had modified the Crown's Special Forces combat uniform into something more useful to the Factions. Most of the camp's civilians worked for or with the master tailor. They produced clothing for multiple Factions. That production kept the vast majority of her patrons perpetually busy. However, bolts of cloth were becoming scarce.

"I agree, Master Qun. However, there is no cloth available in the region. The invaders have burned most of the fields and have destroyed almost all of our industry. As you have so accurately pointed out, there is a decided shortage of good quality material available. What would you suggest we do to remedy that," Mari asked? She was polite, but her mind was not in the conversations. She knew the elder ram already had a solution. However, he liked to feel important while attempting to be humble. He pulled it off well, the vixen thought.

"I have a potential solution. In two weeks, we relocate the main camp near Dairhal Bay. When you send scouts to ensure the roads are safe, I could send two of my Procurers to attempt and secure materials from Dairhal Bay. I am sure they have them. It is one of the last cities left unmolested. Dairhal Bay is the main southern trading port," explained Master Qun. The portly ram waited patiently. He was attempting to be as patient as he could. Mari Semineu's mind was not in the conversation, and it showed on her muzzle.

"That is agreeable," was all Mari replied. She smiled kindly at the portly ram. However, the vixen wanted to be alone. With a polite nod, he was dismissed. A quick glance at the young ferret, she noted he surreptitiously held out four digits.

When the elder ram turned to leave, Mari rolled her eyes in frustration. Four more of her patrons wanted her valuable time. Mari had other, more important things to focus on. Her patrons were former professionals in their respective fields. Yet, they now looked to her as if they were fresh apprentices. That was all Zenti's fault. Sighing, she nodded yes to the unspoken question by the ferret. The next patron entered the tent. Mari smiled warmly. This constant barrage of skilled professionals, acting like kits, was grating on her last nerve.

"Welcome back, Miss Mari. We are all glad you had a safe journey. I apologize for bringing this to your attention. However, we still have an issue with procuring medical supplies," began a burley, elder bear. He was the camp's chief surgeon. He was tasked with maintaining the medical supplies and the critical care of her patrons.

"Doctor," she greeted him cordially. "Please tell me about your current predicament." Though her words were not spoken in anger, the inflection of the word 'your' stung the elder bear. He began a litany of issues. With him, it was always an ordeal. Mari dutifully listened, yet the events of the day continued to haunt the vixen.

Letting her mind drift for a moment, she forgot all about the bear standing inside her tent until he cleared his throat. She turned to face him with a blank expression trying to hide the contempt she was feeling. She wallowed in that contempt for needing Zenti to come to her Faction's aid. Moreover, there was the contempt she occasionally harbored for her patrons. Their inability to make choices for themselves irritated her no end. This was all Zenti's fault, all of it. Not only had he set her up to be the central figurehead of the Faction, but she was the muzzle that Mitdonians thought of when looking for hope.

Mari Semineu also had a measure of contempt for herself for not putting a paw pad down a little more firmly with her patrons. They were adults and needed to step up and carry their weight. However, the deep contempt she felt was that she did not control her temper. The bear's nasally voice droned on. He hit a particular pitch that rudely brought the vixen back into the present.

"Excuse me, ma'am, what is your suggestion on the matter of collecting more medical supplies," asked the bear standing a few feet away from the tent flap?

That simple question was more than Mari could handle. Though she knew they were all capable of making the decisions independently, they insisted that she be directly involved. It was a waste of her time dealing with mundane tasks. Any of her subordinates could handle these requests. Coupled with the meeting with Zenti and her frustration at losing control, the vixen snapped.

"Get out! Get out! Get the Heavens and Hell out!" Mari screamed as the frustration of dealing with the various civilians bombarding her tent with trivial minutia finally boiled over. The rather burly-looking bear backed away from her as she brandished a pen like a sword, glaring at him with bared fangs. Shoving the chair way, she leapt up and advanced on him. Her fur stood bristled. For such a dainty vixen, she was a fearsome sight to behold when she was angry.

"Yes, Ma'am," he said with a quick bow before rushing out of her tent backward as she threw the pen after him. The elder bear burst out of the tent. He regretted bringing what he knew was a trivial matter to her. However, like all her patrons, he wanted to see how she was doing.

"Don't call me ma'am," Mari shouted as she chased him out of the tent.

Mari's patrons waiting outside her tent scattered out of the way of the stumbling bear. Others went about some trivial busy business within the camp. Several females went about cooking as soldiers began to see to the evening's patrols. On the far end of the tents, a group of graying members gathered. They began heated discussions, all with the pretense of staying out of her way. She ignored them and turned back to her tent, hoping for some peace and quiet.

Looking skyward, the late evening stars seemed a

little brighter. Mari snorted in disgust. Looking at the stars, the vixen whispered an apology to all those who ascended for losing her temper. According to the Orra teachings, that is where the departed resided. She wished she knew which of those bright stars her parents were.

Ascending to the stars was the core of the Orra faith. Mitd had only one religion. The Orra teachings were the foundation of all things on Mitd. She knew that her parents were not physical stars; those were planets. However, the thought of them looking down upon her tamed her bitter mood. Looking over her shoulder, her anger faded into one of disgust. She wondered what her father would think of her temper. He passed to the stars a decade ago, and still, she acted like a kit throwing temper tantrums. How disappointed would her father be, she wondered?

The night air smelled sweet, and for a moment, Mari could almost taste spring. Stopping, she went to the cook's tent and fixed herself a cup of hot tea. Her patrons greeted her with kind neutrality. Though they knew the petty administrative duties fueled the vixen's temper tantrums, they still heavily relied on her. However, when the moment dictated, Mari Semineu was a true leader. While the tea steeped, Mari buttered and honeyed a thick slice of bread. Her mood was softening, and she engaged in polite return greetings, but nothing more in-depth.

Returning to her tent, she picked up the toppled chair; it was then she really looked at the mess in the tent. Rolling her head in disgust at herself for letting things get this far out of paw, she thought of tidying things up. That brought on another wave of anger. The vixen was a neat nick. The anger at the sight of the messy area washed over her. In disgust, Mari flung herself back down into the chair. Letting her shoulders slump, she tried to drain the emotional duress. Slowly she sipped the tea and ate the bread hoping the momentary break would help bring a measure of tranquility. However, it was not to be.

Visions of her and Zenti's past tried to break the dam of hatred she felt for him. Those memories crashed upon her anger-built walls. Wave after wave of memories attempted to erode the hatred of him. Those memories reminded her of the sacrifices he had made and the blood he had shed just to keep her from harm's way. There were numerous occasions where Zenti abused his Gift just to ensure she was safe.

Mari recalled the laughter that they shared at the little things that the newly mated experiences brought. The battles they fought together erupted to the forefront of her thoughts. Some of the actions they fought left emotional scars, while others left more physically telling damage. She ran a paw over her eyebrow and muzzle, tracing the long narrow scar. She had been stupidly careless when **THEY** gave her the scar. Zenti had been uncontrollably reckless to save her. That recklessness cost both of them a lot of pain the day she got the scar. However, Zenti bore the brunt of physical damage. He sustained multiple broken ribs and a fractured forearm.

That old memory triggered the events of today. Again, the clearing came to mind, and Mari could smell the lingering smoke on her clothes. Mari looked at the stains on the back of her skirt. The blood was from the dead hyena she tripped over. With that memory, the vision became too much.

Tearing the skirt off, she tossed it on the cot where she earlier collapsed. Ripping off her smoke imbued blouse, she flung them across the tent. Mari growled in rage as the wave of memories crested. Zenti betrayed her. Mari put on new clothing.

The conflict grew inside Mari. She wanted to hurt Zenti for what he had done. However, she could not publicly seek revenge against Zenti while struggling to be the leader her father had wanted her to be. Growling again, she forced a modicum of control over her temper. She knew that if Zenti possessed an expanded Gift, then Mitd truly needed him. She fought the desire to scream again as her whole body shook from the pent-up rage.

Damn Zenti for still living. Why could he not be dead? Why did the war go so badly that she needed to seek him out? What did he possess that made her still love him? Again, she screamed aloud and kicked over her chair. No, she did not love him; she hated him and despised the very breath he took. How could she have trusted him, let him be so close to her? How could she have given herself to him? In the end, all he did was betray her.

Wrapping her arms and her tail around her, Mari shook violently. They did little to protect her from the onslaught of memories. Streams of tears flowed down her furry cheeks.

Picking the chair up again, Mari sat down heavily. She closed her eyes and tried to gain control of her emotions. The vixen shook; this was maddening. How could just seeing him affect her so strongly? Picking up the roster of her camp, she started to immerse herself in some mindless work in hopes that it would drive the memories from her head. However, that little voice reminded her that perhaps Zenti was a victim also.

~   ~   ~   ~

Zenti crouched in the shadows of the trees on the low hillside. That hill was just on the far outskirts of her encampment. Unseen, Zenti had watched for the past two hours. It was nearing midnight, and Mari's patrons went about their evening tasks. The camp never slept. With one-third always awake and working, the chance for surprise was significantly diminished. Guards walking patrols passing within a few yards of the silvery-white wolf, but they never saw him.

Nor would any guard see him without advanced invader technology. However, the technology was not needed to avoid patrols. Zenti knew the patrol pattern well; he developed them for her Faction. However, technology or not, if he did not want to be discovered, no one could find him. He scanned the camp with a pair of captured invader's binoculars. One-third of the camp was up and active as anticipated. The night shift busied themselves with preparing for the needs of tomorrow. That was one of Mari's concepts. It worked very well.

Dialing in the binoculars on Mari's tent, Zenti scanned the line of patrons that waited outside. Steading his shaking paws, the silvery-white wolf slowly exhaled in an attempt to regain control. He was tired from the multiple battles over the past few days. He opened a ration pack and dug out the meat package. He needed more protein, but protein took too long; what he wanted was sugar.

Zenti wanted to follow her after ambushing the second squad of soldiers. Though the battle had been brief in the clearing, it had taxed him. However, the comment made by the hyena who escaped concerned him. After starting after Mari, Zenti decided to track the hyena before seeking her out. He followed the hyena for over an hour before losing his trail. The effort further exhausted Zenti. His rations were low and could not provide instant energy. The lack of energy-sustaining food made the trek to Mari's Faction camp considerably slower. Zenti was still tired when he arrived at the low-lying hillside. This land was filled with mineral deposits. It formerly belonged to the Milter Mining Company. However, recent events left the area abandoned.

Finishing another pack of rations he had taken from

the dead, the silvery-white wolf leaned back and looked to the stars. They seemed a bit duller than he remembered. Perhaps his memory was fading at the simple pleasures life brought. Maybe he was just tired. Looking back down to the camp, he wondered if Mari's patrons could feel the anger welling up inside her. He could feel that anger rising as patron after patron entered her tent. Several patrons brought her a bouquet of flowers or a mug of something to drink, and it would calm her a little. Those small offerings of kindness elicited a warm feeling of love. He could sense them even at this distance through his Gift. However, it was very taxing. The occasional feeling of warmth and love brought Zenti some hope that Mari might be maturing.

Her patrons loved her; what right did he have to love her as well? Holding this position until the dark of midnight's full embrace kissed him with the cold of night, the white wolf watched as Mari's patrons continued to line up to see her. The camp was busy with preparations for tomorrow's meals. Zenti proudly noted that the Faction camp ran with incredible efficiency for a civilian occupied base. General Haverick Waxton's instructions had stuck with her. The Talent of Empathy was draining his strength. However, Zenti persevered a little longer in hopes the traces of her anger would fade.

The past hour had brought more frustration for Mari, and Zenty could feel her emotions taking control when a burly-looking bear entered the tent. The white wolf could feel the conflict through his Gift flowing from Mari. Zenti wanted to reach out with his Gift and calm her. Like every

time before, he resisted. The vixen needed to learn.
However, it seemed Mari had forgotten the self-control
lessons from her father. It was something she desperately
needed to learn. Moments later, through the Gifted Talent
of Empathy, Zenti felt Mari's emotions snap. He stood up
beside the tree just in time to see the resulting emotional
explosion.

The emotional backlash through the Gifted Talent of
Empathy was too much for the exhausted white wolf.
Drops of blood began to form around the corners of his
eyes. Reluctantly Summoner Zenti Semineu released the
Gift. A wave of relief washed over his exhausted body as
he continued to watch in hidden silence.

Backing peddling out of the tent, the bear tried to
maintain his balance as the vixen stormed out after him.
Mari had lost the emotional battle Zenti felt from within
her. Smiling, he watched as the hotheaded vixen cleared
the line of patrons. From experience, he was sure the
patrons were just asking for guidance on petty issues. If
she could ever learn to harness her temper, her greatest
weakness could become her second most outstanding asset.

He watched as she circled the fire just outside her
tent. She stopped and took a deep breath as she usually did
when things were getting out of paw. Mari had not
changed in the past thirteen months. She was still the one
that excited him, and as always, the one her patrons loved.
Was he really willing to kill everything on Jayden just to
save her from the invader's plans? How many more would

die by his paws? Was the price for Mari's freedom and
safety worth paying? Those were all rhetorical questions to
which he already knew the answers. No price was too
high. Sadly, in the end, it might not be enough. In that
case, it would be better if all of Jayden passed to the stars.
Death was better than serving under the yoke of the
invaders.

He watched as she went to the cook's tent and then
came out with a cup and a slice of bread. He smiled, and
he bet that it was hot spiced tea and buttered bread with
honey. He could always calm her down with that. It was a
secret passed on by her father before he died. Zenti thought
of the late Haverick Waxton as he widened the binoculars
viewing range. The lion was a great male and an even
greater father to his two kits. Mari and Rini Waxton
wanted for nothing. Memories of his own loving father
tried to force their way back into the white wolf's memory.
Zenti crushed those memories and locked them away again.
After twenty years, he was unprepared to deal with the loss
of his family.

Mari returned to her tent, and a few moments later,
he heard her howl in rage. She was losing the battle to her
emotions as wave after wave of rage rolled out of her tent.
Zenti always held on to a little of his Gift. It was the Talent
of Life Sensing. It did not tax his body if he were not
actively using it. However, it did allow him the ability to
sense emotional outbursts. Those who were afraid or angry
were easy to perceive. Had an Oracle been near, they could
have fed from the torrents of raw power using the Talent of

Sync.

That questionable Talent allowed a Gift to drain the Void energy that all life possessed. It was considered unethical by almost all the Gifted. Zenti knew that Talent, it was a foul-tasting act to drain someone of their Voidal energy. However, Zenti knew he would need the Talent of Sync to accomplish a future task.

Again, Mari howled in rage, and the wave of emotional suffering rolled over the encampment, yet no one felt it as he did. From the day of their mating, he had experienced her emotions as if they were his own.

"Day of mating," Zenti whispered, and his own fatigue-fueled emotions began to take control of him. A feeling of sorrow filled the white wolf. It came from knowing the depths he had and would sink to for her. He felt her continued emotional assault.

Summoner Zenti Semineu released his Gift entirely. That act should have cut off any emotional bleed that any sentient being project. To his great distress, it did not. He found he could no longer fully let go of his Voidal access. It was as if the Void called to him and refused to release him like a predator refuses to release its prey. The rage Mari projected was overwhelming. At that moment, he knew what the Shaman Torit meant. He and Mari were inexplicably linked to each other and to the Void. He could no more rebuff his connection to Mari than he could stop breathing and still live. No longer able to control his own emotions, he allowed the pain and sorrow to take voice.

~   ~   ~   ~

A deep, mournful howl pierced the night's air, causing the camp to panic. It was all-encompassing, with a power that vibrated the very air. The Faction camp's occupants felt the howl's fiery yet unseen tendrils. Though it did not physically burn their fur and skin, it felt as if it burned their very essence. They began to rush about defensively, searching for the howl's all-encompassing source. Pups cried, and some of the graying patrons screamed conflicting orders. Zenti heard the confusion from the camp's patrons. They were terrified. However, he did not care. So strong was the wave of Mari's emotions that they seemingly came crashing down up him. Her anger assaulted his own emotional state. Zenti tried to regain control, but he lost the battle. The rage from her emotional assault found him no longer caring who feared him. There was no separating the emotional volcano erupting between the two of them in the bleak darkness of midnight.

~   ~   ~   ~

The vixen stiffened at the sound of that sickeningly sweet howl, a howl she knew all too well. In the early years of their mating, she recalled how every death Zenti caused with the rage of his Gift would tear at his very soul. At times it would overwhelm him, and he would cry out in sorrow. Was it still the same? Did he feel each death still?

She gasped, and her paws flew to her muzzle. Did Zenti continue to touch her emotional rage?

Mari recalled the times they would lay under the stars. She asked what the Gift was like. What was it like to touch the Void? At first, Zenti could not explain it. As the years passed, the war turned from occasional raids to full-time assaults. In those years, Zenti found a few words to describe what the power of the Void was like. Most of the concepts she still could not grasp.

What she understood back then was that Zenti could feel her emotions. No matter his physical condition, he found time to come when she battled the emotional rage bottled up inside. When Mari asked why the white wolf kissed the tip of her ears, and told her it was because he loved her. As the years of war continued, Zenti became more distant. He hunted alone and stayed out of her camp for weeks at a time. However, when she needed him the most, he was there. Like a warm summer sun, he comforted her when her emotions raged. The vixen knew Zenti had come to her when she needed comforting the most. That is why he was here. Her heart won a brief battle against her mind at that moment, and her hatred subsided.

Wrenching the flap of the tent open, she scanned the hillsides. Her ears turned forward, then flicked left and right. However, she found no trace of Zenti's presence. Her few soldiers reacted professionally while the rest of her patrons rushed around, some screaming of invaders. Her patrons were getting hysterical.

A male otter pup was crying near her. She picked him up. Moving to the center riser used for the public address, she soothed the little male. Over the camp's public address system, she spoke to them all in measured tones. The calmness in her soft voice helped in silencing them.

"Hush," she said softly, then kissed the male otter pup on the forehead. She turned to her patrons and continued. "That howl is not to be feared, for it is not a foe. It is not a soldier calling for backup, and it is not **THEM**, so calm yourselves. Remember your training and get to your posts. Continue to tend to your duties. Trust in me when I tell you that tonight you are safe," she said. The pup stopped crying.

"Little Gevek, go to your tent and sleep. You should not be up anyway. It is late. Go to your mother; you are safe," Mari said and licked his cheek. Holding him securely, she looked down at her patrons.

Though she was speaking to him, everyone had stopped to listen. Gevek's mother hurried up to Mari. Handing the pup off to his mother, Mari casually went back into her tent. The camp stirred, though only in hushed tones. Mari looked at the unkempt tent in disgust. However, she did not have the will to clean; instead, she sat on her cot. Why had Zenti followed her? Deep inside, she knew he would. There were too many things left unsaid between them. She saw that look on his muzzle in the clearing. Moreover, why had she not warned her patrons? Just where the Heavens and Hells[4] was her head?

Clasping her paws to her head, Mari tried to beat the cobwebs out as if that would do any good. She got up and started to straighten the room but just sat back in her chair with a thud as mental exhaustion overwhelmed her. The rage was subsiding. However, thinking back to what she witnessed Zenti do a few hours ago, how could her patrons not be safe tonight?

"Ma'am." Came a voice outside the tent. "Excuse me, Ma'am; there are things we really need to discuss, please. Do you have time," came the shy voice? Mari sighed.

"Yes, what is it?" the vixen snapped, her voice not as harsh as before. She sat up in her chair, brushing the loose strands of her fur from her eyes.

Pulling open the tent door, a young male rabbit looked in. With a look of concern, Jolet entered tentatively. The brown and gray split leg robe the male rabbit wore blended with his brown fur. Highlights of white and gray splotches made him look very young. He bowed his head briefly before holding out a piece of parchment.

---

[4] *Dear readers. Jaydonians do not have a heaven or a hell. The literal translation means 'place of joy and place of suffering.' It is a common curse phrase.*

He was her third in command and the liaison between her and the camp Elders. His face looked younger than his actual age of seventeen, mainly due to the white heart-shaped patch on each cheek.

Glancing around the tent, Jolet noticed the unusual mess. Her quarters had always been sparse. Miss Mari had but a few changes of fatigues and the occasional everyday outfit; otherwise, the quarters were continually in good and neat order. The desk was a jumble of papers and maps. The once neatly shelved books were now scattered about. Many were open to random pages as if having been searched and then tossed aside. Her cot had clothing thrown across it, and he thought he could smell a trace of smoke. Clearing his throat, he summoned his courage and began.

"These are a list of concerns that the Elders have made. Do we have time to discuss them, please," Jolet asked? His paws trembled as he held out the papers for her to take.

"Yes, we have time," Mari said, trying to forget what had just happened a few hours ago. Looking up at the rabbit, she noted he was trembling as he extended the list in her direction. He stretched his arm as far as it would reach. She could smell the trepidation in his musk. Sighing lightly, she smiled an empty smile hoping it would bring a little calm to him.

"Thank you, Ma'am. First, the Elders think we

should move the camp again. The rumors of soldiers in the area have everyone skittish and ready to run. They feel if we could move now, we might be able to hide from them until some of the other factions can come to our aid. With almost all of our soldiers on loan to General Breymore, they feel we could be vulnerable," began Jolet. He fidgeted at the end of the statement, blurting it out so fast that he was not even sure of what he had said.

"We will be moving camp in two weeks," Mari replied.

"Yes, Ma'am. I explained that to the Elders. They insisted that I present this request," said Jolet.

Though her voice had grown soft, the rabbit knew Mari was in a foul mood, which frightened him. He had served with her for eight months earning her respect with his diplomatic skills. Jolet brought a welcomed organization between her and the Elders. He was good at tedious duties such as record keeping, which served him as liaison quite well. The rabbit had witnessed the unfaltering kindness Mari could and quite often did show. Besides, he knew from his participation in many battles that she had a raging temper. The angrier she got, the more dangerous she became.

"I went to meet with one of the other Faction Leaders tonight," she said softly, really trying not to get mad at him. It was not his fault that she was in a bad mood; it was Zenti's fault. Raising a paw for him to hold his words, she drew a deep breath, trying to silence the rage growing inside of her head.

It was then she realized it. The entire Faction camp was silent. It was never this quiet; whether at rest or hiding from an attack, there was always some low noise. Getting up, she pushed her way past the messenger and threw open her tent's door, her mood turning foul again.

In her camp's center stood Summoner Zenti Semineu, like a phantom of death come down upon them. Her patrons all stood voiceless, staring at the silvery-white wolf, not moving. A pup cried but immediately went silenced as its mother's paw clamping down on his muzzle, punctuated by a soft growl. However, in the silencing growl, the vixen heard a measure of fear. Mari sensed the fear of the whole camp. The monster of the many rumors was amongst her patron in the fur. No one said a word, and Mari was sure that many of them held their breath. Summoner Zenti Semineu stood patiently, with his paws behind his back. The silvery-white wolf looked up.

Mari nearly flinched when Zenti caught sight of her. Suddenly she felt vulnerable, naked even. Crossing her arms, the vixen wrapped her tail around her and tried to ward off the feeling. Inside she raged again, but her body was trembling. With but a glance, he evoked both fear and loathing in her. Her heart wanted to soften to him; her mind reminded her she needed him. She waited, undecided on which emotion would win the war rekindling within her.

Zenti entered the camp between the guard's rounds, then, unopposed, walked to the campfire near her tent. There the silvery-white wolf waited in silence. The light from the fire pit created shadows across his body. The silver tint to his fur seemingly shimmered. He did not need to look around to know the feeling of the camp patrons and soldiers. As exhausted as he was, his Gift came to him, allowing him to feel every emotion but one. It had not escaped Zenti that Mari's patrons had become silent, though he really did not care. His mood was foul from her emotional outpouring. He had blocked her for the first time. It was time for her to learn the truth. Maybe she would grow, perhaps she would turn away. It mattered not. He could not longer stand the emotional assault that was pushing him towards the brink of the Void.

"May I enter," Zenti asked quite plainly? "Your patrons have nothing to fear of me."

The white wolf stood relaxed, unfazed by the silence that surrounded him. For all the silver-white of his fur, bathed in an eerie soft burnt umber glow of the campfire, Zenti seemed dark as pitch. The evening skies cascaded down a soft white light seemingly on him alone, adding to the visage. For a moment, Mari felt a wave of desperation roll over her. Mentally growling at herself, she crushed the feeling.

"Come in if you must," she snapped a response at him. The desperation she felt was a feeling that Zenti projected from his Gift. She had witnessed him use it, in the past, to considerable effect against their enemies. "It is better than you frightening my poor patrons half to death."

Mari stood to the side and opened the tent door. Her tent did not have a flap but a full-length thin wooden door with an upper screen. A slightly scandalous feeling came over her even though she knew that this meeting would be nothing of the sort. Zenti must have figured out what she wanted of him earlier. It could only mean he saw the value of aiding her Faction. He always saw a situation for what it was. The purpose of the meeting must have been clear to him. Why had Zenti allowed his emotions to get in the way of their earlier meeting? That was not his usual response to a stress-filled situation. Zenti was levelheaded and focused.

As he walked toward the tent, he removed the hunting knife and the pistol from his belt. With his Gift, he let the two weapons hang suspended in the air in front of the partially opened paw of a uniformed guard. The male just stood there dumbfounded, not knowing what he should do. Weapons were not allowed in Miss Mari's tent, except her own. Zenti paid the cheetah no attention and entered the tent as if he were an Elder, not a former lover.

An enraging shiver snaked down Mari's spine, which she quickly shook away. How dare Zenti act as if he were someone of importance in her Faction camp. However, she wanted to know what he wanted. More importantly, she wanted to see if he would help her Faction. Nodding to the confused soldier to take the suspended weapons, her smile told him that all was well. She entered the tent after Zenti.

Jolet was just inside the doorway, and Mari tripped over him. She had forgotten entirely about the brown rabbit. Jolet caught her before the vixen fell to the ground. Wrenching herself away from him, she thought of growling at him. However, she was the clumsy one. Zenti must have avoided the stunned male. She gave Jolet a weak but appreciative smile.

Moving with casual purpose, the vixen sat at the desk, ready to take notes. Mari motioned with a silent glance, and Zenti sat on the edge of the cot. She rubbed her forehead and looked back to the messenger, who was shaking from head to paw pad. Mari continued where she and Jolet left off.

"As I was saying, I went to meet with one of the other Faction Leaders earlier this night. Jolet may I introduce the Adviser to the Northern Faction, Summoner Zenti Semineu," offered Mari. Her demeanor was all business, "you may continue." It was only when the rabbit hesitated that she looked at him closely. He appeared to be a few shades paler.

"Z..Z...Zen...Zenti? This is who you went to meet with, ma'am?" The color had gone from the rabbit's muzzle. His ears folded flat to the back of his skull. "Ma'am, do you know what he is?" Jolet continued stuttering the words. He was shaking as if he was underdressed and completely shaven during a mid-winter snowstorm.

"It doesn't matter to me what he is, Jolet; I have nothing to fear," she looked at her former lover with a slight look of misgivings because of what happened earlier. "I do have some knowledge of what he can do. Would you please just continue?" The messenger paled further and stuttered again.

"But Ma'am, he's dangerous, he," Jolet began. She cut him off with a deep growl. She bent over the corner of the desk and glared at the brown rabbit. Her body showed off significantly, which she did not like, though she hardly realized it at the moment. The hackles on the back of her neck rose, fangs bared, claws digging into the edge of the wooden desk bringing her muzzle within inches of the scared rabbit.

"If you call me 'Ma'am' one more time, you are going to learn how dangerous *I* can be! Would you please just get on with whatever it was you wanted to discuss," Mari growled?

Jolet gulped at the rebuke as she slowly sat down in the chair. It was starting all over again; she could feel it as she struggled to get control of the anger building in her. A tiny twinkle of a smile crossed Zenti's eyes, and she thought she noticed it, but his look was as of death when she looked back at him again. Looking back at the rabbit, her glare caused him to jump.

"Yes, Ma…um yes, Miss Mari. Back to our first concern, the Elders think we should move the encampment. There was a report of a platoon or so well-armed soldiers in this area," he said, his voice still shaky.

"What if I think that this is as good a place as any to station the camp," she asked. Jolet stuttered again.

"Well, Ma-," he coughed, catching himself, "I don't think that the eld…," she leaned over the desk at him again and glared.

"Oh, would you just shut it! There are soldiers everywhere at this point. We are as safe here as we are anywhere. It would be better not to attract attention to ourselves and live like this rather than move the camp and possibly fall into an ambushed on our way! Besides, we can hide most of the patrons down in the mine shafts," Mari replied. The abandoned Milter ore mine, in the low hills, made for a very protective location.

"I will tell them," Jolet said, writing her words down. "The second concern they have is that you seeking out the Faction Leaders may be attracting too much attention. Moreover, we know that *THEY* will depart for *THEIR* temple in three weeks and be gone for four months. Might that not be a better time to seek aid from the other Faction Leaders?" He glanced at Zenti but turned away, quickly lowering his eyes to the white wolf's impassive gaze.

"I wasn't planning on seeking anyone else out until then," she said softly, sitting back into her chair. The only reason she had sought out Zenti first was that she knew there were walls to be overcome between them. She needed those walls gone before attempting to join with other Factions.

She also wanted to confirm for herself the unimaginable rumors of his actions and exploits. However, after the small demonstration only hours earlier, perhaps these rumors might not be so far exaggerated.

She only glanced at Zenti as he sat there quietly. He looked like a school pup waiting outside the headmaster's door. Just because Zenti was sitting there watching her did not mean that he was on her side. It did not mean that there were no walls between them, no wounds to tend, or feelings to address. This was not going to be a comfortable conversation in the least. However, an honest attempt had to be made, or there would have lingering doubts in the future.

Zenti had grown stoic, and his look was as distant. In these moments, Mari was worried Zenti was lost to another memory. In their nine years together, she had learned how to read Zenti. Something was different; something was wrong. A sigh escaped her muzzle as the rabbit noted her reply. Jolet began reading the next item on the list.

"We have a shortage of medical supplies, and our food stores will need to be rationed," Jolet began. He looked up at her, saw the boredom in her face, and knew that he best hurry. However, the Elder's list was exceptionally long.

"Um, please, this list is long and should never have come to you. I know it is not my place to say this, but the Elders lean too much on you," Jolet said. He looked a bit guilty for having taken so much of her time. "Perhaps I can get them to shorten it or makes some choices on their own," he offered as he glanced between her and the wolf. Even he could feel something was very wrong here.

Zenti began rubbing his temples with one paw Mari noticed out of the corner of her eye. This meaningless conversation was wearing on his patience. It was then she saw the back of his paw. Several scars were visible that she had not noticed before. Giving a sigh, she snatched the list from the nervous rabbit and rolled it up.

"Come back tomorrow, and I will have the decisions for you. Until then, get out of my sight," Mari said tersely, trying to control her temper. Relieved, the rabbit quickly nodded and bowed before rushing out of the tent. She sat back in her chair and pinched the bridge of her muzzle just between the eyes. The vixen rubbed the fur in slow circles. This was maddeningly frustrating. She had enough to deal with without Zenti being here. Had the earlier meeting been successful, she would have introduced him with a forewarning. Zenti just showing up only exacerbate the challenges she already faced.

"Remember, he is just the messenger," said Zenti without feeling, "it is not he who needs to feel your wrath concerning the petty details." He did not look at her but just stared at the canvas floor. Mari snapped her head up, ready to spit a rebuke. However, she paused.

Be calm; you need him, she told herself as she looked at the white wolf. Indeed, he looked to have a metallic tinge to his fur. Sitting there, rubbing his temples, he seemed distant and aloof. She wanted to yell at him and remind him that he was the one causing her anger. He looked tired, and if she pushed, he would just leave again. Calming herself, Mari took a moment and gathered her thoughts. Zenti Semineu, though exhausted, never looked this weary before. Something had changed in him. She reached for her cup of spiced cider.

"Why did you come here," Mari asked softly? "If you had some desire or need to speak with me, you could have and should have done so in the clearing." Turning, she looked at him, her eyes skating up and down his body as he sat on the bed, rubbing his temples. There were various scars all over him. She could clearly see them now that she was this close and under less duress. Most of the wounds had not been there before he betrayed her. Thick knotted scars crisscrossed his body. They were not there when they had parted thirteen months ago.

The vixen wanted to know what had happened. Who had dared to inflict such wounds upon someone as strong as Zenti Semineu? Who had the skill to get that close to him?

Alternatively, perhaps she had just not seen them. After all, they had not gotten this close in that same clearing some thirteen months ago without the distractions. Some things never change, she thought. In that same clearing thirteen months ago, twelve traitors died at their paws.

Stupidly then, just as she had done today, she blamed Zenti. When the last traitor died, she screamed at Zenti, blaming him for setting yet another trap. Memories of how she felt betrayed earlier today forced her to begrudgingly accept that Zenti was not the perpetrator of those attacks. Mari shook her head in frustration.

Perhaps that clearing was cursed. No, the vixen knew it was either Zenti or she that was being hunted. The clearing was just a patch of land, and there were too many unanswered questions. She had been as stupid today as she was thirteen months ago. For once in thirteen months, her heart and mind agreed.

"You were in no mood to speak to me earlier," Zenti whispered. He did not look up when he spoke again. "I knew you would be angry and would not trust me. Had the soldiers not followed you, we might have had some time to talk in peace." Zenti looked over at Mari. The hollowness in his voice echoed the emptiness in his eyes. She had never seen him so subdued. She knew his Gift took a lot of him; perhaps this new expansion of his Gift took more out of him than he realized. Zenti had always been reckless when it came to using his Gift to defend her. The white wolf looked away again.

100

Zenti's words hit her, *following you*. The soldiers were following her, not him. She was being hunted by soldiers of the Crown and those loyal to the invaders. How was that possible. What had she done to anger the Crown? Mari thought for a moment and realized it was not the Crown who wanted her. If the King wanted her dead or captured, he would dispatch the Royal Assassin. That foul killer would not need an army to capture or assassinate anyone. Looking at the silvery-white wolf, she was unsure of what she saw. He looked as if the weight of the world had been set upon his shoulders. Something was wrong. Hate him or not, he was in emotional pain, and the reason she was loved by all came to the surface. Miss Mari Semineu was exceptionally kind and caring.

Getting up, she paced to him and gently lifted his muzzle, forcing eye contact. Her heart ached as she fought down the urge to feel hatred and disgust for him, 'for the sake of the planet,' she reminded herself, 'for the sake of all Jaydonians.' As she looked at his empty black eyes, it fully dawned on her that they, too, had changed. No longer were they golden. In the clearing, her anger had not allowed her mind to see that Zenti's eyes had changed. The Gift was consuming him. Neither her heart nor mind gave comment. Something deep within Mari Semineu stirred.

He had left her for dead, abandoned her to the whims of her captors. Some mate he had turned out to be, her father would have been disgusted. She thought, but that tasted of a lie. After thirteen months, those words were like bile in her muzzle.

"What is it, Zenti," Mari asked softly? There was a slight hiss laced in her words. The vixen was still hurting. She wanted nothing more than to spit vile hatred at him for leaving her. How it pained her to sit here in this tent with him this close and not be able to make him pay for her hurt. Yet, something deep within tugged at her anger, pulling it deep down into her very being.

"The war against the…" he caught himself again about to use the invader's species name, "*THEM* will end here soon. I will move to the next area, and I will not return." Zenti's eyes told her that he genuinely believed this. "Peace has to come to this island. I have been told the war rages over the entire planet, and I know how to end it." Zenti looked away, having not missed the slight hiss in her words. When his mate hissed, he knew it meant she felt nothing but contempt. This contempt was directed at him, and his ears lowered ever so slightly.

"Really, how do you know this," she asked with a soft excitement in her voice? What did Zenti know that no one else did? Could it be true? He was always able to see grand strategies like others saw a kit's jigsaw puzzle. Holding the side of his muzzle gently, as she had so many times before, she maintained his attention so he would not look away. Mari forced him to face her. This was a familiar play to act out for them, and both knew it. He would hide things from her and allow her to pull tidbits out of him. He taught lessons this way. Zenti was teaching her a lesson, which confused her. Who betrays you then teaches you a lesson?

"Your patrons, like many others, fear what I have become," he began. He looked at her face and, for the first time, stroked the fur of her muzzle. It was just as he had done so many times before when she was concerned for him. However, he knew her concern was not genuine but forced.

"I cannot lose you again, and you cannot wage this war and win," he said. Zenti let his paw fall away, his shoulders slumping in an exasperated gesture, and continued.

"*THEY* get all of their supplies at a Port of the Stars. That is out on the far point of Morgan's Reef. I have surmised that if that Port of the Stars were not there, they would soon be defeated without the aid they receive. I cannot have you fighting *THEM*." Again, he reached up and stroked her muzzle.

"Please take your patrons to safety. Nothing will be safe on the far east end of this island. What you saw today was unplanned, and it took a lot out of me. Things, my vixen, have changed within me. I am someone you will come to despise for what I do. I don't want you to see me in that light." He choked a bit as he said the next words. "I want you to remember me as I was, not as I will be."

Mari bent low to him, her voice soft and reasonable. Zenti remembered that calming voice so well. She always spoke that way when his anger was about to get the best of his action. It was Mari's calming voice of reason that saddened him even more profoundly, knowing what he must do to secure her life and future.

"But I can't just give up because that would mean giving you up, and whether you're in my life to love," she paused, "or to hate. It is still better for our entire species if we resolve our differences so our kind can win this war."

She ran her thumb under his eye, and again she felt the knot of scars beneath his fur. Keep letting him believe that there is a chance, keep the calm in your voice, and let him hear the Mari of old. Keep your anger buried, she told herself. Yet again, something deep inside her tugged at her bitterness.

"I refuse to fear what you are or what you will become. I owe you that much for what you have done so far for Mitd. What you have done for my sister and me in the past is a deep debt," she said. The words found their way out from a heart deeply blocked off by the walls of her mind. As her thumb ran across the fur on his brow, she could feel a multitude of scars there as well. Mari moved closer, looking within his fur, her paws running through the strands. Never had she known him to have so many wounds.

"Do you really wish to know what I am, Mari? Do you really wish to see what your 'death' did to me? It is not too late to look away," Zenti offered. His words were solemn and hollow. Sorrow poured out of his voice like water from a fountain. She looked into his eyes and forced herself to maintain that eye contact.

"I need to know if you are all that the rumors say you are. This war has to end, and I have heard fantastic stories. Today you killed forty crown soldiers without so much as raising a paw. I hear you have burned whole towns, wiped out whole companies, and destroyed military outposts," she said, looking him deep in the eyes. She would know if he was lying. He never lied to her.

"Actually, it was more than that today. A group of Crown's soldiers followed the two platoons I killed when we were in the clearing. They were of mixed regions, which has me concerned," Zenti said, knowing Mari knew of the organizational command structure of the Crown.

She could see he was not lying, and it did concern her that the Crown was sending soldiers after the Faction Leaders. This was contradictory as the Crown was the one to establish the Faction forces. Why would the King want her? Mari looked at Zenti with questioning eyes. She wanted to know the truth of these rumors of him. The vixen wanted to understand why the Crown forces were hunting her.

Moreover, she wanted to know the truth as to why he abandoned her. Placing her paws on either side of his head, she forced him to look at her. There was no time like the present to end this mating yet gain his aid. Zenti did not attempt to look away.

"I am all that you have heard," Zenti said, then paused; the vixen growled at him to continue. "I am much more Mari. You need to take your patrons away from me. I am not safe to be around when I call on my Gift," he said and gently brushed her paws aside as he tried to stand.

She was not ready to let this conversation die. Mari put both paws on his shoulder and pushed him back down onto the cot. The look on her muzzle made it clear that they were going to resolve their issue tonight.

He did not fight her on this but looked up to her muzzle. She could be a little willful, Zenti thought and wanted to chuckle. However, if he did, it would only make her angry. Mari Semineu was not a little willful; she was a lot willful. It is what made her both successful and a pawful.

"Are you sure you want to see what I am, Mari? What your 'death' truly made me?" he asked. "Are you sure you are ready to know what the Gift has done to me?"

Taking his muzzle in her paws again, she firmly held his face; the look on her face was determined. She was stubborn and willful to the extreme, and when she got her mind fixated on something, Zenti knew it was a fight not worth waging.

"I won't look away," she said softly, "I want to see what you have become. I want to know what has become of the mate I knew. I want to know what vile events could

have taken such a good soul and turned him into the
monster that everyone says you are. I have heard all the
rumors about you. Now I want to know the truth from your
muzzle. You owe the memory of my father that much. He
trusted you. He had faith in you, and you have betrayed
that. I want to know why you betrayed me and what price
you were paid to do so," Mari said.

She set her knees against his. Her anger was rising
at his betrayal, and she was again losing control. Deep
within her being, she found a balance between the rage and
the need to know the truth. She set her gaze upon him.

Zenti knew she would not look away; she was too
stubborn. She would refuse to turn aside, refuse to hide;
she had never been one to run, and now was no different.
She would face reality. She would either overcome or
accept it if needs be. That had always been Mari
Semineu's second greatest strength, right behind her
compassion. Mari Semineu was both a great leader and a
willful kit. Tonight, one of those two personalities would
begin the journey into oblivion.

Mari looked at Zenti, looking at her, and knew what
he was thinking. He knew her all too well, and he knew
she would not look away. Drawing a deep breath, she
steeled herself, not knowing what to expect. This was the
wolf that had betrayed her, and while he deserved whatever
punishment it was that he had been dealt, she still had to
stay there and face the truth from him. Not out of her own
inner pride, but to save her species. If Summoner Zenti

Semineu felt he could stop the world, then she believed him. She had seen his resolve and knew that there was nothing he could not achieve. The price he would pay for his betrayal would never be high enough. Still, if he could save Jayden, then she would accept that as just compensation.

Zenti felt her claws dig into his lower jaw. Holding his muzzle tight, Mari looked into those cold black eyes. He knew better than to fight her on this. Too many times, she had gotten control of him this way. She was stubborn, willful, and determined. Those were all the reasons he still loved her. However, he could hear the bitterness in her voice, and when she looked into his eyes, he saw a fire in hers. That fire told him she wanted him to suffer, even if she needed and wanted his help in this war. She wanted him to feel every moment of pain that she had. It was as apparent as the sunrise on a clear morning what she wanted to see. The pain and suffering he had endured.

No, he did not need to be Gifted to know that she hated him still, and the only reason he was here with her is that she needed to know what he could, and would do, for their species.

Closing his eyes, he allowed his mind to drift deep within, finding the strength to overcome the sorrow that he felt. Yes, Mari only wanted him to win this war; she did not care about the event's truth. He knew her well. Mari knew just how to gain his help. She wanted to see that he had suffered for his betrayal of her. So be it, Zenti thought.

Mari watched him close his eyes as he had done many times before. He could call on vast reserves of strength that allowed him to perform incredible feats. She also knew that he had exhibited several facets of his Gift in the past, where others only possessed one or rarely two. It had made him very dangerous before, but what she saw earlier this day made her mind race with a touch of fear. Slowly she settled to her knees but did not let go. The vixen caught her breath when Zenti opened his eyes, and she found herself watching the day of her betrayal through his mind's eye.

This was impossible. Summoners did not have the Talents of Oracles. However, Summoner Zenti Semineu had wholly called on an Oracle's Talent of Union. Zenti had touched her mind with verbal thoughts in the past. They had shared entire conversations within the depths of their mind. That was, according to other Gifted, she knew, a common Talent of the Gifted. It was a minor aspect of the Talent of Union. However, to see from the perspective of another was a Talent historically known only to an Oracle. On the rare occasions she and her sister Rini talked, she learned a good deal about Oracle's Talents.

In the past, Zenti had displayed a variation of the Talent of Union. On occasions, Mari had been able to see through his eyes. But that was from his perspective; this was entirely different. According to her sister, only an Oracle had the full ability of the Talent of Union.

Mari regretted the distance between her and her

sister. Mentally Zenti growled at her wandering thoughts. Somehow he knew she was drifting into memories. Her view of the silvery-white wolf, sitting in her tent, faded. In her mind, she was viewing his life as if she were a ghostly observer.

Mari saw Zenti at the edge of the lake, kneeling down for a drink. She remembered that lake. It was where Zenti abandoned her. They had stopped to refill their canteens. She watched as a flash of light overwhelmed her sight and recalled that flash of light happening on that day. It was fresh in her mind as if today was that day. When her eyes cleared and the lake came into clear view, Zenti was gone. However, she was not alone. *THEY* were all around her. The vixen recalled having nowhere to run and no sign of Zenti to defend her. She was reliving that vision like she was a disembodied spirit. How was this possible? Zenti was gone, and she was all alone again by the lake.

Her body shook in fear, yet it refused to respond. Mari knew she was in the tent in her Faction camp. However, in her mind, she was linked to the past through the Talent of the Union. A familiar warmth caressed her body. It was Zenti calming her fears, and her body ceased trembling.

For almost a year and a half, she wondered how *THEY* knew where she and Zenti would be that day. She tried to reach into his mind like she could in the past. She wanted to see if she could find some answers from within. She found she could no longer find the way in as before.

Zenti had always been able to block her out when he felt he needed to protect her from his inner madness, but this time was different. Before, the vixen could find a crack in his mental armor, now she could find nothing to allow her inside. He was in complete control. She knew this could not be a lie. The Gifted Talent of Union could not implant memories.

In a way, she felt a wave of relief come over her. Perhaps she really did not love him still, and he did not love her. If this were why she could not find a crack in his mental armor, it would make her task easier to win him over to the fight. If he could be controlled instead of being this rogue monster that everyone claimed he was, maybe Zenti could be stopped from killing his own species.

Mari was no lover of those who supported **THEM,** but she had heard convincing arguments about why some of her kind did. Some could not fight; some had pups to protect. Some feared what would happen to their extended family. Still, Mari was glad. If Zenti was blocking her, he could not concentrate on touching her mind deeper than she wanted him.

She remembered how to build walls, just as Zenti had taught her, saying that he wanted her to be able to protect herself from the times that his mind raged. Perhaps it was all over between them, and just the anger and hurt remained.

Control and focus, she reminded herself. See what

you need to see to get Zenti to help, to make him want to help his species. Do not let the anger well up, Mari thought and began building those walls. Her mental pain diminished to the point of greater control, and the walls formed, shielding her mind from his.

Zenti's ears lowered even further as he felt her trying to crack through his walls but failed to raise her own sufficiently. She was never very good at it, he supposed, too much emotion not yet under control. Her thoughts betrayed her feelings, making it easy to confirm what she really wanted from him.

Zenti's heart sank as Mari's thoughts spilled over into his, her real purpose revealed. She wanted the monster to win the war, not the wolf to win her heart. Sadness welled within him as he began to open up his memories for her to see. She wanted to see the monster, so be it.

Outside the tent, the guards backed further away as a rolling wave of fear and depression hit them. It was Summoner Zenti Semineu's Gifted Talent of Revulsion. The guards did not know why they felt afraid, but they were sure they did not want to be near Mari's tent.

Chapter 3

Royal Oracle

Steaming water lapped at the decorative tile around the rim of the large inground tub. A polished brass paw rail led down shallow steps. Soft, subdued lighting from stained glass, floral print, wall sconces illuminated the bathing chamber. Servants had just finished drawing a fresh bath. A young female raccoon servant checked the depth of the water and its temperature. Nodding that the water was as high as they dared fill the rectangular tub, the raccoon once again ensured that it was at the proper temperature. She ran a paw over the tiles depicting the former Kings and Queens of Mitd feeling the tile's radiant heat. The water needed to be sufficiently hot without making it uncomfortable for the Royal Oracle.

Steam rose from the water, filling the room with wet warmth. The clear water gently distorted the crown seal inlaid on the bottom. Oracle Rini Waxton stood at the rim of the tub, her bathrobe loosely tied about her waist. The lioness was lost in thought. She looked down upon the gold and silver inlaid emblem that had been the first and only seal ever used by the royal families in their one-thousand-year history. The water gently rolled, and the insignia shimmered. Rini was lost in its exquisite complexity.

The young lioness studied the Crown Seal through the water as she thought about the metals that composed the real one. They fascinated her in their contrasting value and commonality. Garamite, a brilliant golden, moderately hard metal that was workable in a normal fire, had numerous uses. However, Garamite had been almost mined out five hundred years ago. There was very little remaining. That which was left was usually reserved for the Royal Family with very few exceptions.

Kredomis, however, was almost as plentiful as grains of sand. It was not a true metal but a silvery, powder-like substance that was the byproduct of crushing and separating a common metal used in making low-grade steel. Though workable under low temperature, it was nearly useless except for jewelry. It polished to a high sheen, but a ring could be crushed with relative ease. It was not conducive, nor did it suffer the adverse effect of weather.

However, when heated by the fires of a Summoner's Gift, the powder formed one of the hardest metals known. The process was so physically damaging to the Summoner's health that only a few hundred tons had been manufactured in a thousand years. Most were reserved for the Crown's use only. Once tempered in the forge of a Summoner's Gift, Kredomis took on all new traits. It became highly conductive and was nearly impervious to the ravages of time or weather.

The Royal Crest, comprising of these two metals, was indeed a beauty to behold. This watery copy could not begin to do justice to the grandeur of the one possessed by the King. The Royal Seal that the King wore was a unique piece. No other royal family member possessed one. The first Mitdonian King had the casting destroyed when the seal was completed a millennia ago.

The lioness studied the Royal Seal inlaid into the bottom of the tub. Three rings of Kredomis orbited a central star of Garamite. Tiny golden rays reached outward, holding the rings in place. On each ring was a large gem, one a deep fiery blood red on the outermost ring. The second gem, positioned on the middle ring, was of lush, vibrant sea green. Seated on the innermost ring was a brilliant clear gem with a unique, multifaceted cut.

Each gem had various smaller precious stones orbiting them. Those smaller gems were all held in place by the Kredomis. The whole of the crest was held together by tiny rays of woven strands of Garamite. Rini had always admired the beauty of the seal. His Majesty had always been gracious when she wanted to look at it. The graying wallaby even draped it around her young neck once.

When asked what the three-stone represented, the elder King explained it was about family. He kissed the young lioness on the tip of her nose and told her that she would know what he meant one day. He asked Rini to be patient in such a kind voice, the lioness acquiesced.

"Mistress Rini is there something wrong with your bathwater," asked a very apologetic manx? The feline female stood just behind and to the right of the young lioness. The orange and white-furred female held a silver tray of bath soaps and oils.

"No," came the single dismissive answer as Rini untied the loose looped knot and shrugged off the bathrobe.

The robe crumpled in a pile next to the edge of the large sunken tub. The manx did not react to the lioness's terse answer.

Stepping into the warm water, Rini Waxton held her crippled hip. The lioness was a kit when one of **THEM** shot her. Pressing on her hip joint helped her to keep balance. Every step hurt, and she silently cursed all those who had failed to help repair the damaged hip joint. Though both surgeon and Gifted Shaman alike tried to heal her wound, it would not properly heal. However, the one she cursed the most was that damned white wolf. Her injuries were the fault of Zenti Semineu. He did not directly cause the damage. However, it was him the invaders hunted. Had he not been trained by her father and been part of the training camp, her family would still be alive. As it was, her family was dead, and she was crippled for life.

Though very painful, walking down into the rectangular tub was the best therapy Royal Oracle Rini Waxton enjoyed. She could walk, though, with a hitch. The worst part about her injury was the random times the hip just shifted in the socket. That particular pain was like lightning shooting down her leg. Unless someone caught her, she immediately collapsed in a heap. Growling with each step, Rini forced herself to descend the steps. Though there was a boom chair installed especially for her, she detested how it made her feel like a cripple.

The water soaked her golden, cream-colored fur as she settled down into the tub of hot water. Damn, it felt good against her groin and abdomen. Sliding beneath the surface of the water, she enjoyed it soaking her thoroughly. She needed this. It was a little over ten days after her bleed cycle ended, and she could feel the onset of a breeding heat. That is not what she needed right now, especially since the panther Hayden was at court. Slowly she surfaced, but just enough to put her muzzle above the water. The lioness floated in the steamy water and tried to push the thought and scent of General Hayden out of her mind. It was difficult, as the male panther was incredibly handsome and charming. Rini growled again at her predicament.

Curse Hayden; why did he have such an alluring musk? And curse this damned heat, Rini Waxton thought. It always seemed to come on strongest when Hayden was around? No other male caused her so much discomfort. The fact that he was more than twice her age did not seem to matter. To make matters worse, Rini wanted his attention.

"Would you like soaps or oils, Mistress," asked the manx? Rini nodded at the ruby-colored container.

The young female manx began to pour the oils into the water until a light sheen covered the surface. The scent of cinnamon oil filled the bath chamber as the steam rolled off the water's surface. Setting the appropriate scented soap by the tub's edge, the manx made sure the towels were warming nicely by the heaters. The manx enjoyed serving Oracle Rini Waxton when the lioness was not being a bitch.

In a week when her full heat hit, Rini would be unbearable. Quietly the manx left the bathing lioness alone.

"Bring me something warm and sweet to drink," Rini called aloud, knowing that there would be servants just outside the bath chamber. Looking at the other room servants, the manx nodded at the warming tray of refreshments.

Rini was shortly rewarded with a goblet of warm spiced wine. Motioning the otter away, who was hanging up her bathrobe, Rini laid her head back into the cradle specially formed into the side of the tub and began to relax. The water soaked the short, cream-colored fur around her neck. The Vision she had received earlier today still baffled her mind. Why was her sister Mari repeatedly in her Gifted Visions?

Moreover, why did all the Visions end in disaster? Those memories lingered in her mind. Being unable to release a memory was an Oracles curse. It did not happen very often, but when it did, the mental backlash was maddening. Though soaking in delightfully hot water, the lioness's body shivered at the horrors her Gifted Visions brought.

Letting the hot water embrace her very being, the young lioness drifted off to sleep. The King went to extraordinary lengths to have the tub modified so the lioness could sleep in the water. The unique head cradle prevented her from slipping under the water. The contoured tile bed below the water allowed for a comfortable rest. The King, an elder wallaby, was indeed a remarkable male and monarch. His kindness was touching.

The lingering Visions, like the sore muscles, vanished within the water's warming caress. Rini lost track of how long she soaked, though she knew that several times the servants came to test and warm the waters. The lioness slipped in and out of a floating sleep. Sounds of hurried activities brought her out of her respite to find the room filled with servants preparing her garments and other items for the evening's dinner party. Groaning softly, the young lioness rolled her hazel eyes, not wanting to get out of the hot, scented water.

"Pardon the intrusion, Oracle Rini, but the dinner party is less than half an hour away. You have already rested through the reception. Her Majesty sent word to remind you that your presence was missed," said the young manx servant in a respectful but fear-laced voice.

Like all Oracles, Rini Waxton's mood could swiftly change. It was difficult for an Oracle to maintain their own mental timeline. At any given moment, they could have a Vision of someone else's. However, Rini Waxton had deep-seated anger issues on top of an Oracle's ego. That made her nearly impossible to deal with at times.

More than once, the manx had felt the mental slap from Oracle Rini when she had displeased the lioness in her servant's capacity. It was not a pleasant experience. She winced as Rini stood abruptly, expecting a rebuke, but none came. It was funny how Rini, only six years her junior, could evoke such power with a simple movement.

The water streamed off the wet fur as Rini stood waist-deep in the tub. The lioness debating if she really wanted to exit the soothing waters. A regretful sigh escaped her muzzle as Rini closed her eyes. The Queen had issued a polite summons; how could she refuse? Focusing on her Gifted Talent of Levitation, Oracle Rini Waxton slowly floated out of the tub. The lioness stepped on air as if it were the tile beneath her paw pads. Rini did not enjoy using her Gift to compensate for her disability, but this matter required expedience. The manx held up a towel.

The oversized towel had been warming by the fire, and the moment it hit her fur, it felt divine. The lioness just simply stood there as always, letting her servant dry her body. She only moved when the manx began drying the inside of her legs and tapped Rini's groin allowing for easier access. Though she could have used one of the forced warm air fur dryers, the lioness appreciated the personal attention of being dried off by paw.

Rini thought of the place she was in now. The King himself had given her this beautiful room. This room once belonged to his daughter. No one spoke of the King's late daughter. How she passed to the stars was a mystery. One day the King had a beautiful kit, and the next day he announced she had passed to the stars. The elder wallaby was devastated. However, life went on, and so did the King.

Rini recalled the day the King permanently took her in. The lioness was a little more than a year past her Gifting Day[5]. When she was wheeled into the King's private office, the elder wallaby did something unexpected. He dismissed all of his guards and pushed the young lioness around the castle, finally bringing her to this room. It was his late daughter's room. From the moment the King met the young lioness, he never saw her as anything other than wonderfully unique. Over the years, the King had almost spoiled her to the point she felt like his actual daughter. However, though Rini was fond of the old wallaby, the lioness's true loyalties were for the Queen. It was the Queen who ensured she received the best of every possible advantage. It was the Queen who recognized her Gift and nurtured it.

The manx finished drying her mistress's body when, for a moment, she found herself kneeling at Rini's paw pads. She looked up at the sad young lioness. Rini was absent-mindedly stroking the fur on her servant's muzzle while she stared down into the tub. Not moving for fear of breaking the moment, the manx simply waited for the moment to end. This was not the first time this had happened, and the manx had learned not to interrupt the gesture. She simply accepted it for what it was: a young, extremely talented, and overused Oracle attempting to show a crumb of kindness. The manx prayed to Orra that

---

[5] The Jaydonian Gifting Day is their 5th whelping day, what you call a birthday. However, birthday is an incomplete translation.

her true thoughts were hidden as she softly continued to dry the fur on her mistress's legs.

The sound of a cup shattering broke the moment, and the manx found herself kneeling at empty space as her mistress raged off into the other room. Turning her back to the entryway, the manx quickly wiped the tears from her eyes and left the towels on the floor while getting another warm one from the heating rack.

"Thanks for ruining my mood; who dropped it? Wait, do not tell me, just get the Heavens and Hells out of my room after cleaning up the mess. Your services are no longer needed. Report to the head of housekeeping for your new duties, and be fast about it," snapped Rini, not caring that she was standing among these servants without any clothing. The lioness stomped off to her dressing room. Quickly the servants obey.

The manx was waiting for Rini in the dressing room when she returned and patted the lioness's fur with her dry paws to find any remaining wet spots. Drying the few damp areas, the manx dropped the cooling towel and began brushing Rini's fur. The golden, cream-colored fur had subtle tones of short brown hairs, loosely spread over the length of Rini's body. The lioness stood still while the manx trimmed the fur in various parts of her body. Tapping the inside of Rini's thigh, the young lioness opened her leg, allowing the manx to trim the fur around her groin. Cleaning the trimmed fur away, she waited for her mistress to give a nod of approval before setting the scissors and brush down. Rini examined herself in the full-length mirror and smiled approvingly.

The manx began to dress her mistress, offering first her undergarments, to which Rini batted them away. However, the manx simply sniffed the air and picked them back up. With a sigh, the young lioness lifted her paw pads one at a time as the manx slipped the panties on her. The manx snapped them behind and around Rini's tail and made sure the fur did not bunch up. Even after a bath, she knew it would not be long before Rini's heat-driven musk would be detectable. The panties had a descenter lining in the crotch, which would mask all but the strongest breeding heat musk. Rini thought of General Hayden briefly and shivered.

"Spicy and sweet or soft and flowery," asked the manx as she pointed at two jars on the counter? Rini must have just thought about that dashingly handsome panther Hayden, as her scent just spiked. However, the manx did not react to the musk.

Rini shrugged her shoulders, and the manx chose the jar with the sweet spice-scented oils. She rubbed it on the outside of the panty's front panel. Deciding it would not be enough, the manx then lightly applied the oil over the pantie's crotch.

The manx continued to dress Rini in clothing that continued to amaze her. Rini had always dressed remarkably simple, despite all Rini's airs and all her outrageous temperament. The skirt was soft linen light brown in color, complementing the lioness's fur. The blouse was a light blue-gray with embroidered flowers running up the ribs and wrapping around the shoulders. Delicate vines with sporadic floral buds ran down the length of the outside of the arms.

The styles were thirty years old though the colors were fresh and crisp. The manx thought that Rini must dress like this because of her late mother. The manx learned of the lioness's mother from all the stories Rini told. Her mother was a simple soldier's mate. However, the manx knew General Waxton was no simple soldier. His mate was a strong-willed, well-educated female who stood out in a crowd. Rini rarely talked about her parents without falling into a sad mood. Their death was well known in the inner circles of the upper military echelons. The manx had several lovers who were active military personal. Occasionally they shared tidbits of information when the manx inquired sweetly.

The manx rubbed the sweet, spiced oils on the lioness's hips, lower rib cage, and across Rini's underarm pits. By doing so, the manx was making it perfectly clear that Rini's heat was growing heavier. Though she did not say as much, there was no mistaking the way the servant paid close attention as she rubbed the scented oil in carefully.

Rini knew that the manx was right; she was in a bad state of heat. With the correct male's musk, it would erupt into a full breeding heat. It needed to be solved before that happened. The time just did not feel right to the young lioness to conceive. Rini was not about to let her body dictate her actions. She stood there with no objection, letting her paw maiden, Elli, dress and prepare her for the evening's events.

Elli, Ellsinore Brendma, had been given to the lioness as a paw servant shortly after Rini's initial Vision. That Gifted Vision happened when Rini moved to the Crown City for medical treatment. That was about a year after her mother and father were murdered. The King personally assigned Elli the position. At first, Rini would call her by her full name, but soon it merely became Elli. The manx soon became like a best female friend instead of a servant. However, both knew their station in this relationship, but that did not stop Elli from being the only friend the young Oracle had.

More than once, the manx had overstepped her bounds when serving. However, with those bounds crossed, Elli had kept Rini firmly rooted in base sexual reality. That base sexual reality, if left uncontrolled, would have gotten the lioness mated off by now with several kits. That was a fate Rini Wasxton was not ready to be saddled with. No Oracle wanted kits until their midlife. Kits, and a family, over-complicated issues, especially Visions.

No, Elli was an excellent paw maiden. Not only did the manx reminded her of the necessity of decorum on certain lowly matters, but she was a female who also had an excellent taste in males. On more than one occasion, over the past five years since the lioness's Coming-of-Age[6] date,

Elli pointed out a few lovers that were more than merely enjoyable but also superbly memorable. Rini lifted her arms to allow Elli to tie the ribbons around her lower ribs and neck. When neatly tied, Rini sat down so Elli could brush out her fur.

Rini looked at the manx's reflection in the mirror as she finished fluffing out her hair. Reaching back, Rini stroked the manx's side. Rini laid her head on Elli's midriff for a brief moment. Elli was an attractive female. Though not petite, the manx was a thin one hundred twelve pounds. However, Elli's five-foot-eight-inch tall frame was fit. The manx's fur was a light orange with streaks of cream white here and there. They both knew this was as close to showing the kindness of a friend that the young lioness could ever express. Standing as Elli finished her hair, Rini leaned down and kissed the manx on the cheek before quietly leaving the dressing room. Rini Waxton was a thin one hundred nine pounds and four inches taller than Elli. However, it was not the physical height that made Rini Waxton formidable; it was her Gift.

Elli heard Rini set down a cup a few moments after leaving the dressing room. She listened as the door open and close again. The manx went about putting the dressing table back in order. Hanging the towel up by the fire for drying, Elli heard one of the other room attendants' comments on what a bitch the young lioness was being. A

---

[6] A Jaydonian is considered an adult at the age of eleven. Compared to most other species in the universe, this would be the equivalent of eighteen to twenty years of age. By age eleven, Jaydonians are fully matured.

comment was made that she must be in an awful heat to be so much nastier than her usual self. It was true that Rini was a bitch most of the time.

Turning from the dressing room fireplace, Elli quietly moved towards the door. The same room attendant who had mouthed off about the lioness's mood opened the door for the manx as she approached. A swift fist caught the young doe hard on the muzzle. Like a stroke of lightning, the blow sent the room attendant sprawling across furniture, knocking over a pastry and teacart.

"Do I need to stress my point, or has it been clearly made," the manx asked calmly? Elli tossed a pawkerchief to the doe sprawled on the floor. "And don't get any blood on the rug. It will only anger the Oracle even more. I am sure, once she learns of the comment you just made, Royal Oracle Rini will not be pleased."

The doe went pale at the thought of the Royal Oracle finding out about her verbal slip, and she began to beg the manx not to tell. As the manx left the room, she offered a brief reply. 'Perhaps the young doe should not be in the city when the dinner was over. It might not be a bad idea to visit the other side of the island, even.' Elli made a parting comment about an Oracle's ability to pick up on latent memories. The doe paled even more.

Elli fumed as she walked down the hall towards the servants' kitchen entrance. Guards stood in an ever-vigilant watch, not moving from their stations along the way. Elli served Rini daily and was known to each of them. Their duty was to protect the Royal Oracle. The guards knew better than to be anything more than just a shadow to the young Oracle. However, Elli was very approachable, and the manx made their job easier. They noted Elli's phlegmatic look and surmised one of the other serving staff must have angered the manx as much as they had angered her mistress. They knew Oracle Rini Waxton was a bitch[7], as much as Elli knew it. However, the guards had more sense than to vocalize it, even in private.

"Rini is a bitch most of the time, but no one calls her that, not to where I can hear it. No one talks about my mistress in that manner ever. No one understands her better than I do," said Elli in a soft hiss more to herself than anyone in particular.

The lioness was never given a moment's rest concerning her Gift. When Rini was a young post-Gifting Day kit, she was not afforded everyday playtime that other maturing young were allowed. Rini Waxton was not allowed a typical education either. Instead, she had nothing but private tutors since coming to the Crown City. As the daughter of one of the most respected generals, Rini would have been cared for without question. However, Rini Waxton was Gifted. That elevated any consideration that General Haverick Waxton's daughter might have been granted.

---

[7] The term bitch has two meanings on Jayden. A female who was in heat or a very nasty tempered female. The difference is in the tonal inflection.

The Queen recognized that Rini was an exceptionally Gifted Oracle from a young age. It was the Queen who began grooming Rini almost the instant the young lioness permanently settled in. Had it not been for the King, the Queen would have kept the Pre-Coming-of-Age[8] lioness at her studies all day long. However, the King seemed to know precisely when the young Oracle needed a break. He would come into her tutor's room and sweep the young lioness away on one of the little outings that he had planned especially for Rini. The King was remarkably skilled at knowing when the lioness was faltering. Elli turned the corner and headed toward the kitchen.

Throwing the kitchen door open, Elli almost knocked a cook's assistant on her tail. The manx barged into the room. Everyone in the room skittered out of the way, clearing a path for Elli. Making a beeline directly for her mistress' private cook, Elli shoved a lingering dishwasher out of her way. Rini's personal cook looked up from the well-organized prep table and began to tremble at the scowl on the manx's muzzle.

"Is dinner ready for our mistress?" Elli asked in a flat, unwelcoming tone as she picked at various foods from the serving boards. The manx noted the flavor and consistency of each item.

Elli became more frustrated and grew impatient as the young bovine stood stammering about something that

---

[8] This is a period between the ages of five (their Gifting Day) and eleven (their Coming-of-Age Day) when a Jaydonian was expected to mature emotionally into an adult.

did not directly answer the question. Elli growled before verbally lashing out at the stammering bovine. The young female bovine was an excellent cook. However, she was not the brightest.

"Just shake your head yes or no. I do not have all night waiting for you to decide which words won't anger me, so get on with the answer!" she growled, to which the bovine nodded yes in a quick, head-jerk motion that caused Eli to simply sigh.

Rolling her eyes at the cook's trepidation, Eli picked at a few more items before looking up to the bovine. Rini was exceedingly particular about her food. The lioness was not picky in some trivial sense but demanded attention to quality and detail.

"The meat is not to her liking. Find a better cut before you put it on her plate. Make sure the plate is hot, not lukewarm like the one used for her breakfast," Elli said. No one understood Oracle Rini Waxton like she did. That lack of understanding led to mistakes of carelessness. Elli turned to leave the kitchen, then turned back to the young bovine cook.

"Your mistress is on the verge of entering a breeding heat. I suggest you tailor her meal to help reduce that unfortunate situation. I would hate to find a new cook because you failed to take that into consideration," said Elli. The frightened bovine quickly nodded. Being a cook in the Crown City meant safety from the war. Elli walked away, leaving Rini's personal cook trembling in terror. Elli was not a temperamental bitch; she just hated incompetence.

The manx left the kitchen and quietly walked down the hall to her quarters. She needed to change into clothing that would be more appropriate for the evening. Waiting for her at the door was a middle-aged badger. His dress marked him as a messenger, and he gave her a sealed note to which she offered him a quarter Breng[9] and thanked him before he walked away. It was customary for servants of a higher status to tip those of a lower rank. It reflected the comradery between servants.

Entering her room, Elli opened the note and sighed deeply as she read it. Looking around the modest room, she shook her head. Rini Waxton was kind and generously rewarded loyal service. Though not lavish by royal standards, the gifts Rini gave Elli were cherished. However, Elli had little time to enjoy them.

"Why are things never easy," Elli said to the empty room as she threw the note into the fireplace? The manx watched the special paper burn a bright blue. The night had suddenly become busier with the arrival of the message.

The manx looked at the clock and realized she did not even have time for a quick shower and growled to herself. Her musk was as heavy as Rini's. Quickly she spruced up and put on the appropriate serving attire based on the evening's protocol. Carefully she misted on a light-

---

[9] BRENG is the monetary currency of Mitd. It has various forms, including coins, notes, and electronic tokens (The latter is rarely used).

spiced perfume in strategic spots and headed out to serve her mistress.

＊＊＊＊＊＊＊＊＊＊＊＊＊＊＊＊＊＊＊＊＊＊＊＊＊＊＊＊＊

Standing fifth in line while waiting to be announced, the panther's cool and calm demeanor suppressed a pounding heart with cold calculation. His sharp military dress and detached stare projected a male worth of his notoriety. A personal summons by the King could mean only one thing. With skillful manipulation and planning, he had planned this event to unfold a year from now. However, the King gave no indication that this summons was related to his plans. That created a moment of fear.

Still, it presented an opportunity to conquer one final enemy; fear itself. Overcome the power of the fear, and the universe would follow. The panther crushed the feeling of trepidation like it was one of his enemies. Still, doubt lingered, and the panther needed to solve the mystery of his summons.

Indeed, he thought everyone could smell the terror that his heart wanted to project but did not. The panther thought of how many battles he fought. He recounted how many engagements he had won just by being the Commander of the King's forces. How many wars never started because his reputation preceded him? He felt as nervous and scared as the day when his late mate whelped his first little kit, Lizta. That was nearly twenty-five years ago. Much had changed since then.

Now he stood here, by the King's specific command, waiting in line like a commoner. He was to be the guest of honor at a state dinner that had no practical purpose. The invitation implied tonight's state dinner was to reassure the Lords, Barons, and Governors that the King and Queen were still in power during these trying times. The panther had been invited to many state dinners, but none were explicitly by the King's command. Tonight was an exceptionally uncommon event. The King rarely conducted any business, leaving it all to his mate, the Queen. The King had occupied himself with a project so secretive, even his mate did not know what it entailed. Another guest was announced, and now there were but four ahead of the panther.

'Can you not hurry this up,' the panther thought to himself as another formal introduction commenced. A fat male lion, the Governor of a trivial province, and his mate were escorted to their seat in the Grand Ballroom. He did not enjoy the tedium of State Functions. It was all formality, pomp, and circumstance. To him, they were a useless waste of time. Unlike military ceremonies, which served a purpose, these Royal functions served no discernible purpose other than stroking egos.

How could he have unlimited patience to spare on the battlefield, and yet here, in the Crown City, he had none? This was something he would need to work on;

these days, he spent more and more time in the Crown City. Maintaining his calm visage, the black panther bowed to a noble female hyena as she exited the Grand Ballroom. He could see that a more significant number of Royals were present, more than was expected at such an event, and wondered exactly what was transpiring.

"Good evening, General Hayden, it has been some time," came a familiar voice that shrilled in his ears. True to his nature and station, the panther stepped out of line, noting he was only three away from being seated. General Hayden bowed deeply to the elderly ferret before him.

"M'lady Corinth, to what do I owe the pleasure of being noticed by your grace," Hayden asked? He waited for that light touch that always granted him permission to stand erect in her presence. The touch came swiftly, almost as he finished the words.

Meeting her gaze with a soft smile and a compassioned look, he noticed that she seemed younger. Her black fur did not appear as gray, and the folds of skin around her brown and black muzzle that come with age were no longer present. It was not a trick of makeup or grooming; they were simply gone. The female ferret's gray eyes sparkled with mischief as she smiled at him. Making a mental note of that oddity, Hayden continued his attentions to the Queen Mother. The panther smiled at her as a son would.

"Walk with me and do me the honor of sitting by my side tonight," Lady Corinth said. The elder ferret's voice sounded softer, yet her tone still had that shrillness of an elderly female.

However, when she spoke in a more genteel manner, the shrill was almost undetectable. She smiled softly at General Hayden while motioning for a servant to come forward. Hayden offered the elder ferret his arm as was expected. Lady Corinth, the Queen Mother, passed her cane to her servant and leaned heavily on the panther. Moving slowly, the two proceeded into the Grand Ballroom.

The tall, high ceilings were lined with paw-woven banners representing each of the thirty islands that made up Mitd. Each banner bore a specific island's seal, listing the date they were conquered, with some having more than one date as they attempted to break away.

The wooden floors were polished to a brilliant shine, and the tables were set in a box-like pattern about the room, leaving the center open. Golden fabrics draped over the rectangular dinner tables, barely kissing the floor in the front. They hid the paw pads of those seated. The lighting was soft, casting an almost enchanting glow to the room as it cascaded off the arched mirror-paneled ceiling. However, the moniker Grand Ballroom seemed oddly out of place. For all the fine trappings, the room was surprisingly common, though in retrospect, so was most of the Crown City. The King had a decided taste for the mundane. The nobility thought it was unbefitting; the citizens adored it. That simple act of the King, though distancing the elite, endeared the citizens to his reign.

Stepping into the room without announcement, the soft light reflected off the carefully placed gems and shards of Garamite in Lady Corinth's dress. The effect caused the full-length dress to sparkle. The result created a majestically radiant air about her.

The Herald turned back to the doorway when he saw the Queen Mother standing before the room. The opossum quickly caught his grave error of not immediately announcing her. He bowed deeply and turned to the room. Stepping up and clearing his throat loudly, he tapped a small crystal chime that reverberated throughout the great hall. The crystal chime's unique tone indicated High Royalty was entering a room. Standing, every guest looked to the Herald. He gained the room's undivided attention as he spoke.

"May I present to you Her Royal Highness, Queen Mother of our gracious King Taimus Corinth the Seventh, Lady Quinel Corinth. As if coached, the room bowed in unison. The Queen Mother entered the room on the arm of her escort, Hayden. The Herald continued.

"And presenting our magnanimous King's Guest of Honor, Commander of the Southern, Eastern and Western armies of his Majesty's Armed Forces. Recipient of the Crown Defender Shield, Crown Lance and the only living recipient of the King's Cross, I present General Ra-"

A quick snarl, searing eyes, and a flash of fangs from the panther cut the Herald short on the attempt to introduce him formally by his full name. Gulping heavily, the opossum cleared his throat and tugged at his collar.

"I present General Hayden," corrected the Herald, quickly bowing his head, not wanting to continue the eye contact with the panther.

"Come now, my dear, we mustn't scare the poor Herald," chided the elder ferret. The toothy grin she flashed at the panther momentarily held the air of a mischievous kit.

Hayden turned to apologize to her for his rude behavior when a quick wink and the mischievous grin turned into a wicked smile. Quinel Corinth was playing with him; how unlike her. The panther noticed the elder ferret was leaning on his arm rather heavily and wondered if perhaps she was losing her ability to walk without aid. He steadied the Queen Mother as if she were his own family. Shrill voice or not, she was the oldest living member of the royal family and deserved his undivided attention.

As the two reached her place at the King's table, it dawned on the panther that the Herald had addressed him as the King's guest of honor. Seating the Queen Mother, Hayden followed her command as she patted his chair and sat beside her.

He had been a guest of honor before. After each of his military victories or other services to the Crown, the panther was acknowledged warmly. However, the invitation had always been at the Crown's behest, never directly by His Majesty. Looking down at the ribbons and medals on his chest, Hayden could not recall having done anything recently worthy of such an honor. In reflection, he could not remember having ever been seated at the King's table or treated with such attentiveness as he had been treated today.

General Hayden continued to present the air of a commander serving the needs of the Crown. Attentively he listened to the polite chatter of the Queen Mother. They were not directed at him but at other members of the King's Personal Advisers. However, his calculating mind continued to work this puzzle out.

His plan to become the Crown Champion was still developing. In another year, that plan would be complete. With several more key victories, he could cement the most prestigious military position on Mitd. The Crown Champion officially commanded all the Mitdonian forces, including the various Factions. Though he did command all the Crown's Military Forces, he only technically commanded the Factions. When his plan succeeded, and it would succeed, he would control all the military assets on Mitd.

Perhaps he had been set up and made to wait in line just to be pulled out by the Queen Mother. This was all very unsettling, and his sharp mind went to work on solving the mystery. Everything to the panther was a puzzle to solve. Life, like war, was a battle to be won. To win any contest, and thereby any conflict, one had to have a plan. Any plan required insight, imagination, and the creative ability to adapt to any situation. A great planner's ability to adapt required the skills to solve all the mysteries that any potential possibility might present. The panther was the best at logically solving problems, bar none.

It took almost half an hour to introduce the remaining guests. As the last introduction was presented, he noticed that Oracle Rini Waxton had slipped in and quietly taken her usual place at the King's table. Oddly enough, that was where the late princess once sat. Hayden pondered if the lioness would be adopted into the Royal Family. The thought moved slowly and carefully through his mind as he listened to the droning of the Herald's final introduction. Perhaps Rini might be worth sniffing after. Several members of the Royal Court had made polite, suggestive comments to him on the possibilities.

"She is stunning, is she not? She will make a fine mate to the one who can learn how to control her," said the Queen Mother as she took Hayden by the muzzle with one claw and turned his face to hers.

"I know what transpires between you and the Queen; make no mistake concerning that. Though my son sits on the throne, and I love him dearly, he does not know what is best for the future of our species," the elder ferret said. She patted the panther gently on the muzzle as a grandmother would do a kit; however, the look in her eyes was deadly serious.

"And you would know what is best for our species," Hayden asked sharply? The panther remembered his manners and to whom he was speaking. Too many Royals in the past were military 'leaders' with disastrous results. The ferret scowled at him briefly, then the wicked smile returned before looking down at her goblet.

"Oh, not I, General Hayden. Those designs are best left to those more versed and educated in such matters. I am aware that you and several others have designs on shaping our future and the future of this planet. I also believe that little lioness has a large part in these grand plans," the elder ferret replied. Lady Corinth looked at her empty goblet rather than paying him attention.

Hayden snapped his claws, pointed, and a servant filled her empty goblet. Growling at the apologetic female mouse, the panther's bared fangs reinforced the displeasure in his eyes that the Queen Mother was made to wait for anything.

"My Lizta is older than she by half again her age," Hayden began when she cut him off.

"Oh pish, Rini Waxton came of age over four years ago. In case you have not noticed, whenever you are around, her heat sends every male in this palace out of his mind. The fact she is nearly thirty years your junior is irrelevant. Do not be a stupid kit. Our future as a species depends on how we proceed with these invaders. Though I do not know all the scheming, I know that their technology is far greater than ours is. We can benefit, as a whole, by bringing these schemes to fruition," the Queen Mother whispered into Hayden's ear. The panther began to respond, but he was cut short with the King and Queen's announcement.

"Lords, Ladies, and distinguished guests, I present to you their Majesties, King and Queen Corinth!" Proclaimed the Herald. The room stood in unison and bowed.

"Such an empty introduction for two such powerful Jaydonians," whispered Hayden more to himself than to the Queen Mother as he returned to his seat.

"All part of the matting arrangements and agreements," replied the Queen Mother. "Neither can be introduced above the other when in the other presence. This way neither is exalted above the other. They had to flip a Breng on who was introduced first, and each odd year it changes," snickered the elderly ferret, who was the only one not to bow, much less stand. Hayden gave her a quizzical look. Though he spent more time in the Crown City than before, he was not interested in Royal intrigue. However, that would need to change soon.

"They make a wonderful pair in public," Lady Corinth replied to the panther's raised eyebrow. In his late seventies, the King was a handsome elder wallaby with tan fur and darker brown blotches. He was on the heavyset side but carried it well with a gentle smile and an easygoing manner. The Queen was a very overweight forty-six-year-old kangaroo but bore it with such a regal aura that she did not look fat. Her fur was a soft cream color that was uniform and well maintained.

As the King and Queen approached the table, they stopped, each to one side of the Queen Mother. Both kissed her on the cheek at the same time. They commented on how beautiful she looked before moving to their respective seats. The Queen Mother sat in the second seat on the King's right-paw side. The first seat on the King's right was currently unoccupied. It was reserved for the Crown Champion. The King took his seat while the Queen addressed the gathering as per the mating arrangements.

"Honored guest and members of the Royal Family," the Queen began. Her voice was strong and assured when she spoke. "Tonight, we celebrate a grand event. We will dispense with the traditional ceremonial pomp and be amongst friends enjoying each other company over a fine meal. Let us begin the feast; the main course is only good while served hot. Please do not wait on the ceremony. Eat and enjoy our Guest of Honor's favorite dish," said the Queen, to which immediately dinner was served.

Servants assaulted the room, quickly bringing plate after plate of food to be placed before the guests. Course after course of the best food the land had to provide was sat before the guests. Tonight was to be enjoyed over casual conversation. The various dishes continued to be served about the room.

Hayden did not engage in conversation but simply enjoyed the meal. It was a delicacy from his home province. Only a select few master chefs could prepare this delicacy, and even fewer could prepare to perfection. The rare combination of spices was difficult to properly achieve. The Qua'mar was a deep freshwater trout-like fish. It could only be caught twice a year when they migrated to shallow water to spawn. Its flesh was very temperamental, making it hard to properly prepare.

As he quietly ate, Hayden found himself surrounded by a room of chattering busybodies, gossiping about this or that. Yet no one seemed to be paying him much attention. He preferred it that way. Meals were meant to be enjoyed without being interrupted with polite platitudes.

No conversations were directed to him, and the ones that drifted his way were polite but succinct. He soon found himself not to be the center of attention, leaving the panther to wonder exactly why he had been invited. Was this part of the plan; was he to be kept in complete darkness? This was frustrating; however, he smiled politely and continued to enjoy the meal. The main course was served, eaten, and cleared. Next came the dessert and sweet sherry, his favorite. Servants placed the final dish before the guests.

The panther's keen mind deduced that perhaps his personal staff had presented his dining preferences to the Crown. With the unobtrusive observation, the panther realized that some of the guests wanted to speak with him yet refrained. That observation lent credence to his personal staff theory. The King, tapping his crystal goblet, drew the room's attention and then relinquished control to the Queen.

"Before the night grows old, and our minds become a bit duller with the evening's libations, the Crown has an announcement to make," said the Queen, raising a paw to quiet all the talk. "It has been a century since the Crown has been at a full-scale war and a century since we have needed to appoint the Crown Champion. In the past, the invaders were content with raiding our land. It is evident they have altered their plans. Therefore, a dire need has arisen for the appointment of a Crown Champion. Again, she raised a paw to quiet the murmuring.

"Our battles to date have been what the Crown considers a draw. Our losses have been many, but so have those of our invaders. Soon our invaders will be heading to their yearly worship for four months, giving us a chance to recover and lick our wounds. Now will be the time to act in unified force. Currently, the Faction leaders follow General Hayden, that is, except for three," the Queen said and looked to a far table.

"Minister Quinn," the kangaroo began and hesitated until the Minister looked at her. "Three months ago, you gave our good King your personal assurance that the Southwest Faction would be giving its support to the Crown. I understand it is lead by Commander Taxz. Why have we not seen his forces," the Queen demanded in an accusatory tone?

The male squirrel flinched at her accusation. The Queen was known to make examples of those who displeased her. The squirrel also knew the kangaroo's penchant for making public examples. A slight shiver ran down his spine, yet he steeled himself and answered.

"Commander Taxz has failed to report as ordered, my Queen. Only one and a half squads under his command have reported for service," replied the Minister, now standing head bowed in humiliation. Minister Quinn had hoped that this day would not come or that Taxz would have been killed.

The war in the southwest was on a limited basis. The only viable resources grown in the southern islands were fruit crops. It had been a daily struggle for the Minister to get just what little information he had thus far. Reports were sparse, but he knew Commander Taxz had been training Royal Troops in combined arms tactics. That information came from those civilians who had been delivering supplies to the now-empty Faction training camps. None of the Royal Troops had been located.

"And where have he and almost a full division of the Crown's soldiers gone," the Queen snapped with evident anger at his unacceptable response?

"My Queen, those that returned did not know the final destination of General Taxz's or the Crown's troops. They were on training maneuvers. It seems former General Hetchon set forth orders with which we are not familiar. Our scouts have not been able to locate him in almost four weeks," the Minister replied in a broken voice. The squirrel stood before his Queen with slumped shoulders, folded ears, and lowered head.

He noticed her disquieted look, which needed no explanation. She was exceedingly unhappy at this development. The only positive aspect of this public humiliation was that he could tell the Queen was refusing to let her anger get the best of her. That fact might just save his life.

"There can be only one leader of the military on this island. Those rag-tag Faction leaders have met with some success, but we need to end this war, and I will not put it in the paws of a group of uncontrollable Faction leaders. Therefore, all Faction leaders who are not in the Crown Champion's service will be considered traitors to the Crown by tomorrow evening. The Ministers who govern those Factions will also be subject to the discretion of the Crown Champion," said the Queen, which silenced the murmuring room. This was disconcerting to many of the governing representatives. The Factions were civilian militia, not Crown troops. Their creation was to protect the civilian population against all threats, including a corrupt government. That was a Royal decree five hundred years old.

"General Hayden, come kneel before the Crown," commanded the King as the wallaby stood. He rounded the end of the splittable where he and the Queen were seated. Hayden made his way around and stood briefly before kneeling before the King.

"I proclaim you, General R. Hayden, the Crown Champion, with all the responsibilities, privileges, and penalties. You are now in command of all the Royal

Military forces the Crown possesses. You are hereby commanded to rid our lands of these invaders," stated the King as he draped the sash over around Hayden's neck.

The room exploded with applause as Hayden stood, turning to face the guests. The panther inwardly smiled at the turn of events. However, the timing was too early. This should not have occurred for another year. Those were his plans of becoming the Crown Champion. Because of this advance in the timeline, there would be complications.

Turning to face the King and Queen, he bowed. He noticed that the King beamed broadly while the Queen hid behind an ever-stoic mask of regal aloofness. This should have been a moment when an extraordinary male would have been graciously pleased. It was not every day one became the second most essential force on Mitd. The panther wondered whose paw was behind this sudden naming of a Crown Champion as he looked over to the empty chair reserved for the Royal Assasin. Something felt wrong.

Taking his seat by the Queen Mother, Hayden sat quietly for a moment as the room got back to the post-announcement chatter. His thoughts were interrupted as the Queen Mother patted his paw and whispered congratulations.

Smiling, Hayden thanked her with the deserved reverence and respect. He succeeded in trying to hide the smug yet concerned feeling inside. This was a particularly excellent turn of events for his plans if he could adjust his timeline. Of course, that one depended on one other group. However, Hayden felt confident he could achieve the needed adjustments. A servant filled his goblet, placed a plate of sweets before him, and left the freshly chilled pitcher of refreshment. The Queen Mother turned to the panther.

"Now, as I see it, dear kit, we have a situation at paw. That bumbling son of mine has given you the second greatest power in the land right behind the King's Royal Assassin. That aunt of yours has the ear of that little Oracle sitting over there. How you proceed next is especially important to the survival of our species. How you handle the King's orders and manipulating the Queen's control over our young Oracle is essential. If you can keep it in the sheath[10] and quit sniffing[11] after what that white wolf used to have, you just might find yourself with a title greater than that of the Crown Champion," whispered the old ferret. She clamped a bejeweled paw on the panther's muzzle as he started to protest.

"Oh, don't even pretend to be wounded, dear," began the Queen Mother. "In all the right circles, it is well known, Sir, that you have had designs on a certain vixen. Though she is exceptionally pleasing to the eye, one could say almost intoxicating to scent, there is something more

---

[10] This is a Therian colloquial term referencing a male controlling his sexual urges. Not all races have a sheath that a portion of their genitals are protected by.

[11] This is another Therian colloquial term meaning to seek sexual intercourse.

that drives you to chase that tail. Do not deny it. There is more to your desire than wanting to mount her. I can sense there is more to your machinations than the fact she was mated to a particular white wolf. The fact that Summoner Zenti Semineu has become an immense pain in our collective royal asses is not why you sniff after Mari Semineu." The elder ferret took a sip of her sparkling wine before continuing.

"For whatever reason, my son does not dispatch the Royal Assassin after Zenti is beyond me. No, dear kit, I think you know Mari means much more to our species than even you do. However, she is out of your grasp, but that little lioness is not. Oracle Rini Waxton has a pivotal part to play in the future. Even my addled brained old Oracle has Visions of that," the Queen Mother whispered into Hayden's ear before kissing him on the cheek.

For the show of it, the elder ferret made Hayden help her stand, to which the whole room came to attention. Waving everyone back to the evening festivities, she held a stoic yet pleasant smile when no one sat. The Queen Mother turned to her son; she smiled at him. He was an old fool, but the citizens of Mitd loved him.

"An excellent choice, my son," she said and patted her son on the cheek while looking at Hayden. "Now, if you will forgive me, I grow fatigued and will retire. I will allow our Champion to return, but I wish to request his assistance in escorting me to my chambers," the ferret said. Patting her son on the shoulder, she leaned heavily on General Hayden's arm.

Both the King and Queen stood, kissing the Queen Mother on the cheek again. Along with the entire room, they waited until the doors to the Grand Ballroom closed behind the Queen Mother. The room indeed returned to the evening's festivities.

"What do you think she and Hayden were so intently speaking of," asked the King in his usual oblivious manner? The Queen simply shrugged, shaking her head and ignoring his question. The elder wallaby sighed at his mate's dismissive attitude. Beneath the graying whiskers, a contented grin flashed briefly.

****

As the grand double door closed behind them, the Queen Mother waved off her servants, telling them to clear the hall of guards. She leaned heavily on Hayden's arm, patting him matronly-like on his forearm. The two turned down a now empty hallway. Still keeping her arm wrapped on his for the sake of appearance, Hayden felt the elderly ferret's weight grow lighter until she was no more than a decoration. He looked at her, perplexed at the new development.

"React as if I am still leaning on your arm. Let our movement go slow and steady," Lady Corinth whispered to the panther as she turned his head back to face the corridor. Hayden obeyed as she continued.

"Now listen to me, kit; I don't want to have to repeat myself, so no interruptions. You need to find a way to contain, preferably kill, that cur white wolf. However, I highly doubt that you have the skill or power to do so. Still, use every asset at your disposal. Those assets have expanded considerably now that you are Crown Champion. Also, you need to stop sniffing after Mari's tail and get her back into the Crown's service. You have no idea just how important to the longevity, even the survival, of our species she is. In the wrong paws, she will forever alter the way our species develops, grows, and is ruled," said the Queen Mother. Her voice did not have that nasal tone as she spoke, Hayden noted.

"Do not think for one moment that you have been told everything that our young Royal Oracle has had Visions of. You are no more than a pawn in this game. However, suppose that pawn plays his role correctly. In that case, he will find himself greater than any mere Crown Champion knighted," she said as they turned down the corridor toward her chambers. Putting a paw on his muzzle to quiet a perceived question, she continued.

"Don't, I'm not done. The technology our allies possess in the field of medicine alone is beyond anything our scientists can dream of. I am living proof of that," she said as she stood fully erect and looked at him eye to eye. Age had taken her ability to stand fully upright. For the first time, the two stood muzzle to muzzle.

"You are playing with forces that are beyond your control and imagination. Those two Waxton bitches are the key to our dominance over our allies, and we do not need your libido ruining our plans by sniffing after Mari. Oracle Rini Waxton would be a better choice in so many unique ways. Take care, kit, and focus on the task at paw. Unite our forces. Bring Mari back into the fold and find a way to kill that useless bastard cur of a white wolf," the elder ferret hissed at him. She looked the panther in the eye with a determination and anger he had never seen from her.

Opening the door to her chambers, she immediately put all her weight on his arm, and as the servants came, she demanded her cane. Hayden made note that even her servants were unaware of the changes in her. The panther did not betray her secret. He continued the ruse that he was honored that she would lean on him.

"Take care, kit. I fear the medalling freedom that we allowed our allies to take in experimenting on Summoner Zenti Semineu has backfired. Since his escape a little over fourteen months ago, he has grown in power. I suspect he will continue to grow, according to my sources. My son tells me that even the Royal Assassin core fears him. Kill Summoner Zenti Seminue quickly," Quinel Corinth said before entering her chambers, leaving him standing in the hall alone.

The panther bowed at her dismissal. As Hayden strolled along the hallways, he whistled a merry little tune. Guards snapped to attention while others bowed. However, Crown Champion Hayden paid them little heed. A missing piece of information provided by the Queen Mother expanded his scope of the landscape. With an uncharacteristic smile, though small, the black panther began mentally altering his plan. The revelation of the Queen Mother ensured accelerating the timeline would not be an issue. True to the nature of those who only tasted power, the Queen Mother flaunted her snippet of power. He did not have a mere taste of power, he had a feast, and the Queen Mother added another dish to the bountiful table before him.

****

The Grand Ballroom continued to host the dinner guests when General Hayden reentered. Returning to his place of honor, the panther took his seat to the right of the King. He was now the Crown Champion, the Right Paw, and it was his to occupy. Hayden looked at the empty chair of the Left Paw. A dinner setting for the unknown Royal Assassin sat unused. The Royal Assassin never attended any function, yet a place was always prepared.

There was a saying that every King of Mitd had embraced. *A King needs only two things to effectively rule. A Crown Champion to defend the King's honor, and a Royal Assassin to ensure it is questioned very little.* In due time, the panther thought, I will know who the Royal Assassin is, and dispatch you do end that cur of a white wolf. The Queen Mother was wrong. The Royal Assassin feared no one; even the panther knew that.

It was not long before the party moved into the usual circles, flowing into the various chambers by the time Hayden decided to retire for the evening. However, he found himself congratulated repeatedly to the point he was becoming exasperated from maintaining a constant smile. Of course, duty required the Crown Champion to be the Crown's visible paw, just as the Royal Assassin was the Crown's invisible paw. One dignitary or member of the Royal Family guided him from room to room. Hayden was paraded about like a new possession with which to win favor. Though he grew tired of the conversations, he persevered with a respectful attitude.

"Pardon the interruptions, M'lord. I have an important missive for General Hayden," said a sharply dressed young officer as he first bowed to the noble, then saluted the panther. Hayden took the folded note, read it, then begged to withdraw. 'Matters of the Crown,' he explained and left the tiresome party behind.

Making profound apologies to all, Hayden followed the young officer down the hall and into a private reading room. Much to his relief, the room was filled with fellow officers who crisply saluted. Without warning and with the practiced effort that only seasoned academy-trained officers could pull off, the officers fluffed off the salute. That disrespectful act was followed by a multitude of rude gestures ending in a raucous round of laughter.

"I thought you might need saving, sir," said the young officer who had pulled him away from the barrage of nobles. The young jackal beamed at the panther's reply.

Most officers looked up to General Hayden and tried to win his respect.

"Thank you, Captain. You are the true hero tonight," smiled Hayden as he slumped into a comfortable, deep-cushioned chair.

General Hayden relaxed his usual aloof visage and, with a worn smile, gladly accepted the snifter of brandy. One of his former fellow academy classmates handed him a cigar and proceeded to light it for him. The rich flavor of tobacco impregnated with sweet brandy kissed his taste buds. At the same time, the scent wafted into the air around his head.

The reading room was large, with almost two dozen cushioned chairs nestled aside coffee tables. They were scattered about in pairs, set back to back with a coffee table on one side and a dual-headed reading lamp on the other. They were not meant for conversation but for individual readers. However, tonight the chairs were currently rearranged into a circle. Books lined the walls, and there were racks for periodicals and newspapers. Twenty royal officers waited for the Crown Champion to speak. The panther savored the silence but not for too long.

"My esteemed colleagues, a mighty task has been set before us. By now, I am sure you are all aware that we are to unite the Factions and defeat the invaders. I am open to comments and clear thoughts concerning this task," stated the panther bluntly as the smile left his muzzle.

"All work as usual, eh Hayden," said a portly old bear. Gray covered most of the bear's muzzle, betraying the young chipper voice. However, there was no mistaking the graying military officer was of importance when the room quieted.

The bear swaggered through the doorway, not from pride but from age. Dressed in simple military attire, not of pomp and circumstance, but of functional needs, the bear commanded respect. The room came to attention except for the panther, who remained seated as the old bear moved to the chair beside Hayden.

"I have been well taught," said Hayden as he stood and hugged the old bear. "It is always a pleasure to have the Academy's Commandant attend functions outside the academy. How have you been, Sir?"

"I am well, son, for a bear of my age, though I was not invited. However, as you well know, watching the enemy's movements, the observant can gather what will happen next. I thought I might offer a paw in congratulations after I put the pieces together," the elder bear said, taking a seat next to Hayden. The Commandant also accepted a cigar and a light.

The intense sweet scent of the aromatic cigars began to fill the room. The officers took the elder bear's comment to mean the invaders. Hayden knew the deeper meaning of the Commandant's statement. The elder bear must have deduced Hayden was to appointed Crown Champion. The panther gave a slight acknowledging nod.

"Sir, what if we could plan a massive strike on **THEIR** island starport? We have one old battle cruiser that we have hidden, four light cruisers, and six destroyers. The invaders have no known offensive navy. Can we not simply launch them all at the same time?" asked a young ox sub-officer.

"A solid tactic, lieutenant. However, scouts report that the island starport defenses have a far greater firing range than either the destroyers or light cruisers. This leaves only the old battlecruiser to bring a limited amount of firepower to bear for almost half an hour. Each ship would be targeted one at a time and sunk. If we send the smaller ships in ahead of time to better coordinate their combined firepower, the result would be the same," replied Hayden. However, he nodded in approval at the ox's misguided but solid insight on the assessment.

"Have our scouts noticed any new development in the invader's flying craft?" asked another sub-officer.

"History does not record the invader's aircraft, and presumably spacecraft, as having any weapons systems. Though I find that a bit odd, the historical and current records are well researched," said an Under Captain.

"Uniting the Factions is the best course of action. Gather the support of the citizens, reestablish the cohesion of our forces, strategically strike their bases, and retake the ground we lost," stated another officer.

"Correct choice, Major," stated the old bear while Hayden nodded in agreement. The middle-aged Cheetah only nodded but did not smile.

"Our first Faction contact will be the most important. Mari Semineu is beloved by our kind; she has led a continued string of successful raid campaigns causing setback after setback over the past year. She should be our first contact," replied another officer, to which Hayden paused for a moment before continuing to savor the brandy.

The room was silent as he took a deep draw on the cigar and let the sweet smoke roll off his tongue while tilting his head back, watching the smoke lazily roll towards the ceiling.

"Do we know where she is?" asked Hayden, still looking at the ceiling, to which an affirmative reply was given. Looking back down into the room of his fellow academy officers, the panther took another sip of his brandy. Casually he sat the glass on the side table. He stood and straightened his uniform, to which the whole room, sans the old bear, came to attention. Hayden looked down and smiled at the Academy Commandant, then gave a series of orders to which the room emptied. The officers hastened to see that the Crown Champion's orders were carried out promptly and adequately. It was more of an attempt to please the panther out of a respectful fear than of duty. General Hayden made or broke careers with but a single word. One soldier remained as a guard outside the reading room doors at Hayden's order.

"You have a gift for grasping a situation, making a decision, and then commanding people into action, General Hayden," came a new voice after the last of the officers had left. It emanated from a side chamber.

The tall, lean, furless pale-skinned male spoke the harsh, guttural, Jaydonian language flawlessly, Hayden realized. That was an improvement since their last meeting. The male moved across the room and poured himself a glass of brandy before sitting across from Hayden and the old bear.

"I see you do not require your mask. Have things changed over the past few months, Commander Winslow?" asked Hayden, replying to the newcomer perfectly in the invader's own language.

"Just a brief respite to taste the sweetness of your evening air, dear General. Forgive the slip, Crown Champion," the stranger said in between sips, obviously enjoying the subtle hints of cherry the brandy had to offer.

Hayden and the Commandant both raised their glasses in a small toast. The newcomer watched the panther and bear over the rim of his drink after returning the toast. It was an attempt to gauge a reaction to his lack of a mask and proper use of the Mitdonian language. He found none from either Jaydonian as expected.

"We know where she is, of course. I just needed an excuse to empty the room and give them busy work so we could talk. The scent of your cologne is subtle but unique. I doubt one in a million could detect it," said Hayden.

"However, if we leave in the next few hours, we can be near her location within two days of high-speed continuous travel by motorcar." The panther took another sip before dipping the tip of the cigar in the brandy. Holding a cigar up for Commander Winslow, the furless male smiled but shook his head no. Hayden continued.

"According to our contact in Mari Semineu's Faction camp, her situation is a bit precarious at the current time. It seems the main body of her force is currently on loan to General Breymore. We are currently unaware of his exact location. However, with Mari's Faction forces in a weakened state, I would recommend a small-sized raid that she could easily repel. It would make getting her on our side easier if we were to come to her aid at the last moment," said Hayden in that matter-of-fact tone. It was clearly a statement of intent and not just idle a recommendation.

"I am sure that an arrangement can be accommodated, though that is not why I have come all this way. It seems our white wolf friend has turned up again. Of all the places he could have surfaced, this one will be of interest to you. It seems fortune smiles upon us this day," said the pale furless male, to which he noticed Hayden's ears literally perked up.

"And pray-tell, where would this be?" asked the panther, attempting to hide the adrenalin rush. The panther was glad that Commander Winslow's species did not possess a Jaydonian's heightened senses.

"The white wolf is within two days of Commander Mari's current camp. It is our understanding that his visit was requested according to our sources. The request was for a Faction Leader, but our contact was not privy to the missive's content. It may not have been directed at him. I cannot stress just how fortunate it is that the wolf cur is close to one of your artillery detachments," replied Commander Winslow.

"Have they made contact yet," asked the bear?

"Not yet, according to my last communique, but that was a day ago. He was two full days away from the camp. However, we lost contact with our scouts," said the furless male, taking another drink while trying to hide the disappointment on his face. The reason for the loss of contact was officially unconfirmed, yet Commander Winslow suspected the cause. However, there was the probability that the scouts were intercepted and killed at GiaDat.

"Let me guess. You lost contact with your scouts at the crossroad village of GiaDat, correct? How many did you lose," asked Hayden in a flat tone of voice? He successfully portrayed concern for his allies' losses while hiding a content smirk at their demise. Allies did not mean friends.

"I see news travels fast. Have you restored your communication lines as of yet," Commander Winslow asked? Hayden detected a slight smirk at the loss of communications thought out the island. The invaders were swift in cutting communication lines across the island.

"We have other ways of communicating. I understand you lost a full company of troops to that rogue white wolf," stated Hayden returning the slight smirk, not trying to hide it this time.

"And you lost almost seventy of your loyal supporters in GiaDat," retorted the furless male. "However, it is fortunate that we have located him for you," said Commander Winslow.

"Very fortunate, indeed; I believe that we can be of mutual assistance once again," said Hayden as he stood.

"Two days by motorcar is a long time for him to escape. May I offer a token of my species gratitude to you, Crown Champion Hayden? I have a vehicle that can make it there in hours. That should give you plenty of time to coordinate your resources," offered Commander Winslow.

"A very kind token that will not be forgotten," replied Hayden. The only vehicle that could make it that far in hours was one of the invader's aircraft. The two Jaydonian males stood. It was clear that this conversation had reached a positive conclusion.

The furless male stood. He was half a head shorter than the panther. The elder bear leaned heavily on the arm of the chair as he stood. Command Winslow looked at the padded armchair. The furniture's unique inward arcing seat and open lumbar support were odd-looking. Like all

Jaydonian furniture, it was designed with digitigrade legs and tails in mind. It always amazed him how they could walk on digitigrade legs. However, the Jaydonians were much faster than any of his species.

Giving each a simple nod in salutations, all three departed, each going their separate ways. They kept to themselves, with the pale furless male slipping back into the shadows of the side room. Hayden left the room last. Dealing with these allies was dangerous. However, it was necessary if his goal of winning the favor of Miss Mari Semineu bore fruit.

The Queen Mother was correct in saying that Mari Semineu was a pivotal element in shaping Jayden's future. However, Hayden was unsure of the role the vixen would play. There were too many unknown variables in his equation. However, time was a friend, not an enemy. There were other options in play that even Commander Winslow was unaware of. He was not the only invader that wanted the services of the panther. True to his nature, Hayden refrained from smiling at the fortunate turn of events as the door closed behind him.

Cigar smoke from the reading room filled Elli's nostrils. She stood in a tiny nook behind the floor-to-ceiling banner that concealed the nearly forgotten space. It was a doorless servant's nook. A broom, dustpan, feather duster, and a few rags were kept here by the servants. It was for emergencies, which rarely happened in the reading room. Only a pawful of servants even knew of its existence. The old castle, though modernized, held a few secrets that very few remember.

In silence, she waited until the sound of the door latch clicked, indicating the last of the three had finally left the room. Stepping from behind the banner, the manx slipped out onto the balcony from her hiding spot. Elli took a breath of the fresh evening air. With a few deep breaths, the manx cleared the heavy yet sweet scent from her nostrils.

Ellsinore Brendma was grateful for the information provided to her earlier. However, she wondered how her source knew that the meeting would include an invader. Though it was not stated as such, only one group needed to wear a breathing mask to survive on Jayden. According to the news reports, the invaders needed those masks.

Little was known about the invader's origins, but they shared a few things in common with Jaydonians. They were bipedal, stood wholly erect, and were approximately the same height. The invaders had both males and females in their midst and kits if they were called that. However, not much more was known. Two things were certain. First, they could not breathe Jaydonian air as it was rumored to kill them. The other was that the invaders could be killed.

Stepping back into the reading room, Elli collected a paw full of glasses to complete the servant's illusion before leaving. However, she could not dismiss the facts that an invader was colluding with General Hayden. More importantly, the invaders did not die right away when they breathed the Jaydonian air. Something was not right, and her contact would want to know this vital information. Elli made her way back to the kitchens through the back halls. With her paws full, the manx pushed open the door with her backside.

With little concern, she clumped the glasses into a pile. Elli did not care as to what condition she left them in; that was not her job. She was the paw servant of Oracle Rini Waxton, not the dishwasher. Just the fact that she was seen carrying the dishes served its purpose. The kitchen workers stopped and held their breath as Elli moved about. She seemed in a foul mood, and none wanted to cross her path. How they wished she would be a little more like her usual self. Her mistress must be in a horrid mood. Elli was usually a sweet individual.

Moving about the kitchen, the manx collected and ate various bits and pieces of food. Picking them from the variety of leftovers in the cooking pots, Elli refused the offer of a full meal. Elli was a personal servant to the Royal Oracle and amongst the manx's peers that made her nearly nobility. A server offered her a plate for the impromptu meal but was refused, with Elli saying it was only a quick snack. Partially sated, the manx left the kitchen and headed to the wine cellar, much to the cook staff's relief.

Entering one of the many smaller wine cellars, Elli randomly picked a bottle of wine in passing. She did not check the wine's vintage. Instead, she headed to the empty bottle storage, where crates of empty bottles filled the room. Elli ignored all but a specific stack. The manx quietly slipped behind that stack of boxes and stepped into a narrow, concealed passage. She noticed the dust on the walls and reminded herself to bring supplies to clean the narrow hall, lest she gets her clothes dirty. That would not do at all for a person in her position of service.

Following the passage for a short distance, the manx stepped into what appeared to be a small closet. Then, looking through a narrow slot in the wall, Elli hesitated a few moments. She marked the label of the bottle with two numbers and a letter. Upon seeing the path was clear, Elli slipped into the adjoining cloakroom. Straightening her clothing, the manx exited the cloakroom, casually entered the room full of nobles, and headed directly for her mistress. It was not uncommon for servants to use unseen passages to deliver food or spirits. However, a limited few knew of that passageway.

Standing a respectful distance from the conversation, Elli waited quietly for acknowledgment. When the lioness gave her a brief glance of acknowledgment, Elli presented her with the bottle of wine. Rini dismissed her with a dissatisfied look. However, the lioness did not miss the message on the label. To anyone else, it would have meant nothing.

Half an hour passed after Elli had unobtrusively slipped back into the cloakroom and then back down the concealed passageway. What noble ever cared about the coming and going of a servant unless they were not serving? Stopping in the kitchen to fill a glass of cold water for her mistress, Elli continued. Though the act of serving Rini was genuine, it was also a ruse to keep her fellow servants distracted from her primary objective.

Exiting the kitchen, Elli made her way to a small room filled with several tall floor-to-ceiling cabinets. This room was used to store extra dishes and was rarely used. Making her way to one of the cabinets, Elli pulled a small keyring from her deep hip pocket. Inserting a specific, non-descript key into the lock, the manx did not turn it. Instead, she lifted the key with considerable force. When she did, the entire lock moved an inch upwards. Elli then turned the key counterclockwise.

That act unlocked the whole cabinet fixture and automatically opened it up entirely. Swinging on a pivot point, it was nothing more than a false panel hidden behind the pretext of a cabinet. Behind it, there were no shelves, and nothing occupied the back wall. The cabinet itself held fine table linen. No sound could be heard as Elli opened the secret door.

Closing the panel automatically locked the door again, resetting the exterior linen cabinet door lock in the process. The manx entered a small meeting room hidden behind the cabinet's rear panel. A small end table, two chairs, and an old-style oil lamp were the room's only furnishings. Elli sat the glass of water down, reached for a knob on the bottom of the oil lamp, and turned it slightly. The lamp did not light, nor did the manx attempt to light it. She sat in one of the two chairs and waited in the near dark.

She did not need to wait long when the only other door in the room opened. Oracle Rini Waxton stepped in. The door closed behind her automatically. The instant the door closed, the lock automatically engaged, and the room filled with soft lighting from the ceiling. The lamp remained dormant. Elli stood and offered the lioness the glass of cold water.

"Mistress," began Elli as Rini took a drink, "they have found the white wolf near the village of GiaDat and are planning a trap for him as he heads to your sister's camp. It seems that she has possibly sent word of a meeting to him. However, if Miss Mari did or not was unclear. Hayden appeared glad they have found Zenti, and the panther seems to think that he can sway Mari to his cause. He plans on leaving in a few hours after the event is over tonight."

"Very well done. I suspect that the Queen will want to know of this new development. Anything else," Rini asked? The lioness's tone was abrupt and harsh, to which Elli shook her head yes.

Oracle Rini Waxton hated Summoner Zenti Semineu. The young lioness despised him for being the source of her parent's death. However, Oracle Rini Waxton loathed Summoner Zenti Semineu because she could not clearly see the white wolf in any of her Gifted Visions. The loss of Rini's Visions of the white wolf began just after his capture and subsequent escape. She was not alone in that deficiency. No Oracle on Mitd had Gifted Visions of him. Why this oddity occurred was unknown.

There was something about the silvery-white wolf that obscured an Oracles Gift. That infuriated Rini Waxton.

"For a few moments, there was a conversation in the invader's language. I believe that Hayden was talking to an invader. I cannot be sure because the cigar smoke was thick in the room. I could not pick out the familiar stench associated with one of **THEM**. However, his name was Commander Winslow. Have you heard of anyone by that name," reported Elli?

However, the manx did not expect an answer. Rini was just short of losing her temper. Elli wished she did not have to tell any news of Summoner Zenti Semineu. Deep in the recesses of the manx's memory, there was something about the white wolf that scared her. The feeling was more than him being the most feared Summoner on Mitd. However, Elli could not recall what.

"Thank you," was all Rini said in her usual dismissive manner without answering the question posed by the manx.

The young lioness left the room, exiting through the door she had entered. Her paw servant was left in the room all alone. Elli sat down for a moment, wondering what she had done so wrong to warrant the dismissive treatment from her mistress. Elli sipped the water for a moment and reflected on Rini's expression. A few more sips of water and the manx determined that it was at receiving the news of Zenti Semineu that evoked Rini's dismissive nature.

Elli took the water glass, turned the knob on the oil lamp, and left the room. The manx headed back into the wine cellar. Finding the small wine cellar empty, she then returned to the kitchens. Depositing the empty water glass on the table, she served herself a sizable plate of meats and cheeses along with a small variety of sweet foods and sauntered off to her quarters. Along the way, she stopped by the quarters of one of the Crown's Shamans. The elder female ewe was Gifted, though her Talents were limited. However, Elli had visited her often, and with a brief smile, the old female handed Elli four small vials of clear liquid. Both females, young and old, shared a familiar grin. Elli thanked the elder female and returned to her room. Humming a little ditty, the manx opened the door and smiled.

Waiting for her was a handsome young fox from one of the lesser royal's serving staff. On his master's last visit, she had a most pleasurable encounter with the male fox. Upon confirmation his master was invited to this event, Elli contacted him. The male fox was given instructions to come prepared to spend the evening in a little frivolous play. If his master or her mistress did not need them, he would be at Elli's disposal until no longer needed. Elli grinned a wicked grin at the male fox. Her needs required his talents.

****

Rini returned to the evening's event but not to the social groups she had left. She did not enjoy social gatherings, which were too chatty about the things to come and Visions not understood. Oracles avoided casual crowds. The chance for a random Vision or the continued pestering of those who wanted to ask for an Oracle's Vision was too demanding to enjoy a social gathering.

Wandering aimlessly, Rini found herself amid the line of Royals who would be heir to the throne should the King die. She felt at ease, knowing that none of them would ask for a Vision for fear it might lead to their untimely death if they were next in line. Inwardly the lioness smiled; here, she was relatively safe from the pestering.

The room was filled with the finest that the land had to offer. There were exquisite, centuries-old, paw-crafted furniture. A set of crystal goblet from the first King and items from every subsequent King adorned the room. Articles from the first King were so detailed that no crafter had been able to duplicate them. Paintings and tapestries hung from the walls depicting all the royal family members. The more modern inventions and luxuries that one would expect to be in a chamber fit for royalty were also on display. Rini moved silently about the room, exchanging pleasantries when engaged but quickly found herself looking at a family portrait of Hayden when he was her age.

What was she thinking, hoping that the panther would sniff after her? He was the mysteriously handsome type who was strong, rugged, and charmingly sophisticated. He was also a member of a distant Royal Lineage. Rini moved on down the line of portraits, studying the rest of the Royal Families. Funny she saw how, in the King's royal line, all the firstborn males looked remarkably alike. The resemblance followed them throughout their life.

The King had always been of the same species. If the King died before his heir had achieved the age of ascension, the Queen Mother would rule until the heir became thirty. That sad event had only happened once to the third King. It never changed; the ruler of Mitd had always been a male. Every one of them was of the Corinth linage. Never had another member of the Royal Family sat on the throne other than the eldest male or the Queen Mother.

In the past, many of the other Royal Families did not agree. Several times they attempted to secede from the Kingdom. Legally they could. It was part of the Mitd laws that allowed a portion of the population to secede from the Kingdom. However, that portion of Mitd had to follow the rules of secession. Any citizens must be allowed to leave the new Kingdom if they did not want to be separated from Mitd's original Kingdom. Sadly, that amount of freedom led to several wars over the past millennia. The citizens of Mitd understood the value of being one Kingdom. Only once in the history of Mitd did the population of Mitd attempt to usurp the throne. That was not part of the law. That war happened nearly five hundred years ago. It was a war in which the citizens of Mitd were misled into rebelling. It did not end well for the rebel leaders.

When a state attempted secession and failed, it was repatriated. Only a few had attempted such an act with any chance of succeeding. When a state secession failed and followed the secession rules, the Corinth Lineage offered reconciliation to that state's people. If unmated, the King would offer to take the best-suited female of Royal Lineage as his Queen to unite the conquered state. Most of these attempted secessions were in the outlying Isles that surrounded the mainland of Mitd. Very few states attempted secession after the war five hundred years ago.

However, no matter the Queen's Royal Lineage, the male offspring was amazingly enough, always of the Royal genus. All Royal males were of the wallaby breed. Males were the first whelped into the royal line, Rini noted and wondered why that was. That one-thousand-year oddity ended with King Corinth VI. It was a sad event that many claimed would be the end of the Corinth rule.

King Taimus Corinth VII had no male heir, nor was he the first male whelped to King Taimus Corinth VI. The first died shortly after being whelped. He was of the Lion genus. King Taimus Corinth VII was his second male whelped; he was of the Royal genus. Rini could not help but again marveled at such a striking resemblance to each King as they aged.

Those royal kits which did not ascend to the throne had offspring of different breeds, but never the royal genus.

Rini was puzzled with the royal line until a deep-throated cough startled her. Turning, she saw the King standing quietly behind her.

"Forgive me, your majesty; I did not hear you approach," said the lioness as she curtsied, but the King's customary correction did not come. It was exceedingly difficult for Rini Waxton to curtsy. The damage to her hip made it a risky endeavor. Often, she fell. The King and Queen had given her a special dispensation to prevent her from attempting to do so. Oracle Rini Waxton was stubborn and persisted. Usually, the King would prevent her from showing respect, but there were the occasional lapses. However, the King's paw did not linger before tapping her on the shoulder, indicating she could rise.

"Word has reached my ears, dear one, that they have found the white wolf. He is quite the royal pain, don't you think? I would like to know have you seen him in your Visions as of late," the elder wallaby asked? His smile was soft, and his words warm. Instantly Rini felt at ease. Offering a paw, he helped steady the young lioness as she struggled with her balance. King Taimus Corinth VII was tall and robust for a male of his advanced years. He was also exceptionally kind. It was a kindness that one did not expect from a monarch.

"No, your Majesty, I have not. Not alone, but always with my sister. Even then, the Visions are obscured. Others, too, have searched for him in their Gifted Visions. I am ashamed to admit that I seem no more able to summon a Vision of him than I could of some long-dead relative. It is exceptionally frustrating. I do so apologize for not being of more service to the Crown," Rini said in a profoundly sorrowful voice, which honestly reflected her feelings. At no time in the past fourteen months had she, or any other Oracle, been able to see Summoner Zenti Semineu.

Rini Waxton wanted to faithfully serve the King, who had shown her such exceptional kindness. King Corinth VII was also her late father's friend and had opened his home, the palace, to her. He treated her like a daughter. She did not consider her service as an Oracle a duty to this King. It was a pleasure to serve such a wonderful male. Anyone who loved General Haverick Waxton as much as King Taimus Corinth VII did was to be adored in the lioness's eyes.

"After all the service you have been to the Crown, you still apologize for not being able to find this one. No, my dear, 'tis the Crown who is exceptionally honored and grateful for all you have done. You have put yourself at the whim of the Void to serve the Crown, to serve me. Zenti Semineu is a tough one to see, be sure of that. I must see General Hayden before the night is out. However, I would be ever so grateful if you could find some time this evening to simply enjoy yourself," winked the old wallaby. His voice so warm it could melt any frozen heart. Kissing her on top of the forehead, he nuzzled her cheek the way a father would. To Rini Waxton, this male was family.

The elder wallaby left Rini in a calm, peaceful state. She curtsied as he went and thought she heard a soft rebuking growl from him. The lioness blushed. Standing alone amidst the Royal Portraits, she found her self-calm and Vision free, which was a rare state for an Oracle. For whatever reason, King Taimus Corinth VII left her in such a peaceful state that the horrors of a Gifted Vision fled. Watching him leave the room, Rini felt the warmth of his smile slowly fade, leaving her to wonder just what it was about him that made everyone be at ease. It must be his simple kindness, the lioness thought.

Turning back to the line of portraits, Rini again found herself lost in the linage of royals until she came to the current King and his late daughter's painting. Princess Arietta was a very pretty little wallaby by all standards. Rini Waxton looked at the portrait and thought of Arietta's fraternal twin. Prince Taimus was the first Royal male heir that was not whelped the same genus as his father. Princess Arietta was of her father's genus and the first of twins whelped. That made her the oldest. Of the portraits that hung in this Royal Gallery, not one contained an image of Prince Taimus the VIII. The records indicated the Prince was of Rini's genus, Felis Leo.[12]

Prince Taimus and Princess Arietta were not the current Queen's offspring but the late Queen's offspring. Rini never knew the late Queen, and there was only one portrait of her. It hung in the King's private study. She was the mother of the fraternal twins, Princess Arietta and

---

[12] Dear reader, the translation of these Chronicles into your language borrows from the Etymology of your species' words for better understanding. The Mitdonian language is not easily translatable.

Prince Taimus the VIII. The late Queen's name was never spoken. However, Oracle Rini Waxton did know her name. Queen Kynza was a small female of the otter breed. The twins were her first pregnancy, and whelping a large kit like Taimus caused fatal internal bleeding. Queen Kynza died shortly after whelping.

Queen Kynza's death directly led to a royal war a year later. Rumors and innuendo ran wild that King Taimus was furious that the Prince was not of his linage and had his mate killed during the whelping. The King's son, Prince Taimus VIII, current whereabouts were unknown.   The male lion was sent away shortly after his whelping. The combination of rumors and the newly whelped Prince's disappearance was the final catalyst that ignited the war between the Royal House of Corinth and the Royal House of Kveth.

Rumors continued to fly, of which the prominent most was that the House of Kveth kit napped the newly whelped Prince to protect him. King Corinth VII unleashed his military might against his distant royal relative. However, King Kveth's state was a military rival for the Mitdonian Crown.

The two royal houses fought for almost four years, with neither side gaining an advantage. The cost to both Houses was devastating, and the citizens of both Houses demanded a truce be called for. The two Kings met, and, though nothing had been worked out the first day, they agreed to meet again as the talks were promising. Later it would be discovered that King Kveth was in feeble health and knew the war would be his demise, so he had agreed to the truce talks. King Kveth knew one more thing that accelerated the peace talks. His daughter, Queen Kynza Kveth Corinth, died of natural causes, not at her mate's paws, King Corinth VII, as was the rumor. King Kveth's own Royal Oracle confirmed this. A costly war had been fought over a lie. However, there were forces at play beyond his control or knowledge.

During this war, the invaders increased their attacks against the Mitd Realm. The effects of three combatants warring wreaked destruction on an unfathomable scale. It became clear that a continued war between the Mitdonian Royalty would spell the inevitable doom of Mitd. An armistice was agreed upon while the final terms of peace could be drafted. The process was slow, taking years to reconcile the atrocities that the tri-party war inflicted.

A few years later, during this peace process, Rini's family was slaughtered by the invaders. Rini believed that **THEY** were searching for Zenti Semineu and her family paid the price. The lioness was a few weeks shy of her Gifting Day when her family died. Rini was too young to understand why Zenti and her sister, Mari, took her to the Crown City.

After the invaders slaughtered her family, Zenti and Mari brought her to the first Gifted Shaman they could find. The Shaman's Talent of Healing was limited. However, the Shaman healed the internal bleeding but could offer no more aid. It was several weeks before proper medical care could be found. That medical care was at a Crown Field Hospital. When the King learned of them, Zenti, Mari, and she were hurried to the Crown City. However, the damage was considerable, and Rini's recovery repeatedly suffered setbacks.

Rini shoved those memories out of her head. The lioness looked at the portrait of the King and his late daughter. It was here in the Crown City Rini learned she was Gifted. While Rini recovered at the Crown City, a chance meeting happened with both Royal Monarchs. The youngest daughter of the Royal House of Kveth also was visiting the Crown City. However, Rini did not meet Princess Amatta Kveth at the time, but she did meet her father, King Kveth. There was an uneasy ceasefire between the Royal Houses. Neither King could agree on all the terms. During one of the many breaks, both Kings visited the hospital. The young lioness shared a Vision that there would be peace, but not during King Kevth's lifetime.

Meanwhile, Factions loyal to either house continued to skirmish for the following year. Rini was still undergoing a series of surgeries during that stress-filled year. To promote a lasting peace accord, the Kings had once again agreed to meet. During those peace negotiations, the young Gifted Oracle Rini Waxton revealed a most profound Vision when she saw Princess Amatta for the first time. That prolific Vision shook Princess Amatta and changed the course of the Royal House War.

The opposing King died that same night of natural causes, bringing his youngest daughter to power. Princes

Amatta knew that she would eventually lose the war. As was the long-standing custom, the two kingdoms' unity rested on the two families binding common ties. Princess Amatta decided to accept the mating clause as protocol dictated. However, there were misgivings on both sides of the accord. Amatta was the younger sister of Kynza Kveth, King Taimus Corinth VII's late mate.

During most of this time, Rini Waxton spent many months recovering from surgery or visiting various hospitals and specialists. She spent very little time at the Crown City, but the new Queen, Amatta, took great interest in the young lionesses' care.

Another year of bickering between the newlywed couple was solved when the young and upcoming Oracle Rini Waxton had another groundbreaking Vision. During all these years, Prince Taimus VIII had not been returned. With Rini's Vision solving the power struggle between the King and his new Queen, the King made a tough yet sad decision. King Taimus Corinth VII proclaimed his son, Prince Taimus VIII, must have perished. He announced that the young Princess Arietta was to be the next in line to the Crown.

Though Queen Amatta had not conceived a kit, she was furious that her offspring would not sit on the throne. To the shock of all Mitd, Princess Arietta died in her sleep a short time later. Rini was away for more surgery when the young princess suddenly died.

It would be another six months before Rini returned to the Crown City. There was nothing more that could be medically done for the young lioness. Her return was bittersweet. Princess Arietta was dead, and the King was devastated. Looking at the princess's portrait, who would be only a few years older than Rini now, the lioness could not help but feel for the young wallaby.

"I would have like to have known you, Princess," said Rini in hushed tones. "We only met a few times while I was recovering, but your kindness had a profound impact on me. Your father took me in after my last series of surgery and treated me like his daughter. I could not help but think that I would not be where I am now if you had survived."

"She was beautiful, was she not?" came a familiar male voice that sent a shiver down Rini's spine. His scent caught her nose. The lioness experienced another shiver, but this time it deeper within. She was glad Eli had made her wear panties to hide the musk, which she would now have to change, and she growled lightly at that lack of her self-control.

"I am sorry I startled you," exclaimed Hayden when she turned to face him.

"I was growling at some minor detail I need to work on and forgot to today, not at you, General," Oracle Rini Waxton said. For a moment, the lioness thought she saw a smirk cross the panther's muzzle as his nostrils flared ever so slightly. However, she was flustered by his musk and struggled to maintain her civility and her composure.

"To what do I owe this pleasure, and did your meeting with the King go well," she asked? Rini hoped to catch General Hayden, unaware the King was looking for him.

"We have arranged a brief meeting with His Majesty and my staff in an hour. I thought we could take a walk in the gardens, perhaps even see a shooting star tonight," the panther said as he offered the lioness his arm.

"I think perhaps another night, my hip is bothering me a bit," Rini said, fighting her body's urge to give in to his request.

"That is exactly what His Majesty said when I asked how you were doing. You seemed exceptionally quiet this evening. The King was the one that suggested that a short walk might help," said the panther, and before she could refuse, Rini was on his arm being whisked gently outside in the cool evening air.

Together, arm in arm, they walked for a little more than half an hour without speaking. Rini Waxton found herself closer to the panther's body than she would have admittedly liked. However, Rini's body said otherwise. She found she could not pull herself away; Hayden's musk was so heavy and intoxicating. Much to both of their dismay, they saw no shooting star before Hayden begged to take his leave of her.

"I would like to have the pleasure of your company again when I return," Hayden said.

"Your duties call so soon?" Rini asked, holding his paw tightly. This walk was what she dreamed of; it was not an Oracle's Vision. This was the dream of a young female in a breeding heat.

"I must attend to the capture of the white wolf traitor and will be leaving the Crown City immediately after my audience with His Majesty. We know exactly where he will be two days hence," Hayden replied and beamed a little. Pulling the panther close as if to whisper into his ear, the young lioness kissed him softly on the lips before speaking.

"I would take it as a personal favor if you made sure that he died very slowly and painfully. You would have my unlimited gratitude," Rini said as she stepped back from Crown Champion Hayden.

Smiling softly, Hayden asked where Rini wished to be escorted to. Here, she replied, as the evening air was enjoyable. Rini explained she thought staying outside might do her good. It seemed King had been correct, that the walk would help her hip. However, it did little to sate her heat.

Rini watched as the handsome panther strode away in that typical confident manner that he had. Levitating a stone from the pathway, she flung it as far as she could in anger, which did little to release her body's own frustration.

"Mistress," called Elli as soon as Hayden disappeared out of sight. Rini to jump at the sudden start.

"Yes?" she started to snap, but it came out more of an exhausted whine. Rini turned to face her paw servant as the manx approached. Movement caught Rini's attention. Looking up, the lioness watched as a meteor glowed across the sky to brilliantly fade away.

"I have something for you that will hopefully bring you a small amount of comfort," Elli said, holding up both paws. Rini could tell in one paw was a fresh pair of panties, to which the lioness lowered her ears just a little. In the other was a key.

"I was informed of your chance in counter with Hayden, and I knew that you might want to change before returning to the party. However," Elli drew the words out, "there is an extremely handsome young fox who was watching you all evening. I have taken the liberty of preparing him for you. I must say that you will not be displeased in his performance, or dare I say his attributes and stamina. He is waiting in my chambers for you. I have prepared the spare room off of your chambers as usual. You will find two vials on the nightstand to help our young fox recover," said the grinning manx as she offered both items to her mistress.

Stepping close to the manx and taking the key, Rini caught the fox's heady mixed musk along with Elli's scent, and again she shivered deep inside. In the silence of the cool evening air, Rini wrapped her arms around her paw servant. They embraced deeply with Elli letting a small whimper as the lioness softly buried her claws in the arch of the manx's back. Rini's musk caressed Elli's senses, and she shivered. Looking at the manx, the lioness's eyes said everything in gratitude that words could not. Rini licked Elli's muzzle before slipping off, leaving Eli quietly cry happy tears.

"Forgive me," came a voice shortly after the lioness left the gardens. It came from the side of one of the many fountains that graced the pathways.

"I noticed you when you served Oracle Rini this evening. I hope everything is alright?" the male otter asked. He had a quizzical look on his muzzle and then looked at the path that Rini had just departed down.

Turning, Elli knelt swiftly upon recognizing the officer, who in fact was the King's young nephew. He was the son of the King's late younger brother. The young Lord's father died in a boating accident some years earlier. This young otter was the future King of Mitd should their majesties fail to have an heir. That possibility was becoming highly likely now as Queen Corinth was almost past the age to whelp.

"Forgive me, M'lord, I did not see you standing there. How may I be of service," Elli asked as she knelt at his paw pads?

"I had hoped to ask permission of our Royal Oracle for the pleasure of your company for the rest of the evening," stated the sharply-dressed otter. He reached down, offering Elli a paw up. "However, I see, I am too late." He said rather disappointedly.

"I am flattered that the King's nephew would take an interest in me," Elli said as she took his paw. Allowing the handsome otter to help her to her paw pads. The act brought her muzzle close to his.

They stood close to each other for a few moments before he lifted her arms around his neck. The otter draped his arms around her waist. His musk, through the light perfume he was wearing, was sweet and thick. Oh, Heavens and Hells, how the manx hated being in heat at the same time as her mistress. It just complicated matters and, though the handsome young fox was very gifted, Elli had not been sated.

"I highly doubt that my mistress will need my service for the rest of this evening," Elli said, placing her paw on the back of the otter's head.

Gripping his neck firmly, the manx boldly, with unabashed passion, kissed the otter on the lips. Pressing her body against his, she was glad she was having the same desired effect on him as he was having on her. Taking the otter by the paw, the manx smiled at him with a sly grin before leading him away.

~   ~   ~   ~

From the third floor's balcony, a shadowy figure watched as the whole series of events unfolded below.

First was the interlude between the lioness and the panther. The shadowy figure knew that was a dead-end relationship.

However, the young lioness needed to see the panther for what the male feline was. Next was the interlude between the manx and the lioness. The young Oracle needed a protector, and the manx was on the shortlist. Lastly was his nephew and the manx. To test the loyalty of both his nephew and the manx, he brought them together. Betrayal was all too common when there was a Crown at stake.

Smiling contently, the elder wallaby stepped back into his private study. Gathering his Royal notes for his upcoming meeting with the Crown Champion, the wallaby hummed a merry tune. He closed the door behind him, quietly congratulating himself on the achievements so far this evening. Now, there was only one more puppet to make dance.

Chapter 3 Royal Oracle

Chapter 4

Joined Past

A warning to the reader. This passage was most challenging to translate. How I received the telling of the story is one that I have never fully encountered. It was almost as if I were an observer, yet a participant. Please read it carefully. This passage is from the shared memories of two extraordinary beings, seen from the other's mental perspective. I have separated each vision, dividing it for what I hope is easier reading. ~Sanura

"Zenti," Mari whimpered in an unsure voice? The vixen's heart nearly failed as the present ceased to exist.

A moment ago, Mari Semineu was in her tent with her former mate, Zenti. She was holding his muzzle and looking into his eyes. Quite literally, in a blink of an eye, she was back in the ruins of a munitions' factory with Zenti. The building looked just as it had been seventeen months ago. She and Zenti had gone on a scouting mission investigating a rumor. Even now, Mari remembered the information that prompted them to explore the factory's ruins. By way of those fleeing the ravages of the war, reports of a crashed invader's flying vehicle at the munitions' factory was something that needed to be followed upon.

However, the memories of then and the reality of the now were confusing. Mari wanted to focus on the here and now. She did not want to be back in that factory. It was there that Zenti betrayed her. It was there that she became a victim of the war. She was not seeing through her eyes but from someone else's point of view. What she was seeing was real to her. Yet, in the haze of her peripheral vision, Mari could see the blurry images of her tent. She could see the shadowy image of the white wolf seated in front of her. She fought the vision with reluctance. The vixen wanted to see why Zenti betrayed her, yet seeing herself in the factory again, caused fear to wash over her. She began to tremble uncontrollably. However, Mari was unsure if the fear was from the memory of the factory event or the raw power she now felt from Zenti's Gift.

'Just let the memories flow, Mari, don't fight them,'[13] Zenti softly brushed her mind, encouraging her back into the vision.

The vixen was just as scared now as she had been that day that **THEY** had captured her. Mari continued to tremble, though a deep calm began to fill her. She was struggling to process exactly what was happening. The vixen was back in the factory and under attack. This experience was edging on insanity.

Mari watched her phantom-self; she was taking the same actions just as she recalled them. Mari's phantom-self was backing away while **THEY** advanced on her. One invader aimed a gun and fired, but she dodged to the left. A sharp pain burned her upper arm now, just as it had that day. The invader's bullet grazed her phantom-self and lodged into the wall behind her. However, the vixen could

---

[13] For the ease of understanding, any words *'such as these'* (inside prime symbols) represents a telepathic communication between parties.

feel the impact of debris as the bullet struck the wall. Mari felt that pain again, in the present, and tried to grab her arm. However, she could not move.

Watching her phantom-self duck into the same alley just as she had that day, Mari tried to make since it all. Again, it was as if she was there, running for her life, yet she remained in her tent with Zenti sitting on the cot. How could he do this? Only Oracles could share memories; what was it that he now possessed? A mental growl from Zenti brought her back to focus. They had share non-verbal communications through Zenti's Gifted Talent of Union. That Talent allowed those in the Union to 'talk' and 'hear' through a simplistic form of telepathy.

Looking at her phantom-self's arm, Mari could feel the pain. It hurt now just as bad as it had then. Her phantom-self watched as the blood covered her fur. At this moment, looking at her phantom-self's wound, Mari knew the bullet had more than just grazed her arm. Watching the events unfold, she thought her phantom-self was perhaps a little slower than she remembered. This shared vision, or whatever it was known as, was maddening. Mari was losing her ability to perceive the present reality. Before the vixen had a chance to gain some small amount of control, her phantom-self had slowed down. Mari watched her phantom-self move about in the imaginary factory ruins.

Present-Mari watched her phantom-self do all the things that she had actually done on that day. However, was the pain burning her arm now, or what it a memory of pain? Was this some trick Zenti's Gift implanted in her? Mari could not tell which was tangible and which was a memory. When a second bullet ripped through the phantom-Mari's shoulder, she felt the searing pain again. She watched her phantom-self crumple to the ground from the impact of the shot.

"I nearly died that day," she said softly to herself as she watched the soldiers carry the phantom-vixen away. Self-pity began to rise until a deep, guttural, telepathic growl from Zenti pushed her back into focus.

Another flash and the vixen was sitting in the jail cell. Mari remembered that someone had stitched up her wounds and kept her from dying. However, her shadow-self, just like her present-self, never learned who kept her alive. Seventeen months ago, Zenti abandoned her on the outskirts of those factory ruins. He vanished, leaving her to suffer at the paws of the invaders and those who served them. Mari watched her phantom-self and wondered how this memory could be possible. However, her mind did not drift, and she realized her present-self was intently studying her phantom-self.

The cell that she was locked in was a small ten by ten cubical with no windows. There was only a cot attached to the wall opposite the solid steel door. A single light dangled from the ceiling's electrical wires, which her captors randomly turned the light on or off. There were days the light was never turned off, and there were days the light was never turned on. Mold covered the walls, and the cell reeked of stagnant water.

A shabby mattress and a thin blanket were all that was in the room to keep her warm. She had been held captive for almost a month. However, it was not until she was freed that she confirmed it was a month. Mari watched her shadow-self scratching tiny marks in the wall for every time food was slid through a small slot in the steel door. Mari's phantom-self had been unconscious for a time, though she did not know how long. She had simply woken up already in the cell.

Mari saw no one, her food being shoved through a narrow slot in the metal doors. For a moment, she could taste the foul excuse that passed for food. The only thing she could be thankful for was it contained a lot of liquid. There was no water in the cell except in the toilet. Mari's present-self watched the food slot open. The vixen hoped to see who fed her from this shadow of a memory. However, there was no way to see who provided for her. No jailers and no interrogators came to extract information. It was as frustratingly maddening now as it was seventeen months ago when Zenti abandoned her.

Mari Semineu's present-self watched her phantom-self grow deeper in despair. *THEY* did brutal things to her species. The bodies of those who were known to have been prisoners had been badly mutilated. Mari remembered her days in the cell. Every moment she was awake was a moment waiting for the torture to begin.

The first few days, she expected Zenti to come crashing through that door and free her, but as the days went on, depression began to set in. Her mind wandered into that dark realm that all those in prison experience. The heart wonders why they are abandoned and forgotten. The realization that her mate was not coming to save her took root.

"I never considered that you might be dead," whispered Mari as she kneeled at Zenti's paw pads. It was only now, seventeen months later, that she began to look at those events in a new light. However, Zenti did not brush her mind, nor did he attempt to discuss the matter with her. She could almost physically feel the mental wall he had build to keep her out of a place that he welcomed her in the past. Anger flared up within Mari that he would block her. It was the same anger that she felt when she saw him again thirteen months ago. With a gentle growl, Zenti brought Mari back into the shared memory.

As her phantom-self became angry at Zenti's abandonment of her, she also became more depressed. Quickly the phantom-vixen began to hate Zenti for easily leaving her to fend for herself. Rarely did her phantom-self consider his fate. Even now, Mari did not credit his past actions. Mari of the present watched this Gift fed memory. Somewhere, within the vixen kneeling at the white wolf's paw pads, she lost her connection with the present and let the Gifted memory almost completely blanket her thoughts.

Mari's feelings welled up in her present-self as she watched the memories of the past. She was living them all over again. A wave was building inside, making her want to break the contact and shove him away. Deep in her mind, the need of her species again pushed its way forward, reminding her of why she wanted to be here seeing this. However, there was something else. There was a small voice, an echo of her Mother's wisdom. 'No matter how angry you are at your mate, at least listen to their explanation. There are times, my Little Ray of Light, that you are the problem.' For once, Mari Semineu let the wisdom of her mother's words seep into her brewing temper tantrum.

Zenti felt the wave of depression rising from Mari. She was beginning to allow the full effects of the Gifted Talent of Union to embrace her. The shared memories would be as freely complete as his grasp of the Talent of Union would allow. Zenti knew he was still growing in this Gifted Talent, but this sharing could not wait until he had more mastery of it.

The silvery-white wolf felt Mari's depression roll into an emotional waterfall. Depression was swiftly followed by anger and soon hatred. He could feel something that tasted vaguely of the Gift but was not wholly the Void. Her emotions were all too fast and unnatural. This much emotion was a product of manipulation. Zenti wanted to delve deep into the manipulation, but Mari let all her feelings out at once. The Talent of Union only showed what was real. It was not like the Talent of the Broken Heart, which could manipulate memories. However, with her temper and outpouring of emotions, he dare not tell her now. She would never believe him. Summoner Zenti Semineu steeled himself for her emotional torrent. Mari needed to experience the truth, not hear it third paw. Someone had gone to great lengths to separate them, but the question was why. Pushing her back into the memory, Zenti knew this would get exhausting quickly if he did not find a way to keep her focused.

Mari watched her phantom-self in the cell. Her present self knew that she was only there for a month, not years. However, Mari knew that even now, she was not emotionally prepared to be a captive. The wave of emotional destress and confusion crashed down upon her phantom-self. That flood of emotions pounded at the vixen's memories. She did not relive each day of her captivity. Instead, the vixen's inability to control her memories and emotions allowed them to batter her mind.

~   ~   ~   ~

Quietly Zenti allowed the raging sea of emotions to toss Mari about like a rudderless ship in a storm. He wanted to protect her from that emotional storm but knew she had to weather it or drown. It was breaking his heart, but every life lesson requires you experience it. The white wolf knew from experience that those life lessons will be painful.

~   ~   ~   ~

Mari watched as her phantom-self had just pushed the food bowl back into the slot when a crash from outside the cell room door startled the phantom-vixen. She stumbled into a corner when a heavy thud against the door frightened her. The shadow-vixen jumped back as fear ran through her body again as the door began to open. *THEY* were coming for her.

Mari's present-self relived the terror of that moment. Her memories of that day co-mingled with her present-self. She now knew it was only a little over a month of being locked in alternating light and darkness. Yet, like her phantom-self, she remembered someone was coming for her. The vixen's present-self reacted the same as her phantom-self. Like that day, Mari's heart raced, she began to sweat, and her body trembled.

The vixen's present-day memories could not suppress the phantom-self's memories. The phantom-self knew that someone was probably coming to start some form of information extraction. Being familiar with the tactic, Mari thought she was ready to endure an interrogation. However, the vixen's phantom-self forgot all her training as she continued to believe she had been abandoned by Zenti. The phantom-Mari was already defeated.

With the terror of that moment flooding Mari's present-day self, she tried to block the memory. Mari tried to force herself back to the present but was guided back into the memory. Mari watched as her phantom-self huddled in the corner. The door to the phantom-self's jail cell flew open and light flooded into the room.

Present-self Mari watched silently as a sleek panther, his black fur glistening like armor, burst through the door. The phantom-panther picked her up and carried her like the kit that she had been back then. It was the panther Hayden that took her to safety, not Zenti. The vixen's present-self felt the emotion from her phantom-self. The panther was her knight and savior.

~   ~   ~   ~

"I remember that day, the door opened, and it was Hayden who came to get me. He's the reason I didn't go to the gallows," said Mari as she kneeled at Zenti's paw pads. Anger at Zenti flared to the surface of her mind like a bonfire. Like her phantom-self, Mari's present-self raged at her mate for leaving her there to be tortured and executed. Mari unknowingly dug her claws deeper into Zenti's chin.

Nothing he could show her would ever convince her that he had not abandoned her to save his own life. She felt the brush of Zenti's Gift as it pulled her memories out into him, viewing what she had experienced that day. Then without warning, Mari was looking as if seeing through Zenti's eyes.

~   ~   ~   ~

Not only could Mari view objects through Zenti's eyes, but she could also feel what Zenti felt as if it were her own body. This was confusing. However, she did not fight it. Instead, she allowed herself to see what the betrayer Zenti saw and felt. When she and her sister Rini, the Crown Oracle, spoke civilly, she knew that a Gifted could not manipulate actual memories. If a Gifted used the Talent of Broken Heart, and the memories conflicted, the ruse would soon be uncovered. Therefore Mari knew this was what really happened to Zenti, and she relished his betrayal exposed.

Zenti was wet, and his body felt as if it were tingling with static electricity. Mari's present-self felt the additional weight of wet fur of Zenti's past-self as he dragged himself out of the water. Mari's present-self watch with eager anticipation.

Looking through the view of Zenti's phantom-self, she looked up from the water's edge. Zenti's looked around for Mari. The white wolf was alone on the edge of the water's bank. Looking up, the sun was remarkably close to where it was when he lost consciousness. How long had he been out, and why had he not drowned?

Zenti's thoughts were playing back in her mind as if from a video reel. The central view was in focus. However, the peripheral sight was a little blurry. Sitting on the bank of the water, Zenti's phantom-self turned when he felt the presence of another. Mari's present-self could see that it was an invader. However, a flash of pain shot up Zenti's back, and he convulsed violently. The last view in the phantom-Zenti's eye was of one of the metal rods the invaders used to stun those of her race. Stars flashed in Mari's present-self's eyes. For an instant, she began to lose consciousness.

In that brief moment, Mari almost felt the connection to Zenti sever. Yet she could feel him here and now, focusing her mind back on the images. She realized that Zenti passed out in the vision, yet the connection felt so strong that she thought it was real. Zenti slumped back to the water's edge, right where he had previously fallen.

~ ~ ~ ~

Mari's present-self opened her eyes, expecting to see Zenti sitting on the cot in her tent. She expected to hear the chatter of her patrons in her Faction camp. What she saw was undiscernible through tear-blurred eyes. There was a constant ringing in her ears. In a moment of brief confusion, the vixen wondered what Zenti had done to her. However, her vision cleared when she blinked. But Mari Semineu had not blinked, and she knew it. This was still Zenti's view, his experience. She remained linked to him through the Gifted Talent of Union.

How was this possible? According to several Oracles that she knew, though their Gift's were limited, they all agreed that the Talent of Union was very taxing on the body. Mari knew Zenti was tired several hours ago when they met in the forest clearing. What did it cost him to hold the Talent of Union with her? A soft mental growl called the vixen from the periphery of the Union. Mari found herself back, viewing the world through Zenti's eyes. The blur cleared as Mari felt tears running down the phantom-Zenti's cheeks.

The vixen gasped as pain wracked her body momentarily until she felt the cool, numbing effects of Zenti's Gift. He had used the Talent of Reflection to reflect the pain of someone wounded upon himself. That allowed a Gifted Shaman to stabilize the injured party while they or a doctor tend to the injured. Once again, the wolf who had abandoned her was taking the pain she felt away and absorbing it. Mari realized Zenti wanted her to feel the suffering he was subjected to, but only a portion. The vixen's ears folded back in acknowledgment of what he was doing so she could see the betrayal from his perspective.

~   ~   ~   ~

Zenti's phantom-self next awoke in a destroyed factory's basement rubble, or what he thought looked like a factory. Mari thought it looked like an iron mill. In fact, it looked very much like an iron mill Zenti recalled from their travels. Mari was unsure exactly which iron mill this was, but she remembered it. Zenti was projecting his experiences into her mind. Mari felt the phantom-Zenti try and sit up only to find himself bound to a metal slab. Heavy metal clasps were around his wrist, ankles, and waist. They secured him to the metal slab with strands of woven metal cable.

The vixen felt the pain as it seared through Zenti's body. She felt the white wolf's phantom head turn. Through partially dry eyes, she could see blood pooling at the edges of the slab. She thought she saw movement out of the corner of his eye, and again he tried to sit. The ensuing pain washed over his body. Darkness overtook the phantom-Zenti and ostensibly her. Through the Gifted Talent of Union, Zenti helped her remain lucid.

~   ~   ~   ~

The subsequent shared memory the vixen saw through the phantom-Zenti's eye was herself. The feelings he projected were one of a smitten pup. Mari wondered where this memory took place. They were both young. The vixen smiled to herself, reacting to the warm feelings he was projecting from the memories. Looking through his eyes, she realized that this was his first time seeing her outside the training camp. Mari's present-self recalled that, while at her father's training camp, Zenti Semineu had only one focus. She never knew he had ever noticed her.

Mari vaguely remembered that day. Her father sent her out into markets to buy her mother a present, as was the custom of a young female just Coming-of-Age.

"I was eleven," she recalled, "it was my whelping day. My Coming-of-Age party was that evening. Dad wanted me to pick out a gift for mom as a thank you for raising me."

She could feel phantom-Zenti's emotions and blushed, noting that he thought she looked very enchanting as she walked the cobblestone streets. The noise of the fair, the crowds, and vendors hawking their wares distracted him. When Zenti looked back, Mari was gone. Nonetheless, Mari felt the rush of Zenti's memories.

~   ~   ~   ~

Mari's present-self's own memories of the fair began to surface, and she again became confused as to where and when she was. Zenti could feel Mari's memories rising, creating more confusion within her. The vixen was losing the ability to tell when and where she was. The memories of events played twice in her mind, once from each other's perspective. Mari saw Zenti's memory and her mind attempted to consolidate them into one cohesive memory. That was a potentially maddening effect of the Gifted Talent of Union. The viewing participant could quite literally get lost in the two memories. That event usually drove the viewer insane. This consolidation of views was distracting her focus.

~   ~   ~   ~

"*Let me make this easier,*" Zenti said mentally. His words brushed Mari's mind softly, then his thoughts made her gasp.

Touching the vixen's mind, she could feel the raw power of Zenti's Gift as it coursed through her. Again, she felt as if she was him. She now looked down at herself, kneeling in front of Zenti. She was in her tent, and it was the present, not the past. Mari realized that she was physically looking through Zenti's eyes. This was incredible. This was the Oracles Gift of Transference. Mari then felt Zenti intertwine their memories, allowing them to experience the events from the other's perspective.

Together the memories ebbed and flowed between them. Then, slowly, Mari's own memories were but a shadow. Though they were not forgotten, they were subdued, leaving her with their collective memories. They were getting the rare chance to see and feel what the other was experiencing, without the constant burden of their own memories overpowering the shared memory.

"I knew you could brush the mind of others, but I never knew you had this Gift," she said in bewilderment. The vixen was seeing his memories from his perspective without remembering them from her own. This was an incredible leap in his Gifted Talents.

"Who taught you this. Since when does a Summoner

learn the Gifts of an Oracle," Mari asked in an accusatory tone? None of this made any sense to her. Summoners did not have the Oracles Gifted Talents. Minor aspects, yes, according to her sister Rini. But this was not possible, thought Mari as she watched her body talk to Zenti. However, it was a fantastic feeling and experience.

Her sister Rini had told her once when times were still better between the two of them that sharing memories this way was the best way to learn the truth. Still, it was incredibly taxing to the Oracle. Rini warned that a viewer could get lost if the Oracle succumb to the Void. However, Mari began to see and feel what Zenti felt with clarity. The vixen relished the idea of seeing the betrayal without confusion. Now she would see the genuine coward for what he really was. Still, she wondered just where he had learned this Gifted Talent. However, Zenti did not respond. Mari thought she could sense a feeling of sorrow gently washing back from Zenti for a fraction of a moment.

~   ~   ~   ~

Mari's thoughts touched him like a hammer to an anvil. After ten years, Mari still had not learned to shield her thoughts properly. Some things never change, Zenti thought quietly, hiding that from her. Yet the chance to see what each other saw, to feel what they felt, was uniquely fantastic. However, it was an exhausting event. Mari wanted to witness his past, if only to placate him into helping her, so he would pay the price. He fully opened the Union between them, and they lived the other's life.

~   ~   ~   ~

My dear readers:

I hope you will accept that reading this particular chronicle is like watching two lives playing simultaneously in a hologram. I attempt to bring this to you from multiple perspectives. These are the memories of two very hurt individuals, both with burdens unimaginable. Through a unique ability, I have access to the memories of all the people in Mari and Zenti Semineu's life.

Not only will you relive the life of these two extraordinary individuals, but also the lives and deeds of others. I present the beginning of a most beautiful tale of the most remarkable spirits I have even had the honor of chronicling. Please digimark or bookmark this chapter. These memories are the roots and limbs of a mighty universal tree, known by many names but meaning the same thing...Hope ~ Sanura

~   ~   ~   ~

Mari was standing on the training grounds' outer ring, dressed in a loose-fitting gray shirt and overalls. It was three days after her Coming-of-Age party and the first time she had ever seen Zenti for more than just casual interaction. Zenti Semineu was not the approachable type. Though friendly and respectful, he was all business, all the time. He was not the typical young Mitdonian. All the young vixen knew of the male white wolf had come from watching him train his Gift or leaders within the new recruits. He was well respected in the camp but very much a loner. He did not attend any of the parties unless ordered to do so. He did not engage in the comical play of the other young recruits. In short, she thought he was quite the odd one. Mari had come to see her father, General Haverick Waxton, the camp commandant. He was charged with the training of the recruits in unconventional warfare and was always busy.

Her father had made arrangements for the vixen's mating. Pre-arranged matings were old-fashioned. The vixen was determined to demand that her father listens to her position. She needed to stop this arranged marriage that he had announced at her Coming-of-Age party. The vixen was so intensely focused on her goal that she did not notice she had entered the training grounds.

On her way across the training ground, a spear nearly impaled her. One of the first-year male recruits had thrown one towards her. Females were not allowed on the training ground once they came of age. It was forbidden so that the young males would not be distracted and subsequently injured. When an of-age female did come on to the grounds, the recruits were given permission to drive them from the area, though they were not allowed to harm them. However, that rule did not prevent a recruit from defending themselves if the female did retaliate.

"Shove off!" Mari yelled at the recruits, but they had advanced on her. They were demanding to know why she on the training grounds. It was not long before one of the recruits threw a punch, and Mari was in the scuffle. All three males pulled at her hair and tail, along with hitting and punching her arms and legs. They were sending a message, not trying to inflict permanent damage.

Mari surprised them, though; she fought back a lot harder than they could have expected for a female. The young vixen fought to inflict injury. She was outraged that they would touch her. She was also outraged at the archaic rules that stated females could not train in the arts of unconventional warfare. Mari fought with tenacity.

Though it was longer than the three males had expected, Mari was overcome and soon had her face buried in the dirt. The three of them, one with a knee on her back, taunted her. They humiliated her by laughing at the blows she had landed as weak. The three males did not relent, saying how the training ground was no place for a female and that they would teach her a lesson she would not forget.

~   ~   ~   ~

It was three days after the fair that Zenti saw her again. Mari wore the gray blouse and coverall of a female recruit. However, females were not allowed to train in unconventional warfare. Mari was the daughter of General Waxton and expected considerations. Her father did not make an exception to the rules for her. Still, the vixen was trained in paw to paw combat and rifle drills like the other females. Mari had just passed her Coming-of-Age date. However, the war dictated that those within a year of that day could be trained in basic military skills. Regardless, of-age females had a separate training ground.

There the vixen was bold as brass on the male's training grounds. Zenti officially was a second-year officer recruit who had earned the full commissioned rank of lieutenant. However, his training started long before. By now, everyone knew the white wolf. He was a fixture on these training grounds since he was seven. Zenti Semineu was a Gifted Summoner of considerable power. However, seven years old was too young to train in the arts of war. Exceptions were made for the young Faction fighter. Zenti had fought for over a year with one of the most feared Factions on Mitd. His reputation preceded him as a Gifted. Within a year, he was respected for his desire to free Jayden and feared what his Gift could do.

Today was two years after the white wolf was officially accepted into the unconventional warfare program. Zenti had been at the camp for nearly seven years. However, for the first five years, Zenti only trained his Gift. General Waxton forbade Zenti from participating in formal combat training. That upset a few of the recruits as it meant Zenti received preferential treatment.

However, during a visit by the elder Shaman Torit, the recruits quickly learned why Zenti needed to be trained separately. The violent Gifted battle between Shaman and Summoner was terrifying to witness. Everyone knew of the legendary Shaman Torit. Until that visit, the recruits did not fully appreciate the pre-Coming-of-Age white wolf's access to the Gift. They quickly learned that Summoner Zenti Semineu was a rage-filled young male with a propensity for pushing his Gift to the extreme. That was five years ago when Zenti was only nine.

Today Zenti was in command of a platoon that was working on their marksmanship. He had finished his platoon's drills when he noticed Mari Waxton crossing the training grounds. Three young recruits immediately began yelling and screaming that she should not be there. This soon turned into a fight, and though she gave as good as she got, three to one are never great odds. Mari Waxton went down.

Zenti noticed that General Waxton was watching yet did not say a word or stopping the fight. For a moment, Zenti wondered why the General would allow his daughter to be attacked. However, the reason the General did not intercede was unimportant. Without thinking, Zenti moved to defend Mari from the males. It was disgraceful to attack a female. The young white wolf would not tolerate that from his trainees or any male soldier.

~   ~   ~   ~

Mari heard a single gunshot report and watched as the first of the three males went down hard. The vixen caught a brief glimpse of the shooter and noticed the bright green pistol. It must have been a rubber-training round from the color of the firearm, the vixen thought. It stuck one male square in the back. When the feline fell muzzle down in the dirt, she could see no blood. That confirmed it was a training round.

The second male, shocked, stood up and turned away from the vixen. The last of the three did not notice the reactions of the other two. The ferret continued to punch her arm, causing it to bruise. Free from the other two males, Mari clumsily flipped the ferret assailant over her. He attempted to kick her, but the vixen grabbed his booted paw pad.

Lurching back, she bit the ferret above the digitigrade ankle. The ferret yelped in surprised pain. However, he lashed out at the vixen, who groaned in return when the ferret kneed her in the muzzle. Rolling over, she got him back for kneeing her. Mari kicked out with both booted paw pads and hit the leaping ferret square in the jaw. The blow was hard enough to make him bite through a corner of his tongue. Mari sent him flying backward a few feet before landing on his rump, blood pouring from his muzzle.

~   ~   ~   ~

Zenti watched as the male feline he shot with the rubber training round tried to crawl away. Walking toward the only one standing, Zenti watched as the vixen was kneed in the muzzle. The vixen responded to the attacking ferret with both booted paw pads to the jaw with lightning-like reflexes. The ferret was sent reeling. The male ferret landed hard on his tail, blood pouring from his muzzle. The second now stood, not knowing what to do. He was choosing to fight or flee, though the choice could easily be seen on the badger's face. He decided to run and turned from the advancing Zenti, wanting no part of his rage. The vixen pushed herself up and spat in the direction of the running badger.

~   ~   ~   ~

"WUSS!" she yelled after him before dragging herself to her paw-pads. The vixen began dusting her clothing off. With the back of her paw, she wiped the slow trickle of blood from her muzzle. The knee to her muzzle cut her lip. She was sure it would swell. Turning, young Mari saw the white wolf advancing and brought up her fisted paws, ready to attack him if he came too close to her.

~   ~   ~   ~

What spirit, Zenti thought, as the vixen pulled up and raised her paws, balling them up in fists, she would use no claws here. Young Zenti laughed. Circling, slowing towards the crawling feline, the white wolf kept his eye on the vixen. The female fox was incredibly angry.

The ferret began to slowly get up, staggering a bit from the force of Mari's double boot to the jaw. Before he could stand fully upright, Zenti drove him back to the ground again with a swift boot to the back of the knee. The male feline Zenti had shot with the rubber round began to recover his wits but found himself firmly pinned to the ground under the young white wolf's other boot. Looking back at Mari, Zenti smiled and gestured at the kneeling male he had just driven to the ground. It was now a fair fight of one on one.

~   ~   ~   ~

Mari did not move but only watched this newcomer with curiosity. She thought he was coming to hurt her or join the fight and throw her out of the training grounds. That is what most males usually did to of-age females. She watched the white wolf with a keen eye. She knew of him and never heard of him laying paws on a female. She wondered if she would be the first female he threw off the training grounds. However, he did not; he had helped her, maybe not fully protected her, but had helped her. Slowly she shook her head, wondering if he meant for her to kick the younger male feline.

"I didn't come here to fight," the young Mari said quickly before nodding thanks to the male wolf and then hurried away. Looking for her father, who was previously standing on the porch, Mari noticed that he had vanished. However, Mari had a feeling that she knew where he was.

~   ~   ~   ~

Zenti watched as she gave what could be considered a quick bow and skittered off. He then looked down at the male that was under his boot with disgust.

"I'll give you a choice. You can get up and kick the feline's ass," began Zenti with a quick nod at the feline, "or I can kick yours," Zenti half-growled, "At what point in time do you hit a female, regardless of the rules? Take your pick; I need to get back to the next platoon's practice."

Removing his foot from the male's chest, the white wolf stepped back and waited. It was a short wait as the ferret chose the lesser of two beatings and jumped the kneeling male feline. Zenti turned and walked away.

~   ~   ~   ~

Mari's present-self felt Zenti's disgust at what the males had done. It was strange to feel what his emotions were. There was a depth of honor in him she had never known. Mari's present-self made a mental note of that.

How could this coward have lost such a strong streak of honor? However, the stream of memories did not subside, and she did not fight them. She wanted to know the coward Zenti Semineu from his own memories. Mari recalled what she did after leaving the training grounds. Instantly Zenti felt Mari's profound guilt at what she did next.

~   ~   ~   ~

The office was hot despite the open windows. A big paddle fan on the ceiling steadily turned. Behind a desk sat General Haverick Waxton. His rugged lion features were well-groomed, like his manners. His mane was closely cropped but predominate enough that it helped define him as male. He portrayed a figure of leadership and control. The office was clean, sharp, and in good military order. Pictures lined the off-white walls. Those photographs recounted General Waxton's achievements. There represented former classes, various military personal, and photos of the General and the King. Mari knew the King and her father shared a very close bond.

The door flew open, and a disheveled young fox stomped in. Blood dripped from the cut on her muzzle as Mari stormed up to the desk and slammed her fist onto the polished hardwood surface. General Haverick Waxton looked up from the desk at his daughter and calmly smiled.

"Arranging a mating for me, you can't be serious!" Mari half-pleaded, half screamed as she looked across at her father's war-worn muzzle. "Do you know how old century that is?"

Her father softly smiled, patiently letting his eldest daughter vent her frustration. The lion had years of practice. His mate, a vixen breed also, had the same hot-headed temper as his daughter. The lion smiled, knowing at least his daughter came by it honestly. However, Haverick Waxton detested screaming. Mari was on the verge of pushing her limits.

Pointing his claw at the chair behind her, obediently, Mari sat down, folding her ears back slightly in embarrassment and apology. She knew screaming would end any hope of compromise. Her father poured her a cup of tea. She knew the aroma; it was designed to relax and calm. She took the subtle hint and breathed a frustrated deep breath. He handed her the cup then refilled his own, making her wait patiently.

Like his mate, he knew his daughter. Neither were irrational, just high-spirited and willful. He knew one more thing that was his fault; both were spoiled.

"Mari, it's a good match, don't be so difficult," he answered her statement in his calm, deep voice. However, it did not carry the tone of finality but opened the door to continue a polite conversation. Haverick Waxton was laying a trap for his daughter. It would not work on his mate, but it presented Mari with an opportunity to grow. She was now considered an adult by law, having reached her Coming-of-Age Day. Still, he treated her as if she was still a kit. Mari jumped at the offered bait. Inwardly the lion sighed.

"Difficult? Other females my age are mating for love! What are you doing is setting me up," the vixen shouted.

Quickly she let her excitement retreat and sat back down when he gave her a stern look over his cup of tea hovering just below his nose. In many ways, she was still a kit. Perhaps he had been too accommodating with her, just like he was with her mother. However, the calm never left the lion. When he spoke again, his voice was peaceful.

"The times are trying, my daughter. You have always been strong-willed, and that will get you killed one day. The match is not for love. The match is for survival. *THEY* have become more and more aggressive in taking our race and our resources. What has prompted this change is a mystery that needs to be solved. However, I fear one day the invaders will come to take all that we have. I need to have you safe when that happens. An Oracle told me, long before you were whelped that the Monster will roam and devour this land before our Saviour will come. I need to know that you are safe from harm," her father said as he stood up and moved around the desk to her.

Haverick Waxton detested calling the invaders by their colloquial name. However, Mitd was not ready for the truth. The Saviour needed to be raised first, according to the Orra Prophecy. The lion's sources said this event would not happen on Jayden but high above it. It made no sense, but one did not question an Oracle's vision lightly. However, the Oracle he knew was crystal clear on one fact;

the Monster of the Orra Prophecy would come before the Saviour. That spelled the doom of Jayden, but Haverick Waxton was not about to give up hope.

Haverick kneeled before his daughter. The lion began wiping the trickle of blood off the fur on her muzzle. Mari pouted. Her father was treating her as if she were a kit with food on her chin. Every Mitdonian knew of the Orra Prophecy of the Monster and Saviour. Most considered it a bedtime story to scare pups and kits into compliance. However, General Haverick Waxton had knowledge that others lacked. He knew that the Prophecy was true. He also knew that the Monster had been whelped already and was growing. Oracles were rarely wrong, especially this one. The lion looked at Mari and sighed.

"What would I ever do if any real harm came to you?" her father said as he pulled her close to his chest.

~   ~   ~   ~

Mari's present-self touched the scar on her face as she watched the memory, "So much for that wish," she whispered. Ten years ago, her parents passed to the stars. For nine of those years, Zenti protected her as best he could, then he betrayed her. The thought flared up her anger, but the calming power of Zenti's Gift gently quelled it. He guided her back into the memory.

~   ~   ~   ~

"I don't need protecting from **THEM** or any monster!" the young vixen insisted, "I can take perfect care of myself."

    The old lion pulled his daughter's muzzle to his chest. He laughed at her fiery determination. His laughter rumbled against her cheek as she listened to him, treating her like a little kit. Pulling away, Mari glared at him.

~   ~   ~   ~

    Her phantom-self raged at her father. Yet deep inside of those memories, Mari's present-self cried for her next words her phantom-self would utter. They were petty, hateful words towards a male she deeply loved, respected, and missed.

    "I hate you!" the phantom-vixen yelled, pushing her father away. The phantom-vixen ran out of his office and raced across the training fields.

~   ~   ~   ~

    "I hid in the forest that night after it started to rain," Mari said softly, speaking mainly to herself as she watched the memory. The vixen's present-self began to softly cry at the bitter words. "I hate you. How can I ever take those words back? I'm so sorry, dad." Looking at her present-self, through Zenti's eyes, Mari briefly lost herself in the memory of running into the rain-filled night. Though exhausted, Zenti allowed the Talent of Union to continue to flow between them.

~   ~   ~   ~

The vixen could feel the rain on her fur. It was not real, but the memory was so strong Mari felt wet. Here in her tent, holding on to a past love she now hated, the memories continued. Mari did not want to return to the past anymore. However, it was too late, and the memories too strong. The present fought to remain in control but failed. Mari remembered finding a hollowed-out tree stump. Lightning had destroyed it a decade before she was whelped. It took nearly a century for that species of tree to rot away. She and Zenti's memories began to merge again.

Mari's phantom-self huddled tight into the large crevasse caused by the ancient lightning strike. She did not want to be found. Somewhere inside, Mari's present-self wished she were back in the knothole right now. Zenti nudged the present aside, bringing her back into focus with such ease that she found she could not resist. That act shocked her. Was it another new expansion of his Gifted Talents? She was not looking through the phantom-Zenti's eyes again. Mari started to question how he could do this when Zenti growled again. Mari knew that growl. It was Zenti's 'I have had enough' growl. When mated, each had a growl that signaled the other had pushed too far. When that happened, a fight was about to begin. For the first time in thirteen months, Mari yielded to her logical mind's desire to fight with Zenti, and the kit inside became silent.

~   ~   ~   ~

The phantom-white wolf heard the door slam as he headed to his barracks. Looking back just in time, Zenti watched as the little vixen rushed out of the General's office and off into the dusk. After a long moment, the office door opened, and the General stepped out. Those on the training ground stopped and turned to face the lion at attention. Zenti stopped as well, turning completely to face the lion.

The general was tall, with a bulky muscular frame. He was still powerful for a male in his late age. Time had not diminished this decorated warrior. Zenti moved forward when the General motioned for the white wolf to come.

"Sir," answered Zenti as he saluted.

~   ~   ~   ~

In that instant, through the Gifted Talent of the Union, Mari felt an immense wave of love and respect from the white wolf for her father. She never knew just how deep the love Zenti had for her father until this moment.

~   ~   ~   ~

"Go find her, son. Take a moment and change out of your uniform. I fear there are too many traitors in the area. I would hate for you to find yourself in a compromised position. Mari hates it when I try and take care of her, but what is a father to do," the lion said? Haverick Waxton shook his head in exasperation. As Zenti saluted and turned to trot off, the General called to him in a less military tone.

"Mari does not know who her intended is, Zenti. Perhaps she should not find out just yet. I think that if the two of you became acquainted first," the lion let his suggestive voice trail off.

~   ~   ~   ~

Young Mari tugged the collar of her coveralls tight as the rain intensified outside. Ahead, the vixen noticed a broken, twisted, and splintered tree trunk. Though dead for the past ten years, the tree still stood. The last winter storm must have toppled the tree. However, enough was remaining to huddle up in and hide.

"I'm not going back," she told herself determinedly, "I refuse!" Huddling down deeper, she felt the wet chill soaking through her clothes and fur.

~   ~   ~   ~

Zenti exited the main gate after changing into something less conspicuous. He tried to pick up her tracks, but it became a challenge. It would have been easy, but the heavy rains of spring came up shortly after he left the compound. After nearly an hour, the rain began to wash her tracks away entirely. Luckily, he had followed her to an area where there were only a few hiding places. The white wolf started a systemic search. Using the Gifted Talent of Life Sensing, he finally found her huddled up in the knot of a dead tree trunk. The rain began to come down harder, turning everything to mush.

The rain had soaked through his clothing and fur, the cold cutting to the bone. Kneeling, he looked inside the knotted split in the dead tree and found Mari huddled as deep in as she could. The rain ran down his muzzle.

"I am not going back; I will die before I go back!" she screamed immediately. Phantom-Mari glared at him over her rain-soaked muzzle. She tried to huddle further back into the hole. She recognized him; this was the same wolf that had helped defend her. He was just another lackey sent by her father to recover her. Summoner or not, she was not a kit anymore. Her father had no right to send a soldier after her.

Zenti knelt there in the rain, looking at this rain-soaked vixen. She bared her teeth and set her jaw in the act of defiance. Mari Waxton growled at him; no one had done that in six years. It was as if Orra had come down from the stars and taken a living, breathing form. He knelt there for what seemed an hour, just looking into those green eyes of hers.

"Would you just go away!" Mari yelled finally, "I am not going back. Kneeling there watching me isn't going to make me change my mind. There's nothing you can do to change my mind!"

When he continued to watch her, she reared back and kicked him hard in the muzzle. She slithered lower in the hole, trying to stay out of his reach as he went reeling backward, landing hard in the mud with a splat.

~   ~   ~   ~

She moved like lightning as her booted paw pad caught him entirely by surprise, knocking him on his tail. He had been listening to her yell something about not going back, but he was just too lost in her eyes to hear what she was saying.

The cold, muddy water not only further soaked his shirt, but mud began to ooze into his pants. The shock brought him back to the rain-soaked reality. Looking up into the sky while trying to shake the stun of being kicked in the muzzle, Zenti could only see darkness. The thick, coal-black clouds blotted out the stars. Whether Mari Waxton was a visage of Orra or not, he was getting tired of the screaming. However, he controlled his temper. When General Waxton approached him about being his daughter's protector and mate, the lion had warned him that his daughter was 'willful.'

"Hey, what the Heavens and Hells is your problem?" Zenti growled as he leaned up. Mud dripped off his pants and fur, "I came out here to find you as a favor to the General, not to be whipped on like some pup. Now come out of there. Let us go find someplace where I can relax. I'm not going to drag you kicking and screaming any place, but I would like a hot drink and a warm soak at the Pots."

"You can go by yourself," phantom-Mari said stoutly as Zenti glared at her. Rain poured down as he sat there in the mud. The rich Jaydonian soil oozed into his pants, soaking his backside. Growling lowly at the situation, the white wolf rolled onto his knees, then stood. Had the white wolf not used the Gift to locate her, he would have never known Mari was hiding in the tree stump. A tree stump was a great hiding place, one he would need to remember.

Moving around the stump, Zenti looked down into

the low side hollow. Mari was huddled down as far as you could get. The white wolf had to admit she had chosen an excellent hiding spot. He stood there looking down at her for a moment longer, then reached out his paw.

Rainwater ran down his paw and rolled off his claws. Mari looked at them closely. It was then she noticed his claws were ivory white, with no trace of black or brown. The sight of pure ivory white claws sparked memories of a bedtime story her mother told her about ivory and onyx claws.

However, in her anger, the young Mari Waxton could not recall that story. Her awe quickly ended, and she crossed her arms and turned her head away from him. She had no intention of returning to the camp or accepting an invitation to the Pots with this white wolf. He may be someone of importance in her father's command, but out here, he was just another male. The vixen growled at his offer of assistance.

"You know what?" Zenti's phantom-self muttered. Quick as a stroke of lightning, Zenti reached into the tree stump. He grabbed Mari by the scruff of her neck and yanked the vixen out of the hole. Zenti held her dangling off the ground. Mari was kicking and trying to get away. Zenti pinned Mari against the tree stump. He had grown tired of this kit-like game.

Shaking her, he growled a deep, low, long growl, fangs bared that immediately quieted her. No one had done that since her Gifting Day party six years ago except her father. Even her mother did not growl at her in that commanding tone. Mari gulped as she thought she saw a flash of red in Zenti's hazel-colored eyes. However, she thought there were a lot more golden than they were brown. It was hard to tell in this light. However, the fiery red flash was clear, and the vixen quickly remembered she was talking to a Summoner.

"I come out here; I try to be nice, but you insist on being a brat," the young Zenti growled. Mari squirmed in his grasp, "C'mon, we're going to go find somewhere warm to stay rather than some stinking old knothole!"

Zenti lowered her to the ground but did not let go of the nape of her neck. She tried to resist, but he was much stronger than he looked. Why did her father send this brut to collect her? Why did her father not come himself? She started to protest.

"No! No! No! No! N-," Mari stopped objecting when she realized that he was not taking her in the direction of her home but instead to the east towards the Pot's hot springs.

~   ~   ~   ~

He was half pushing, half dragging her along the path with no intention of returning her to her father until she had cooled down. Ten minutes into the walk, she quit the last of her struggling and began to follow his guiding lead. His long strides were taking a toll on her. His hurried pace took them in the direction of the hot springs.

The evening air was crisp, and it was still raining.

However, it was a bit lighter than when the white wolf found the vixen. The clouds were moving by fast as the wind picked up. It was a miserable trek to the hot springs. At least the young fox was no longer fighting him. Easing his grip on the nape of her neck, Zenti began to guide her with little effort.

It took them another good ten minutes to get to the hot springs. The white wolf had not said a word to her. Nor had he slowed down. She also noticed he had not let go of her neck. Mari thought his grip was a bit too tight.

~   ~   ~   ~

Zenti began to calm down when Mari stopped fighting. He quickened his stride to get himself out of this rain. It was a colder rain than usual this time of year, the white wolf thought. With a sigh, the young white wolf conceded that maybe he was chilly because he was tired. Over the past weeks, he had pushed his Gift too hard. What he really wanted was some warmth in his body.

The darkness in the woods brought a kind of solace to Zenti. He hated groups of any type, preferring to be alone. However, he knew things were changing, and leaders were being made every day. He knew that this was his calling and had embraced the path of service to the Crown. What he had learned from General Waxton in the past two years was invaluable. The training would be helpful in a tactical situation and in strategic ones as well.

Every bit of knowledge he gleaned from General

Haverick Waxton he was using to hone his Gifted Talents. However, it was his other Crown duty that benefited the most. His daily training duties were a simple ruse to establish him as a military leader. The bulk of his personal training occurred late at night with the general. Only Lillian Waxton knew that her mate was training the young white wolf in secret.

~   ~   ~   ~

Through the Talent of Union, Mari's present-self felt the most profound feeling of love. It stunned her that Zenti genuinely missed her father. However, the shared memories continued to flow, and she found herself effortlessly returning to their past.

~   ~   ~   ~

A shiver ran down Zenti's spine as the cold rain penetrated his fur, seemingly to the bone. Shifting his regular sight to Gifted sight, Zenti scanned the area with more clarity than any normal eye could have. Taking the vixen by the wrist, the white wolf quickened his pace with the Gift.

~   ~   ~   ~

Mari noticed that Zenti quickened his pace, and soon the vixen was running to keep up with him. In several instances, Mari's phantom-self had to catch herself when she stumbled. The white wolf was speed walking, and the vixen was practically running so he would not rip her arm off. She was sure that if her shoulder joint and his grasp were tested to find which was stronger, his grip would win.

"Would you slow down? You're hurting me," young Mari half whimpered. To her surprise, he did not slow at all but instead scooped her up into his arms and kept walking.

"Forgive me for carrying you, but I am tired. I want out of this wretched cold rain. I need nothing more than a hot soak in the springs and a warm drink to take the chill off. So please do not fight me. I just want to relax," Zenti's phantom-self said with such a soft plea that she found herself willingly complying. With incredible ease, the white wolf carried the slender vixen along the path.

It was not much further until they reached the hot springs, which was a popular spot. The rains had kept most all but the hardcore patrons away. Zenti could see the cabana up ahead. The promise of a hot soak was within reach, and it quickened his pace. The smell of sulfur filled the air.

The Pots were a series of hot 'pots' feed by hot springs. Most of which could fit three or four comfortably. The army training camp maintained these pots for recruits and citizens alike to enjoy. The pots themselves were natural formations. They were caused by erosion created when the hot spring waters bubbled up. Mitdonian records show that the hot springs were here for at least a thousand years. Until a little over one hundred years ago, they were unusable. The spring waters were scalding hot. Tectonic shifts altered the flow of the underground waters, which reduced the water temperature to tolerable levels. Several minor modifications over the past one hundred years made them quite enjoyable.

The area was open to the skies apart from one structure: the cabana. Each pot had a small overhang that blocked a portion of the weather but was otherwise open to the air. The guard, who also doubled as a concession's operator, was the only attendant on duty. Each pot held a metal ladder and circular metal bench attached with heavy rods drilled into the surface rock. A simple clothing rack was beside the ladder. There were no changing rooms and anyone who came out here fully understood that drawback. Most of those who visited the Pots knew that many patrons soaked sans clothing. Whole families came to soak, kits and all. Nudity was not an exception but an accepted norm at the Pots.

Zenti dropped the young vixen to her paw pads just outside the entrance and walked over to the cabana where the guard was. Returning shortly with two glasses and a large kettle of something still steaming, the young white wolf headed for one of the far pots. The evening air was cold, and Mari saw that Zenti was shivering.

Zenti motioned for her to follow. Surprisingly, she followed him obediently, looking him over curiously. Her paws were folded before her as she had always been taught when in the presence of a male. It was the Mitdonian way to signal a female was uninterested in a male. The well-worn path was muddy from the rain but felt well packed under their booted paw pad as they traveled to a far Pot.

"You don't actually expect me to be so taken in as to get into one of these with you naked, do you?" she asked. Mari could not believe that he possibly expect that. They stopped at an empty secluded pot.

Setting the two glasses and the kettle down by the pot's edge, young Zenti ignored the vixen as he took off his boots and poured the water collected in them out. He then took off his shirt and spread it across the rack that each pot had beside them to hang clothes on. Though they would not dry, the rain would wash the mud out.

Next, he unbuckled his pants and did the same with them as well as his underpants. Turning to face the vixen, the white wolf ignored her comments as he climbed into the steaming water. Zenti's phantom-self sat down until the water was just under his chin. Steam rose rapidly from the addition of the cold water that soaked his fur. Mari thought Zenti looked somewhat ethereal sitting there in the mist for a few moments, much like a floating head before the steam cleared.

"I don't care if you take your clothes off or not," phantom-Zenti said as he stood and poured two glasses out of the steaming kettle, "but I'm sure you know as well as I do that these waters will ruin your clothes. Besides, I am tired and want nothing more than something warm to drink and to just relax. I am not interested in sniffing after your tail. It is not mine to take or expect. You can just stand there in the rain, soaking wet, and remain cold. You can get in dressed and ruin your clothes, or you can lose the clothes and not worry about it." Zenti sank back into the blissful water.

Mari weighed her options, struggling inwardly for a long moment. It would not matter if she were past her Coming-of-Age Day; if she ruined these clothes, her mom would whip her tail. The vixen crouched down like an embarrassed pup and pulled off her boots. Removing the overalls, she folded them across the rack. She took off her shirt, wrung it out carefully, and then draped it over the stand as well before removing her undergarments and hanging them up. Slinking down into the pot, she felt the warmth of the water as it caressed her body.

She had never sat in the pots this way before. The vixen had always worn an old pair of shorts and a worn shirt. For a moment, Mari understood precisely what her female friends meant by being free. The lack of clothing made the flow of water quite enjoyable. Mari decided to join her female friends the next time without any clothing.

She turned to face Zenti and huddled down in the water. Glowering at him, she tried desperately to stay as far away from the white wolf as was physically possible. How was it possible that her father had sent this pervert after her? She thought about it angrily until she noticed Zenti's eyes were closed and his head tilted to the skies letting the rain massage his face. He was not looking at her. What kind of young male did not look at an available female. Not that she was *available* to him.

The moment the vixen stopped moving in the water, he opened his eyes and reached for his glass. Zenti stretched for the pitcher, but he had set it out of his reach. Growling a little at his stupidity, he closed his eyes again and opened his paw. The kettle moved closer to his outstretched paw, and she wondered how he did that. It must be his Gift, the phantom-vixen thought.

Zenti filled his glass again, wishing they were a bit bigger. Taking a deep drink, the warm honey mead coated his throat. He could feel the brew eating away at the cold in his bones. He finished the glass and looking over to Mari sitting in the water. He smiled to himself as she tried ever so hard to become part of the pot's opposite wall. The look on her muzzle was one of disgust, which he found utterly amusing.

'Well, this whole adventure of her father's is starting out on the right paw,' Zenti phantom-self sarcastically thought. Nothing about this situation would lead to a positive outcome. When Haverick Waxton said Mari was was 'willful,' it was an understatement. However, Zenti would not retreat on his promise to care for her when they were mated.

Leaning forward, he poured a third glass and motioned for her to take hers. He ached, and the warmth of the mead and water was melting those aches away. A blissful ignorance caused him to ignore her and everything around him. It was a sweet mead, all flavor; little alcohol, he thought. Mari crossed her arms, refusing to look away from him, watching him in suspicion. However, the vixen could see that Zenti Semineu was lost to the blissful oblivion of the hot spring water.

"My father isn't going to be happy with the way that you're handling this situation," Mari finally said. The vixen tried to inch further away from the young white wolf.

She wanted to blend into the wall but found it impossible. Seeing she could not meld into the stone wall of the pot, she huddled at the far side. Mari crossed her arms over her chest, which was below the water. She tucked her knees up under her chin as she crouched there. She again ignored his nod to her full glass and continued to glower at him.

"The General will probably not be pleased. He rarely is at my brash actions. However, that is why I am at the top of the class. I do things the unconventional way and to the extreme," replied Zenti. He let those last words trail off, leaving the statement open to interpretation. "So, we can be sociable, or we can just sit here, me enjoying the warmth, and you being all pissy. Take your pick. I really don't care." It was a lie; he did care. Being disrespectful was not what he desired for their 'first date.'

Zenti's white fur was thoroughly soaked, and true to his word, he went back to his mead, letting his head rest against the edge of the pot. Without looking away from the dark sky, he offered her a suggestion.

"I would drink the honey mead before it gets cold. It goes from delightful to awful in no time," Zenti said while closing his eyes. The cold rain tingle on the now warming skin beneath the fur.

Pushing the mead back, Mari looked away. She disliked how things were turning out. However, the vixen did not want to be ignored if she was forced to have company either. Mari slid down, sat on the bottom of the pot, and pressed hard against the wall. She wrapped her tail protectively around her before she looked at him again.

The water was just below her chin.

"Why did he send you after me? I would have thought that my dad would come after me himself," she asked slowly, trying to keep a civil tongue. It was a lesson her mother said she needed to learn. Mari had been 'learning' that lesson for nearly six years.

"He has pressing matters," Zenti convincingly lied, "If you're not going to drink that, pass it over. It is too good to let go to waste. Not that I want to drink that whole kettle by myself. I am expecting a rude surprise when I get back from those pups who attacked you. Tell me, what has gotten your tail in such a knot? You said you were not going back with such a strong emotion."

Zenti rubbed his muzzle while not trying to look at her. That was becoming more and more difficult. She was even more beautiful, soaking wet, he mused.

Passing off the mead, she looked up at the cloud-covered sky, watching as they rolled by. She saw through some of the breaks that the stars were becoming visible. The rain began to lighten up to a misty drizzle though the air still had a chilly bite about it. Mari Waxton sat in the hot spring pot and let the water peal the chill away before answering the white wolf.

"My Dads got me in an arranged mating to some male I don't even know," Mari said stubbornly, "'It's a mating to keep you safe,' he tells me. It's idiotic, antiquated, and about as intelligent as buying a bride like they used to two hundred years ago."

Pouring her mead into his glass, he saw a young couple headed to a pot just down the path. As they got closer, he finished his mead quickly and got their attention. The male skunk and female weasel approached. Mari slid deep enough until the water was lapping at the bottom of her jaw.

"Here," said Zenti as he stood and offered the two newcomers the kettle and the two glasses. "Take this, I have an early morning, and my company," nodding to Mari, "is not interested. It is still hot and over half full. I would hate for it to go to waste. Please take it. Someone should enjoy it," Zenti offered while standing up in the pot.

The water came to just below his navel as he handed the kettle and glasses to the couple. It was when he reached up that Mari noticed the long scar down his left ribcage. The couple took the gift and, with a few pleasantries, continued towards another secluded pot. Zenti sat down in the delightfully hot water and let the warmth bore deep into his sore muscles.

"An arranged matting, I would say it is old-fashioned. But I have several friends who have been mated that way. Some are even still mated today," Zenti said with a sarcastic snort at those words. One of the few friends he had was miserable in his arranged mating. However, he did not expound on that statement when the vixen glared at him.

"Well, Heavens and Hells forbid; I don't want my life chosen for me," Mari snapped, forgetting her modesty as her temper flared. Mari disapproved of a female's life being dictated by fate or the whims of another. There was no force on Jayden that would compel her to do anything she did not want. Orra, herself, could not make Mari Waxton do anything she did not wish to.

Getting out of the pot, Mari used the fur brush to strip some of the hot spring water out of her fur. The vixen was so angry that she did not realize she was nude before this male. With a determined glare, the little vixen put her clothing back on before walking away. She was returning the way they had come. She did not look back at Zenti, who remained sitting in the hot springs pot.

"Stupid soldier," Mari growled to herself, braiding her wet hair as she went. The vixen hated it when her hair got into her eyes. "Who does he think he is? No male could ever understand how a female feels when her fate is not in her own paws."

Only when she got outside of the hot springs did young Mari realize she had forgotten to grab her boots. Slumping her shoulders, she debated on turning around and heading back.

"Well, I can't exactly go back now," she groaned at her blind anger. That self flaw always seemed to land her deeper in trouble. If Zenti Semineu was any kind of respectable male, he would bring them for her. She did not care. She could return in the morning, and they would be at the cabana.

Mari continued walking, which quickly turned into a jog, then into a full sprint when the thought of Zenti following her crept into her mind. She did not want to see that stupid soldier again. The vixen did not want to talk to her father or discover who this unknown future mate was. The ground was squishing under her paw pads as she ran down the path.

It felt good to run, to feel the cool of the evening air on her still warm fur and skin. Mari Waxton let the calm of the night air help her focus. The fresh smell of rain calmed her to the point where she slowed down. When the vixen's anger fled her body, she stopped and plopped down on a log. Mari Waxton looked to the sky. The rain was now nothing more than a drizzle. There were patches of starlight, and the phantom-vixen wondered why she could not be like other females. Why did her father choose a mate for her? She was now of age and considered an adult. What gave him the right to decide her life? It was unfair.

~   ~   ~   ~

Zenti had not turned his head away or looked to the stars when the vixen exited the pot. He took in her wet body, altogether finding it more intoxicating than any mead. Mari stormed off without a word. The white wolf lay back in the pot. He decided it would be best to give her a few minutes. She had no place to go but home. The night had not turned out the way he expected. He had hoped Mari would just talk with him.

Zenti Semineu could not ignore Mari Waxton's natural beauty. If Mari ever lost that kit-like attitude, she would be a fantastic mate. She came from a linage that the Crown respected. Her education was excellent. What he knew of her was from casual observation and from those around her. However, he was reluctant to pursue such as her. Not because she was unattainable, but because he knew that there was a price that he would have to pay to fulfill what Orra placed before him.

The Gift was not without a price. The power of the Void could, and occasionally did, drive the Gifted insane. The more you drew on the Gift, the more you touched the Void, the more swiftly the Voidal madness came. Most Gifted barely caressed the Void for fear of going mad. The white wolf looked at the still waters in the pot. The reflection of the few stars that shone through the slightly clearly sky called to him. No, he should not have accepted the General's offer. He had no future to offer anyone.

Young Summoner Zenti Semineu knew that he would not merely caress the Void but fully embrace it. The price he had to pay to fulfill the Orra Prophecy was his alone. Whoever was with him would be left alone and empty. The white wolf gazed deep into the still waters as if he were looking into a mirror. He found no answers but the one he knew in his heart; the price was steep.

~   ~   ~   ~

"You knew ten years ago that you would have to pay a heavy price? I hated it when you would tell me that. I thought it was just the Voidal madness all Gifted fear," whispered Mari's present-self. Zenti said it rarely, but it deeply bothered her. What did he know that even her sister, an Oracle, did not know? When she and Rini were on speaking terms, Mari would ask if the Void demanded a price. Rini would snort a reply. The Void never demanded a price. The Voidal madness was a result of abusing the Gift, nothing more.

Zenti's present-self did not reply to her questions. Mari could barely feel his present-self at all. Drifting back into the shared memories, Mari realized that Zenti never wanted to hurt her. What changed to make him betray her? Or had he betrayed her? The past's shared memories supplanted the present's thoughts, and Mari once again saw Zenti's past.

~   ~   ~   ~

Mari Waxton was spirited. However, the white wolf was tired. Let Mari Waxton spend her anger on her way back to the camp. Zenti decided she would probably vent her rage and then stop for a rest. Most who were angry at the unfairness of life usually could not hold that anger for long. Looking at the half-empty clothing rack, he saw her boots. It had been five minutes, and she had not returned. He was reasonably sure the vixen would not be coming back. He let himself soak for another ten minutes and then reluctantly got out of the never-ending warm water.

Zenti shook out his pants and decided not to get dressed. Instead, he wrung out his undershirt, shook it in the air several times, and then pulled it on. The undershirt was a long-cut design, and it hung mid-thigh. He preferred that style as he hated clothing that bound his movement. Another benefit is that it covered his sheath[14], allowing a

---

[14] Therian males have their genitals predominantly housed inside their groin area, with a sheath that the male member retracted into.

modicum of decency. Mitdonians did not have an issue with nudity, but most wore clothing for the sake of society.

Picking up Mari's boots, the white wolf knew they would need to be returned. He emptied out the little bit of water in them and headed back towards the barracks. On his way out, he stopped by the cantina and got one of the bath wraps. Zenti promised to return it tomorrow. The attendant, a retired soldier, nodded. Zenti turned and headed down the path. The vixen would want to dry herself if he guessed correctly.

The rain had stopped, and a soft mist hung in the cool night air. The remaining warmth of the ground continued to rise as the cool of the wet night descended. The bugs were singing their nightly songs, breathing life back into the surrounding woods. It was distractingly calm, and the white wolf thought of a time before the invaders came to his home.

Losing himself in the evening's beauty, Zenti dreamed of a peaceful time. One of his favorite things to do was sit on the deck of his parent's desert home after the evening meal and listen to the animals' sounds. The warmth of the desert air had always calmed him as a pre-Gifting Day pup.

It was one thing that deeply saddened the white wolf. He missed the quiet moments that his father insisted that the family take. As a pre-Gifting Day pup, young Zenti would be required to sit on the open deck in the fleeting warm air until he released the stress of a hot day. It was the memory of his father's calm, compassionate, and loving manner that helped hold the Void at bay. One day, it would not, but until then, Zenti Semineu had his father's life lessons to draw from.

"Thank you, dad," the phantom-white wolf said to the evening stars. Spring was such a wonderful time of year, where all things were coming alive again. He wondered if he would ever be able to return to what his father had wanted for his family to experience, the happiness of a spring evening.

~   ~   ~   ~

Half an hour after the vixen left the hot springs, she found herself sitting on the outer hill that overlooked her home. Quietly Mari Waxton stared down at the world she had always known. Her father was probably waiting for his soldier to bring her back. General Waxton commanded respect from every soldier. Her father expected Zenti to waltz through the door, carrying her hoisted over his shoulder like a sack of potatoes. However, Mari thought that the white wolf would not do that. It had been half an hour, and he had not come after her. It was not easy to just walk away from one of her father's soldiers.

~   ~   ~   ~

Walking along the path, Zenti replayed the day's events in his mind. The recruits were getting younger, though he was young himself at the age of fifteen. However, there were things in his life that had already made him hard and uncaring. He remembered his home being assaulted by **THEM**. What an empty name for such a hate-filled species. There were those of his species that would aid the invaders. However, no matter how hard he tried, he could not abolish the memories of his family's slaughter. Those memories were fuel to feed an ever-demanding fire.

Zenti was an obedient pup. His family died while he hid where his mother had put him. His mother told him to remain hidden, and no matter what, do not make a sound. She told him the invaders would kill him, and she believed he was too special to pass to the stars. His mother made him promise. Like a loving son, the pre-Gifting Day white wolf promised.

Zenti had turned five the day it happened. It was his Gifting Day, the day a pup ceased, and the future adult began to develop. On a pup's fifth whelping day, they were treated like a pup until the last hour of that day. As the final minutes faded away, the pup was no longer afforded the leniency of youth. Adulthood was a short six years away, and no time could be wasted.

However, the day the invaders came lingered in his mind as if it were only an hour ago. Zenti remembered one of the invaders was left behind to make sure there was no one left alive. He remembered standing motionless behind the curtained nook as the invader made its way around his family's partially destroyed home.

Zenti recalled feeling anger and hatred. It was the same as now; he badly wanted to make the invader burn. It would only be fitting. The invaders had piled the bodies of his family in front of the smoldering remains of his home.

The white wolf recalled how when his father's body was tossed on the pile, one invader threw something on the stack, and the fires leapt to life. Zenti did his best to obey his mom. He hid but watched as all but one invader left. The stench of burning fur and flesh filled his nostrils, and something in him awoke. The invader screamed.

The next thing Zenti remembered was the partially charred body of one of his family's murderers. The five-year-old white wolf was hacking at the chared invader's body with a kitchen knife. His Gifting Day brought him the loss of all he loved. However, where Mother taketh away, She also giveth[15]. On that life-altering day, Orra gave him the Gift. The Gift allowed him to focus all his rage on the murderers of his family. That day he agreed to pay any price Orra asked to cleanse Jayden of the invaders.

Zenti pulled short when he stumbled upon Mari sitting on the hill. The white wolf was so lost in memories that he had not even known where he was when he came upon her. Young Zenti looked at his paws. They were still glowing fire red as he unconsciously called on his Gift. His paws were as red as the day he had killed the invader. Struggling, Zenti dominated the rage the Void was fueling and gained control over his Gift.

~   ~   ~   ~

The memories briefly faded, and present-Zenti could

---

[15] A common Mitdonian blessing. Mother refers to the Creator, Mother Orra. The saying reflects the belief that when one door closes, another opens. You are presented with a choice to close the door or walk through the new door.

feel Mari shaking while she grasped his muzzle tighter. The memories of rage and hatred he possessed even as a young pup had flooded her mind. Present-Zenti had lost focus and allowed the connection to go too far. He reached out and mentally wrapped her mind with the calmness of a midsummer's night after a harvest. Slowly Zenti brought Mari back to the vision. Again, tapping into his iron will, Zenti blocked the raging hatred that festered inside for twenty years.

~   ~   ~   ~

Phantom-Mari was so wrapped in her own thoughts that she did not notice Zenti coming up the path. Deep inside, the young vixen knew that her life was about to change. It was a gut feeling, and it felt ominous. It was more than being forced to mate a stranger. Though that was unacceptably bad in her opinion, it was not the deep-seated dread she felt. Something deep within screamed in terrified warning. At the vixen's spiritual core, she knew Orra was presenting her a choice. However, she did not know what choice. More importantly, Mari did not know if she even wanted to make a choice. The war had taken away the years any kit needed to enjoy life while growing up.

Mari thought about the six years a Jaydonian had between their Gifting Day and their Coming-of-Age Day. It was not a long time for a kit to become an adult. Mari thought it is unfair that Jaydonians are given so little time to adjust to their body's changes. Lost in thought, the vixen remained oblivious to her surroundings.

Sudden stabbing pain in her arm forced phantom-Mari out of her self-pity. She cried out at the sudden burning pain. Grabbing her arm, she saw the blood. Turning, she looked around. Mari saw the attacker and her eyes widened. The attacker was one of **THEIR** soldiers stepping from the cover of the trees. A gun pointed at her; she had been shot by the invader. He wore a military uniform similar to the Mitd Special Forces. The ever-present clear breathing mask covering his nose and mouth revealed the features of her attacker. His furless face and chin covered by that clear mask marked him as an invader.

Immediately Mari tried to scramble away, but the pain raced through her body when, with her wounded arm, she attempted to push herself off the log. She cried out again, feeling tears spring to her eyes as she did. Turning her body sideways so that the invader might not notice, she palmed the small hunting knife in the inner pocket of her clothing. Her father had taught her to carry a small hunting knife for safety. The vixen began to cry louder. It was also something her father also taught her. If someone were intent on killing you, they would kill you as quick as possible. However, if they had other designs for you, acting helpless would possibly cause them to lower their guard. Mari was not deluded about her situation. The invaders did not capture Jaydonians. However, they were known for their arrogance and that she might use it to her advantage.

She mimicked, holding her wounded arm exaggerating the injury. Though it hurt, she could still move her arm and paw. It must have been a grazing shot. She had helped bandage several of those superficial wounds on soldiers at her father's camp. The vixen knew it was all Mitdonian's duty to fight for their freedom or help in some way. Not only could she fight, but she also knew she needed to fight. However, her father's teaching had not been lost on her. 'Don't fight stupidly,' he would tell his recruits. 'Beating an enemy by using dirty tactics was not dishonorable. Living to defend others was honorable. Use any advantage to win.'

Mari wondered what an invader was doing so close to the training camp all alone? According to all the briefings, *THEY* were cowards and never traveled alone. Again, the vixen whispered thanks to her father for forcing her to attend his briefings. Though she wanted to learn, being force was not something Mari Waxton enjoyed. The invader eased closer. She tried to steady her nerves as she shook from the pain of the wound and her fear.

~   ~   ~   ~

Zenti pulled up short when he almost stepped out into the clearing where Mari sat. After witnessing her fighting ability, he did not want to risk another kick to his muzzle. He was not concerned with the vixen hurting him but did not want to hurt her by accident. The day had gone badly enough, and surprising her would not help ease the tensions. He stepped out into the small clearing and moved towards her. He stopped a few feet away and to her left. Zenti was about to speak out when the peace of the evening was shattered.

Mari cried out in pain a moment after he heard the sharp report of the pistol. Looking up, he saw one of the invader's soldiers advancing on them. It was a male and was motioning for the vixen to get up and move away from Zenti. However, Zenti could tell Mari did not know he was in the clearing with them. The invader must have been aiming at me, thought Zenti. Mari was unaware she was blocking the line of fire.

Zenti again looked at his paws; they still were glowing red. He wondered if the faint light had given them away or if somehow, the invaders were able to track him because of his Gift. However, this was not the time for investigating that possibility. Zenti decided it might help to develop his Talents to hide the visual effects of his Gift. The invader moved closer to Mari and him. The young vixen had not moved, and the invader motioned for her to move again. Zenti stepped up and round Mari, putting himself in front of Mari to defend her.

Reaching reached out his left paw, Zenti lowered his right and dropped Mari's boots. Using his now empty right paw, he motioned for Mari to move behind him. Zenti tried not to touch her with his right paw. It was now glowing red-hot. The white wolf's shoulders slumped a bit as he was too tired to call on his Gift to fight, but he knew he had no choice. The invader hesitated, and the expression was one of stunned bewilderment. Zenti surmised the invader did not expect to find him.

~   ~   ~   ~

Quickly Mari hid behind Zenti, her arm bleeding as she held her paw over the wound. The vixen pressed the handle of her knife tightly to the injury. Still, the vixen had the knife for protection. Before she knew it, she could hear the screams of the inhabitants below. Mari knew almost all the residents in the small village. She had lived there all her life. She could hear them screaming as they died. The light from the flames and explosions told her that the village was burning. The war had finally come to her father's military training camp.

~   ~   ~   ~

As Mari ducked behind Zenti, she brushed his paw that shielded her. Zenti noticed Mari did not scream in pain. His paws were holding onto the Gift and were red hot. However, the moment the vixen brushed him, he felt envigored. It was the first time in weeks that he experienced the Void coursing through him unfettered. He was so tired, but with that brief touch, he felt vibrant. A coursing power surged through his veins, and without hesitation, he unleashed a stream of blinding red flame at the invader. Zenti could hear the screams of the village below amid the sound of gunfire. Rage burned in him, and he could feel himself about to lose control when a sharp pain cut into his lower leg. The pain was intense enough to break his hold on the Gift.

~   ~   ~   ~

Mari's present-self felt the phantom-Zenti's leg burn. She knew that feeling from personal experience; he had been shot. The vixen could still see what he was seeing. However, their beginning is not what the vixen wanted to see. Reliving that sharp pain for Mari's benefit taxed the silvery-white wolf's concentration. The shared image of their first meaningful meeting blurred, and it brought him back to the present.

Zenti could read Mari's thoughts. She did not want to see the beginning of their relationship. The vixen needed to see the real reason that he 'abandoned' her. So be it, thought Zenti. The silvery-white wolf had never denied his vixen anything she wanted. However, one can not look at a tiny area of a painting and expect to comprehend its true beauty. He would show Mari the whole picture in small bits. As exhausted as he was, Zenti opened the Gifted Talent of Union and took her back to when the old Zenti died, and the monster he became was born.

~   ~   ~   ~

In an instant, Mari knew that she was no longer viewing their beginning. She had just been thinking that the beginning was not what she wanted to see. The vixen could see that Zenti was back on the metal slab, his body bound to it. Mari could see through his eyes again, and for a moment, the vixen was briefly confused. However, the Talent of the Union was now firmly established, and she found that flowing through her and Zenti's past was much more effortless. Mari was seeing Zenti seventeen months ago, not ten years.

The room they were now in was dimly lit except right over the blood-covered slab. However, even those lights were dim compared to a proper medical facility's lighting. Mari could make out the various forms of medical equipment and some sort of machinery. Before she could get a solid look through Zenti's tear hazed eyes, one of **THEM** hovered over Zenti. The white-robed invader began to insert a needle into Zenti's neck. She felt the sharp pinch as the needle entered Zenti's flesh.

~   ~   ~   ~

Again, Mari experienced everything the silvery-white wolf did. However, she knew it was but a mere fraction of a connection. The effects Zenti's mind and body suffered were being shared with her through the Gifted Talent of Union. She knew that Zenti greatly subdued those effects, or she would have been overwhelmed already. The vixen fell back into the shared vision. She wanted to see what torture the invaders used to make Zenti betray her. However, deep in her subconscious, a seed of doubt germinated.

~   ~   ~   ~

Lashing out, Zenti engulfed the invader in flame. The white-coated, male scientist screamed in pain. Zenti's anger was so violent that the scientist's furless skin was burned off within moments, and the muscle began to char. The intensity of the fire started burning away the meat on the extremities and exposing the bone. Mari was shocked at how fast the fires of Zenti's Gift could consume flesh so rapidly. The vixen was also shocked that she could not feel Zenti had touched the invader.

Zenti could not freely move. He was still strapped to the table. Mari felt the pulsing of raw power coursing through Zenti. To her amazement, the vixen understood that this must be how the Gift felt. It felt like standing in front of the stream from a fire hose under full pressure. She did not fully understand how, but Zenti found a wave of new anger that fueled his Gift's expansion. It was incredibly intoxicating. Zenti's rage was opening him up to the raw power of the Void. Her sister Rini had attempted to explain what it felt like. Mari was living it as a phantom-self of Summoner Zenti Semineu. She felt the madness that the Void was rumored to bring. It was snapping at her like a rabid wild animal. Is this what Zenti experienced every time he touched the Void?

Then quietness came over him. Mari, through the shared sensations, could smell the bitter gas mixing with the burning flesh. She knew that her own species would flood a room with a knockout gas if there was imminent danger. Phantom-Zenti faded a bit. Through blurry vision, Mari watched as a gauntleted fist came crashing down on the phantom-white wolf's muzzle. The darkness of unconsciousness overtook the stricken Summoner.

~   ~   ~   ~

With unconsciousness came the memories of the hill above the burning village and Zenti's young Mari. Their memories once again intertwining, taking the two of them back to when they first met. Mari wondered if this was part of Zenti's plan or was his exhaustion diminishing his focus. However, the pain from the blow Mari felt was not on Zenti's muzzle but hers. With the phantom impact to Zenti's muzzle, the vixen briefly felt the darkness of unconsciousness. In an instant, Mari found she was back on the hilltop where their younger selves face the single invader.

~ ~ ~ ~

Young Mari squeaked in fear as Zenti fell before her. He was not unconscious, but it seemed like he was not moving now.

"You're the one we have been looking for," the invader crudely screamed in the Mitdonian language. The white wolf's actions had taken the invader by surprise, affecting his aim. The male invader had fired wildly and, through sheer luck, hit the white wolf in the thigh. However, the invader's uniform was on fire.

The furless male soldier was beating at the flames burning his uniform sleeve. Ripping his uniform jacket off, he sneered down at the wolf in disgust. That was the way **THEY** reacted to any of the Jaydonian species. To an invader, a Jaydonian was nothing different than an animal. Mari would never forget seeing the photographs of recovered Jaydonians. Their bodies were mutilated. The invaders were ruthless.

The invader advanced on them. Having dropped his hot pistol, the soldier pulled a combat knife from a hip sheath. Moving slowly, the soldier cautiously advanced on the two when Zenti moved slightly. In a motion quicker than Mari expected, the invader dashed up to the prone Zenti. She had never been in a real fight, and this was the first time she had seen an invader in the flesh.

The soldier booted Zenti hard across the muzzle, but

the blow did not solidly connect. The invader momentarily lost his balance but did not fall. Zenti moaned and barely stirred. Panic made the vixen brave the moment the soldier kicked Zenti. Mari darted after the discarded gun the invader had dropped. Her bold action startled the soldier. The weapon was still warm, and a slight wisp of steam rose from the mud and water-covered metal.

"Don't come near us!" Mari yelled. Her eyes were wide with fear as she held the gun in trembling paws. The invader laughed at her. Mari knew **THEY** never took a Jaydonian seriously unless it was one of the Gifted.

"What do you think you're going to do with that? You don't even know how to shoot it," said the invader. The furless male raised the knife. Holding the knife out in front of him in a thrust-ready posture, the furless male snarled, "You have no gray in your fur. You must be just a pup. You cannot do anything but serve our needs, you pathetic excuse for an animal!"

No, it could not end like this, phantom-Mari thought. The furless soldier leapt at her. She could see his bared teeth through his clear breathing mask. Surprisingly the vixen found the invader's teeth unimpressive, and the invader's act of growling like a Jaydonian was quite comical. Mari pointed the gun directly at the soldier's chest, just like her father taught her. The invader let out a deep-throated yell as he lunged for her.

Mari had trained with her father's recruits. However, if she failed in training, all she ended up with was a bruised pride. This was real, and the knife was not a practice weapon. The vixen panicked, pinched her eyes shut, and braced herself for the attack. *No,* the phantom-Mari mentally screamed as she squeezed the trigger. The single pistol report echoed across the crest of the hill and slowly faded. The phantom-vixen opened one eye to a squint to see why she had not been injured. Her muzzle flew open, and she opened her eyes wide. Mari watched in complete disbelief as the invader staggered backward for a moment before crumpling to the ground in a heap.

Was *IT* dead? The little phantom-vixen dropped the gun as she began to tremble in fear. A whimper escaped her muzzle, and a shiver ran down her spine. She began to cry. Sobbing, young Mari buried her muzzle into her paws and cried large, frightened tears. They rolled down the fur of her cheeks. She tried to rub the tears away, but the blood on her paws from her injured arm only mixed with them. Streaks of thinned blood covered the phantom-vixens muzzle.

~   ~   ~   ~

Zenti slowly regained full consciousness. The combination of exhaustion and the shock of being shot had temporarily overwhelmed his body. The first sounds he heard were that of a kit crying. Memories of his past flashed to the forefront of his mind. He saw himself for a moment back at his home with the burning bodies of his family. The crying continued; it was a familiar sound. It was the sound of a kit having to grow up too fast. It was a sound he once made.

Quickly he looked around for the soldier and found

the body piled in a heap, dead. He looked over and saw the gun lying at Mari's paw pads. She had sunk to her knees. Slowly he got up and gingerly moved up to her. Shaking his head, Zenti tried to clear the cobwebs away. At his first step, the pain in his leg returned. He had been injured before, and using his Gift, he numbed the pain receptors in his leg. It was a struggle, but he knelt before Mari. Wrapping his paws around her, he drew her close to him and hugged her tight.

"That is just what I felt when the shock and rage went away, and I realized that I had taken a life. Even if it was an invader's life," Zenti whispered into Mari's ear. "I'm sorry, I was not fully strong enough to defend you."

"I can't do this. I can't be the warrior my father wants me to be," the phantom-vixen whimpered. From down in the village, the sound of screams and gunshots filled the air. Zenti stood up and offered her his paw. Mari shook her head no.

"We don't have time for this, Mari. We need to get to the village below. Grab his gun, and let's make our way down. You know the old cobblestone path that is partially overgrown? That is the best way to get to the training camp unseen," the phantom-white wolf said in an unmistakably commanding voice. He took a step and stumbled a bit when he put his full weight on the injured leg.

"I know the cobblestone path," Mari said as she stood. She noticed Zenti stumble. Heavens and Hells! He had been shot, and it looked like the bullet went all the way through. There was blood on the front and back of his leg fur. Oh, Heavens and Hells, it must hurt, she thought. Again she heard the screams and immediately thought of her family down below. The thought of her family under attack triggered something deep within.

"I can go alone," the little vixen said quickly, wiping the tears from her blood-covered muzzle while putting on a brave face, "You're hurt; going down there will only get you killed. I am small, light, and quick. I can get down there and help them evacuate."

Before Zenti could reply, Mari grabbed her boots that he had brought and was off. She struggled to put them on as she hobbled down the path. Running as fast as Mari could, her small, feminine body disappeared into the brush. She raced down the old cobblestone path, skidding as she came to the slope of the hill.

"Dad!" Mari yelled, desperate to be heard over the noise of the fighting.

~   ~   ~   ~

Zenti heard her running down the path, sounding like a pack of wild mounts, and sighed. Then Mari began yelling for her family. He growled something about naivety and ripped a long strip of the invaders uniform as a bandage for his leg. Zenti quickly searched the body for anything useful. Picking up the gun Mari had left, the white wolf growled again at her kit-like actions. Zenti looked to the stars and wonder if he had made a mistake in agreeing to General Waxton's proposal. Zenti would have to teach Mari several basic lessons, or she would be dead in no time. He wrapped the towel around his waist and tied a half bow in the draw strip.

The invader had a radio, but the heat of his Gift summoned fire had melted the outer casing. Zenti tossed the radio aside and took the extra clips of ammunition from the invader's body. The white wolf knew that the invader's radio equipment had a tracking device installed. With nothing of further use, he headed for the old cobblestone path. His leg hurt, but he did not have the energy to spare to start even a little healing. The phantom-white wolf did his best to make his way to the buildings below yet remain unseen.

The invader who found them was alone. Therefore he must not have been expecting to find anyone on that hilltop. He must have been an observer who would report the movement in the village and training camp below. Zenti thought about the invader's statement, "you're the one we have been looking for." Did that statement reference Mari or him? Surely the invader meant him; they always were hunting the Gifted. What would they want with Mari? However, the invaders also seemed to be interested in the upper echelon's offspring of the Mitdonian influential population. Perhaps Mari was the target. However, phantom-Zenti pushed that thought from his mind and focused on the task at paw.

The path came up behind and slightly above the barracks, which seemed undisturbed. Zenti was reasonably sure he would not be seen approaching from this direction. Taking a moment, the phantom-white wolf surveyed the situation.

Zenti saw dead bodies everywhere; they were all his species. Fires flickered in the small village of Hasha just a mile away. The destruction of the training grounds was methodical. It appeared the raid had been designed to remove a possible military threat. Tonight, the small village of Hasha celebrated its one-hundredth anniversary of founding. The citizens were participating in the festivities. The bulk of the recruits planned to attend. The training camp was guarded by a minimal presence.

The villagers should have listened to General Waxton. However, the village Elders demanded that the troops and recruits attend. The village Elders boasted there had never been a raid on Hasha. General Waxton, on Shaman Torit's advice, objected but was overruled by the Elders, who threatened to involve the King. Zenti wondered what General Waxton and Shaman Torit knew that others did not?

The white wolf made a mental note of that thought for later dissection. Thinking of General Waxton, the phantom-white wolf saw Mari run to her father's home. Somehow, she managed to cross the training grounds unseen and unmolested. The phantom-white wolf shook his head in disbelief at her blind luck. Slowly he began to make his way down to the barracks.

~   ~   ~   ~

Mari darted across the training field, dodged through the training grounds, and up to her family's home unopposed. She stopped for a moment as she skirted the body of a dead leopard lying beside the door and gasped. She knew and played with his kits. The male leopard was one of her father's personal guards. The male had been shot several times in the back of the head. Mari gasped again when she realized he had been executed. Noise from inside her house drew her attention away from the blood-soaked leopard.

Quietly phantom-Mari slipped into the long, central hall. The main hall ran the house's length and connected the porch with all of the house's rooms. The pictures on the wall looked undisturbed. Knowing precisely where to place her paw pads, the small vixen avoided the floorboards that creaked. Phantom-Mari heard talking coming from the living room, and though the front hallway door was closed, the second door near the end of the hall was cracked slightly open. She peeked in, covering her muzzle as she saw one of **THEM** was in the living room.

"Where are the others," the invader demanded? Mari could see her mother and her little sister, Rini, huddled on the floor in the corner while the male invader aimed a gun at them. The invader was speaking to her father in Mitdonian. The male invader was speaking the Mitdonian language surprisingly well, a fact that shocked Mari. The invader's language was nearly impossible to understand. It lacked the subtle undertones and inflections of the Mitdonian language.

"There are no others," Mari's father said firmly.

It laughed the hideous laugh common to all their

species; it sounded nasally and high pitched. Mari was unsure what to make of that development as the invaders were just intelligent brutes. Though they were technologically advanced, they were no better than wild animals. Learning the Mitdonian language should not be possible beyond a pup-like speech level for an invader, the phantom vixen thought. Those were the reports the media propagated. However, her father had a different view of the invaders.

The invader moved over to Mari's mother and sister. Mari's breed was like that of her mother, a fox. Her sister, Rini, was of the lion breed like their father. Mari's mother hugged the nearly five-year-old Rini close to her chest. The invader pressed the barrel to the elder vixen's forehead. He did not look back or give Mari's father a chance to correct his answer.

"You shouldn't lie," *IT* taunted. The transparent mask muffled the invader's words, though not enough that the phantom-Mari could not hear them. *Bang!*

One shot and her mother's head jerked back, then the elder vixen's limp body crumpled to the floor. Mari's paws flew over her muzzle again, and she felt sick. Her baby sister, Rini, cried out. Stroking the fur on her mother's face as blood poured out of the small entry wound. Blood splatter covered Rini's muzzle. The little lioness tried to stop the bleeding, but the sticky blood only coated the little kit's paws.

"Mommy!" the five-year-old yelled, "Mommy wake up!"

Her father stared, his mouth agape as though he were lost. Hot tears welled in the phantom-Mari's eyes.

~   ~   ~   ~

Entering the rear of the barracks building, Zenti quietly slipped past the common shower and moved up to the bunkroom. Quietly but painfully, he climbed up on a cabinet and investigated the adjacent bunkroom through the ventilation slots. He saw a room full of the dead. Two male invaders were coming down the row between the bunks, kicking the dead, flipping them over, and looking at their muzzles as if searching for someone.

The phantom-Zenti waited and watched, then as the invaders continued down between the bunks, he knew the invaders would pass through the door right below him.

Backing away from the edge of the cabinet and hugging the wall, Zenti waited in ambush as the two came closer. He had the gun, but if he used it, the sound would bring more. Laying it down on the cabinet top, he pulled out the hunting knife he always carried and waited for the right moment.

Zenti wanted to use his Gift, but if the enemy could somehow track him by its use, he might bring more invaders. Already the death inflicted by the invaders was too high. Focusing on the situation at paw, Zenti ran his probable course of actions through his head. This needed to be two quick kills to prevent a warning cry.

That moment came, and the two soldiers walked

through the door. Zenti let the first one pass by. As the second soldier passed through the doorway, the phantom-white wolf pouncing. Landing hard on the second male soldier's shoulders, Zenti drove him to the floor. A split second before the invader's head hit the floor, Zenti forced the male's chin down into his own chest. With the target's head down, the phantom-white wolf drove his hunting knife to the hilt in the invader's skull. The soft tissue around the base of the male invader's skull offered no resistance. The blade sliced between the first and second vertebrae killing the invader instantly.

Without wasting time to remove the knife, he opened his palms, and flames engulfed the lead invader's head. The fear of attracting more attention was less significant than the need for swift kills. The Gift summoned flames were small and concentrated. The male invader took a deep breath to scream, but the fire completely melted the invader's clear face mask. Flames raced into the male invader's open mouth and poured down his throat. The fire was brief, no more than a few seconds. Releasing his Gift, Zenti thrust his claws into the male's neck and ripped his throat out. The body dropped to the floor, and Zenti turned.

Zenti wiggled the hunting knife free from the dead invader's skull. He did not search the bodies; instead, he moved on towards the front of the barracks. The phantom-white wolf retrieved a gun as he went by the firearms rack. Though the invaders' weapons were comparable to Mitdonian weapons, they were designed for the smaller grip of the invader's furless fingers. In general, a Jaydonian's digits were longer and generally thicker.

The sound of fighting had moved deeper into the village. Though only a mile away, Zenti could hear the gunfire. Cautiously he looked around at the open parade ground between the barracks and the General's quarters. There were bodies everywhere, buildings burning, and the screams of pups and adults pierced the air from the village. Seeing the path was clear, Zenti slinked from shadow to shadow, making his way towards the General's quarters.

~   ~   ~   ~

"I ask you again," the phantom-Mari's eyes snapped up as *IT* spoke. The invader stepped over her mother's body and advanced on her father. "Where are they? There are only two of them that are rumored to be here. Now, where are they?" asked the invader. He hissed like a Jaydonian feline as he spoke to her father in Mitdonian.

IT aimed the gun at her father. To Mari's surprise, her father's muzzle became calm. In that instance, Mari knew all the tales of her father's bravery were true. The male lion was facing death with unwavering courage. Mari wondered who the invader was looking for?

"I am telling you that we have no Summoners here," her father said. If he were still in shock from watching his mate's murder, the male lion did not show it. The phantom-Mari remained frozen in fear as she watched from behind the partially opened door. Zenti Semineu was a Gifted Summoner, and her father was protecting him. Who was the other, she wondered? Why would her father defend Zenti Semineu and not his own family?

"You're lying to me again," ***IT*** said softly, aimed the barrel at Rini, and shot her through the stomach. A cry died in Mari's throat as she watched.

"No, please no, not my little sister," Mari whispered and watched as ***IT*** aimed at her father again.

"Now, would you like to rethink that answer one more time," the invader asked of the lion?

Mari could see that her father was hurt, but she did not know how badly. He was such a strong male, so how could he look so helpless?

~   ~   ~   ~

As Zenti raced across the parade grounds, a shot rang out. Ducking behind a bale of hay used as a bullet catch, Zenti peered around. Seeing no one, he continued across the way, pulling up just outside the steps to the General's quarters. It took him only a few moments to reach the porch when a second shot rang out. This time he could tell it was from inside the General's quarters.

"Heavens and Hells, I am too late," young Zenti growled quietly.

He moved up steps in a single bound. Picking up the discarded saber from a fallen officer just outside the door, he looked down and knew the leopard. He had a mate and four kits. The phantom-white wolf growled deeply at the loss of such an outstanding father.

"It is happening all over again," Zenti growled. The

memories of the slaughter of his family flashed in his mind. "This war is going to end one way or the other no matter the price I have to pay," he hissed as a new rage found its way into him, "The dead shall be avenged."

Focusing on the anger within, Zenti prepared to enter the house. He could feel a new rage and hatred rising. He could feel he was about to be beyond rational control. The white wolf knew he needed to be in control. Focusing, he heard talking, which helped him concentrate on controlling that rage.

~   ~   ~   ~

"I already told you," Mari's father pleaded bravely, "we have no Summoners, here, none. If we did, they would have reacted by now. Don't you think that you would be fighting them instead of interrogating me?"

The phantom-vixen watched as the invader's gun did not lower. Her father was protecting Zenti and another Gifted Summoner. The Gifted was indeed Orra's gift to Her kits, and they were to be protected at all costs. General Haverick Waxton, her beloved father, was not failing Orra's laws.

"Wrong again," *IT* said.

Mari's world went silent as one last register from the gun rang through the air. It all seemed to go in slow motion as the bullet hit her father in the chest, and he crumpled against the legs of the desk. Through the crack of the door, Mari could see the blossom of blood on this chest as he lay sprawled on the floor. The gun lowered. Without so much as a pause, *IT* walked out the first living room door and into the hall. Mari watched as the invader passed by the second door she was at. The soldier had left her father for dead.

~   ~   ~   ~

A third report rang out as the white wolf entered the hall. He stiffened as he heard footsteps coming toward the front hall doorway. He saw Mari hiding down at the second door looking in through a slightly opened crack. Her color was gone, and she looked as if life itself was draining out of her.

The male invader walked into the hall and saw the little vixen huddled there. He raised the gun for yet another kill. The saber flashed in the dim light, and the male invader's body crumpled to the floor. However, his head rolled back into the living room. A sad satisfaction crept over phantom-Zenti that the invader's death was all too fast and painless.

.   ~   ~   ~   ~

The front living room door opened, and phantom-Mari saw *IT* step into the hall. He looked directly at her and raised the gun. There was a flash of light, and *IT* began to fall. Mari did not wait to see why but scrambled away from the falling body. The vixen still held one paw clamped over her muzzle to stop her from screaming, the other helping her scurry into the living room. She sat there for what seemed like an eternity as she looked at her family covered in blood. Mari's heart was in her throat as she looked at the severed head and took in the fact that *IT* was dead. However, what killed the invader? Her sister, Rini, whimpered. Rini was alive!

With that only thought in her head, Mari was immediately up, and she raced to the corner of the living room. Fear overrode her desire to know who or what killed the invader. She reached Rini and looked at all the carnage. Blood covered the floor and walls. Her mother was dead in a heap on the floor. Her little sister lay beside her, alive but barely.

"Mari," came her father's weakened voice? She turned to look at her father when footsteps behind her caught her attention. Grabbing her father's fallen gun, the phantom-vixen aimed it at whoever was in the doorway.

~   ~   ~   ~

As the invader's body crumpled to the floor, Zenti looked to where Mari was crouched, but she was gone. The second hall door moved. Uncaring, the white wolf stepped over the body. He entered the first door, kicking the severed head out of the way. There he saw another reason why he hated the invaders. The General's wife lay dead with a single bullet to the forehead, and his youngest kit lay bleeding on the floor from a gut wound. Beside the desk lay the General with Mari at his side. He took a step forward, and the floor creaked under his weight. In a flash, Mari had a gun pointed at him. The little vixen was shaking like a leaf, yet Zenti simply stood there. The saber clattered to the floor. Mari knew it was the white wolf who had killed the invader.

At the recognition of the white wolf before her, the vixen dropped the gun. Tears streaked down the fur on her cheeks. Before she knew it, she ran to Zenti. She was crying like a small kit, even though she thought she was not one. She held onto Zenti tightly, sniffing and sobbing, her face buried in his ribs. He did not hesitate to pull her tight, but for only a moment.

"Mari, we need to save your father and sister. Pull yourself together, dear vixen, and let us save them before we mourn the fallen," Zenti whispered. Dear vixen is what Haverick Waxton repeatedly called his mate, Lillian. It struck a chord in the young vixen. Zenti's late father also used a similar term often when addressing his mate.

Pulling away from him, Mari's phantom-self nodded gently, obeying his military-like command as she would if her father had given one. Labored laughter came from her father as he lay there.

"I'm glad to see that you two get along so well," her father said gently as the phantom-Mari turned to him, looking worried and confused at his condition. The lion pointed to his youngest daughter.

"What," Mari asked as she went to get Rini? She wanted to keep her father talking.

"I said I am glad to see that you two are getting along," the lion said softly. Haverick Waxton watched his eldest daughter wrap her little sister in a blanket, trying to keep the pressure on her hip wound.

Zenti moved to the General's side and opened his shirt. The wound was terminal, and by the look on the general's face, the lion knew it too. Zenti started to take off the General's shirt to use as bandages when the lion put a paw on his, stopping him.

"Nothing you can do for me, pup. Best get to taking care of my kits since I am not going to be around to do it anymore," coughed the lion. Blood filled Haverick's spittle as he spoke.

"Dad," said Mari as she held Rini tight? The vixen looked at her father. She could see the tired look on his muzzle.

The lion smiled tenderly and reached his arm toward her. Mari bent to take his paw, bringing little Rini closer to their father. That small act allowed General Haverick Waxton the last chance to stroke the fur on the unconscious Rini.

"Mari, my dear," Haverick Waxton said softly, "I would like you to meet your future mate." The little vixen's jaw hung open. Mari stared at the young male white wolf kneeling before her father. Zenti was still wearing the bath wrap and the long shirt from the pots.

"You!" Mari's gaze snapped between her father and Zenti for a moment. The vixen slapped the white wolf hard across the muzzle, "You sneaky two-faced minx kit," she screamed but stopped when Rini whimpered a little. Mari's movement brought the small lioness kit temporarily back to consciousness. The pain caused Rini to quickly pass out again.

Such spirit, Zenti thought, rubbing his muzzle again.

The old lion half coughed; half laughed. Blood trickled out of his muzzle. However, the elder male lion managed a smile.

"Son, I think you're going to have a very sore muzzle before your time is done on this rock," he took a deeper breath, tears running down his cheeks.

"I am afraid you're right, sir. That is the second one today," said Zenti, wiping the red spittle away from the lion's muzzle.

"Really?" the General asked in amused surprise. "What did you do to piss her off?" Haverick coughed as the words struggled to find a voice. General Haverick Waxton breathed heavily as blood flowed more freely now from the stricken lion's muzzle and nose. Mari remained silent. The vixen was watching her father die, yet he still had a sense of humor. All the phantom-vixen could think about was how much she wanted to be like him.

"I went after her," was all the white wolf replied.

Zenti looked at the wound on Rini. It was not really a gutshot, but an upper thigh/lower hips wound. It was bleeding but not life-threatening if they could get her to a shaman or doctor soon. However, the hip was probably shattered.

~   ~   ~   ~

Mari held her little sister tightly when Zenti moved the blankets over the wound to inspect it. There was not as much blood as she would have expected, and the light concern on the wolf's face meant perhaps that her sister would be ok. She looked at her father, and the elder male recognized the lack of immediate concern on the white wolf's muzzle. Haverick Waxton knew his daughter would live. The lion knew Zenti Semineu did not react in an uncaring manner when the situation dictated.

~   ~   ~   ~

"Why were **THEY** here, sir, and what were **THEY** looking for?" he asked as he tried to make the old lion comfortable, putting a chair cushion behind the lion's back. Still, more blood was trickling down the General's muzzle, it's color a blacker red.

"They were looking for you and Mari," the lion managed softly through the blood. "Take care of my daughters. Be careful, Zenti. You are going to be hunted, and I fear it will be unrelenting. You, son, are a rare and exceptionally Gifted Summoner, and I fear the invaders know that. Take the greatest of precautions and trust only Torit to heal your wounds." General Waxton's look became grave. "I know who and what you are, Zenti Semineu. The King told me the day he sent you here. Don't let my kits come to harm, please, son."

~   ~   ~   ~

Young Mari listened to her father's voice and tried to burn every tiny inflection into the deepest parts of her memory. He was everything to her, and Orra was calling him to the stars. Tears poured down her cheeks. Her father calling Zenti son in the same tone as he called her daughter struck an indelible chord.

Again, the lion coughed, and more dark blood gurgled out of his muzzle. There was a crackling and a muted popping above the room in the attic. Before Mari knew what had happened, she, holding Rini, had been swept up in Zenti's arms. He quickly raced out of the house through the back door and into an abandoned courtyard. Mari could feel the tingle of Zenti's Gift as he accelerated faster than he should have been able to. The air rumbled above the structure, and a small fire was burning on the roof. It must have been started by whatever caused the pop in the attic. Zenti turned and saw an invader attempting to reload a grenade into his rifle's launcher. Without hesitation, Zenti shot the male invader four times while holding on to Mari.

Struggling against Zenti's grasp, Mari managed to get away from him and started to run back to the house. Zenti dropped the pistol and took Rini from Mari before the vixen hurt her injured sister by accident. He knew what Mari wanted to do, but it was too late to save General Haverick Waxton.

"Wait, we have to bring my…" Mari began. The house collapsed, and Mari stopped in her tracks, her eyes wide "Dad!" she screamed and made to run to the house but was instantly caught in Zenti's grasp. She struggled, pulling and wiggling, trying to get out of the wolf's grip until finally she turned and held onto him, crying.

For what seemed an eternity, Zenti let Mari hold him. Holding Rini in one arm and Mari with the other, he nuzzled the side of her cheek until she looked at him. The soft, ruddy red fur of her muzzle was matted with blood and tears. Repositioning the little lioness in his arms, he reapplied the pressure to the wound.

"He is gone, Mari. Nothing we could have done would have saved him," Zenti said with an apologetic look. He saw the sadness on her muzzle. She knew that Zenti was right and nodded slightly. Her father told her war was coming to Mitd. Her mother told her one day she would need to be stronger than any other female on Jayden. Mari looked at Rini and realized that her parents had paid the price to prepare her for war. Moreover, they had begun her preparations for what must come. Mari Waxton would need to be formidable.

Stroking her muzzle with his free paw, Zentie waited until Mari looked at him. When she did, he saw the cold fire of a kit having to grow up too fast. Mari Waxton was not kit by the law. However, that did not mean she was not still a kit inside.

"I am sorry I said nothing earlier back at the pots. It was never my intention to deceive you. I only wanted you to be able to choose for yourself. I would not have made any claims on you had tonight not happened. I still do not.

I do not want a servant. Your father was a good male, and he loved you deeply. I am sorry to say that we cannot stay here and offer your parents a proper burial. I can, however, ensure that their bodies are not experimented upon," he said, withdrawing his paw from her muzzle.

She noted that it glowed red, and then appeared a little ball of flame dancing in his palm. He pointed at the house, and she understood, lowered her head, and nodded yes.

He handed Rini to Mari. Mari watched as a red warmth covered her little sister after Zenti placed his glowing paw on Rini's muzzle. Mari did not understand what he did, but the blood stopped flowing.

Zenti released the little lioness's muzzle and stepped over to the smoldering, collapsed house. Placing his paws on the wood, flames spread from his paws over the whole of the rubble, completely engulfing it. He turned towards Mari, took a few steps then nearly collapsed. Zenti caught himself on a lamppost. However, his head sagged, and shoulders slumped. As he straightened up, Mari could see he looked exhausted.

"We need to leave now," Zenti said, taking the unconscious Rini from the stunned Mari. "There is an old underground munitions supply rail line. It is not serviceable, but we can use it to secure our escape."

"I never knew about that," replied a surprised Mari.

"It was built two centuries ago. This training camp

was once part of a greater military structure. The Crown had the structures closed. The King's late grand-father built Hasha to help the citizens of the area forget this was once a major munitions plant," Zenti explained as he led her to the mess hall.

"Dad never said anything about any of this," phantom-Mari said as she entered the mess hall. "How is it you know about it?" She followed him through the dining area and into the kitchen.

"Your father trusted me with a great many things Mari Waxton," said the white wolf, then looked at Rini. Mari understood what Zenti meant. The white wolf continued speaking as he led the vixen into a meat freezer. Closing the door behind them, Zenti threw a nonstandard locking bolt. When he did, the floor began to retract.

"I will not force anything on you. I will give myself to you, defending you, until you have chosen a mate. I will care for your sister, as I promised. You are not beholding to me. I do this to honor your father and mother," said the wolf respectfully. Mari could tell that the white wolf held great admiration for her parents.

Zenti stepped back, shifting Rini until her wound was pressed against his body tighter. Mari looked up at the wolf through teary eyes. He was not as tall as some of the other male canines. Nor was Zenti Semineu as lanky as some of the felines. Still, nonetheless, he had a presence about him, and when he spoke or acted, those around him followed. She had seen this in the training grounds when he commanded any of the recruits.

Mari had never known him, just of him as the new recruits hated him for his rank for such a young age. However, the older recruits admired him because he never lost a simulation against other training facilities. When he led counter raids against the rebels, he never failed. She could feel a leader's presence. She really had never known who Summoner Zenti Semineu was. She now knew why he was her father's favorite. The white wolf was unafraid of a challenge and possible defeat. He was a natural leader that commanded respect from just his presence. Zenti reminded her of her father.

Now he dropped the aura of command and simply turned away. Zenti began to descend the newly formed steps. He was taking Rini to where the little lioness could get the medical help she needed. Her wound would not kill her, but if it were not treated soon, the effects of the damage would be irreparable.

"Excuse me," she called as she dried her eyes, and for the first time, she really looked at him. As he turned, his white fur almost seemed a tad silver in hue in the lights now coming on in the underground tunnel. She looked at his white claws again as he held Rini and tried to recall the story her mother told her. However, the phantom-vixen but could not.

~   ~   ~   ~

"I only remembered it on the day of our mating as I was putting the silver ring over your claw," said Mari present-self. She became aware she was now back in the tent. The vixen's mind had suppressed the shared memories for a moment. She needed the brief respite. She looked up at the silvery-white wolf sitting on her bunk. As a result of reliving her past, Mari's claws had dug deep into Zenti's jaw. Trickles of blood puddled on the tips. At that moment, she recalled the bedtime story her mother told her.

'One of silver, with claws of white will bleed for all in the blackest night.

Trading love with one of cold, the silver one will lose his soul.

The soulless Monster burns the night, onyx claws replacing white.

The Monster rages, the cold one calms, the war is fought, a Kingdom won.'

Zenti eased her back into the share vision of their past.

~   ~   ~   ~

"What is your full name," Mari asked softly as she watched this wolf? Zenti was holding her little sister like her father would.

"You already know it, Mari Waxton. I am just Zenti Semineu. I promised your father I would care for the two of you. I always keep my promises," he replied as he nodded for her to follow.

Quickly they slipped into the tunnels. The stairs began to retract as the three of them headed off into the dead of night. The old, forgotten tunnel now protected them. The light started to fade behind them. A soft glow appeared ahead, floating midair; the vixen realized that Zenti was lighting their escape path with his Gift. Mari noticed that drops of blood began to drip from the white wolf's nose and ears.

The Gift demanded a price. Zenti was paying the price as he held Rini. Together the three of them traveled the forgotten tunnel to safety.

Chapter 5

Doctors

Mari Semineu, seeing life through her estranged mate's eyes, looked down upon her physical body. She was back in the present. The soft glow of the single electric desk lamp illuminated her tent. She and Summoner Zenti Semineu had just telepathically shared events of their past together. Through the Gifted Talent of Union, the two estranged mates witnessed the events that shaped their lives. However, those shared memories did not explain why her former mate abandoned her. That is what Mari wanted to see.

The Talent of Union subsided, and Mari found herself back inside of her own mind. She looked up at the white wolf who was sitting on her cot. He was bleeding from the nose, ears, eyes, and jaw. The Gift occasionally demanded the blood of the Gifted when they pushed their Gift. Summoner Zenti Semineu abused his Gift repeatedly. However, the blood oozing from the white wolf's jaw was of her doing. She had buried her claws into his flesh as a reminder that the Talent of Union was not the present reality. Mari loosened her grip but did not release it.

"We took Rini to the Elders of a village three days away. I did not realize it then, but you were using your Gift to stabilize my little sister. That is the Gift of a Shaman. How could you have done that," the vixen asked? However, the white wolf did not answer. She could feel him still maintaining the Talent of the Union and decided not to push the question. Summoner Zenti Semineu continued to surprise her with what his Gift could do.

"The village doctors said she would survive as the

bullet had passed completely through her small hip but shattered the bone. They told us we would have to leave Rini there for them to care for her. I remembered the Elders asked us to leave the village when they found out Zenti was a Summoner, though I did not understand why at that time. Summoners were normally celebrated for their Gift and their selflessness in using it to help others," Mari spoke as she recalled the old memories.

"Mari, do you want to continue," the white wolf asked. She could see the onset of exhaustion. The vixen nodded, knowing this might be her only chance to see the truth.

~   ~   ~   ~

Another sudden flash and Mari found herself standing in a cold, dark, dank little room with water dripping from the walls. How was this possible? Just a moment ago, they were sharing memories. Now she stood in a room as if she were a spectral observer.

~   ~   ~   ~

"I told you I would make this easier for you. You are seeing what an Oracle calls the Talent of the Soul's Self. It is a form of soul projection that Oracles can do over great distances. However, everyone could do it all the time; they just do not know how to get in touch with that part of themselves. Oracles can, through the Talen of Union, allow someone else to view what their soul sees. It is that mysterious feeling that someone has; yet cannot explain. You know the feeling that you have been or seen something from outside your body. The Talent of Soul's Self will also allow you to understand a language even if you don't know the language," Zenti vocally said. He dared not risk this conversation in a telepathic form.

Mari Semineu had never learned to gently reply to their shared telepathic communications. Mari did not have the Gifted form of telepathy. Zenti had to open a telepathic link with a diminished state of the Talent of Union. If he were unprepared, her replies were like sledgehammer blows.

"And this is something you know how to do now? So, you are an Oracle now as well as a Summoner. You must think pretty highly of yourself," she snidely replied. Mari's words were laced with bitter sarcasm.

'Do you want to see or not?' Zenti mentally brushed through the Talent of Union. If she wanted an argument, Zenti could force her to continue speaking by blocking out her thoughts. However, that was rude. This was a test for Mari. The vixen became quiet, which he took as a yes. Such bitterness she possessed for him as he opened the Talent of Soul's Self for her to watch the events unfold.

The present faded, and she witnessed the shift in scenery. Mari could see colors, hear the hum of machinery, and smell the vile stench of a laboratory. This was exactly as her sister Rini, when they were on talking terms, described the Talent of Soul's Self. Mari was floating above the room, looking down upon everything. She could move and change her perspective, but she could not leave the vicinity near Zenti's body. This was an incredibly unique Talent, one Rini possessed. The vixen wished her sister, and she was on better terms. However, she was not on good terms with Rini Waxton.

~   ~   ~   ~

Mari saw a nine-foot-long and a little over four feet wide, metal, rectangular table while looking down upon the room. Zenti was chained to this table. With the practiced eye of a military veteran, Mari visually inspected the room. There were a variety of large transparent containers, much like giant vats, surrounding the central table. Those vats lined the walls and occupied a large portion of the room. Some of those vats held members of her species suspended in a liquid. As she looked around the room, she noticed some of the vats were broken.

Cords and cables ran everywhere, and many dangled from the ceiling. A network of grated metal channels crisscrossed the concrete floor where liquids were collected. The metal grates eventually terminated near the far wall. There was a trough-like basin where the run-off drained. The basin emptied into a large floor pipe that ran along the wall's length, no doubt on its way to the sewers. There was a mixture of Mitdonian technology and what could only be invader technology. A tingle of fear ran through the vixen at that thought.

Looking around, Mari decided the room was not initially designed for its current purpose. The damaged hoist equipment suspended from the ceiling gave this room the look of a factory or foundry of some sort. Numerous cables dangled from multiple block-and-tackle rigs. Thick steel beams supported an overhead crane rig. However, it had sustained severe damage. The room with the metal table appeared to be free-standing in the center of this industrial complex. Mari was unsure as her sight began to fade into the shade of shadows the further away she looked.

The walls of this free-standing room were covered with a smooth metal surface. The vixen had never seen a room covered in metal before. The entire room looked filthy. The large floor pipe looked like it was hammered open in several places. On the table lay Zenti. He seemed mostly unharmed, though he was bloody. Mari was confused at the calm, relaxed demeanor of the white wolf. He was not unconscious, but perhaps he was sedated. She was unsure. Questions began to form as to why Zenti was not attempting to escape. His Gift should have allowed him to burn through his metal bonds. The vixen wondered why he had not tried it.

Mari was an unseen phantom as she watched this memory. Yet her paws flew to her muzzle as the door opened. Several of **THEIR** scientists entered the free-standing room. Immediately some went to the various equipment and began turning them on. Others began checking medical equipment. When the last scientist entered the room, she noted **IT** appeared to be the one in charge as the others gave various reports on equipment status to him.

Mari thought the chief scientist scuttled like a fat

vermin on two legs as it approached the table where Zenti was chained. The chief scientist was male. He wore a crisp white smock that covered his rotund body. The clear breathing mask had two squat, oval canisters on each cheek that covered most of the invader's horrid facial features. Mitdonians had a similar chemical respirator, though much bulkier. However, she knew that they offered the same function. The Mitdonian intelligence on the invader's technology was not inaccurate, just incomplete. *IT* leaned over the table, looking down at the stretched-out form of Zenti.

Watching the white wolf feebly strain at the bonds but failing, Mari could feel that Zenti's mind was a haze from being kept semi-sedated. *THEY* knew more about Summoners than she liked and wondered who had been feeding the invaders information.

"Well, we finally have the great Summoner Zenti Semineu. It has been a long time finding you, wolf. You have killed so many of our troops we were beginning to think you were a ghost, but you are just flesh and blood," *IT* said while putting surgical gloves on furless paws.

"We thought we would never be able to capture you. However, we were fortunate enough to have your weakness revealed for us," the male invader said as it poked and prodded at the restrained wolf.

Turning to an associate, the male scientist mumbled something Mari could not fully understand. However, he spoke her species' language with remarkable skill when conversing with Zenti. The vixen could understand the invader's tongue when audible through the Talent of Soul's Self. Mari wondered if Zenti could understand the invader's language. Not wanting to miss one moment of the conversation, Mari let that thought fade. The chief scientist held out a gloved paw if that is what they were called, and an assistant place a scalpel in the open palm.

"This will hurt you a lot. I cannot say that it bothers me one bit," said the invader. His mouth made something resembling a grotesque sneer, thought Mari. "However, I want to know how and why your type can do what they do. I want to know what it is that makes you Gifted. I want to know why you were so hard to capture. What makes Summoner Zenti Semineu different from the other Gifted?"

The male invader ran a gloved finger across a medical device with a glass-like surface that had an effigy of Zenti on it. It looked like a very detailed, computer-generated image. However, it hung suspended in mid-air. Mari had never seen anything like that device. Mitdonian computer seemed archaic compared to this technology. Nine years Mari had fought the invaders. She was happy that they were limited in numbers because their technological superiority would have undoubtedly helped them win the war by now.

Handing the scalpel back to his assistant, the chief scientist looked back at the semi-conscious white wolf. The male invader looked at his watch and rolled his eyes in disgust.

"I am just glad that your species can betray each other. Too bad your little bitch had to die; I would have enjoyed cutting on her as well," *IT* said, looking down at the semi-conscious wolf. "You have cost us dearly, and I would have preferred that she die slowly. It would have brought a measure of satisfaction to watch your reaction to that little fox beg for mercy." The door opened, and the chief scientist looked back over his shoulder.

Three soldiers entered the room, and the chief scientist grumbled something about the three soldiers taking their sweet time getting here. Taking a step back from the steel table, the chief scientist pushed his assistant away. Taking a scalpel from the tray beside the table, he waited for two of the soldiers to roll the sedated wolf onto his stomach.

Mari watched through the Gifted Talent of Soul's Self as the soldiers move up to Zenti. The two soldiers carefully loosened Zenti's chains and stranded metal cords with great trepidation. The vixen could not help but notice that *THEY* were afraid of Zenti even though he was all but unresponsive.

The chains and metal cords were loosened just enough to roughly roll the white wolf onto his stomach. With fear-driven haste, the two soldiers chained Zenti back down, pulling the restraints taught. All the while, the third soldier kept his rifle pointed at Zenti's head. When the soldiers finished securing the white wolf, the three stood in the ready guard stance. The chief scientist nodded, and an assistant stepped back and brought out what appeared to be a fire extinguisher. The assistant thrust the fire extinguisher in the paws, or whatever the invaders called their paws, of one of the soldiers. The male soldier held it at the ready.

"You might want to bite down on this," the chief scientist cackled into Zenti's ear, "this is going to hurt a lot. Conscious Sedation merely blocks certain neuromuscular controls. I have tailored this formula, especially for your species. You will feel everything, but you will not be able to move. I hope you do not pass out too quickly."

A female assistant shoved a block of wood in Zenti's muzzle with a fearful look on her face. Chains hanging from each end of the wooden block allowed her to secure the gag behind Zenti's head. The metal slab lowered until it was no more than waist-high to the chief scientist. The chief scientist waited impatiently before positioning himself above Zenti's back.

A male assistant positioned a pair of curved glasses on the chief scientist's face. They wrapped around from ear to ear. It seemed odd that they were tented a light lavender color. When the head scientist wiggled his nose, the glasses projected a ghost-like image that floated in the air a few feet away. When the male invader looked at Zenti's back, the glasses displayed what he viewed on the ghost-like projection.

For a moment, Mari could not determine what she was seeing until she realized that the glasses were projecting and magnifying what the scientist observed. She

wondered what the invaders called that remarkable
technology.

~   ~   ~   ~

"The technology is known as a Virtual Viewer,"
brushed Zenti in response to Mari's curiosity. However,
Mari was deeply engrossed in what the scientist was doing
to Zenti's body to listen to his thoughts.

Mari could hardly believe that Zenti was chained to a
metal slab and about to be mutilated. The chief scientist
twirled the scalpel with precision and dexterity the vixen
did not imagine an invader possessed. When the female
assistant finished securing the block gag, the chief scientist
stopped the twirling scalpel with a snap. A wicked grin
grew beneath the transparent mask of the chief scientist.
With a glimmer of someone about to exact sweet revenge,
the male invader positioned the scalpel between Zenti's
shoulder blades. In a swift motion, he plunged the surgical
knife into Zenti's flesh.

Zenti did not flinch, though, in his mind, Mari felt he
did. However, through the Gifted Talent of Soul's Self,
enhanced by the Talent of Union, Mari could feel a tiny
fraction of the pain Zenti must have felt. The vixen could
see the maniacal look on the invader's face as he began the
procedure.

The scalpel sliced through fur and flesh, opening
Zenti up like a piece of thick-skinned fruit. Mari felt the
pressure of the cut and the tiny sting. The phantom-vixen
continued to watch as what started as a medical procedure

turn into an event that would make a butcher vomit. Mari Semineu was so deeply engrossed in observing through the Talent of the Soul's Self that she did not realize her physical body trembled at the events. Nor did she feel the tears running down her cheek fur.

At first, the scientist was careful and meticulous with his actions. Slowly the male invader peeled back and separated the skin from sinew and muscle. Mari watched as if *IT* were skinning an animal. The chief scientist worked for a little more than four hours, carefully pealing Zenti's skin away from the flesh below. He revealed the hard cords of muscle beneath once the skin and fur had been peeled away. However, the male invader grew tired of the tediousness. He began ripping the skin away from the muscle like one would the skin of an animal whose fur was not worth saving. An assistant used a fluid injection device for debriding the wound and extracting blood and loose tissue.

Zenti randomly attempted to howl in pain. Between the wooden gag and not being fully sedated, the howls were more a gurgling sound. However, Mari could hear the pain in the white wolf's voice. Soon it was more than Zenti could bear, and he passed out when the chief scientist started to separate the skin from his back. Mari realized that Zenti could feel everything that was happening to him. Through Zenti's great iron-like willpower, he was fighting the sedatives. Mari could feel Zenti attempting to touch the Void yet failing. It became apparent the invaders had found a way to deny the Gifted their access to the Void.

However, it only left them partially unconscious.

Nevertheless, Zenti subconscious mind was still fully functioning. Mari saw, and through the mental connection, felt some of the pain he suffered. To the vixen, the incisions felt like paper cuts. However, Mari knew that Zenti must be shielding her from the complete pain. The vixen had limited knowledge of the Talent of the Union. Mari knew Zenti could do many things that other Gifted could never do. The Talent of Transference was one of them. Zenti was reliving all the past pain, and he was shielding her from its full effect. Mari did not know the level of the past pain Zenti was suffering, but she could feel it, so he must be feeling it.

She watched as the scientist next separated the muscles, sometimes ripping and isolating them in a careful but brutal fashion. The invader was not attempting to cut the muscles from tendons but shift them around so he could get better access to certain portions of Zenti's body. Mari could feel this muscle manipulation. It felt like a rough massage. She knew Zenti was suffering even more than the scant feeling of pain and discomfort she was feeling. What strength Zenti must have to endure even a portion of the pain from the past?

The Soul's Self project of the vixen's ethereal form shivered, and her ears lowered. Zenti, for all his betrayal, was still shielding her from the harms of life. The seed of doubt about Zenti's betrayal of her began to germinate. The phantom-vixen watched as the invader continued his brutal assault on Zenti's body.

When the scientist was satisfied that he had exposed the necessary sections of Zenti's spinal column and ribs, he asked for a circular bone saw.   The dexterity with which the male invader displayed convinced Mari that he was an expert in the surgical field.   The invader exposed Zenti's spinal cord by cutting through several sections of bone. The whine of the high-speed circular saw sent a shiver across the vixen's body.   It sounded like a dentist's drill.

The saw was smaller than those she had seen in the medical tents of her species.   The scientist wielded the tool as an artist used a paintbrush.   *It* was obviously skilled but seemed to care extraordinarily little for the pain being inflicted.   The saw gently ejected a greenish-colored liquid as it cut.   The device must contain a suction device as the fluid and blood were pulled free of Zenti's body.   The assistant continued to excise the blood and tissue as well. However, the female assistant was careful to avoid the chief scientist, who seemed to be in a foul mood.

The male invader placed multiple pairs of tiny devices over various exposed nerve bundles.   Because the scientist was working on Zenti's spinal column, Mari assumed that the devices were being attached to his spinal cord.   The vixen had never seen devices like these before. They were smaller than the head of a needle.   Occasionally the male looked at the tiny devices through the Virtual Viewer.   Mari thought the exploded view of the device made it look like a spider.   The male invader worked at an unbelievable pace.

There were forty pairs in all.   It was a tedious and

time-consuming process. Mari looked over to the diagnostics equipment that monitored Zenti's vitals. There were no cables connected to the white wolf, yet the display showed a multitude of readings. Mari noticed that for all the brutal assault on Zenti's body, the white wolf seemed to be weathering the invasive procedures well in the less than sterile environment. Mari also noted that time seemed to move faster within the Gifted Talent of Soul's Self. Zenti had been in surgery for more than ten hours, yet it only felt like a few minutes.

The chief scientist wiggled his nose. The Virtual Viewer's image changed, showing a full-body view of Zenti. However, the display was one of muscle and bone sans skin and fur. Touching the Virtual Viewer, the male invader began testing each of the devices. The male then tapped the virtual project of Zenti's body. The scientist followed the illuminated blue impulses that raced through the virtual body of the white wolf. However, Zenti's body did not seem to react.

This was a technology Mari was unaware of. Most of the invader's technology recovered from successful combat was severely damaged. What remained were more compact versions of Mitdonian basic military equipment. It was astounding yet frightening that the invaders had such a technological advantage. However, like many of her fellow military leaders, Mari was glad that the superior technology was not military-oriented. The invaders used the same type of weapons that Mitd did. It was an oddity as to why that remained undiscovered.

The chief scientist tested each set of devices. The virtual projection flashed a series of colored lights with each test. Mari realized that each device was recording and mapping the responses to the invader's probe. What were the invader's plans with this equipment? Could the chief scientist really discover the nature of the Gift with this technology?

Hours passed as he tested the nerves. When food was brought into the room, *THEY* took a break to eat. The female assistant covered Zenti's back in a wet, jelly-like blanket before discussing what was to eat. The scientist agreed the food was unacceptable, and the room emptied. Mari watched the silent room and the wolf on the table. She felt numb as she recalled the words, 'I'm just glad that your species can betray each other.' Who was betraying Jaydonians? Was Zenti the betrayer or the betrayed?

The scientist returned. Mari realized an hour had passed in less than a minute of her time looking at the clock. The vixen did not understand the Gift and probably never would. Nonetheless, it was a marvelous mystery, and seeing what Zenti was suffering brought mixed emotions. She was no longer sure of what really transpired or if he even abandoned her?

The chief scientist gave himself an injection, as did the other scientist. However, the military personnel was not the same as before Mari noticed. The chief scientist seemed to become more alert and promptly returned to the procedures after the female assistant removed the liquid blanket from Zenti's back. Mari watched as the invaders tested, injected drugs, and made adjustments to Zenti's body and devices. All was going gruesomely well until medical alarms began to chime. One of the scientists said something about Zenti's heart beginning to fail. An invader military officer commented that the cur white wolf needed to survive for the feline's plans to succeed. This seemed to anger the chief scientist. However, the military officer's tone was clear; do not let Zenti die.

The scientists went into a frenzy to stabilize the white wolf. Again the soldier stressed that no matter the delays, the white wolf cur must not die. The chief scientist started to reply when the officer emphasized his position by pulling out his pistol. The medical scanner blared a warning that Zenti's heart had stopped.

Making a grumbling noise as if it were an enormous inconvenience, the chief scientist claimed that the assistant was interrupting just to be a nuisance. However, he stepped back and allowed the assistant to take care of the emergency. Mari thought she saw the concern on the chief scientist's face. She was uncertain if it were for the loss of Zenti or the pistol still pointed at his head.

The assistant dug into a drawer, pulling two sealed, nearly flat packages out. Ripping them open, *IT* put two patches on the underside of Zenti's chest after the guards lifted him just enough to allow him to do so. A rubber mat was placed between Zenti and the table. The female invader attached the leads to the pads and then to another device.

Holding a small box the size of paw held, compact radio, the female invader presses a button. Zenti's body convulsed momentarily. Mari realized the device was a defibrillator, clearly smaller than a Mitdonian one. However, the monitors showed no signs of a heart rhythm. Another assistant injected something into a Zenti's neck and quickly stepped back. Again, the female assistant pressed the button. Zenti's body convulsed again. This time there was a faint rhythmic beat emanating from the monitors. Mari noticed that the new device beeped, and lines moved up and down in unison with the other virtual monitoring devices.

"Your prize possession is on an auto defibrillator, Lieutenant. Should the wolf cur's heart stop, it will automatically be shocked into starting. Happy," the chief scientist asked in a sarcastic tone of voice? The lieutenant snorted in disgust. At least that was what Mari thought it sounded like. The male ordered additional medications for Zenti, but Mari could not understand what they were. The chief scientist returned to his testing of the neural implants.

Waves of tiny electrical pain pulsed through Mari as she watched the scene with appalled disbelief. It did not take long before the vixen realized that she was feeling the pain as Zenti did. Though significantly diminished, that pain resulted from *IT* tested nerve after nerve, being exceptionally careful not to damage any of them. While the testing continued, other assistants brought in trays of thin strands of metal wires. Through it all, Mari could not help but marvel at the advanced technological equipment in use. Many she could not even begin to comprehend what the equipment or their functions were. However, the gruesome medical procedure quickly pressed her admiration of the invader's equipment aside. Zenti moaned again, and the scientist wave for more sedatives.

Mari could sense Zenti fading in and out of consciousness. He could no longer feel what was being done. However, through the Talent of Soul's Self, Mari knew that Zenti knew he was being operated on. When the chief scientist grew tired, he stopped the medical procedures and left the room. His assistants did not close the incisions on Zenti's back. Instead, they covered his back with a jelly-like liquid blanket and left the white wolf lying there. Periodically Zenti was checked on by an assistant. According to the clock on the wall, sixteen hours had passed when the scientist stopped his butchery. Nine hours later, the scientist and his team returned, escorted by **THEIR** soldiers, and continued the process.

Mari watched as day after day the scientist came in and begin the procedures over again. When they grew tired, the invaders left Zenti lying on the table. Zenti was bleeding, and his wounds were open with nothing but the jellied liquid blanket to cover them. After a few days of medical procedures, the scientist began to joke about how well the surgeries were progressing. It seemed as if the invaders considered Zenti as nothing more than just an unfinished hobby project, Mari noted.

Mari counted a month of days the medical procedures continued. Through the Gifted Talents of

Union and Soul's Self, the vixen experienced Zenti's brutal captivity and torture. The vixen listened to the invaders speak, and, through Zenti's Gift, it allowed Mari to comprehend what **THEY** were saying. Again the vixen wondered if Zenti understood the invader's language. The vixen listened to the invaders speak, and she concluded that it was a guttural language that sounded like gibberish. However, that gibberish did not make those inflicting the brutal actions any less tolerable.

Through Zenti's Gifted Talents, Mari could tell that frustration was the primary emotion the scientist expressed. The main frustration was the inability to find a physical connection with Zenti's ability to summon fire. After some initial challenges, the scientist began inserting wires along Zenti's back. The male scientist intertwined the thin filament wires within the muscles along Zenti's back, shoulders, and waist. In the act of final triumph, the male scientist danced a little jig, then patted the white wolf on the forehead like you would a domestic canine.

Sewing the strips of fur and tissue back together took a better part of two days. Zenti was turned over and laid on a cushion of gel. The chief scientist took one full day off from the butchery. However, Zenti was not moved. The following day the chief scientist began a new series of operations. It was as brutally gruesome as was the work on Zenti's back. Through it all, Mari wondered how Zenti could survive such brutality.

Zenti's chest fur was cut open and then peeled back, exposing his rib cage. Mari watched as Zenti's chest was

opened in the same manner as his back. The scientist
began installing those same style wires across his ribcage,
abdomen, and partly down his hips and thighs. On the rare
moment when Zenti was conscious before the cutting began
again, the lead scientist would speak to him detailing the
procedure. It was as much a lecture as it was taunting
Zenti.

"You are the most puzzling subject animal that I
have ever had the enjoyment of experimenting on. You are
also the most frustrating," *IT* whispered into the wolf's
blood-covered ear. "If we cannot find out what it is that
makes you have the ability to summon fire, then let me see
if we can make you into a weapon for our use. I disagree
with the feline in this course of action. But who am I to
argue with one who your pathetic species holds in such
high esteem."

The procedures continued, and after a particularly
savage surgical session, the male scientist went away for a
time. Though Zenti could not recall how long or short the
session was, days passed as he lay there on the table. The
occasional attendant came to check on him. As the needs
dictated, the attendant would shove needles attached to
bags of fluids into Zenti. It was not always in the same
location. Sometimes it was in the veins in his arms, legs,
and any other portion of his body where the veins had not
collapsed. Yet more days passed, and Mari soon lost all
count before the lead scientist returned.

"Well, I see you are still here with us. Shall I
continue? I will install a device inside you that will allow

me to control your actions and read your body's biofeedback. I highly doubt that your primitive culture could comprehend what I said. You are just talking animals, after all. This will not be painless, but as I count it, you have not paid enough for all of our dead," chuckled the chief scientist. With a joyful glee, the scientist picked up a scalpel and began to cut on Zenti again.

Zenti screamed before passing out. Mari felt a fraction of the pain and also mentally screamed. This was madding, but somewhere a soft voice echoed, '*You wanted to see, you said you were strong enough,*' then Zenti's telepathic voice quieted. In silence, he returned Mari to that dank, wet, cold excuse for an operating room. The scientist moved about, bringing more tiny devices to be implanted into Zenti's body.

Mari watched in near sickness as they installed the tiny devices gently but not painlessly. The scientist began hooking them into the various wires that they had integrated into Zenti's body. Her whole body hurt with the flood of Zenti's memories. How could **THEY** have done this to him? How could Zenti have survived? Mari cringed as the male scientist cut through another of Zenti's vertebrae again. This time it was with an even smaller circular bone saw.

The blood that had left her former mate pooled on the table's trough-like edges until it dripped down onto the floor. It mixed with the filthy water that then ran in ruby-red rivers to the channels. From there, Zenti's spilt blood was further mixed with more dirty water and debris.

Finally, it ran to the collection channel at the far end of the room. Mari looked away from the grisly surgery. Her gaze took in the bodies in the tanks. Those dead bodies watched the macabre scene with sightless eyes as the wolf underwent the gruesome torture. Mari wondered just who they were and why they had not been strong enough to survive. Were they also Gifted, the vixen wondered? Days continue to roll by in the blink of an eye. Mari did not know how long she had been there, but it seemed time was now moving in fast-forward clips.

After thirty more of such operations, **THEY** celebrated the success of having a live Summoner soon to be under the invader's control. The chief scientists gave commands to his underlings. He told an assistant to close the incision, clean the wolf up, and put him away. Tomorrow would begin a time of recovery, and no more procedures were to be done on Zenti for a while. Instructions were given to put IVs into Zenti. The need continued to facilitate the white wolf's intravenous feeding and to replace the fluid loss. However, the white wolf was not to be given any blood transfusions. An assistant asked how the white wolf cur could have sustained such a loss of blood. The chief scientist shrugged his shoulders.

"I do not know. None of the other Gifted we operated on survived long enough to understand much about how it is possible. This white wolf cur not only survived but seems no worse for the ware. How his blood seemingly replenished itself is a mystery we can work on. Again, I stress, he is not to be given any blood transfusions.

The feline made expressly clear that his blood was not to be tainted with another's. Perhaps his blood has special properties. We will test that curiosity in the months to come," explained the invader scientist.

It was the longest speech to his subordinates that Mari had heard as of yet. Mari wondered what feline gave the invader orders. That was a ridiculous thought, as her species were nothing more than animals to **THEM**. However, that was not the first time the invader showed a modicum of respect for the mentioned feline.

"Yes, Doctor," replied his female assistant. The chief scientist moved up to Zenti and admired his work.

"Well, wolf, that was another good month of work. I hope you do not die while the wounds heal. After all the effort invested in you to create a traceable, controllable puppet, it would be such a waste if you died. Though I have learned much about your anatomy, should you die, it will help on the next subject. I have to admit you are a tough one. None of the other Gifted subjects lived," **IT** said. Looking back to the bodies floating in the vats, the male invader sighed. Zenti did not look, but Mari did and counted eight bodies.

~   ~   ~   ~

'They were all Gifted,' Mari mentally whispered to Zenti. Mari wondered how many more places like this there were. The force of the vixen's whisper hit Zenti like a runaway freight train. He was grateful that she had not tried to communicate with him before this.

~   ~   ~   ~

"You are also the first Summoner that has been captured that actually survived past the first few procedures. We had to tailor our work so that they would live longer. However, you survived beyond what we expected, and we are grateful for that. We were hoping for a younger subject to find what secrets your body held as an adolescent. Unfortunately, there was nothing out of the ordinary when compared to other of your species," said the male, then leaned in closer to Zenti's ears. "Well, ordinary for trash like you, that is," *IT* laughed.

The male invader stood, arched his back, and stretched. An assistant brought him something to drink when he pointed at the water pitcher. Finishing his drink, the chief scientist looked back down at Zenti.

"When we were given a chance to capture you, we could not pass up that opportunity. We were grateful for the aid that was rendered in your capture. It was amazing when he told us where you and that bitch of yours would be. I never expected such a gift, especially from him," said the chief scientist.

Mari wondered precisely who the invader was referring to. Someone had betrayed both Zenti and her. The seeds of doubt began to sprout. However, Mari's heart was heavy from the sustained abuse the scientist had inflicted upon Zenti. How had her former mate survived such an onslaught?

Zenti could hear the scientist walk out of the room,

and it seemed like it took hours to put the needles in his arms. Mari could sense that Zenti was grateful that he could feel nothing. It appeared that his nerves had long since stopped responding to the pain. She could feel he was numb to trivial pain such as a needle poke.

~   ~   ~   ~

Mari watched in sickening horror, and soon she felt dead inside. Is that what Zenti felt? Is that what had been lost in him when they met him some thirteen months ago? Zenti was so cold and hate-filled. She had been bitter and hurt. Neither of them relented on the emotional pain. That failure to communicate drove them apart. It forced her to hate him and him to wage a brutal personal war against everyone. Mari refused to think about the horrors that Zenti committed in those thirteen months. Could she have prevented it if she had believed him?

The pain Mari had felt through Zenti was only a fraction of what he must have felt. What was it that drove him to survive? What Gifts must he possess to endure such abuse, what hatred must he harbor? However, Zenti did not reply to those questions, though she was sure he could hear her thoughts.

For the first time in thirteen months, Mari desperately needed to reach out and touch Zenti. She wanted to drive **THEM** away from him and kill everyone for causing him this pain. The vixen could not; it was just a memory, a ghost movie reel playing in her head. While it felt so real, deep down, she knew it was not real, this was the past, and here she could change nothing. However, she felt the unrelenting pain.

~ ~ ~ ~

Zenti saw the sun come up and go down six times before the chief scientist came back. The white wolf was unsure if his memory was playing tricks on him or if he had been unconscious longer. He tried to roll just a little, to move at all. His body burned like fire when he did, and pain randomly raced throughout his body like sand blown about in a storm. Zenti stopped moving, and the pain began to subside when he heard an invader say something about him being awake. The chief scientist came over, and then Zenti could feel pressure here and pressure there as the male touched the areas around the wounds. Soon pain came again, and in a flash, he was unconscious. Mari watched and cried.

The operating room faded, and Mari found her standing in a tiny space, not unlike the jail cell she had been kept in. It was not an ideal place to facilitate the recovery of a surgery patient. However, Mari knew the invaders did not care for their captured subjects, no matter how important they might be. She watched Zenti for a while and those that came in to render a crumb of medical care.

The next thing Zenti remembered was waking up in a cold, musty room filled with straw. He was lying on his belly, still, on a low, flat, bed and when he tried to move his muscles, he cried in agony. However, the muscles responded. He made it all the way to his knees before collapsing, laying down hard and breathing rapidly as his mind fogged in pain.

His eyes adjusted to what little light there was, but he could see walls made of steel. Rolling his head, looking up to what should have been the roof, he noticed that the room was round, and it took him a moment to realize that he was not in a room but in a liquid storage tank. The stress of that movement taxed his body, and he fell back to sleep.

Zenti awoke to one of the invaders dabbing him with a cloth that stank of medicine. He started to reach up to strike at the invader, but he found himself chained through the bed to the floor.

"We can do this easy or hard, and to be honest, I would love for you to make it hard. But as another three weeks are almost to an end, I want to be done as quickly as possible. You are healed enough for the next series of operations, the ones that will allow you to be tracked and controlled when we install the final devices. Yes, wolf, we will control you and one day will learn how you summon your magic. Your species will come to despise you. What better weapon could we ask for than one of its own Summoners," the invader said? The male invader slapped Zenti on the back of the head before injecting him with something. Moments later, the surroundings began to haze, and the white wolf was again semi-conscious.

Mari watched as guards came in and put him on a

gurney and then rolled him out back into the makeshift operating room. Depositing him on the table, they stepped back before being ordered to turn him over. The chief scientist entered the room triumphantly. Immediately he went to work.

Picking up one of the scalpels from a new tray of tools, he waited as two of **THEIR** soldiers rolled the wolf onto his back and chained him down. Telling the soldiers to leave, he slowly prepared to make an incision. The male cut along the wolf's breastbone, revealing the sternum when an alarm sounded throughout the facility. The chief scientist jumped, dropping the scalpel.

"God damn it!" the male invader cursed before yelling at one of the other soldiers standing guard at the door. "What the blue blaze is going on," the chief scientist shouted at the soldier? The soldier was on the phone nodding as he listened to the person on the other end. The soldier slammed the phone down on the base before answering the question. The scientist picked up the scalpel, not bothering to get a clean one.

"We have a breach," said the soldier.

"Damn it, can we move him safely," asked another soldier?

"Maybe, but it sounds like we're being overrun," the first soldier replied.

Zenti heard the alarms still going off; their blaring tone was barely audible to his ears. He surmised it was an effect of the sedatives. The chief scientist dropped the scalpel a second time and cursed something fierce when an explosion rocked the air. Then there was greater panic as someone opened the doors and yelled that there was a full breach in progress. The sound of gunfire was getting closer, and all of the scientists in the room began to panic. Mari watched the confusion unfold as **THEY** tried to hurriedly staple the sternum incision closed. The chief scientist was yelling for them to finish the incision closure before moving Zenti out of the makeshift operating room. A soldier yelled that an explosion ripped open the outside doors to the warehouse, and they needed to evacuate immediately. The gunfire sounded very close. The scientist looked at Zenti for one long, last moment and made a painful decision. If he could not have the white wolf to work on, then no one would have him. Picking up the scalpel from the floor, he grasped it so he could make a deep cut to the wolf's throat. The chief scientist raised the scalpel to slice. There was a sound, something like clicking and a pop.

Groggily Zenti watched as a red mist exploded from the chief scientist's head before the body crumpled to the floor. Turning his head to where the male invader had been standing, a bear came into Zenti's fuzzy view. The male bear stood with his rifle aimed at where the scientist's head used to be.

Catching sight of Zenti, the bear quickly shouldered the weapon, ensuring it hung out of the way. Zenti heard more gunfire as the bear kicked the body of the lead scientist out of the way. Hurrying, he began to undo the restraints before hoisting the injured white wolf into his powerful arms. Mari noted that Zenti looked tiny in the bear's arms, almost like a pup; thin, furless, and pale against the bear's black fur. The bear's fur was laced with grey strands of age. He was tall, thick, and very muscular with a rugged look.

"Are there any others?" the bear asked the wolf firmly, and when Zenti failed to answer, the bear asked again, this time louder with more clarity. "Are there any other of our species alive here?"

The pain of being moved so gruffly brought Zenti to the brink of passing out; he heard the question the second time and mumbled something that the bear must have taken for no. Zenti found himself being hauled outside at a neck-breaking pace. Zenti tried to speak but failed as he was just too weak.

The bear stepped outside, and the light assaulted Zenti's eyes. The white wolf moaned in agony, snapping his eyes closed. The bear growled orders, and Zenti could hear the unique sound of boots hitting the pavement that only someone who walked digitigrade made. These must be Faction soldiers, but Zenti was too deeply sedated to know for sure. That made it hard to focus on the male bear's voice. Pain wracked his body all over, and the white wolf again teetered on the brink of unconsciousness when the bear stopped moving. Letting his head fall back, Zenti could see a wagon. With the aid of a female weasel, the bear lifted the injured white wolf up into the wagon's bed.

The action caused pain to shoot through Zenti's body. With the constant drip of sedatives gone, Zenti called on his Gift and attempted to cleanse his system of their effects.

Somewhere Zenti heard more gunshots, but they were fading fast as the bear laid him down in the bed of a wagon. Barking a command, the wagon promptly jolted into motion, sending a shockwave of pain across Zenti's battered body. The white wolf tried to hold on to consciousness but lost the battle.

When the white wolf awoke an undetermined time later, he was still in the wagon, but it was not moving. He could hear voices but was just too exhausted to move. He drifted in and out of consciousness for the better part of unknown hours as they retreated from the abandoned factory.

Mari recognized the bear; he was from one of the southern Factions. They had only met a few times, but that was many years ago. However, when the vixen was younger, the bear had come to see her father many times during the war. As the wagon left, the vixen saw what was left of the factory. She realized that it was the destroyed rail car manufacturing facility, just outside the ruined city of Taiir. This had been a heavy industry facility that was the heart of separating, smelting, forming, and producing steel for the whole of Mitd. However, this was not the only place though it was the newest, largest, and most advanced of the several plants scattered throughout Mitd. The steel was produced here. The nearby factory manufactured heavy weapons, armor plating, vehicle armor, rail engines, and rail cars. It had taken three years to build, and the invaders destroyed it in one day.

~　　　~　　　~　　　~

"I know that bear's muzzle," Mari said softly. She had briefly returned to the present. Leaning closer to Zenti, the vixen pressed her forehead to his. Perhaps it would juggle the memory of the bear's name free from wherever it was lodged in her brain. "What's his name, what's his name, what's his- General Riley Hetchon!"

At the recall of the bear's name, a sadness washed over Mari. At some point, she had been told the bear's mate and three of his four cubs had been executed for participating in acts of war. However, everyone knew better. They had been killed just because invaders had not gotten the information about the General's whereabouts. The mate and cubs of General Hetchon were not worthy of taking on as captives.

Mari edged closer to staying in the present, straining Zenti's Talent of Soul's Self. Gently, Zenti coaxed Mari back into the memory. Fatigue was setting in, and the white wolf knew that he could not maintain the Talent of Union for too much longer. Mari wanted to see, and he would pay the price for her to discover the truth. Then she could freely end their lives together. Zenti wanted nothing more than to see Mari happy, and if that meant they go their separate ways, then so be it. The present melded into the memory of the past. Mari was once again watching Zenti's battered body in the wagon's bed.

~   ~   ~   ~

What seemed to be a short time later, though Zenti could not tell, the wagon was driven into a cave. At some point, someone had put wrap-around shorts on him. However, modesty was not a high priority now. Still, Zenti was grateful for the kind gesture. The fading sunlight glistened off the wet moss on the tree branches as he passed underneath them. The wagon jolted, and again the white wolf passed out from the pain. Zenti awoke, not knowing how long he had been in the cave. The weasel that had helped the bear put him in the cart put a canteen to his lips. She let a little water moisten them before trying to get Zenti to drink again. The results were worse this time as the white wolf spilled more than she got him to drink. The pain raced through Zenti once more, but this time he did not pass out. Mari felt the pain; it was far worse than it had ever been.

~   ~   ~   ~

Mari tried to pull herself back to the present. She could feel the tears running down her fur in steady, unstoppable streams as she watched Zenti suffer. How could he have survived? Again, Zenti pushed her back in the memory. She wanted to see this, even if the emotional pain was incredible. Zenti knew life was not fair, and there was always a price to pay in living it. It was time Mari began to see that.

~   ~   ~   ~

"Kajot[16]," Zenti called for with a rough, dry voice

when he was able to speak. He felt his head lifted and something cool touching his lips. Zenti choked on the drink but managed to get some down; it was water again. Looking up, he saw the smiling face of the young weasel giving him a drink from a canteen.

"Kajot," he said again, but before he could say another word, she put her paw on his muzzle to quiet him.

"I don't have any; all I have is water. Now be quiet; you are in horrible shape," said the weasel. The white wolf could tell by the look on her muzzle that she was horrified by what she saw of him.

Gently she gave him another drink and laid his head back down in her lap. "I don't have anything for the pain, either, I am afraid. I'm very sorry," she said, folding her ears back, knowing that Zenti must be close to death.

Just then, the bear came into view, and the weasel looked up at him with a sickening expression on her muzzle. The bear leaned over the side of the wagon and looked Zenti in the face.

"Well, son, it looks like **THEY** did a pretty good number on you," General Riley Hetchon said.

Zenti knew this bear; he had been to see Mari's father many times as conflict spread. He was General Riley Hetchon or something like that. His mind was not completely clear at this moment. Zenti nodded slowly at

---

[16] Kajot is a strong, sweet, potent liquor known for its pain-numbing properties. It is also highly addictive if imbued often.

the bear's statement, and he raised an eyebrow at the shocked look on the bear's muzzle. Even that movement hurt.

"As I see it, son, we have two choices," continued the General, "You can be taken to a doctor or a shaman, though I am not sure what either one can do for you. You're pretty close to death, and I honestly don't expect you to live long, much less make the trip anywhere else." The bear reached down and took the wolf's paw. Lifting it up, he gently patted it in a fatherly sort of way. Zenti flinched as the pain raced through his body.

"Oracle," Zenti coughed, grabbing the General by the front of his fatigues. That action racked Zenti's body with pain, "Breest Isle, no place else."

Zenti's sudden movement caused him to passed out. His head and shoulders dropped back into the weasel's lap. The general sighed and nodded to the driver. The bear climbed up beside the ram, and they were off.

The wagon swayed gently as they pulled out of the cave and onto the road. The movement jarred Zenti awake, and he moaned a little. As they left the cave, Zenti noticed the afternoon sky had changed into late afternoon. The sun was not as bright in his eyes as it filtered through the scattered trees.

It was not a long way to Breest Isle, but it was longer than the bear was comfortable with, and Mari could tell. General Hetchton fidgeted and got that worried look that her father had always had when he was losing at a game of

King's Gambit. The look said he was running out of options. The bear watched Zenti slip in and out of consciousness.

Zenti was awake for most of the trip but just kept his eyes closed; thoughts of Mari, his sweet Mari, now dead, flooded his mind. Memories of the life that they shared replayed randomly in time. Zenti was not sure if he were ready to pay the price that the Oracle would demand. The Oracle of Breest was feared but sought after. This mysterious Gifted demanded a high price for the use of her Gift. That was unheard of. The Gifted never charged for the benefit of their Gift. Donations of kindness were reluctantly accepted, but even then, it required the giver to be insistent. However, the Oracle of Breest was unquestionably the most powerful Oracle on Jayden. Zenti found it funny one of his kind, a Gifted Summoner, was going to see this particularly demanding Oracle. The Gifted did not like to collaborate. It bred unhealthy competition.

Zenti remembered the first time he crossed paths with an Oracle, Mari's little sister, Rini. Her wounds did not kill her, but that traumatic experience somehow had brought about a change. Rini Waxton was just at her Gifting Day. That was historically the day the Gift was tested for. However, that tradition ended with the King's Fist Rebellion. Mitd had been wholly ravaged during that civil war five hundred years ago. Many traditions were forgotten after that war. Did trauma bring about the Gift, Zenti wondered. Due to the pain, it was a question he could not focus on. With that change in Rini Waxton came nothing but bitterness between him and the lioness. Rini's relationship with her sister Mari became terse. Even after ten years, Rini and Mari hardly spoke in more than forced civility.

The white wolf recalled the day he and Mari were mated. The life that day had held a future filled with promise and hope. Zenti also would never forget how Rini had ruined that future for him. At the simple reception that was held at a Faction camp, a few comrades had gathered. The young Rini stood up with the aid of a nurse. The young lioness first displayed she was Gifted that day. Rini growled at her nurse until the elder female marmot relented and helped the young lioness stand. Everyone had their metal trail cups raised, and the customary toast was about to be made. Rini growled until she had everyone's full attention. It was intimidating the way the five-year-old female commanded attention. The young, pre-Coming-of-Age lioness balled up her paws, and they began to glow a pale teal. That was the first sign that Rini was Gifted.

Rini looked at Zenti and told him that his fate was doomed. She continued by saying he would forever suffer in agony and that when the time came, he would make a choice. That choice would take him to Breest Isle. The young Oracle Rini Waxton then shared her vision of the white wolf. The young lioness said that he would do something that none of his kind had ever done. That act, Rini said, would forever change the lives of everyone. That was the last clear vision Oracle Rini Waxton had of

Summoner Zenti Semineu.

~   ~   ~   ~

Mari recalled that day. The vixen's phantom-self watched the events of Zenti Semineu's life unfold. In her ethereal form, created by the Gifted Talent of Soul's Self, Mari gasped at her sister's Gifted Vision's accuracy. Zenti was going to pay the price that the Witch of Breest demanded.

~   ~   ~   ~

Zenti heard the water splashing on the rocks and felt his body lifted into a boat. He must have passed out again for a short while, the white wolf surmised. Opening his eyes, he saw the bear at the back of the flat-bottomed boat poling him across the water to the small rocky isle.

Breest Isle was the name of a small rock outcropping in the center of a large brackish lake. There were no tributaries to a saltwater source, so why the waters were brackish was unknown. The rock outcropping was not large at all. It was perhaps the size of an average home. There were no trees or buildings of any type, with only an old wooden dock jutting out into the water.

As the boat pulled up by the ragged old dock, the bear tied it off at the far end. Lifting Zenti out of the boat, the bear laid him on the dock's rough, sun-bleached deck planks, and Zenti moaned as the bear laid him down.

"Not the place I would choose to die, pup, but since you are dying, I will grant you this request. I know I cannot get you to a doctor or shaman in time. I guess that old buzzard, Torit, got it all wrong about you. I would say it is such a waste of life though, no one has ever returned from the Breest Isle Oracle unaffected by the witches Gift. But the shape you are in, pup," said the bear, letting his voice trail off as he pushed the boat away from the docks and started back to the lakeshore.

~   ~   ~   ~

Mari watched, nervous even though she knew that Zenti would live through this; after all, it was just a memory. However, Mari knew the stories, the legends, the Oracle of Breest. She was known as the Witch of Breest and, by some, the Bitch of Breest. No matter what she was called, Mari knew the Oracle was a fearsome goddess indeed. The Oracle of Breest had no true face. She shifted from shape to shape, with none that was her own. With a short temper and little patience, the Oracle's wrath was something that even **THEY** feared.

However, the Oracle of Breest was on neither side of the war. 'It is not my war,' she would say to those that dared to pay the price to simply ask her guidance. Zenti coaxed Mari back into the memory. Mari thought she could feel the white wolf's exhaustion. How long had Zenti been using his Gift to open the Talent of Union and the Talent of Soul's Self? At that moment, Mari realized Zenti was paying the price to fulfill her desire to learn the truth. He had always paid the price for her.

~   ~   ~   ~

Zenti lay there on the dock, not knowing what to do next. He was unable to move, much less walk. The pain only subsided when he lay still, so he did just that and laid there waiting. He watched the clouds roll by as the late evening sun began to wane. His mind wandered to Mari again, hoping her death was quick at least. However, he did not have to wait long as a fog rolled in on him. The next thing he knew, he was being moved. However, he was not exactly being carried; it felt like he was riding on a cushion of air. It reminded him of the few seconds of flight when a diver jumps a cliff. That was not a sport he enjoyed but had tried.

Zenti saw ritual robes of whomever it was moving him. They were covered with Orra's symbols. The movement was not gentle, nor was the gate steady. The pain of being bounced around, even slightly, was causing him to see lights dancing in his eyes. When the pain overcame him again, he passed out. For how long he did not know, but a voice brought him back to consciousness.

"Welcome back to the land of the living, wolf," said a voice as he faded between the waking world and dream world.

Through the haze of pain, he opened his eyes to find himself in what appeared to be an empty room, except for a shadowy presence. He knew that language; it was of the invaders. Anger rushed through him as he tried to move but found himself restrained. His first thought was perhaps his rescue had just been a pain-induced dream. He found he could not clearly focus, but the scent of the shadowy figure was all wrong. Had he been moved to another facility?

Trying to strike out at his unseen captor, he managed a small ball of flame that leapt from his paws but hit nothing. The pain raced through him at the strained effort, and he fought to remain conscious.

"I expected as much from you; act first and think later," the voice said.

"It works for me when it comes to your species. You are so pathetically stupid and predictable. Now, where am I? Who are you," Zenti retorted flippantly? He was tired of playing the mind games, through his voice failed to hide the pain.

"I knew you were coming, wolf, from the day you were whelped. I had many visions of you. Though I never saw just how badly you had been hurt in any of them. It is utterly amazing that you still live," said the robed shadow. It moved forward, and the room became dimly lit.

The robe was from the Northern Faction crafters who were famed for making ornate robes for Orra's servants. However, this was not one of Orra's servants; its face was one of the invaders. Straining to refocus his vision, he tried to make out any features. The effort was causing his head to ache, and he stopped. The invader was not wearing the typical breathing mask. Was he dreaming, the white wolf wondered?

Suddenly the face looked like it was being stretched,

and then it was a different face altogether. A weasel now looked down at Zenti with eyes bright full of mischief. The musk remained feminine as the female weasel shifted into a male ocelot. Zenti realized this was not a dream. This was the Oracle of Breest.

"Why have you come here," the Oracle asked softly? "You want something, say what it is. I will tell you my price. Be quick about it; I don't have all day."

Zenti looked at her silently, his mind growing slightly fuzzy as he watched her face change repeatedly, but her voice remained the same.

"I want you to undo what the invaders did to me," he managed, and the rabbit smiled at his answer.

"Why?" Her voice was dreamy. It reminded Zenti of water, water that had been made into sound. "Your Gifts will now make invincible in your enemy's eyes. Perhaps a study of your invaders might help you understand more."

He looked away from her shifting forms. The continual shifting was causing him headaches again.

"Invincible is not the word I would use," he coughed, laboring to control the pain and his breathing.

Each slight movement brought intense pain that reflected on his muzzle and in his eyes. The Oracle smiled, her face becoming fishlike, her nose flattening as her eyes became large and round. "Are you sure it's not another reason, wolf," the Oracle of Breest asked? There was venom in her voice. Zenti looked at her questioningly.

Again she shifted. "For love, perhaps?" The Oracle cooed as she leaned closer to the bound wolf.

Her face suddenly was not fishlike anymore-- it was Mari's.

"Mari is dead," Zenti said flatly. "The invaders do not take prisoners and let them live."

"How do you explain your current situation," the Oracle asked in that watery voice again? Her face shifted. She was now a bearded goat.

"I was needed as a weapon of war, that is all. Devices were planted in me so I could be followed, controlled, and used to kill more of my species using my Gifts," Zenti replied. The white wolf rolled his head back in pain, shivering in the cold air of the room. Every movement hurt, and it showed as he spoke.

The Oracle touched what was left of his fur, and he screamed in agony, though the touch was a mere brush. Again, she touched him, and again he screamed. Tracing a claw down his wounds, she felt the metal underneath the skin. The Oracle of Breest ignored the screams of pain at her slightest touch. She continued to probe the injuries, and he continued to scream.

~   ~   ~   ~

Mari screamed as he screamed. This was beyond maddening; what more must Zenti endure. Mari thought she could hear movement outside the tent and figured Zenti must have heard that as well. A rolling wave of fear washed out from him. She had never felt such strong a surge from Zenti before. The Gifted Talent of Revulsion created a wave of fear. Zenti had used it on the battlefield when he would use the Talent to disperse enemy troops. Before Zenti had mastered the Talent of Revulsion, Mari had felt its effect and had reacted strongly to it before.

Wondering why she did not react now, Mari, moments later, felt Zenti employ yet another facet of his Gift. The vixen felt the cocoon of fear peel back from around her mind. She gasped when she realized that not only could Zenti cause a feeling, but he could also protect others from the end effect. Where had this Gift come from? From what she knew of the Gift, only Gifted Shamans could call on the Talent of Emotional Shielding. When Zenti brought her back into the memories, Mari noted that it was not as gentle, and he felt exhausted.

~   ~   ~   ~

The Oracle of Breest stopped, and the pain gradually became less intense as she moved to one side of the room. The light was still dim, and his mind was still hazy as he watched her take a syringe from a shelf built into the wall. The raccoon filled it with a liquid from a tiny vial.

Moving over beside him, the cheetah form of the Oracle of Breest looked his arms over. Continuing to search his body for a suitable injection site, the Oracle gave what sounded like an exasperated sigh. The opossum found one and injected Zenti with something on the inner thigh of his left leg. The veins stood out the most there and had the smallest number of needle marks.

Zenti could feel a burning move up his leg and into his torso. At first, he thought the Oracle of Breest was trying to do more damage. However, moments later, the pain subsided, and he was able to focus better. Was she trying to help him or hurt him? Zenti wished he knew. Rolling his head back to face the ceiling, he relished the freedom from the pain.

"I don't want this technology in me; I don't want anything that the invaders have done. I want to be my old self," Zenti said in a growl. The effort taxed his body but no longer hurting.

"It is too late for that, Summoner. What has been done cannot be undone. What is amazing is that you survived," she hissed in a snakelike voice, "But there are things I can do that will make you a bane to your enemy's existence. The question is, will you pay my price?"

She again shifted, looking like an owl, face wide and round, fluffed with down-like feathers, then sat on the side of the table beside the prostrate wolf.

"What could I offer that you could ever need," Zenti asked, looking up at the shifting face?

"What I *want,*" she said sweetly, "is something that only you can give me. I want your morality, young wolf, the very essence that is you."

"Morality is *that* all?" The wolf laughed, gagging on

the dryness in his throat. "That you can freely have. I lost my Mari, I lost my family, and I have watched countless die by the invader's furless paws. Morality," he coughed. The dryness in his throat felt like sand.

She summoned a goblet from the air; tilting his head up, she helped him drink a semi-thick sweet liquid. He continued to drink until the goblet was empty. His throat tingled, and he thought he tasted a hint of Kajot. That excellent liqueur was a great pain reliever, though addicting. Relaxing his head back on the table, he closed his eyes, deciding if he wanted to accept the Oracle's gift. The decision, however, was not a hard one. What did one need to live for except revenge? What was morality compared to everything he had already lost?.

"Morality it shall be. Take it, though I expect a like exchange. What things will you give me that will make me the bane of the invader's existence? Will it be technology, or perhaps physical? What magical thing could you offer me that will harm the invaders more than I already have? Come now, Oracle, what you offer cannot be done," the words flowed out of Zenti's muzzle, sarcastically mocking her calm tone.

"Oh, pup, it can be done. You were born with the Gifts, yes-plural, wolf. You are what must come. The arrogance of the scientist who worked on you is astounding. That species's lack of understanding of just what you are has allowed the technology to be implanted in you," the Oracle of Breest cooed. "Well, not exactly technology. But what those items were made of. It cannot be undone, pup. Those items have been embraced by your Voidal Gift and have begun melding to your very body. It has already been done, pup. Your escape temporarily interrupted other processes before they could be completed. Those fool scientists cannot begin to know what they have done. It was what needed to happen to awaken your full access to the Void. Amazing, is it not that your companions found you? Is it not even more amazing that they were so close to me," the Oracle said? A wicked smile crossing the spotted muzzle of the jaguar.

"Yes, amazing indeed," Zenti said dryly. He looked at this feline intently. So, the Oracle of Breest had been behind his rescue. Zenti wondered if she was also behind his capture. If she was, then she was indirectly the cause of Mari's death.

"Oh, come now, wolf, you should learn to hide your thoughts better. I had nothing directly to do with your capture. As to your Mari, well, this planet needs her," the chimpanzee said.

"Mari is dead," Zenti growled.

"You are so narrow-minded, pup. All you need to do is pay the price I demand, I will finish what was started, and you will learn just what you are. You will learn what Mari is. Trust me, wolf. You will become hated, feared, and the dead will litter this planet. You will learn who the true invaders are. You will be my personal harvester of souls," the shifting Oracle said. The wicked grin of a hyena smiled down at Zenti.

"If you are true to your word, I will be true to mine. To make the invaders suffer, I will forego the very teachings of my species, the things that make us different. Nothing can bring my Mari back, but I want retribution," Zenti growled.

Zenti's words were filled with anger. Though the drugs coursing through his veins were meant to render him numb to his body wracked with pain, yet he hurt. Zenti focused all his being on breaking the bonds that held him down.

The white wolf howled in pain. It was a screaming cry of anguish that turned into a howl of rage that fueled the inner fire that all have yet fear to unleash. When the howl subsided, he found himself sitting on the table. His wounds were open again, and he was bleeding. His paw pads were bound at the ankles, and his legs were still secured at the thigh, but he did not care.

Sitting on the table, his body covered once again in blood, he looked over to the Oracle of Breest as she stood calmly near the point where she had retrieved the syringe. Grasping the straps, he screamed in rage as he ripped the bindings out of the table around his thighs. In rage-filled agony, as he tore the two remaining straps binding his paw pads. However, this time he did not ignore the pain but embraced it wholly.

"Come, Oracle, take your payment, and give me the gifts you claim to offer. I fear not death; we are old friends, and she will walk in my shadow, filling her coffers with the litter I shall leave behind. Look at me, Oracle, and see if you're willing to give such a great gift," he growled in burning rage. Zenti's paws glowed brilliant white as balefire danced about his claws.

His thoughts were of but one thing. Mari. They flooded his memories like a bursting dam. All he had wanted was in her. All he needed was in her. All he dreamed was in her, but all were dead like her—morality, what a minor price, Zenti thought.

All it took was a smile, and the Oracle was gone. He found himself flung back to the table, his body wracked in pain as he lay there, convulsing. It felt like he was being ripped in half. There was a buzzing down his spine like an angry nest of bees. What followed was a thousand stings, as if those bees were swarming him. The Oracle of Breest appeared at Zenti's head and reached out a tentacle arm.

Instantly, Zenti curled into a ball the moment the Oracle of Breest touched his forehead. His whole body tightened then he began to shake violently. The moment she removed a clawed digit, he stiffened out straight on the table. He screamed as the wires burst forth from his furless skin. The metal wires rose into the air like a strange-looking winged serpent rearing its head to strike, dripping blood with pieces of flesh hanging from the wire filaments. However, they never lost connection to his body.

The white wolf arched backward towards the ceiling. Zenti screamed in utter pain as the implanted chips ripped forth from the base of his skull, shoulders, paws, and chest, tearing his skin and what little fur was left with it.

His whole body burned, it as if he were, immersed in a lake of freezing water. Sick as he was, he fought this new pain and struggled to control its effects. The wires reared back, coiled up, and looked as if they were ready to strike a fatal blow to his head. With blood smeared and dripping down its wire body, the metal stuck out. However, it did not attack him. Instead, it burrowed back into his body. The intensity of the blow slammed him down on the table with such force that the table cracked. Zenti was left there, lying in a puddle of his cooling blood, his chest heaving heavily as he tried to recover.

Blinding lights struck his body as a wide beam painted him from the tip of his ears to the claws on his paw pads. Just as it seemed that the pain had stopped, another pain gripped him, a more profound pain. It was a pain that burned through his bones. It penetrated all the way down to the very core of every fiber of his being. Almost as soon as it started, it stopped, and it was over.

Zenti knew something was missing from him. The warmth of memories was gone, the comfort of the happier times waned, and he found that his memories held no flavor. He felt genuinely empty.

Lights erupted from the ceiling again, and he felt a new pain, this one he was familiar with. It was the dark pain of taking a life, the monstrous darkness that ate at his soul each time he had killed. Yet it called to him, filling him with something new. He could not quite tell what it was, but something much stronger had come to replace what was taken, and it felt very satisfying. It felt familiar and tasted of the Void.

The Void did not embrace him; it was him. It had been part of his life since he was five and touched the Gift for the first time. In that instant, Zenti realized that the Oracle of Breest was not the source but a conduit and the Void took the pain completely away. His body went limp.

"There now, all done. What it took scientist to do in three months, I have undone with the mere call of my Gift," the Oracle of Breest said in an overly sweet manner. She appeared, and she leaned over the cracked table, "How do you feel wolf?" She brushed a soft paw on the tip of his muzzle.

~   ~   ~   ~

Mari's phantom-self could not tear her eyes away from Zenti. The change was almost instant as she watched something leave him. It was like watching a sheet of ice inside him melt away. She did not know what it was, but it was visible. Starting at the tips of his ears and slowly, like liquid, it moved down his body, taking something unknown with it. As the wave of light passed over his body, something happened to Zenti. His body seemed not to reflect the light shining on him any longer. Mari watched the transformation. Zenti's eyes became a deep black, and his claws changed from ivory white to the purest of ebony.

Looking at the cloaked figure of the Oracle of Breest, Mari knew this had to be Orra, the Creator of all life. No Oracle had this power. The vixen was shaking still, feeling the emptiness of Zenti's soul. What Mari witnessed next, as Zenti pushed her back into the memory with even more force than before, shocked and scared vixen.

~   ~   ~   ~

Lifting himself from the pooling blood, Zenti slowly swung his legs over the edge of the cracked table and stood up. He faced the Oracle, a rage burning inside him. His empty gaze meeting that of the Oracle of Breest. In the reflection of the Oracle's un-shifting eyes, Mari witnessed the identical empty reflection she now felt in Zenti.

Zenti could feel the emptiness. The loss of something so fundamental that he knew he was different. Yet, he felt a new power well up within him, unfettered by any morality or feelings. Instantly he closed his thoughts off to the Oracle. He felt the power of his Gift course through him. He also knew, without reservation, the change was not from the Oracle of Breest. What game was the Oracle playing, wondered Zenti?

"Well, Witch, it seems I have kept my part of the bargain; we shall see if you have kept yours," Zenti growled. He stepped towards her on unsteady paw pads. "And remember Witch, you command me not, we have a bargain, and nowhere in that bargain was I yours to command. You gave me something; I gave you something. We are even."

His voice filled with bitter hatred as balls of balefire

surrounding his paws. Heat rolled off them. Moreover, for a moment, the Oracle flinched; a flinch Zenti nor the phantom-Mari missed. *So the Witch of Breest was playing a game*, thought Zenti.

"Of course," the Oracle said with a sickeningly sweet smile, though her voice held a note of trepidation. A ruby gem set atop a small golden orb floated in the air before the shifting form of a lamb. The Oracle of Breest began to fade as though she were just of wisps of smoke, "Your full change will present itself in time. The Void has you now wolf as it was foretold. You are one-half of the Prophecy. I merely opened the door, wolf, you freely walked through. Though you should know, your Mari is not dead. She holds a secret to the Prophecy. You will need the ruby topped orb; its purpose will become clear in time. Our bargain is complete; we are even." In those parting words, Zenti noted something about the shapeshifting Oracle of Breest; she seemed satisfied.

Then the Oracle of Breest was gone. There was a flash of light. Instantly he found himself standing on the cold, rocky shoreline of Breest Isle. However, Zenti found no peace, but he was sure of that familiar taste within his spirit. It was the Void, and it fueled his rage. The Oracle of Breest was a witch of unsavory character, but she was not Orra.

Zenti did not believe the Oracle's proclamation that Mari was alive; only the Gift had kept him alive. The invaders did not let his kind live. His survival was because the Void demanded a price, one he agreed to pay on his

Gifting Day.

The white wolf watched as the water lapped at the fur on his paw pads, one of the few spots on his body that still had some fur. It was chilly and dark outside with but a few stars shining through lightly overcast skies. He had lost most of his fur when the invaders were cutting on him. Zenti now knew it had been three months since his capture. Three months of brutal procedures. He should be dead but knew his Gift had kept him alive. However, the extensive medical butchery, and the lack of grooming, cause the loss of almost all of his fur. For the first time in a long time, he felt cold and alone. All that was left was burning anger deep in his soul.

The white wolf could see the shoreline across from Breest Isle. However, he could not see a boat of any kind attached to the decrepit docks here. That left him with little choice. Zenti waded into the water with what was to be a bone-chilling swim. Winter was in its final death throws, and the cold nip of the spring air caused shivers to run across his furless body. What month was it, he wondered? Was it the fourth or fifth? Three months was vague, and he did not know precisely how long he was captive. The trees were beginning to show signs of buds, so perhaps it was early in the fifth month.

He thought he was fully ready for the brackish water to be on his wounds. Zenti expected that the cold would numb him to the pain caused by the water's salt content. He stifled a howl of agony as the cold failed to deaden the pain caused by the brackish water. Watching the water turn brown then red around him as it washed off the caked-on blood Zenti converted the pain into determination. The water allowed his wounds to begin bleeding again. As the pain flowed through this entire body, Zenti wondered just how much his body had been through.

The salt of the brackish water burned through the wounds, searing his flesh as if a fire burned him. If the white wolf had not been concentrating, he would have been screaming until he passed out. He stood there an unknown time as his body became numb to the pain. Slowly he began the swim across the small lake, diving under the surface to clean the blood from his head and muzzle. He should not be able to move around, much less swim. However, the Void fueled his body as much as it fueled his Gift.

~   ~   ~   ~

Mari watched him quietly, her heart racing just as she felt Zenti's was. What more could he take? What more would Zenti have to go through? She watched as he took the first step on the beach. Zenti's mental scream chilled her to the core as the cold air, and brackish water hit his open wounds, shocking him again. Mari wanted to end this. She no longer wanted to see the pain Zenti was enduring. This was not what she was led to believe happened. Again, Zenti guided her back into the Talent of the Soul's Self. However, Mari felt he was growing exhausted.

~   ~   ~   ~

The day was old and the evening new as Zenti stood on the far shore. He was close to complete collapse and needed rest, but here and now was not the place. Zenti began to march on, enduring the pain until it was just a dull ache. He felt the Void coursing through his body, and it fueled him. If it had not, he would be dead. He traveled slowly down the dirt road and watched as the breeze gently rustled the trees' branches. However, each step became more laborious than the one before it.

Sheer hatred drove each step forward as Zenti focused on the changes that were happening within him. A new scent wafted in as he came to the crossroads. Taking in the area, Zenti saw an encampment just a short distance down the western road. He was not far from Breest Isle and thought it odd that someone would choose to camp near here. As exhausted as he was, his curiosity got the better of his physical condition, and he turned down the west road.

Approaching cautiously downwind, he saw two invaders sitting around a small fire, preparing a meal. The smell made him ravenously hungry, yet the thought of eating was revolting. Quietly he closed in on the camp. Circling into the woods, he checked to make sure there were no more invader soldiers on watch in the surrounding area. When he was sure there were no more in the area, he moved even closer to the camp.

Only as he moved closer to the camp, hidden by the tree line, did the white wolf notice there was one of his species freely moving about the camp. He froze in his tracks, watching.

~   ~   ~   ~

Mari's phantom-self also stared. How could there be a traitor? How could there be someone so cowardly that they would sell out their own kind to the enemy? She knew some served the invaders. But to see one freely interacting with the invaders made her angry. Mari did not want to believe it, but there the raccoon was. The small and fidgety raccoon took in the scents and sights around the camp. Who was this traitor, and why did the invaders allow the raccoon to freely move around?

Looking at their uniforms, she knew that the invaders were scouts, not the regular or heavy assault troops. Why were **THEY** here all alone and out in the open? This was so unlike the typical tactics for invader scouts. What was more impressive is that those two scouts could speak her language.

~   ~   ~   ~

Zenti watch as the three talked as if they were equals. No invader considered a Jaydonian an equal. The conversation was low and hushed, and he could only hear a few words. Straining to listen, Zenti found himself unable to focus for longer than a few moments. Fatigue and hunger distracted him. However, anger sustained him for the moment.

It was clear this fidgety raccoon was there of its own volition. Zenti could not tell if it were male or female, but he could tell that it was always alert. Keeping wind neutral, Zenti moved ever closer until he could hear more than bits and pieces. The white wolf hoped the wind did not shift. The invader scouts were doing most of the talking, mainly asking questions about individual military commanders or encampments. Zenti listened for almost an hour of questions and answers. One of the scouts pulled out a piece of paper and showed it to the raccoon.

"Have you seen this wolf? We were told that we would be meeting a representative of your kind here and that they would have information concerning this wolf," the male scout asked.

The raccoon shuddered at the picture, "That's a wolf?"

"What is left of one, it was stolen from us today, and we want it back. We lost the tracks down by the place you call Breest Isle. As you are the only one here and out in the open, I can only surmise that you are our contact. So, tell me, have you seen this wolf," asked the other invader while stirring the food on the fire?

"I am that representative. I was told this morning to come here and make a campfire in the middle of the road, and you would contact me. I was not told what you expected of me, but I was to assist in any way possible. I have not seen, um, that wolf," he said, pointing at the photo. The raccoon shuddered at the mutilated creature. "Wait, there was a wagon that passed a little way down the road just before dark; I guess it was about four hours ago, it was headed to Breest Isle. I was out scouting the area as instructed."

"Who or what was in the wagon," the cook asked, adding more seasoning to the pot.

"There was a bear, a weasel, and a ram that was driving the wagon. I could not see inside the bed of the wagon. I follow them to Breest Isle but stayed to the edge of the woods. The bear carried something to the island, but I got scared and ran back deeper into the woods," said the raccoon. Again, the raccoon shuddered at the memory. From the look on his companion's faces, *THEY* knew the story about Breest Isle.

"A powerful Oracle lives there. Many who go never come back. This one is evil, a hideous, shape-changing creature that devours the life of all who come near. I saw the bear take a flatboat over to the isle. He laid something on the docks a few hours ago. It could have been a wolf, but I'm not sure," the raccoon swallowed hard and made signs of protection to the sky at the thought of the Oracle of Breest.

"We are not afraid of any Jaydonian Oracle. We will head there, then perhaps this Oracle will be of more value than this wolf. With any luck, we will get them both," one scout said. The other invader gave the raccoon a small pouch, which the raccoon pocketed.

Taking a plate of food, the raccoon bid *THEM* good luck and skittered off into the darkness of the woods.

~   ~   ~   ~

Mari swallowed the bitter taste in her muzzle as she watched the coward scurry away. She watched *THEM* leave the meal to simmer. The two invaders marched off to their mounts, ready to go to Breest Isle. They joked about how easy it would be to capture the Oracle. Gifted or not, at the end of the day, the Oracle was just another Jaydonian animal. Oh, how foolish they were, Mari thought. She could not imagine someone of such power as the Oracle of Breest would surrender to the invaders without a fight. Zenti did not follow *THEM* to their demise. Instead, he headed into their camp once everyone had gone.

~   ~   ~   ~

Zenti slipped into the camp, looking things over before succumbing to the smell coming from the fire pit. The invaders had left the food cooking on the fire, obviously not thinking that the trip and capture would take a long time. The invaders were arrogant and foolish but a formable enemy. However, the invaders had a weakness; it was the underestimation of his species. His body craved the food as he heaped a plate full of something with meat and vegetables.

Zenti's mouth watered at the prospect of real food. He knew he would throw up but ate anyway, and true to course, he did vomit. He tried again, only in smaller portions, and it stayed down this time. He searched the encampment finding little of use. However, he found more food and began to stash it in a bag when he heard a noise from within the woods.

Immediately the raccoon appeared, glancing behind him as he walked as if looking for some unseen enemy. Zenti could see the raccoon was a male. He held an empty mess plate in one paw. It was apparent he was hoping to pilfer another meal from the unattended camp. He finally turned to face the fire. The raccoon froze in place when he turned. He saw what looked like the wolf the scouts were looking for. The ragged excuse for a wolf was relieving the camp of its food and supplies.

"Y-y-y-you're-" he stuttered, but he could not get the words out of his muzzle.

"I'm what, coon?" said Zenti bitterly. Coon was a derogative term for the raccoon breed. Zenti did not hate the breed but hated the traitor the raccoon was. The furless wolf took another small bite of food as he watched the raccoon advance. "What am I coon: alive, a spirit, perhaps curious at why you're consorting with **THEM**? Perhaps I am just deranged from all the damage done to my body, or perhaps I am just hungry?"

Zenti finished taking another small bite. There was no emotion in his deep black eyes as he looked at the raccoon that just stood frozen in place. Zenti continued to eat small bites while he reclined by the fire as if this were his camp. The raccoon still did not move.

"Come now, coon, you were not at a loss for words earlier in **THEIR** company," said Zenti, using the term for the invaders the Mitdonians used. "Am I so hideous and offensive, one of your own species, that you would not make polite conversation with me?" he asked. Zenti looked at the raccoon through the wisps of smoke lazily wafting its way skyward.

The raccoon moved slowly forward and hunched down across the fire from Zenti. He filled his plate again when Zenti nodded at the cooking pot.

"What conversation would you like to have, wolf?" asked the raccoon as he crouched across the fire from the furless male. The sight of the wolf's horribly wounded body almost turned his stomach.

The food was flavorless, thought Zenti, but his hunger found it acceptable. However, it was thick, hardy, and filling. He had found a chunk of bread. Breaking off a piece, he tossed it to the raccoon who caught it, nodding thanks.

"Let us begin with what's in that little bag **THEY** gave you," said Zenti as he took another bite.

The raccoon immediately touched his body, where the pouch was hidden. The look on the raccoon's muzzle was one of concern. He might have been scared, but he was obviously not going to give up the treasure in his possession.

"What do you want with it," the raccoon snapped shakily?

Zenti could tell that this raccoon was a scavenger, a coward who ran and hid, only to face the light when it benefited him personally. What was he gaining by working with the invaders, and who had sent him to this meeting place?

"I want nothing with it. There is nothing that ***THEY*** could offer me that I would be interested in having. However, you seem more than willing to talk to the invaders for the promise of a gift. Tell me, what was it that you offered for obviously such a prized treasure?" Zenti asked, looking for something to drink.

"None of your business!" he snapped. The raccoon watched Zenti with a wary eye through the rising smoke of the fire.

Zenti snorted lightly in retort to the raccoon. The white wolf continued his rummaging through the invader's supplies. Finding a bundle of canteens set into a pile of rocks, propped so they would not fall, the wolf grabbed one and drank it down. Not realizing until now just how thirsty he really was, he grabbed one after another until all three were finally empty. He was still thirsty, though. Maybe it was a permanent state, a side effect of what the Oracle of Breest had done to him.

The raccoon watched in near fear as the three canteens were emptied one at a time and then tossed aside. The male raccoon shifted nervously when the canteens were all empty, and the furless wolf was left licking his chops. Zenti was disappointed that there was no more to drink. He sat down by the fire again, letting the heat warm his skin. Zenti could feel the fatigue creeping in.

However, he did not have the luxury of resting.

"Well, coon, it's of no matter to me what treasure **THEY** gave you. What interests me more is what information you gave **THEM**," growled Zenti, shifting his attention from the empty canteens back to the raccoon. Instantly the male raccoon stood as Zenti took another small bite of food.

Not liking the sound of the wolf's tone, the raccoon backed away from the fire, ready to flee. However, the fear of being ripped apart from behind rooted his paws firmly to the ground. Even though the wolf looked in unbelievably bad condition, something about him reeked of danger.

"I tell them things from time to time. They promise not to kill my family. On the rare occasion, they give me things that I find useful to help my family survive," whimpered the raccoon. He watched the expression shift on the wolf's muzzle, and it terrified him.

Slowly the raccoon put his paws behind him as if being coy. The shaft of the short blade tucked into his belt made him feel a bit safer. The wolf looked worse for the ware. If needed, and it was very possible that he just might be able to wound the wolf sufficiently enough to secure an escape. The raccoon stood there, trying not to show fear. He moved slowly, scooting sideways, trying to keep the smoke between him and the injured wolf. The raccoon hoped to mask the scent of fear that he was emanating.

Zenti could tell that something was up with this traitorous piece of trash. It was something that would have made his fur stand on end had there been any left. He was still weak, and he was sure that the coon was most likely armed with only a knife. He could possibly have a gun. However, Zenti had seen no sign of one when he watched the coon reenter the camp.

"What kind of information?" Zenti asked. He turned his back on the raccoon and began to scavenge for something more to drink. Zenti hoped desperately that there were more canteens, "What was the last thing that you told the invader scouts," asked the white wolf. Still, he did not face the raccoon. It was a sign that he was utterly unafraid of this male. It was also very disrespectful, something Zenti did on purpose.

"There is talk of the leader of the combined Crown Armies making changes to the Factions. It is rumored the leader of a single Faction, a vixen named Mari, will be placed in command of all Faction troops. There is also the rumor that this leader of the combined Crown Armies will take her as his mate," the Procyon said shakily. That caught Zenti's attention, a fact the raccoon did not miss.

"Mari? What an uncommon name. And just who would this Mari be? Why is it of any importance what mate a Faction leader takes to **THEM**," Zenti asked? He tried to mask the excitement of her name, then like a hammer on an anvil, he struck the thought from his head. Mari was dead. The Oracle of Breest was playing with his emotions. That shape-shifting witch was known for her mind games.

~   ~   ~   ~

Mari could feel the raw emotion that the mere mention of her name could elicit from within Zenti. How could he have such feelings for her yet betray her? The vixen felt as if a truck had hit her. Had he betrayed her? Mari almost let go of Zenti's jaw when the memories were pushed to the forefront of her thoughts. She had found a crack in Zenti's mental armor; it was her. Mari reached into the gap in Zenti's mental armor, and for an incredibly brief moment, felt he was near total exhaustion.

~   ~   ~   ~

"She is the Eastern Faction leader; her second in command is missing, presumed dead. As to the mating proposal, some say she rebuffed the cat," the raccoon said quickly. "However, the panther took her as a protégé, a student of a sort. They say that she's the only survivor of the Hasha Massacre."

~   ~   ~   ~

"Hasha was the name of the village we lived in. It is only natural that they would call it the Hasha Massacre. That was ten years ago when *THEY* murdered my family," said Mari as she lived Zenti's memories. The massacre was a long time ago, yet those memories were as fresh as yesterday. The panther this raccoon spoke of was Hayden. Just after he had rescued her, the panther wanted her to command the Factions. Hayden also asked her to be his new mate. Mari returned to the present, but Zenti had more to share with her and again brought her back into the Talent of the Soul's Self. The push back into the memory was less than gentle.

~   ~   ~   ~

"Are you lying to me?" Zenti accused hesitantly. The white wolf's eyes narrowed, noting how very quickly the raccoon was shaking his head no.

"I promise I am not," said the raccoon and noticed the wolf's eyes narrowed even more as he bared his canines.

"What worth does your promise have," asked Zenti? A helpless look came over the traitor's muzzle as Zenti spoke. A heavy feeling of fear washed over him.

Fidgeting, the Procyon grasped the short blade tighter, hoping the wolf was far worse than his voice indicated.

"I have no reason to lie to you, wolf. I have met this Mari. She does not talk of her family, but I know that her sister is an Oracle. She survived the Hasha Massacre too. She and one other, a wolf, which they say-" his words trailed off as the raccoon began to put the pieces together.

THEY were looking for an escaped wolf that was severely injured. He had told the two scouts that he had seen what might have been a wolf on the docks of Breest Isle. Moreover, right here was a wolf that was severely hurt and who reacted to the name Mari. It could not be a coincidence that this injured wolf should appear just a short distance from Breest Isle. *Oh, Heavens and Hells*, thought the raccoon, *this was Summoner Zenti Semineu,* as the color began to drain from his face.

Zenti watched the raccoon as he began to pale. It was evident that the traitor was putting the pieces together inside that pea-sized mind of his.

"Are you Zenti," the raccoon asked nervously. The gears in his mind had worked their way through putting the puzzle pieces together, "Zenti Semineu?"

The wolf's ears perked up at the mention of his name as if he had not heard it in a long time.

"And if I am," Zenti asked callously? The raccoon jumped at the hollowness of his voice.

"Well then, Miss Mari will want to see you, sir," he said eagerly, "This Mari has been looking for you."

"Now I know your lying to me, coon. If Mari were alive, she would have been searching for me all this time," he said as he stood to his full height, which was not tall, but the wounds and sparse fur made him seem more imposing.

However, it was not his size that frightened the raccoon; it was the way the wolf's paws glowed. Deep scarlet red with tuffs of blue balefire flickered at the tips of the wolf's onyx claws. The glow illuminated the night more than the light from the fire did. The wolf advanced on the coon, who backed away, stopping only when the wolf pulled up short.

"I know where she is. I will take you to her. I swear

by the stars that I am not lying," shouted the raccoon. The traitor's voice was a mixture of fear and panic, which almost begged for mercy with just its tone.

It was then that the raccoon's head snapped to the left, looking down the path at **THEM**. *Oh, Heavens and Hells*, thought the raccoon, *I'm dead.*

"Come! Come! This way! **THEY** are coming back. I guess they decided it was not worth the risk of attacking the Witch of Breest," the raccoon whispered. Quickly the raccoon scurried off into the woods, hoping that the wolf would follow him.

Zenti thought twice about following the raccoon. However, he decided that it was probably better to follow a traitor that he knew he could defeat. He was uncertain if he could win a fight with the invaders in his current condition. Zenti followed the little coward. The raccoon was fast and surprisingly good at maneuvering through the dark forest.

Zenti followed the raccoon for several hours as they weaved their way through the thick forest. The new buds were still heavy with moisture from the rain earlier in the day, and the ground smelled musty. Zenti let this sensation flow deep within his nostrils; the war had been so long, and his rage was consuming him more and more each day. The combination had made him forget such simple smells.

"Tell me, coon, why would you want to take me to this Mari? What would be in it for you," Zenti asked? He still did not believe Mari was alive as he kept telling himself that the invaders do not allow prisoners to live. His situation was an exception because the invaders needed him as a puppet.

"Because I owe her that much," the raccoon said with such ease it tasted of the truth. "She saved my neck, so I am doing her this favor. It's as simple as that."

Zenti was anything but convinced over this argument, but his Gift told him the raccoon was not lying about the debt owed. No matter the real reason, Zenti figured that he did not have much to lose since he'd already lost it all once.

~   ~   ~   ~

"I remember him," Mari said softly as she watched the memory, "he was going to be skewered by some of the camp guards. They claimed they had seen him conversing with **THEM**. I intervened because I did not want to believe that one of our own would freely aid the invaders. I know better now," Mari said and felt Zenti brush her mind, bringing her back into focus on the memories at paw. The crack in his mental armor was growing wider. Mari now knew Zenti was exhausted.

~   ~   ~   ~

Mari watched the two travel. The first few days were the most demanding. They were long days as Zenti did not want to sleep for fear of the combination of his wounds and mistrust of the raccoon. Zenti thought he might find himself on the losing end of a battle. His Gift was unimaginably strong, and he used it to keep himself in a state of mental alertness. Every time the raccoon slept, he took short naps himself.

The morning of the fifth day, Zenti found the raccoon tending his wounds after he had passed out. He could no longer hold on to the Gift. The Gift taxed the body, and his body was already taxed to the limit. The male raccoon jumped back the moment Zenti flinched. The traitor begging for a moment to explain.

"I mean you no harm, wolf; I could have killed you after you passed out. I do owe this debt to Miss Mari, and returning, you will pay it in full. I want to be able to sleep again at night," he said, hoping his words had gotten through to the now upright wolf as he backed away. Returning to the campfire, the raccoon stirred the food in the pot on the fire.

Nodding, Zenti sat leaned against the tree trunk he had passed out on. He was exhausted and needed both the food that was cooking and peaceful rest he denied himself.

"I am in no mood for small talk, but the food smells enjoyable, and I am hungry. Let us eat in peace and quiet, and then we can be on our way again. Though I do want to know where you are taking me. Where is this Mari's camp at," Zenti asked the raccoon?

Taking the plate of what appeared to be cooked oats with chunks of some sort of white fleshy fruit mixed in, Zenti nodded in thanks. The male raccoon stretched out as far as he could while offering Zenti the bowl of oats. Being near Zenti while he was unconscious was one thing; awake was quite another.

"Rotika over on the middle eastern shores, three weeks from Dairhal Bay," said the raccoon. Zenti cut the raccoon short by waving his story off. The gesture said, 'I know where it is.'

"Normally, I would say we take the main roads and be there in a week of driving. However, seeing as the invaders are looking for you, we best stay to the back roads, hunting trails, and creeks. It will take us almost a month by paw pad that way, considering the shape you are in. But at least you will not be caught in the condition you are in now," said the raccoon in between bites of his own meal.

"We will take a detour to Ditz, where you will go to the Crown Bank. I will give you a note, and you will give it to the Bank Manager. The manager will give you enough Breng for supplies and for a pack animal. I will require a lot more food than this or than we both can carry," Zenti said. The white wolf held his plate out for more. Zenti nodded thanks when the raccoon filled the plate again.

"Every receipt will be collected when you are done purchasing supplies. I will need clothing, preferably a bath-style robe, loose-fitting pants, shirts, and underclothing. The food will need to be high in protein. That means lots of meats, cheeses, and such. Do not skimp either. Spend all that you need. I will eat three times what you have fixed this morning each meal," Zenti said. With that explanation, the two sat quietly, finishing their meal.

Breaking camp, the two began what would be an uneventful trip to within a day of Rotika. Neither had spoken to the other much more than for necessity's sake. Zenti had grown stronger every day, finding a new strength he had never known. He never even asked the raccoon's name, having felt it was of no importance. The month seemed to pass quickly with them only traveling maybe a little more than ten miles a day to start, and by the end of the trip, they were traveling fifty miles a day.

"Well, wolf, I will go give Mari the message of where to find you. That is if she is still in her camp. If not, I will return with her location, and you can make your way there. At least your fur has grown in, hiding a vast majority of those nasty scars," said the raccoon as he began to leave.

"Take the pack animal with you; I have no need of it now. Consider it compensation for your guide services. I owe you this debt, traitor. I suggest you don't waste that debt consorting with *THEM* again," said Zenti, to which the raccoon nodded. He did not miss the implied meaning behind those cold, empty, hollow eyes of Summoner Zenti Semineu.

Chapter 6

The Dead

Tears continued to stream down Mari's muzzle uncontrollably. The link between her and Zenti remained unbroken, yet her claws had dug deeper into his muzzle. She did not realize that in her attempt to pull him out of the pain brought upon him by *THEIR* scientist, she was causing Zenti pain. Through tear-blurred eyes, Mari did not notice the blood dripping from the wounds she was now inflicting.

The vixen had never felt the link so strong between the two of them. Zenti almost held her telepathically captive. He showed her all the pain that had been the reason he 'abandoned' her. However, somewhere in the darkness of Zenti's mental armor, the vixen thought she found a chink. Mari felt his exhaustion from maintaining the link. It was a brief glimpse into his soul, and in a flash, she found herself in the clearing, some thirteen months ago, as he forcefully closed the small crack. That hard, mental shove pushed her back into the vision.

~   ~   ~   ~

The month of travel had done little more than superficially heal Zenti's wounds. A short, coarse layer of fur had started to grow and, thankfully, had stopped itching a week ago. The fur did not thoroughly hide the scars, but it was a start. With rest and a generous amount of high-quality food that the raccoon had bought, Zenti felt more robust than he had ever been before. However, Zenti's body was still recovering, and in a paw fight, he could potentially lose. That notwithstanding, the white wolf's access to the Gift was like a raging inferno, with seemingly limitless power.

Zenti felt the newness of the power coursing through his body. He was thankful to be able to test the expanse of what the Oracle had unlocked. To him, that is what the Oracle of Breest had done. The witch had removed something that limited his access to the Void. Zenti was unsure what the Oracle released, but he was sure he would figure it out in due time. However, the Oracles of Breest flinched when he called on his Gift back on the Isle of Breest. Goddesses' do not flinch.

At first, Zenti gently tested his access to the Void. But true to his nature, gentle was an invitation to death in his war with the invaders. Over the past month, he had discovered many new Talents. Perhaps, it was more accurate to say Summoner Zenti Semineu created new Talents. However, the white wolf doubted that the Oracle of Breest had actually provided him anything new. It was more as if she had removed all the moral boundaries.

It is those moral walls that cage the preverbal monster inside each of us. Whatever the Oracle of Breest did, she eroded the foundation of those walls. That set the monster free. Each passing day he felt those walls crumble. With each fallen wall, the white wolf began to understand just what the Oracle had meant. However, the Oracle was someone that he found repulsive, but he could not place a claw on why.

Sitting on a tree branch, Zenti looked skyward. The trees were on the outskirts of a small clearing. A home once stood at the center. Now all that remained was remnants of ash. The invaders had burned the house as a warning not to help the Factions. No one had returned, nor would anyone return. All the family members were burned along with the home. Zenti waited with anxious trepidation. This was the location the raccoon had designated for his meeting with Mari. He still did not believe she was alive. However, he hoped, for hope's sake, that she was alive. Zenti wondered why Mari had not come looking for him.

Zenti watched the clouds drifted across a soft blue sky. Golden rays of sunlight danced on lush, fresh green trees. The leave and grass were flush with water from earlier rains. Birds chirped, flitting about, in, and around the branches; they played the games of spring. The land of Mitd, after the bitter embrace of winter, was returning to life. The sweet smell of blossoms drifted on the breeze, and those fragrant aromas beckoned rare memories. Both Mari and he loved walking in the orchards near Eastern Provinces. Those were beautiful times they spent together. That is where the two began their war on the invaders and those who supported them. In the beginning, he and Mari had brief moments for the small luxuries of life.

The morning lazily drifted on. Zenti had arrived at this meeting place five hours early. The time allowed him to reflect, without distraction, on the changes in his life. One of those changes was the simple pleasures Mari and he shared. Zenti recalled those blissful times. Those memories flooded his mind, though they brought no joy. Something indeed was missing from him, and he knew only one way to get it back. Quietly he waited as he pondered how many of the invader's dead would it take to make him feel alive again.

Sitting back in the crook of the forked branches, Zenti drifted in and out of light sleep. It was the kind of sleep that brings fleeting nightmares. He could feel the scientist blades cutting into him again, and he would shudder awake only to drift off again. The interrupted dreams continued to repeat themselves until he could no longer sleep. Looking at the sun, he noticed it was past the noon hour. Zenti began to wonder if Mari would show as he attempted to quiet the butterflies in his stomach. He closed his eyes again and thought of Mari. Sighing, he looked back up to the sky, and to his surprise, the clouds had cleared, turning into a beautiful spring day, leaving him to wonder where the time went? Looking at his watch, another hour had slipped by.

Long moments passed while the silence of the forest punctuated the serenity of the afternoon. Nothing moved, nor was anything seemingly out of place. The sun filtered through the branches of the trees, and Zenti thought of leaving. Something on the far side of the clearing stirred.

At first, he thought it was the trick of lights and shadows when, suddenly, Mari stepped out of the tree line. She was at the edge of the woods, standing a single step into the clearing below. Zenti sniffed the air. It took a moment for her scent to reach him. It was faint and was heavily laced with descenter soap oil.

Had it not been for his Gift heightened senses, the white wolf would never have detected Mari's scent. However, the taste of the vixen's musk erupted in his mind. The white wolf's memories did not fail him as the vixen's scent flooded his nostrils. Zenti marveled at the brain's ability to remember even the tiny nuances of events. No matter how much he might try in the future, he doubted that he would ever forget Mari's scent.

What should have been sweet memories were all bitter now. Everything they had done together, every lesson learned, was but a black and white photograph of a vibrantly colored memory. That hollow feeling was not what Zenti wanted. Since his agreement with the Oracle of Breest, the white wolf felt the beauty of life begin to slip away. Though unsure why Zenti tried to hold on to the memories of him and Mari. However, those sweet memories were slipping through his paws. Zenti looked at the vixen across the way and felt the chasm growing wider between their bonds.

Mari's body was a bit more fleshed out. Though the vixen's muzzle seemed a little leaner. No matter those minor changes, Mari was just as she had always been. Her hair was longer now, just enough to catch his attention. The vixen looked none the worse for the wear, making him wonder why she had not come looking for him. Perhaps she had begun the search for him. Possibly Mari was not done searching when he escaped. However, Zenti knew he was lying to himself.

Mari stepped out of the trees in the warm midday sun and felt the rays embrace her tense body. Basking in the warmth, she felt the tension easing. Mari wondered how long it had been since he abandoned her, five months perhaps? Today she would end her connection and bonds to the vial betrayer Zenti Semineu.

~   ~   ~   ~

Kneeling in the tent, Mari tried to break the Talent of Union. She did not want to see this. Not now, not when the seeds of doubt were growing. However, nothing the vixen did could break the Talent of Union with Zenti. She felt a whisper of a psychic brush. The words were not bitter, but they evoked a bitter taste in her muzzle. *'You wanted to see,"* brush Zenti. However, the vixen relented, and the present again faded into the past.

~   ~   ~   ~

"Hello," Mari called out. The vixen touched the blade that was always strapped to her thigh. Her off paw moved to unsnap the strap on the new gun she had recently added to her other hip. Zenti smiled. She was ambidextrous and a deadly shot with either paw. "Who's there," Mari called.

"Have I been dead to you so long that you could forget your mate's scent," growled Zenti in a low voice? He tried to hide the hurt but was unsuccessful. His Gift carried his voice across the clearing. Shouting attracted attention; attention meant fighting. Right now, he did not want to fight. Zenti needed to understand her attitude. He felt a wave of disgust and hatred emanated from the vixen. Crouching on the tree branches just a dozen feet off the ground, he felt confused at the raw emotions she did not attempt to hide. Mari spun, pulling the pistol, and pointed in the direction of the voice. The vixen hesitated as she scanned the general area of the familiar voice.

Movement caught Zenti's eye, and he watched as the raccoon guide slipped off into the forest. He must have guided or followed Mari to the clearing. It appeared as if the raccoon changed directions many times before Zenti lost sight of him. Reaching out his Gift, Zenti wrapped the traitorous raccoon in the Talent of Life Sensing. With the warm red glow, visible only to someone using Gifted Sight, Zenti tracked the raccoon with his Gift as he traveled westward. Through the heightened senses of the Gift, Zenti followed the raccoon's sounds. Within a minute, the white wolf knew which direction the raccoon was finally traveling. He let the Gift fade, as the traitor was no threat. The emotions pouring out of the vixen regained Zenti's attention. Mari was still angry and made no attempt to hide her feelings.

Zenti repositioned himself. Now, if Mari spoke, she would be talking to him up in the trees with the sun at his back. Zenti was an expert at hiding himself within the shadows. A thousand thoughts were running through the white wolf's mind. Why had Mari left him in captivity?

Why was the vixen not dead? Everyone knew that the invaders did not keep captives. Why had his mate not searched for him? Why had Mari given up on him so quickly?

Zenti stopped the wild conjectures. The white wolf brought his analytical mind back into focus. He would not let his fear of losing Mari dictate or prejudice his perceptions of what might have happened. Mari deserved a chance to explain her story, and then he could come to his own conclusion. Zenti reminded himself that logic was always in control of emotion.

Mari's past-self reacted at the creaking of a branch and fired her pistol in the sound's direction. Zenti watched as a piece of bark explode off the tree. Had he not moved, the bullet would have hit his chest instead of tree bark. Mari shifted her aim directly at him.

~   ~   ~   ~

Mari's heart pounded as she watched the younger version of herself glare hard and shoot into the space that she was sure someone was sitting. Mari recalled that moment. She was convinced that she had caught a brief glimpse of an outline. Zenti leaped just before Mari's past-self pulled the trigger. Through the white wolf's enhanced Gifted reaction, he raced along tree branches better than a wild squirrel. Mari fired several more times. Though the shots were becoming more accurate, Zenti was just too fast. Mari's present-self realized that Zenti was much faster than he had ever been.

"I was wearing a binding that afternoon under my military dress," present-day Mari mumbled to herself. "I had fresh wounds that hadn't quite healed. Every twisting movement hurt," the vixen commented as she watched the dream-self wince a bit. The dream-self vixen had turned too fast and placed too much weight on her wounded leg. A mental growl snapped Mari back to the vision. Mari felt that Zenti was losing his grip on the Gifted Talent of Union. He was pushing himself too hard, but he offered to allow her to see the past. Mari knew there might not be another opportunity to learn the truth or for Zenti to learn the truth of her treatment of him.

~   ~   ~   ~

"You bastard," the younger Mari growled in a low voice! "I didn't forget your voice; I was hoping it wasn't you," as she reloaded the empty pistol. Zenti used that opportunity to expose himself to her. If it was Mari's intention to kill him, then he should make it easy for her. Life without Mari was not worth living. At that moment, the white wolf knew that the vixen was his world, his future, his life, and therefore his death if she wanted it. Still, her words cut deeper than any invader's scalpel.

"You hoped it was not me," Zenti asked in a mockingly, amused tone?. "How loving of you. Perhaps I should have forestalled my return considering the welcome I have received," he said, not moving when she brought the gun around. It was pointed at chest level. The two looked at each other, neither moving nor speaking.

This male was not the Zenti she remembered. His fur was shorter, and she thought perhaps there were a few scars. As the two of them were far enough apart, Mari could not confirm the report the raccoon gave her of Zenti's injuries. Something was different about Summoner Zenti Semineu. The vixen knew the feel of Zenti when he was using his Gift to create a wave of fear. The feeling she got from him did not feel like that. There was something fundamentally different about Zenti. Though she could not place the felling, it was nonetheless imposing. Mari had never been afraid of Zenti. He had never harmed or failed her until he abandoned her. However, Zenti's Gift had always caused her alarm.

The stories of a Gifted falling to the Voidal madness was a significant concern for all Mitdonians. Mari wondered if Zenti had begun that fall. The vixen felt a tinge of fear, and she backed away from the white wolf. For a moment, Mari's shadow-self's eyes grew wide with fear. However, her hot-tempered, kit-like attitude rose to the surface, and she glared at him fiercely.

"You should have forestalled it forever, in my opinion. You left me for dead," Mari snapped. Though her voice was unfaltering, there was an internal fight, and it could be discerned in each bitter word. The vixen's heart was twisting painfully in knots at seeing him.

"It is hard to leave someone for dead when you're lying face down in a pool of water. It's even harder to leave someone for dead when you get out of that said pool of water, and you are then attacked," Zenti retorted. He was becoming angry. However, the anger was for the invaders and their collaborators, not Mari. He knew she was as much a victim as he. Zenti tried to regain focus.

"I nearly died in jail!" Mari screamed, wincing slightly as she moved the wrong way, "But you wouldn't care about that, would you? You didn't even care where I was!"

"I didn't care?" Zenti snapped back, "I didn't care? You were all I thought about!"

"Yes, I'm sure," the vixen snapped, raising her gun level to his head, "I am not your mate!" she said darkly, "I will never be addressed as such again, do you hear me?"

Zenti turned to leave, his anger burning in the tips of his ears. He could smell the hot air rising from around his body. What was more, he could feel Mari's rage, and her hurt, all of it. Mari was a spoiled brat. Zenti wanted to blame her parents. However, that tasted dishonest. Yes, Haverick and Lillian Waxton were doting parents who spoiled their daughters. He could not lay the whole blame on them.

Zenti knew he had to take some of the blame. In the past nine years, not only had he not denied her anything she wanted, but he willing went out of his way to fulfill her desires. He struggled to remain calm, but the thought of her being a spoiled little brat about this was chafing at him.

The air around his body became hot enough to wilt the grass at his paw pads. Was this happen because he was angry, or was this effect of his Gift manifesting because she was enraged? Perhaps it was both? Was this yet another facet of his Gift unfolding? Could he now channel the rage of others? He would have to ask the old buzzard Torit about this new development.

However, Mari's reaction was not what he had expected. Especially from someone who claimed to have loved him unconditionally. Zenti recalled their past memories before being captured and allowed it to wash the anger from him. Zenti exhaled and let the anger flee. It was quickly replaced with yet another deep feeling. The sorrow of loss, not only of his family but now Mari, quickly quelled his temper. If she felt this strongly about him, then it was good things were coming to an end.

"Pull the trigger," Zenti said. The white wolf walked away. However, he stopped short when his Gift enhanced hearing heard the distinctive snap of a branch being stepped on. Looking back to the clearing, Zenti saw soldiers burst forth from the surrounding brush. In his anger-filled sorrow, Zenti had failed to keep a vigilant watch.

Mari spun around and dropped to the ground with a roll, firing on the hostile soldiers. They were not hers; therefore, they were the enemy. Two fell to the vixen's deadly aim as Zenti stepped into the clearing and fired at the soldiers. They did not follow his command and were openly hostile. Though they could have shot Mari at any time, it was clear they were trying to capture Mari.

Three continued to press the attack on Mari while four erupted from nearby scrubs. They were Mitdonian, yet attacked with the invader's shock rods. Zenti shot one and then called on his Gift and burned the other three beyond recognition. When he turned to survey the situation, Mari was standing in the clearing with multiple dead at her paw pads. She had the gun leveled at Zenti. The expression on Mari's muzzle was clear. It said she thought these were his troops until she saw the four smoldering bodies around him. The gun never wavered as she pointed it at Zenti. That act pushed the white wolf further away. Again he turned and walked away.

"Pull the trigger; it will look as if they killed me. That is what you wanted," Zenti growled. Those were the last words Mari heard as he walked towards the forest.

Mari's paws shook, and she tried to pull the trigger. The conflict inside the vixen raged, yet her digit would not move. Why would he abandon her then defend her? However, the vixen's kit-like anger overrode her common sense. Zenti vanished into the trees as she stood there. Mari did not know how long she had remained rooted in that spot, shaking. It must have been for a long while. When she heard Zenti howl, it had the hollow ring brought on by distance. The vixen knew that howl. It was one of rage, a rage she had seen when he was on the brink of losing all control.

When sounds of Zenti's rage-filled howl left the woods, the quiet of the spring day returned. Mari finally stopped shaking and slowly put the gun back in its hip holster. It was over; she had said what she had come to say. Looking up to the sunny sky, the vixen opened her arms and allowed the warmth to penetrate the coldness of her anger. Turning back toward her camp, Mari let the golden ring she had brought with her hit the ground. It was over, and she could now move on.

~   ~   ~   ~

Mari's present-self watched the old memory as tears continued to flow down her muzzle. The vixen had not felt them start again, but she could smell their salty essence. These tears were not for the pain that *THEY* inflicted upon Zenti, but the pain she had inflicted. Then, before the vixen knew what was happening, the world around her dissolved into a watery smear of colors. Mari found herself right where she started the night. She was kneeling before her cot, back in her tent. The vixen was still clutching Zenti's muzzle in her paws as tears ran down her cheeks. Through tear-blurred eyes, she watched as his blood oozed over the tips of her claws.

The vixen had not known back then, but that was no excuse. Mari assumed that Zenti abandoned her and thought that he was more interested in saving himself than her. Her own memories flooded her thoughts of their past together. She recalled every battle they had fought in, every wound he had taken to save her when she had gotten too reckless. Memories surfaced of how Zenti would travel for a week just to get her a bit of fruit that she craved.

It was in this flood of memories that she realized

just who had been the one to abandon whom. Before she could stop herself, she was holding onto him, her arms around his neck, one set of claws digging into his back and the other into her own wrist. She held onto him, silent, as she cried. The vixen laid her head on his chest and sobbed.

"I'm sorry," she rasped after what seemed like an hour of crying. Mari's cheek pressed against the fur of Zenti's chest, her ears laying flat in apology, "I am so very sorry." She felt the multitude of knotted scars, and her ears drooped even more.

His arms hung at his side as she hugged him; he did not hug her in return as he had in the past. She did not blame him; she understood she had acted like a kit. His breathing was deep and slow from the exhaustion of maintaining the Gifted Talent of Union as well as the Talent of Soul's Self. Mari could hear the grating of the metal in his chest as he breathed. Fresh was the painful memories of how it had those knotted scars were formed.

Mari recalled her captivity. It was now evident that her imprisonment was just a speck of discomfort compared to Zenti's torturous ordeal. In the grand picture, all the vixen had done to her was kept in a cell. Someone had tended her wounds. She did not starve, nor was she tortured. Her captivity was civil compared to the brutal assault Zenti endured. The tears continued to freely flow as the memories lingered.

The vixen continued to cry as she thought of the wounds and pain Zenti had suffered at the whim of *THEIR* scientists, and yet the hurt she felt the most from him was her very own words. 'I am not your mate.' In those five words, the vixen had caused more harm than any instrument. What had it done to the male who had given more for her than the whole of Mitd combined? Mari leaned back on her calves and looked up at the most selfless male she had known since her father. There was the look of a lost pup on his muzzle, a look of defeat. However, his black eyes held the cold, hard stare of a soul filled with unrelenting rage. Around the corona of Zenti's black pupils, a halo of flickering red glowed. It was more brilliant now than she had known it in the past. Before, the red halo was just a pale shade of umber around his once golden eyes.

"Remember the town of Dotharian," Zenti asked? His voice was distant and hollow. He saw Mari nod, yes, but she did not stop crying, "The invaders used it as a collection camp. It was there all the spoils of war were warehoused."

Mari understood his meaning of the word 'spoils.' The captured Mitdonians were considered nothing more than war spoils. They were warehoused as if they were nothing more than excess merchandise. However, Mari knew that any 'spoil' of war was soon disposed of. She had found many bodies of those warehoused. What the invaders did to them was now clear to her. **THEY** were looking for the Gifted. That was not the only thing the invaders wanted, but she now understood why so many bodies were mutilated. They were test subjects. Mari looked back up to Zenti.

"There were those of our species who were not immediately executed. Some were slaves to be used and thrown away when they were no longer productive. Others chose to willingly serve them instead of fight for their freedom," Zenti said. The white wolf took a deeper breath, shuttering a little when he let it slowly escape; he was exhausted.

"Until then, I never knew the invaders took prisoners and let them live. They are not really prisoners; they are bodies to be abused until they are no longer useful. Then they are used for target practice or experimentation," Zenti explained. His last words had a haunting finality to them. Mari hugged him again and noticed he did not pull away, nor did he hug her back. The vixen accepted that he might not ever forgive her.

Mari felt Zenti draw a breath, and the grating of the metal in his body could be loudly heard as his chest expanded. What he had endured caused the vixen to sob even more. Again, the lingering memory of what he had suffered because of her kit-like action brought on more tears. She could feel the multitude of wounds on his back, and her paws trembled as she failed in her attempted to find a spot unscarred.

Mari started at the base of his skull, tracing all the way to the base of his tail. Not one spot could she find that did not have a gnarled knot. Though there were many knots across Zenti's back, nothing compared to the digit[17] thick knot that she followed back up from his tail to head.

"Dotharian was the first place I came upon after leaving you. I was full of rage that my mate could treat me the way she did. It was the first place on my list of cities to liberate from the invader's presence. It was there, at Dotharian, that I knew what the Oracle had truly unlocked in me," Zenti said. His voice held a trace of bitter anger. Again, he drew a deep breath and let out a heavy sigh. "It was the place I had chosen to die. Obviously, only one of the two events happened."

Mari bowed her head in shame as the shared memories were fresh in her mind. However, Zenti searched the lingering effects of the Talent of Soul's Self. There was a remnant of implanted memory in Mari's thoughts; someone had manipulated the vixen's memories or perceptions. That revelation helped the white wolf comprehend Mari's bitter reaction to being captured. Someone had implanted the thought it was Zenti who abandoned Mari. However, Mari had rejected everything of their past because she was still immature in some aspects. Summoner Zenti Semineu felt fatigued but knew there was still more to be done.

"Ex-excuse me, ma'am," came a female voice. Mari jumped. The vixen was so lost in the memories of her

---

[17] Jaydonians do not call their digits fingers. Though they share similarities to human fingers, the range of motion that Jaydonian digits have is far greater than most other species in the universe. Also, all Jaydonians have retractable claws. Several species in the universe share this trait as well.

shameful actions that she forgot where she and Zenti were. The female's voice ended that forgetful moment and Mari released Zenti.

Pulling herself away from the wolf, she looked at him. His eyes seemed so empty, not in defeat, but merely empty. Mari hesitated, then leaned into the white wolf's muzzle and licked the blood oozing from the wounds caused by her claws. When Zenti did not pull away, the vixen licked the other side of his muzzle. Mari paused with a moment of trepidation, then licked his lips, pressing her tongue against his gums. That, by all standards, was considered a base animal act. However, it also symbolized the deepest of apologies, respect, or love that a Jaydonian could display.

Mari stepped back and lowered her ears again. Zenti nodded to the tent door. He knew that this moment was over, the truth had been shared, and nothing more could be said on the subject. Zenti also knew how Mari's Faction relied on her heavily. Turning, the vixen headed for the tent entrance and opened the door. Mari's tent was a command tent model. It had a wooden framed door with a cloth-covered top half. When rolled up, the cloth revealed an upper screen. Standing at the door was a young parrot, who jumped as the door suddenly swung open.

Mari winced. The daylight hurt her eyes, but Mari could see clear enough when the parrot gasped. The female parrot offered a pawkerchief as she saw the tear-soaked fur, bloodshot red eyes, and blood-stained claws. Mari smiled at the young female in appreciation and took the offered pawkerchief. Mari wiped her muzzle and claws. Looking at the now blood-stained while cloth, Mari could clearly see the blood in the mid-morning sun. It was in that mid-morning light that Mari realized she had been crying all night.

"What did you need?" Mari sweetly asked of the young Rochet.

The parrot was a small thing, not much past her Gifting Day. She fidgeted as Mari looked down into her young face. Smiling, she lifted the parrot's beak up and gave her a wink of reassurance as she put her paw on her head.

"Ricket says that there are soldiers on the way here. They should be here late this evening," Rochet said nervously. The young parrot tried not to look Mari in the face, partly out of respect, partly out of fear, having never seen her matron cry.

"Did he say who the soldiers were," the vixen asked, while earnestly trying to hide the shaking in her voice? Rochet was too young to join in any fighting, but she was an excellent messenger.

The parrot shook her head, but it was evident that she was still nervous about her patron's current condition. Rochet turned to Zenti, looking through the tent flap. The little parrot began to tremble. Everyone knew of the white wolf Summoner. Mari put a claw on the muzzle of the young digitigrade parrot and made direct eye contact.

Bumping Rochet's nose with her own, Mari gave it a quick, reassuring lick.

"Did you order soldiers to follow after you," Mari asked of Zenti? The vixen gave him a stout glare while petting the young female on the head. This was still her Faction camp. No matter the circumstances, he was no more in command than another visiting Faction Leader.

"No, Mari. I have no soldiers. No one is brave enough to follow my direct lead," the white wolf replied. It was a half-truth. His faction would follow him into battle if he asked, but they did not freely offer to follow the companion of Vzdoch[18].

Still, Mari does not trust me, Zenti thought. Honestly, he could not expect Mari to. It had been over a year since their last meeting when she said he was no longer her mate. The white wolf did not expect anything to change overnight. No matter the truth of events, the past thirteen months had changed the white wolf. Now what fool would follow me, thought Zenti? Vzdoch was his only companion, and they had become the best of friends. No one wanted to follow someone who kept death as his only acquaintance. He shook his head and looked at the silver ring still on his ring digit. Quietly he slipped it off and laid it on Mari's desk when the vixen turned away from him again.

---

[18] Vzdoch is the Jaydonian personification of death. Unlike all other personifications of death, Vzdoch is an escort of the dead to the stars. Though not evil, Vzdoch is feared because she represents the end of life.

"I will take my leave of you now," Zenti said as he stepped outside of the tent.

Even in the light of mid-morning, others stepped as far back from Zenti as possible. Those who did not see the white wolf enter Mari's tent stared at him with a shocked look on their muzzles. It was with that shocked looked on her patron's muzzles that Mari looked Zenti. In the dim light of her tent, she had not noticed that Zenti was bleeding from his eyes, ears, and gums. The closer Mari looked, the more she thought that Zenti had even been bleeding from his pores. However, it was the cold, heartless look in his eyes that evoked fear from her patrons.

"I will be near until I am sure the soldiers that young Rochet speaks of mean you no harm. I do know that the remainder of what was my Northern Faction wishes to meet with you. It is my understanding they wish to discuss plans of some sort. There is a great battle coming, and it is not safe without the force of numbers. I hope you will entertain their offer. I, however, have work to do now," said Zenti. The white wolf's look told her that this 'work' was not war, but execution at best, murder in any other times. When Zenti looked down at the little parrot, Mari slipped into the tent.

Zenti remembered when Rochet was whelped. "You have grown up to be quite the young female. You do your late father proud with the way you report," offered Zenti.

The white wolf thought of ruffling the little parrot's

feather-soft hair but decided that perhaps it would be too traumatic. He knew his reputation. Zenti turned and headed to the south.

"Zenti," Mari called after Zenti. Mari watched as he turned to look at her. She thought his fur did have a silvery tinge to it. "Take your ring with you," she said softly.

He could have smirked at the determined look on Mari's muzzle. Zenti did not think that she had seen him put it down. However, it was apparent a lot had changed since he had last been this close to her. She had grown as a soldier and leader; the vixen was a lot more observant. He made a mental note of that.

Zenti stepped up to Mari and looked at the silver ring in her open paw. He thought of what the ring represented. He understood what it would mean to the future of his species. What the silvery-white wolf knew he had to do would scar the vixen forever. She would have to walk in the wake of his destruction. His heart and mind fought a war. Fighting an action, his heart did not want to take his mind finally won the battle. He looked Mari in the muzzle.

"Last we talked, you ended this mating. Hayden, however, will not be pleased, or have you not heard," Zenti asked? He waited for some response but got only an empty stare, "He is to offer- um how was it put, ah yes- a 'gift that will bring unity and peace' to Mitd. He intends it as a mating gift. In the past month, I have heard a lot about his intentions. Surely, you have noticed how more and more he is always near to you," said Zenti.

"Oh, please," huffed Mari. Zenti smiled inside. That was the attitude of the Mari he knew.

"All of Mitd knows your rebuke of me over a year ago. It has spread everywhere. Everyone knows that I am a betrayer. Rumors abound that I abandon my species at first sight of danger. Now they know I kill both the invaders and our race without remorse," Zenti looked at the ring and then closed her paw around it.

"No, Mari, this ring binds you to a hated. It will only weaken your position as Faction Leader. That creates disloyalty. I did not come here to seek forgiveness or for a reunion. I came so that the truth would be known of me, even if only to you. You are the only one that has ever mattered," he turned to leave again, "remember what they say of me. Remember how I am hated, feared, and a vile betrayer. It could have only come from two sources, Mari. Your father thought I was the best hope for protecting you. I failed in protecting your family ten years ago when the invaders slaughtered them." Instantly Mari's ears folded back in apology. She had said a great many disparaging things about Zenti to anyone who would listen.

Looking out over the Faction camp, Zenti did not miss the fear-filled muzzles of her patrons. "I have failed your father twice now," said Zenti. The absolute emptiness in his voice reminded her of the shared visions. "At least you know the truth."

"Zenti," Mari began, but he held up a paw. The vixen fell silent. There was no arguing with Summoner Zenti Semineu when he reached a decision.

"However, those failures I can at least pay for in blood; both mine and the enemies of Jayden," the silvery-white wolf said. This time he did not stop walking away.

Mari watched Zenti go. It was true. She had heard that Hayden had planned on asking her to be his mate again. However, she had never even entertained the idea that she would say yes. Zenti had drawn the conclusion that she intended to accept Hayden's offer. The silver ring sat in the blood-stained fur on the palm of her paw. Mari wondered how much blood was indeed on her paws because she wrongly accused Zenti of betrayal.

Sighing lightly, Mari headed back into her tent. Removing the key that she wore around her neck from under her shirt. The vixen unlocked her writing desk's top drawer. There lay her ring of gold. She had gone back that night thirteen months ago to where she met Zenti. Mari had gone back and searched until morning for that ring. Upon finding her mating band, Mari cleaned it then tucked it into her dress's inner pocket. That morning, thirteen months ago, Mari Seminue made the longest metaphorical walk of her life. Now the vixen had another long walk to make, one of recompense. Exiting the tent, the vixen watched as Zenti continued to walk away.

Mari did not know the reason she kept her mating band. Perhaps it was as a keepsake to remind her of his misdeeds and betrayal. Mari returned to her tent, wiped the silver ring clean of his blood, placed it into the top drawer beside her gold band, and relocked the desk. Her tent was a mess, and so was she. That was something she needed to remedy before she got to attending camp business.

Opening the tent door, she told the little parrot to bring her breakfast and a basket for laundry. Watching the Rochet run towards the laundry tent, Mari motioned to Jolet to come over.

"Tell the Elders that I will meet with them in two hours. Also, please ask someone to have a shower ready in an hour," she said, looking at her still bloody paws. He nodded yes and moved to implement her orders. She went back inside and began the laborious process of straightening out the mess.

****

Zenti quietly walked out of Mari's encampment and was soon lost from sight. He traveled perhaps another hour, then abruptly pulled up beside a big-branched tree. Though he was exhausted, Zenti climbed some twenty feet up into the tree. Hung within the lush green leave was his backpack. It was right where he left it. Very few would think of looking up in a tree for anything. Reaching into his pack, he pulled a small device from a pouch-like pocket.

It looked like an ordinary wristwatch with two buttons and a central disk. The band itself was made of flexible metal. Zenti slipped it on with practiced ease. He pushed one of the two buttons and watched as a blue disc on the device spun for a few seconds and then stopped. It showed almost a full circle with only a tiny sliver missing. Reaching into another pouch-like pocket on the backpack, Zenti pulled out a pair of oversized sunglasses with an elastic band. They almost resembled ski goggles. He put them on the top of his head, securing the strap behind his ears. They did not appear to be made for his species, but they still fit, though awkwardly.

Zenti waited another twenty minutes. The white wolf had felt the presence of deceit in Mari's camp when he first entered. The Gift allowed for many possibilities if you knew how to manipulate a given Talent. The silvery-white wolf had been experimenting with his Gift since his encounter with the Oracle of Breest. There was unlimited potential in each Talent if the Gifted were willing to pay the price for experimentation.

When a Gifted understood that taxing the body was acceptable to learn or expand a Talent, the rewards were significant. It was when you pushed too far into the Void that the Voidal Madness devoured you. Zenti had pressed too far on occasions but had the willpower to resist the madness. In exchange, his Talents had vastly grown. With the Talent of Life Sensing, when employed with the Talent of Union, the white wolf could detect others' intentions. However, it was taxing to the body. That combination of

Talents was how Zenti determined he would be followed.

Right on the schedule was Mari's third in command. The male rabbit stopped directly beneath where the silvery-white wolf was perched. Zenti thought that the male rabbit was not a bad tracker. However, Zenti had also not been entirely covert when he departed Mari's Faction Camp. He pulled the pair of glasses down and adjusted the strap behind his ears. Zenti then pushed the second button on the watch he had just put on. The white wolf's body faded from sight, leaving nothing but his scent and the scent of Mari's tears on his fur. His species possessed the ability to track others by their musk. The rabbit could easily detect him. That problem was Zenti quickly rectified. Using his Gift, Zenti heated the air close around his body and burned off any lingering scent of sweat, tears, or blood.

It did not take long for the rabbit to find the apparent paw prints Zenti had left at the base of the tree. So, this was Hayden's spy, Mari's third in command, thought Zenti. Though Zenti's primary goal for speaking with Mari was to show her the truth of what happened to him, he also wanted to follow up on a rumor. The last village that he burned to the ground was infiltrated by those who supported the invaders. One of the final traitors he interrogated revealed that Hayden had placed spies within the Faction Camps. Only his Northern Faction had not been infiltrated. The fact that Zenti was still the official, though distant, Northern Faction leader was a closely guarded secret. That deficiency was necessary for several reasons. Perhaps he would need to return and check for any

385

traitors. However, that was not important this instant; the rabbit was.

The white wolf had never been fond of General Hayden or the losses he would inflict on his own troops just to achieve a victory. However, Zenti did respect his ability to win battles. Hayden would use any strategy or tactic but one. That one tactic Zenti intended to exploit. With a few final adjustments, the white wolf was satisfied with the fit of the glasses. Looking down at the rabbit, the white wolf smiled.

The glasses were invader's technology, as was the wristwatch-like device. The glasses distorted the view of most everything around him, but they were necessary when used with the PRISM device. That was the name of the wristwatch device. Zenti was unsure of the exact acronym's meaning. Still, it was only a matter of time before he could fully comprehend the invader's language. However, with a bit of practice, Zenti had become accustomed to the distortions caused by the glasses.

The white wolf might not have an ounce of love for the invaders, but he knew the invader's technology was superior to their own. Why not turn the captured technology to his advantage, thought Zenti? The rabbit, Jolet, started searching for Zenti's prints that circled around the trees' base. Zenti watched and counted. How skilled was this spy at his craft?

After a few moments, Jolet concluded that the white wolf had climbed a tree. Taking out a pair of binoculars,

Jolet searched the trees several times before giving up. Putting the binoculars away, the rabbit pulled a two-way radio out of his pack. Zenti knew the large communications device was not the invader's technology. Was this rabbit just a spy for Hayden or a traitor to Mitd? Zenti called on his Gift and his senses instantly sharpened.

"Seeker to Lost-and-found, come in," Jolet said in a low voice. The rabbit had a good enough grasp of the invader's language. Jolet now had the undivided attention of Summoner Zenti Semineu.

"Go ahead, Seeker," came back the voice.

"I am afraid I have lost him. He has just vanished," answered Jolet.

"A new Talent of his Gift," asked the voice?

Zenti could not place the accent, but the unknown speaker's words were in a broken form of invaders' language. However, it sounded like one of his breed speaking. Zenti thought that the rabbit had a better grasp of the invader's tongue than the unknown speaker.

"Very possible," replied Jolet.

"Very well, what did you learn last night," asked the voice?

"The conversation was minimal. It seems as if Mari wanted to learn what had made Zenti betray her. I have three recordings discs of nothing but silence with only a hushed comment or two by Mari. In the later parts of the recordings, there are the sounds of crying. Zenti said almost nothing after he asked if she really wanted to see what had happened to him. I am not sure what transpired between the two of them. However, the recording device worked perfectly. Honestly, it just seems for almost twelve hours, something happened, but it did not occur verbally. I do not know how to describe it. I could hear breathing and crying and the occasional words. Still, it was not muffled, and everything was adjusted correctly," Jolet said into the radio in a hushed whisper.

"Anything else to report,'" the voice asked?

"Yes," said Jolet, "Zenti gave Mari his mating ring. He said something about being hated, and it would only cause her harm. I gathered from the tears just before the conversations restarted that Mari had seen what had really happened. Perhaps she had forgiven him and wanted him back. Also, Zenti said he had 'work' to do and that only blood would pay for his crimes or something similar. It is all on the discs," the rabbit reported. Zenti noted that the rabbit spoke in hushed tones, suggesting he thought his target was still around.

"Very well, look for him a little longer. A platoon of soldiers should be at her camp in a few hours. You being gone will not be missed for another hour or so. Return to camp before then," replied the voice.

"As you command," said Jolet. The rabbit was about to turn the radio off when another came on.

"If you find Zenti, do not try and kill him. You are

more valuable where you are in Mari's camp than as a corpse. He will kill you. He has grown much stronger than he was ever intended to. You alone will not be able to harm him. Lost-and-Found out," commented a smooth, sophisticated voice over the radio before ending the call. The new voice spoke the invader's language fluently. Zenti almost growled at the new speaker's voice.

"What do you think I am, an idiot," said a sarcastic Jolet to the radio after he turned it off?

Zenti knew that disembodied voice, and his fur stood on end. It was the panther Hayden. Was the panther involved with the invaders? Zenti looked down at the radio the rabbit was using. It was one of his species radios. Though he could not tell the model from this distance, its general size and shape limited its range to no more than ten miles. Zenti thought that a ten-mile radius was a pretty big area to search in just a few hours.

Zenti watched as Jolet searched some more, and when the rabbit moved away from the base of the tree, Zenti turned the PRISM device off and removed the glasses. Zenti took a moment to shake off the disorienting effects of the glasses. It only took a moment, but he knew he needed to work on reducing the disorientation effects. When Zenti's head cleared, he then took a scrap paper and wrote a brief note to Mari.

Jolet completed his search, which led him back beneath the tree Zenti was in. With a disappointed look, Jolet began the trek back to Mari's Faction Camp.

However, the rabbit was secretly relieved that he had not found the white wolf. Jolet regretted that the war had devolved to a point where Jaydonian felt the need to switch allegiances. However, he felt the war was about to be lost. Though he loved Miss Mari, Jolet knew that if the vixen returned to Zenti, Mitd would turn into a slaughterhouse. Jolet was sure that the butcher's bill would be excessive, and it would be the white wolf who would collect the tab.

Zenti waited a short while longer as he watched the rabbit slip into deeper woods. Jolet was just about out of visual range when Zenti acted. Rapidly tapping the first button on the device, Zenti released the PRISM device from his wrist, and he put it away. Focusing on a large branch above Jolet, Zenti called on his Gift and shattered the limb at its base. The wood cracked loudly. Jolet looked up, but the Gift splintered branch fell towards the startled rabbit at an alarming speed. The rabbit was so distracted that he never saw the blurred form of the silvery-white wolf rapidly approaching.

Jolet jumped aside, barely making it out of the way, as the piece of thick tree branch fell in front of him. Looking up to make sure no more were falling, the rabbit screamed in terror as a large shadow covered his body.

＊＊＊＊＊＊＊＊＊＊＊＊＊＊＊＊＊＊＊＊＊＊＊＊＊＊＊＊＊＊

"Ma'am!" Mari looked up suddenly as Ricket, older brother to Rochet, burst into Mari Semineu's tent. Ricket was dressed in his usual vest, pants, and forest green cap. He had his rifle slung across his back.

Mari smiled at Rochet's older brother. He was also of the parrot species, and the vixen thought he was as cute as his younger sister. Rochet was excitable, but he was also observant and very dependable. Mari waited for him to catch his breath. The young male must have run all the way from the forward observation post.

"Soldiers have been sighted, and they'll be here in a few hours!" Rochet blurted out.

Smiling, Mari raised a paw for the pre-Coming-of-Age parrot to calm down and gather his thoughts. Though she loved his enthusiasm and his dedication to freeing Mitd, he needed to calm down.

"Now start all over, Ricket, like I have taught you," Mari said. The vixen was ever the teacher. She was good at it. She should be, her father, General Waxton, was the best teacher, and the vixen wanted desperately to honor her father's memory.

"One of our scouts on the western roads spotted a platoon of Mitdonian soldiers on the march towards our camp. At their current pace, they should be here by nightfall. Their uniforms are devoid of insignia," said the young parrot.

Giving a stern nod, the vixen snaked around her desk then around him. On the way out of the tent, the vixen patted Ricket on the shoulder in appreciation. Stepping outside, she noted that it was well past noon. After Zenti left, Mari spent an hour in meetings with the Faction Elders and then a light lunch. The vixen had returned to her tent to contemplate the Elders' needs. However, she had given very little attention to the needs of the Elders. Instead, during that time, she had just sat and stared at the two mating bands.

Mari wondered how long she had been sitting there looking at the two rings before Ricket interrupted her thoughts? It was now past two, and she pondered where had the time gone. Mari rechecked her watch to just make sure she was not mistaken. What was it she had been thinking about, where had her mind wandered? However, her patrons and soldiers were counting on her leadership.

"Start evacuating to the tunnels," Mari ordered, "female caregivers, pups, and the elderly first. Any patrons who are capable of fighting will set up defenses. Those not working are to go to the armory tent and arm themselves for defense. This may be the remnants of a combat team who got separated from their main body. However, we cannot be cautious enough. There are traitors everywhere. Where is Jolet?"

Ricket gave a nervous shuffle but kept his eyes on his commander. The young male was still afraid to offer his superiors an unfavorable report. However, he had been steadily improving and quickly straightened up.

"No one's seen him in the last few hours, ma'am," Ricket answered. Mari sighed; she hated being called that.

"Find him and tell him that I want him to roll-check all of those evacuated," ordered Mari.

Ricket saluted and headed off to carry out her orders. Mari set off, pushing her way through the crowd of citizens heading towards the armory tent. Truth be told, it was only called the armory because it sheltered a few guns and some body armor. Her Faction camp was significantly reduced in strength. Most of the combat troops were on loan to other Factions. Those soldiers who were here were recovering from battle wounds. Her camp also was the home to many displaced civilians.

Mari entered the tent and grabbed an armored vest. Her personal body armor vest was being repaired. Slipping the vest on, she tested it for fit. It would suffice. The vixen also selected a scoped rifle. Though she preferred an assault rifle, she knew that her place was in command. She could not command from the front defensive lines, but she could single out enemy leaders and neutralize them.

Checking the rifle's ammunition, Mari picked up another three magazines before heading out of the tent. The vixen passed other troops who had begun preparing crew weapons. There were a plethora of heavy weapons, but most were being repaired. With her Faction's reduced fighting capacity, it had become a temporary repair facility for other Factions.

There was a bustle of controlled chaos as the camp evacuated into the tunnels. Describing the decrepit holes in the ground as a tunnel was being generous, Mari thought. The tunnels were filthy abandoned mineshafts. Though there were no tall hills or mountains here, only sparse patches of forests, low rolling hills, and open plains, the area was rich in minerals. However, the lack of heavy equipment meant that those minerals were mainly inaccessible. These shallow mines had been played out years ago. They were poorly excavated, and the minerals were haphazardly extracted. Now the mines were too toxic for a long-term stay. Since the start of the war, there were just not enough workers to clean them out or dig deeper. With the destruction of most of Mitd's heavy industry, the ability to produce new equipment was severely limited.

Most of Mitd was generally in this wretched condition. The invaders, and those who supported them, had not stuck at the key cities directly. Instead, they had destroyed the manufacturing facilities and the mining operations. It was a brilliant tactic, one her father would have employed. Denying an enemy of their base materials and their current stockpiles was a proven tactic. However, Mitdonian law prevented the destruction of civilian infrastructure in Barrony conflicts. **THEY** were under no such restrictions.

The few soldiers, all of who were recovering from various battle wounds, scurried as best they could to their positions. They began setting up a crossfire as well as secondary and tertiary lines. Mari looked over her troops. They were well trained, though most were still physically nowhere near ready for heavy combat operations. However, most of the time, the battle never wait until you were fully prepared. Mari knew they did not have enough heavy firepower here. There were just the recovering wounded and civilians. However, everyone knew the consequences of failure.

A little over four hours to secure the camp had passed, and Mari was pleased with the way her staff handled the critically wounded and Elders. Had the camp been more than a recovery center, they would have been ready in a quarter of that time, but she was still pleased with their progress. Those who served under the vixen had faith in her ability to lead. She was Miss Mari to all. Why Mari did not know, yet those who served the Crown and Jayden loved her.

Mari barked orders, and soldiers fell into place. Just then, Jolet came up behind her. The rabbit snapped to attention when she turned to face him. The vixen started to chew him out for not being here in the camp when he abruptly handed her a piece of paper. His eyes looked a bit glazed, and his fur was unusually disheveled, she noticed.

"A message Ma'am, a mutual friend from the Pots, asked me to deliver it," the rabbit said as he handed Mari the paper. Mari noted that the rabbit seemed disoriented the moment she took the note from his paw. Jolet began to scurry off, but Mari stopped him and gave him orders to roster all those hiding in the caves. For a moment, the rabbit looked lost but quickly regained his composure.

He saluted again sharply and darted off. Mari noticed that he had a substantial abrasion on the side of his head. Before stepping into her tent, Mari looked at the area again. Her keen eye made sure all was in preparation.

Satisfied, she stepped into the privacy of the tent and opened the slip of paper.

'*Hayden comes with his troops to talk to you. It was Hayden who sent this spy after me. The panther is in the company of the invaders, who are nearby. There is a plan being formed. I am not sure of what, but if Hayden works with the invaders, you best watch your tail. I have gone hunting. Let us see what I can find. Jolet is a spy for Hayden. Keep him on a short leash, though personally, a noose would be my choice. He will not recall this conversation with me but will remember everything else in time.*'

Mari was about to throw the note away when she noticed a splatter of blood at the bottom of the page. Touching the drop of blood, an image of Zenti rushed through her mind as if he were right there. It was a visage of him kneeling before her on the day she accepted his paw in mating. Stunned that a drop of blood could evoke such a memory, she wondered why she could feel that.

Was this another aspect of Zenti's Gift? Her sister, Rini, said that Blood Memory was a Gifted Talent possessed only by Shamans. She wondered again what it was about Summoner Zenti Seminue that allowed him to have such Gifts. The Gifted on Mitd had many and varied Talents. Those many Talents fell under three classifications of the Gift, each with their own unique ability.

There was the Summoner, the rarest of The Gifted.

A Summoner's Gift involved manipulating one of the elements through touch or contact. It was also the most physically demanding of the three Gifts. A Summoner drew power from their body, and, with overuse, it would shorten their life span considerably.

The Shaman was a healer who had limited divination Talent. That Talent was mainly known as the Talent of Blood Memories because they required a drop of the seeker's blood. Shaman's had the greatest of the healing powers of any Gifted. The Shaman could be extremely dangerous in a fight because not only could they heal a wound with a touch, but a Shaman could also inflict wounds.

Lastly, there was the Oracle who had the Gift of 'Dream Sight.' However, the non-Gifted simply called it Visions. They had limited healing ability and were amazingly effective defenders. It was easy to defend against something when an Oracle knew what would happen before it happened.

Most of the Gifted only had one Gift, though they possessed a few shared minor Talents. It was rare for a Gifted to use two Gifts, and when they did, they were only mediocre at each Gift. How was it that Zenti had shown her aspects of all three Gifts? Mari thought about the shared memory and how the Oracle of Breest said Zenti had access to multiple Gifts. There were more significant issues that required her immediate attention.

She stuffed the note into her pocket. Mari had

incoming troops to contend with. However, the vixen
could not believe Zenti could use all three Gifts, yet the
blood on the tip of her digit suggested otherwise. The
vixen rubbed two digits together and when she did, another
memory stirred inside of her. Mari Waxton Semineu
recalled her dying father's final warning. The dying lion
said something about the invaders looking for two
Summoners. Did he mean Zenti had two Gifts?

Jolet came to her tent. With the clearing of his
throat, the rabbit interrupted Mari's memories. The vixen's
fur stood on end when she saw Jolet. However, if Zenti
had not killed a known traitor, then there must be a reason
the rabbit was still alive. Perhaps the rabbit would be
useful in the future. Biting away her initial instinct to kill
the traitor, Mari stepped outside and listened to Jolet's
report. The rabbit was, if nothing, efficient. With Jolet's
information, it seemed that everyone was accounted for.

The moment Mari knew that everyone was where
they were supposed to be, she grabbed the little traitor by
his ears, punched him in the stomach, and drove him to his
knees. Yelling for Ricket, Mari glared down at Jolet's
fearful muzzle. Ricket and a companion came running.
Waiting for Ricket and the weasel to stop and salute, Mari
threw the rabbit into the weasel companion's grasp.

"Get this traitor out of my sight, string him up by
his ears and paw pads if he resists. Put him in one of the
empty sheds where we store food. I will deal with him
later," the two soldiers nodded and headed off with the
rabbit in tow. Mari turned back to her troops. There was a

look of confusion on their muzzles. Jolet was her third in command. How could he be a traitor? Mari saw the confused look on their muzzle. Pulling Zenti's note out of her pocket, she let it wave in the light breeze.

"This is proof Jolet is a traitor. Hold steady," the vixen ordered her soldiers. "We are not here to miss! Remember our defensive tactics. Shoot and kill as many invaders as you can, and accept any Mitdonian's surrender. We must obey the Crown Laws. I have faith in you."

Mari's troops nodded in understanding. Mitdonian law demanded that if one of their species surrendered, you must accept it. Though seemingly an odd order during a war, Mitdonians did not wish to kill each other without the chance to surrender. However, that was increasingly hard to comply with these past few years.

Mari smiled at all of them. Male and female alike. They were brave, and to Mari, they were the closest thing to friends that she had. These brave stragglers were her patrons, and she was proud to have them by her side.

"Thanks to all of you," she said in the calm, measured tones that brought them peace. "I am so proud to be fighting beside so many good patriots. We are fighting for the survival of our kind. I do not know what to expect but be prepared to act according to your training. You are a credit to our King and Mitd. Remember the flanks attack first once the enemy has advanced past our mid-perimeter marker," Mari said to the defenders.

The soldiers took their positions and made one final

check. It was not long until a perimeter communication's scout came into camp and made his way directly to Mari to report.

"Ma'am, there are two squads of our troops about thirty minutes from here. Their uniforms suggest that they are under the command of General Hayden. They are not moving in a skirmish format, but simply marching directly towards us," reported the ram.

"Circle around and watch for any support troop activity. Do not take any shot of opportunity, and do not expose your positions. The information you can provide is more important than kill you could score," Mari ordered.

"Yes, Commander Mari," replied the ram.

"Instruct Mova to take the route opposite of yours," ordered Mari. The ram saluted and immediately went to find Scout Mova. The two separated and traveled in opposite directions, making a wide circle to flank the approaching soldiers.

"Ricket, go tell your sister I have a job for her. She is to take the video recorder and position herself over there. I want her up in a tree recording this whole event. She is our Watcher. She is to go to the Northern Faction camp if this turns bad. Tell her where that camp is, please," Mari ordered the older of the parrot siblings. The pre-Coming-of-Age male saluted and ran off to find his sister.

The vixen watched Ricket instruct the little female parrot, who then skittered along the edge of the woods until she was lost in the trees. Good, Mari thought, one less kit to worry about if Hayden attacks. Mari needed a new Watcher anyway, as her last Faction Watcher passed to the stars three days ago.

Watchers were an essential part of the Faction armies as they took vital recordings of the enemy's actions. These recordings improved the tactics of each Faction and the King's Army. The vixen's last watcher was a graying soldier who was past his fighting prime. The otter passed to the stars in his sleep. Mari was glad to give Rochet a chance to feel part of defending Mitd. Giving last-minute orders, Mari repositioned her troops accordingly and began the half-hour wait.

Hayden's troops appeared out of the woods right as predicted. They marched rank and file right down the middle of the dirt road as they came into sight. A Sergeant called cadence as the soldiers approached with their rifles shouldered. They did not look ready for battle, marching as if on parade. These were members of Hayden's personal guards, not an enemy. Confusion washed over Mari's troops, and they looked to Mari for guidance.

Mari kept her aim; she knew this trick. The invaders had used it before. Often traitors were sent in ahead of the invader's troops as skirmishers. However, Mari never expected this cheap tactic from Hayden. She surveyed the area and could make neither heads nor tails of the situation.

"*THEY* may be behind the troops," Mari barked.

"Do not be fooled by simple tricks." The vixen's ears lay flat to the side as she focused on the soldiers coming towards her. The invaders were cowards, ready to use the delusional soldier as heady bait for her troops to kill first. Well, she would not fall for this ruse. Her scouts should have reported back by now. Mari wondered where the invader's troops were. However, the vixen was not going to take a chance.

"Aim!" Mari ordered. With focused control, the vixen steadied her heartbeat. This was not the first battle she had been in. The vixen's grip was relaxed, her aim true, and her voice soothing to her Faction troops.

Hayden strode to the front of his troops and called a halt just outside the camp's perimeter nearly a quarter-mile away. He noticed that the encampment looked empty. However, the panther knew that there were troops strategically positioned. Mari Semineu was a successful Faction Leader. The vixen was every bit her father's daughter, and General Haverick Waxton was an exceptional soldier. The panther advanced within thirty yards. However, his troops held their position.

"Hail Faction Leader Mari Waxton, I come for talks. May I enter freely," asked Hayden? The panther spoke in the same manner as if he were addressing a group of officers at a banquet.

His voice was controlled, with a soft deepness that commanded attention. The male panther was tall, lean, and incredibly attractive for a male in his middle years. He was widowed many years, and though he was highly sought after, he had never remated. A brilliant tactician with a penchant for winning at any cost, any female would have willingly lifted their tail for him. Admired by the masses, General Hayden was the quintessential military commander. However, he was also a potential traitor if the vixen were to believe the note Zenti sent.

Mari stepped from behind a stack of crates, her gun still aimed at the panther. He was well over six and a half feet tall with a lean, sleek, and muscular body. His short black fur was well-groomed, as was his sharply pressed military uniform. Nothing looked out of place, just as if he had stepped out of a dressing room. There he was, strutting as if he were some sort of premier ballerina, thought Mari.

"Why do you call on me so suddenly and without advanced warning? You, of all Mitdonians, know the protocol," Mari demanded. "Answer quickly, or I may shoot, and I warn you, my gun is aimed well lower than your head."

"I come for talks of unification. I have information about our common enemy that I wish to specifically share with you. Perhaps you will entertain the idea of working with the other Faction Leaders. If you grant me an audience, I have a plan that just might destroy *THEM* for good," began General Hayden.

He spoke to her as an equal, which was stunning considering the male panther's rank. His smile was genuine, though Hayden detested using the common name his Mitdonians had given the invaders. To all those who knew General Hayden, the male was unapproachable, except by a select pawful. Even those did not understand the scope of power the panther wielded. There were many minor rebellions and two Barrony wars in the past twenty years as the invaders increased their attacks. Strategic thinking was as natural to the panther as breathing. He had crushed every rebellion with astonishing ease. Mari was unsure of the panther's true intentions, but the looks on her patron's muzzle were one of hope in response to the General's words.

"That still does not excuse the breach of protocol. Many could have been injured or killed here," snapped Mari.

"The King has granted me permission to offer you the command of all Faction Forces on Mitd. You will be the first-ever General of a combined Faction Army. Can we talk this over in somewhat less of an open place?" Hayden said, casually lowering his helmet to protect another part of his body besides his head.

Hayden knew Mari Semineu very well. Beyond her impressive command ability, superior ability to handle a firearm, and her legendary temper, the panther knew one other thing. The vixen would not hesitate to deprive him of a specific body part just to make her point. That was one of the reasons Mitd loved Miss Mari. She was wholly unafraid when backed into a corner. However, she had two major flaws, and Hayden knew them both.

"What needs to be said can be said to me here," Mari retorted darkly, her gun still aimed at the panther.

Her soldiers looked surprised at the abruptness of Mari's answer. Still, they did not waver in holding Hayden's shocked troops under their sights. Several of the panther's soldiers had started to un-shoulder arms.

"Shoulder arms, soldiers! Now, or I will order my troops to open fire," Mari commanded, to which Hayden's troops came to attention and shouldered their weapons. Mari Semineu's reputation for kindness was matched by her proven battle record. Not one of Hayden's troops doubted the vixen would order her troops to fire on them.

Hayden did not look back but heard his troops come to attention, and his eyes briefly narrowed at his troops obeying the vixen. Mari smiled internally as she watched the troops respond instantly to her command. The vixen did not miss the slight sneer on Hayden's muzzle as his troops took her orders as readily as his orders.

"Can I at least have a chair? It has been a long march, and I am a bit tired," said Hayden. He was not appealing to Mari Semineu's generosity but to those of her patrons. "Would a drink be too much to ask as well?" He was extremely casual in his manner, bordering on arrogant. He kept twitching at something on his side; however, the distance prevented Mari from seeing what it was.

Mixed emotions ran through the vixen's thoughts as she debated between trusting her feelings and believing what she had felt from Zenti's message. Was it too early to rely on Zenti, she thought? However, the vixen knew the Gift did not create lies. Mari growled to herself at her indecision. Looking around at her patron's, Mari's gaze landed upon a graying badger. In his muzzle, she saw the determination of a seasoned veteran. The look on his muzzle was one of distrust and suspicion directed at the panther.

"You assume too much of a welcome from me after what I have heard of you, Hayden," Mari snapped. "The answer to both of those questions is yes; it is too much to ask. Now speak or so help me; I will shoot," she watched him flinch and inwardly smiled. Mari knew the one weakness of General Hayden. The panther detested not being in control of a situation.

"Very well, though I wish to protest this discourteous treatment by the civilian resistance forces. Nevertheless, as you want to be to the point, I have information that the invaders will be bringing in a large shipment of arms into the area. The shipment will be followed the next day by a troop convoy. If we can capture the arms before the troops can arrive, we will have a tactical advantage. I want to send a message to the invaders that we are not to be trifled with," General Hayden said. Mari detected a hint of anger in his voice. She smiled.

"Would not a single messenger have sufficed? Surely this tidbit of information does not warrant the caliber of an officer such as yourself," Mari said, then decided to test a theory. "Since when did the great General

Hayden become a messenger?"

"Because there are traitors everywhere. Does this answer your question?" the panther hissed, "This is so unlike you, Mari; what has gotten your fur up?" The vixen was being exceptionally hostile, which was far beyond her routine hostilities toward him. It was clear Mari did not favor him for some reason, only known to herself.

"Like you don't know," she snapped before lowering her gun very slowly. However, her glare did not relent. "Ricket, escort General Hayden to my tent and stay there with him until I come back."

Ricket saluted and quickly went to salute Hayden. The young parrot asked the panther to follow before heading towards Mari's tent.

"Stand down," she called to her troops, "I apologize. It seems my information may have been incorrect. Set Hayden's men up in the far clearing away from our camp. Continue to keep a vigilant watch. Extend my apologies to my patrons and begin bringing them back into camp."

None of the soldiers were irritated with Mari; they trusted her implicitly. The vixen was annoyed with herself. She did not know if she should believe her instincts or Zenti's information. However, there was one way to find out. Giving a low growl, she headed for the shed where Jolet was confined. She wanted to be calm but felt her temper rising. Jerking the door open to the temporary storage shed, Mari stepped in and slammed it closed. The rabbit twitched at the rough entry.

Jolet hung suspended by his paws just so the tips of his paw pads barely touched the dirt in the shed. The light was dim, and she dismissed the two males guarding him.

"I am in a foul mood and would just as soon cut your throat as to talk to you. However, what happens next fully depends on you," Mari said, bolting the door closed, "so start talking." Jolet fidgeted as best he could from his current suspension, and Mari glared harder, paws on her hips.

"What is it that you are seeking to know?" he asked hesitantly. However, his attitude was anything but humble.

Balling her paw up, the vixen struck him hard across the muzzle at the flippant tone of his voice. Blood splattered from his freshly split lip.

"First off, this business of you spying on me and Zenti for Hayden. How long have you been working for the panther," Mari demanded? Embarrassment began to grow inside. Just how much had the rabbit already found out about the meeting with Zenti. Moreover, what other secrets had the rabbit passed on to the panther.

Jolet could not possibly know about the intimate nights that she and Zenti had spent together in the past, could he? No, the rabbit had not been in her Faction long enough. She pushed that thought away, bringing her muzzle close to Jolet's. The vixen grabbed the rabbit by the collar and shook him as hard as she could.

"If you want to know about my past affairs, is it not fair to ask me such information" Mari growled?

"Ma'am, I'm sure I don't know what you are asking of me," Jolet said, trying not to be flippant again. However, he failed, and as soon as he replied, he knew he had screwed up.

She drove her fist into his stomach. In a follow-up motion, her knife was instantly out of its sheath, pointed at his throat with the tip pressing precariously close to the rabbit's jugular. Blood began to trickle down the blade as it cut through the fur and bit into the skin.

"Don't lie to me, rabbit," Mari growled. She ran the tip of the razor shape knife under his fur. With a slow, deliberate cut, she began skinning a small section of fur away from Jolet's throat with the tip of her knife. "I don't like to be lied to!"

Thoughts raced through Jolet's mind. He could lie about Hayden wanting to know the details of Mari's Faction command structure. He could lie that he was tasked with finding out if the vixen were still in love with Zenti. However, the knife and her anger were genuine. Jolet decided on a half-truth.

"Hayden wanted to know how deeply involved you were still with that wild animal, Zenti. He has become such a liability to our cause for peace," Jolet said. That was not a lie. Zenti had repeatedly hurt both the invader's and Hayden's plans for almost fourteen months, thought the scared rabbit. He knew the truth of General Hayden; the panther wanted to broker peace with the invaders. However, the rabbit was unsure as to why General Hayden sought peace.

"How deeply I am involved is none of his business," Mari snapped, her muzzle still close to his, "but I know that that is not all of it; what else is there to tell me?"

The rabbit fidgeted again, not knowing exactly how to answer or just how much he was willing to tell her. She must have seen the indecision in his eyes because she pressed the knife deeper into his throat, and he knew that she would cut it from ear to ear with no hesitation.

"What more do you want to know, ma'am," asked Jolet? The rabbit's arms were beginning to hurt. Apart from the tip of the knife in his neck, so far, Mari had not actually tortured him. Jolet decided to continue to play the helpful innocent.

****

After Jolet left the woods with Mari's message, Zenti took a wide path towards the Faction camp. Zenti headed westwardly. The white wolf suspected that is where the invaders would be stationed. The invaders were not wholly predictable but underestimated his species ability to adapt and learn. Zenti was not disappointed as he saw the command center from a distance. It could not be considered a complete command center. It was just a pawful of soldiers and a makeshift communications table. However, Zenti knew that there would be more invaders in fire teams about a mile ahead. The invaders thought so little of his species as soldiers that the invaders employed only a limited number of tactics.

The silvery-white wolf had learned so much in the past year since Mari rebuked him. Everything that Mari's father, General Waxton, had taught him was valid. Zenti had just never let go of wanting to protect Mari. In restricting his use of unconventional tactics, Zenti had never risked losing Mari.

Strange that when you have nothing to live for, you can achieve so much more, Zenti thought. Cautiously he moved closer to the makeshift command center.

Zenti recalled how this realization had begun. It started by being reckless, and the white wolf laughed at this illuminating event. It commenced on the first attack after leaving Mari in the clearing thirteen months ago. That was at Dotharian. It was in that small town where he first learned that the invaders did take prisoners for slaves. The white wolf learned that those slaves were then worked to death or that they would be killed for sport, target practice, or experimented on.

Zenti decided that it would be better to kill even the slaves than try to free them. If his species were unwilling to fight for their freedom, then they deserved to die. However, Dotharian gave him a new perspective on that line of thought. He remembered standing in the center of the town as it burned. From when Zenti was a pup, the smell of charred flesh and fur had forever been etched in his brain.

The white wolf fully expected to die the night he attacked Dotharian. However, much to his surprise, Zenti found that his Gift had grown exponentially more powerful. In the past, his rage and hatred fueled his Gift in ways that no other source could. In Dotharian, the white wolf discovered that his anger could barely feed his Gift.

The Gift is never one-dimensional if the Gifted is willing to open themselves up to the madness that is the Void. When his rage failed to fuel his Gift beyond what he knew it could be, he found another source. The Void itself was at his whimsical desire. Dotharian was also where Summoner Zenti Semineu learned that he had both a Shaman's and the Oracle's Gifts. Deep within his heart, he knew what he was and what he needed to do. With his newly expanded Gifts and Talents, Zenti chose not to merely touch the madness of the Void but to embrace it with unbridled passion. In making that choice, Zenti also earned his reputation in the city of Dotharian.

The first place Zenti attacked was where the prisoners were housed. They were held in the Dotharian zoo. It was a small, cramped facility designed for animals. Most of the prisoners were savagely beaten. However, it was in them he found the few who were willing to fight. Zenti found the spirit of those who chose to willing to pay for the price of freedom. It was that spirit that the silvery-white wolf respected and admired. Those brave spirits Zenti spared to spread the word of his deeds or to continued to fight again. A video had been taken of the attack on the town. The sound of the invader's language broke his reminiscing and brought Zenti back to the present.

Pulling up short, Zenti heard a conversation just ahead. Moving closer, he saw the invaders, five in all. Three appeared to be guards, and two were looking over a table. The two standing over the table were officers. Though he could not make out what was being said, the gestures were clear enough; the two were planning an attack. No more than a dozen feet away from the table lay two Mitdonians. One was a ram, but the other he could not clearly see. Both were dead. Zenti suspected that they were scouts from Mari's camp.

For a moment, Zenti thought of reaching out with his Gift. However, he was still unsure if the invaders could track him using his Gift. Though he would need to resolve that issue, this was not the moment to do so. Quietly he circled to the rear of the invader's group. The three guards were walking a circular patrol around the makeshift command camp. The radio equipment was small, which Zenti deduced that it could only control no more than a company of soldiers. The question was, where were they? Typically the invader's main troops were close to the command center. Perhaps this was a trap set for him. With the traitor Jolet knowing that he was with Mari for nearly twelve hours straight, anything was possible.

"Perhaps these useless waste of flesh can learn,"

Zenti whispered to himself as he watched the patrolling guards.

Before, they would keep their forces in one location. It made it easy to attack. The invaders feared his Gift and the fire he could summon. The best strategy sometimes was the most direct, and Zenti waited until one guard's path neared him. The fear of whether the invaders could track him using his Gift was a distraction that could cost him the advantage of surprise. Acting swift and decisively, Zenti called on the Talent of Shadows. Zenti blended in with the shadows cast by the trees of the evening's dusky light. It was a taxing Talent, and the silvery-white wolf steadied himself on the nearby tree. He was tired. However, there was work to be done.

The guard neared, and like a specter that haunted the dreams of the fearful, the silvery-white wolf attacked. The invader never even screamed as Zenti drove him to the ground, crushing the male's throat, then ripped it out with his claws. The rush of adrenaline coursed through the silvery-white wolf's body. Oh, how he relished the hunt.

****

Mari glared at Jolet; the rabbit was not sharing everything he knew. The vixen cut the rope binding one of the rabbit's arms. Jolet now hung one arm. She pulled the remaining rope tighter so that his paw pads dangled just above the dirt floor.

"You would do well not to lie to me again," Mari growled. "You know more than you are letting on."

He started to open his mouth in protest, but Mari placed the knife's tip in a non-lethal spot on his free shoulder. The vixen drove the blade deep into the rabbit flesh just above the collarbone with a swift thrust. She followed it swiftly by delivering a fisted hard into his solar plexus. Jolet wanted to scream but found no breath. His eyes began to water as the pain from the knife was excruciating, yet still, he could find no breath.

"Well, rabbit," began Mari, "we have two choices here, and they are both yours to make. I can leave you strung up here, slit your wrist and let you slowly bleed out. That is one option. Your other option is that you can tell me everything I want to know, and I will make sure you spend the rest of your miserable life in prison. Perhaps before the gray of old age comes to your muzzle, someone will feel pity for you and set you free. But that won't happen as long as I live."

Jolet honestly did not like the odds of either of those choices. However, he liked the idea of prison much better than the concept of death. If he told Mari everything, perhaps Hayden would be able to free him tonight after the attack.

"I have been in the service of Hayden for over eight months now. He has had a lot of success against *THEM* and has a plan to defeat the invaders. Yet, you and the other Faction Leaders have had as much success with less support and supplies," explained the rabbit as he gasped for air. When he took too long to continue his answer, the vixen tugged the rope tighter. Jolet whimpered.

"He wanted you to be part of his plan. Hayden even convinced the King to give you a commission as the head of all the Factions after the King made General Hayden Crown Champion. When the panther learned of Zenti's agreement to meet with you, Hayden asked me to observe and report what transpired. To date, as you know, ma'am, Hayden has won every battle against *THEM,* and he feels that if he can unite the Factions, he can win more," whimpered Jolet. With a heavy, sobbing sigh of defeat, the rabbit's eyes pleaded for mercy. He was in extreme pain, and the blood, though not gushing, was not stopping. Mari had known precisely where to insert the blade to cause intense pain but not cause massive hemorrhaging. Jolet saw the unrelenting anger in the vixen's eyes, so he hurriedly continued.

"Zenti has also won every battle, but all by himself. The cost of his victories is in the blood of our own. His Northern Faction troops are wild and uncontrollable. They slaughter everything in their path, and Zenti leaves nothing unburned," said Jolet, and Mari eased off on the rope ever so slightly.

"Those who support the invaders do not deserve mercy," Mari hissed. Since the rabbit was talking, she eased off the rope a little more. Though he deserved any punishment he received, he was providing potentially valuable information. At the release of tension on his shoulder joint, Jolet continued.

"Those that help **THEM** just so they can live, Zenti executes. General Hayden thinks that this will lead to a mob of renegades flocking to the invaders' protection just to flee the wrath of Zenti. The General believes this course of action will lead to a standing army for the invaders. He asked me to report what you and Zenti talked about. He also wanted to know all of Zenti's movements after leaving the camp," explained the rabbit, then stopped speaking.

"Zenti has liberated more of Mitd than Hayden has. The citizen of Mitd should never fear a liberator who has no desire to assume command than a General who wants to lead all Mitd. It is a choice of being a slave to Hayden's leadership or living in fear until the invaders are defeated. For one, I would prefer the temporary fear of a mad Summoner to the benevolent leadership of a dictator. Make no mistake about this rabbit; Hayden had dreams of domination," growled Mari.

Tears were flowing down the rabbit's cheeks. Mari could not tell if they were from the pain or from the shame of spying. Giving a heavy sigh, she pulled her knife from the rabbit's shoulder, sliced through the rope that was holding him off the ground, and watched him fall to his knee. Before Jolet could move, she kicked the traitor onto his tail.

"If I find out that you're lying to me, so help me, I will skin you alive," Mari hissed before turning and storming out of the shed. "Keep him in there and fetch him a medic," she ordered the guards outside the door.

Jolet sat down on the floor of the shed and leaned against a crate. Putting a paw to the bleeding shoulder, the dejected rabbit waited for what came next. He knew better than to have gotten involved, but General Hayden was persuasive. However, more persuasive was Summoner Zenti Semineu's burning of all cities, towns, and villages of those who aided the invaders. Not all citizens had the courage to fight, thought Jolet. The pain in his shoulder and the guilt in his heart made him re-evaluate his loyalties. Jolet continued to cry with each tiny movement.

Stomping across the camp, Mari's ears were flattened to the side of her head in anger. Reaching her tent, Mari threw open the door. Ricket was attending General Hayden. Holding the door open, Mari told Ricket that he could leave without allowing anyone near unless the camp was under attack. Turning, she closed her eyes and took a deep breath. Entering the tent, Mari closed the door calmly and walked over to Hayden. The panther stood when she entered the tent.

"You had me spied on," Mari growled once they were alone. "You sent Jolet to spy on me when Zenti was here. What did he tell you," she hissed?

When the panther hesitated with a nonchalant look on his muzzle, she struck him in the chest with both paws, driving him into the chair. Hayden sat down hard in the chair but maintained his composure. Casually he took a plum from a tray of fruit that Ricket must have brought in while she was with Jolet.

With a relaxed, collected, and calm demeanor of a polished Elder, Hayden did not even look up at Mari. The panther took a bite from the plum, letting the juices run down his long canines and over his chin. Stopping the flow of plum juice with a single digit, the panther licked the excess away.

"Zenti is a traitor to Mitd and to you," Hayden said. Turning his head up to look at Mari in a slow, accusatory way. "That white wolf cur has caused more harm than good. I need to know if one of the most powerful Faction Leaders is on the side of our species or just interested in lifting her tail." The panther's words were cold and bitter, and he realized his mistake the moment he made it.

The second that those words left his tongue, Mari balled up a paw and drove it into his muzzle. The blow sent the plum flying to the ground. Mari's teeth were bared dangerously as she grabbed him by the collar and came muzzle to muzzle with him.

"How dare you," the vixen growled, "you who have had thirteen months to learn about me. In that time, you should know me a lot better than that, Hayden." Mari drove her fist into his muzzle again. She hit the panther hard enough to split his upper lip.

Her ears flattened further as she growled low in her throat. How dare the panther make her out to be a common whore or a primal animal in a breeding heat. Mari hit him yet again. The vixen's anger was rising, and the panther could see this ending up in a duel.

For a moment, Hayden's ears folded just a little. Mari's reaction was not what he had precisely expected. Well, at least not with this much bitterness. The fur around her neck was standing on end, and her jaw was clenched. Hayden figured he had better change tactics, or this conversation would get bloody, knowing Mari's kit-like temper.

"So, if he was not sniffing again, then what was he up to," Hayden asked? The panther pulled a pawkerchief from his jacket pocket. He waved it in a mock gesture of surrender before wiping the blood and plum juice from his muzzle.

He might as well be direct, the panther figured. The vixen, it seemed, was not in a game-playing mood. He did not need to win Mari over to his cause. Many Faction Leaders were being pressured to perform and were getting their soldiers killed as well as themselves. The loss of experienced Faction Leaders made it easier to control the newly promoted ones. Having Mari on his side would make that more manageable in the long run. Still, he was quickly losing patience with the temperamental vixen. Tempting her with rewards and promotions would not work. Mari was neither stupid nor that gullible, but he had to make a faux attempt at it.

However, the panther really needed to know what the white wolf cur was up to. Mari was the only Faction

Leader to speak with Zenti. The other leaders were in fear of the Summoner. Moreover, there was one more thing that the panther knew; his species needed Mari Semineu. Hayden was not about to lose the kingdom or the planet to some bitch in heat whose puppet master was a bloodthirsty monster.

Mari crossed her arms over her chest, her glare not diminishing. She watched the panther with fiery green eyes as he calmly cleaned his muzzle. However, the vixen had not missed the subtle gesture of the white pawkerchief. She curbed her anger for a moment. Though she may be hot-tempered, she was also pragmatic. General Hayden wielded tremendous military power and social influence.

"Whether or not the wolf that was once my mate is sniffing around is none of your business, panther," stated Mari. Her tone held a finality to it.

Hayden may have been planning to ask her to be his mate, but that did not mean that she was automatically entitled to agree. It did not mean that he had any right to be jealous or push his noses into her business. However, Zenti insight had always been correct in the past. Even if Zenti was unwilling to consider their future together, he still had an uncanny insight into the unfolding events. She glared at the panther while assessing the situation.

"That reply does not answer my question," Hayden said flatly. "What was that wolf cur up to?"

The panther had to find a way to get Mari out of her defensive posture, or this would be a long discussion going nowhere. He could just pitch camp and then wait for the oncoming attack. That was the alternate plan. Let the invaders attack and then come save the day. The panther would have preferred that this meeting go a lot smoother. However, even he could tell something had transpired between that white wolf cur and Mari. That something did not bode well for his peaceful plans of bringing Mari into his fold of supports.

"I called him to meet me," Mari said flatly. The vixen's stance did not change as she watched Hayden. However, the vixen did ease a few steps away. It was the only acknowledgment she would give to Hayden's feeble attempt at an apology. Mari could feel her temper getting out of control and made no attempt to regain it. The panter's smug look instantly ignited the anger in the vixen. Let this conversation go wherever the wind directed, Mari thought.

Hayden realized that this conversation was not going anyplace fast. He decided that perhaps a strategic withdrawal would be best, at least until the attack. If the wolf cur were not here, he would still be in the area. Hayden was sure Zenti would come to Mari's aid if the invaders attack her camp. Hayden was counting on Zenti to come to her aid. That is why he had the alternate plan well organized. Standing, he bowed to Mari, excusing himself to go set up camp.

"Don't you dare walk away from me, Hayden," the vixen snapped before the panther could leave, "You leave this tent, and you can leave my camp as well." Hayden stopped, and Mari continued, "If you want information from me, you should ask me directly. You shouldn't suggest that I am a bitch in a breeding heat. Moreover, you should be more courteous."

"I do not have time for courtesies, and as to the suggest you're a bitch in a breeding heat, he was your mate. You are the one who tossed him, not that I blame you. But in a world of mystery, filled with danger, one never knows when one might be meeting one's doom. Allow me to set up my camp and direct my soldiers. Perhaps we can discuss this over an open dinner at my camp. I will invite the Elders of your Faction," offered Hayden. The panther bowed his head as if he were through with this conversation and politely waiting to be dismissed. Yet Hayden could smell the lingering scent of the wolf still in the tent. That scent infuriated him, but true to the consummate professional he was, the panther kept it to himself.

"Fine," Mari snapped, "leave. However, I expect the invitation to be offered in person. If you send a messenger, I will not come."

"Agreed," was all the panther said. It was a minor victory. Getting Mari Semineu to concede any point was a victory. She was such a spoiled kit but a brilliant leader. Though Mitd needed a charismatic leader of its population, Mari Waxton Semineu was destined to lead far more than just a war-torn island. The vixen was destined to lead the stars; she just did not know it yet. The panther was not about to allow that white wolf cur to be the vixen's mentor. Oracles were rarely wrong, especially this particular

Oracle.

Hayden turned and sauntered out of Mari's tent and then out of the camp. His calm demeanor leaving all those patrons who knew Miss Mari Semineu confused at just what to expect next. However, those in the camp knew one thing. With Summoner Zenti Semineu and General Hayden in the area, a peaceful evening was not in the works.

****

Zenti drove his onyx claws deep in the throat of the closest invader, silently solving one problem. Taking the dead guard's rifle, Zenti took aim. The invader's equipment was of better quality but no more lethal than its Mitdonian counterpart. Before the other invaders even knew the silvery-white wolf was there, two shots rang out in rapid succession. Two more invaders were dead before they hit the ground. The two standing over the maps tipped the table over and dove behind it, sending papers and equipment scattering everywhere.

The Talent of Shadows was taxing on his already tired body. Zenti released the Talent. As a result, the silvery-white wolf was more visible. Activating the PRISM device, Zenti pulled the companion goggles down over his eyes and vanished from sight. The PRISM device had a limited power supply. They were not readily available to him; therefore, he preferred to use his Gift. However, he knew his own body was in no condition to hold on to his Gift. The PRISM device did not mask sound or scent; that was a significant weakness. Zenti moved towards the two remaining invaders.

However, the white wolf did not move carefully enough and rustled the bushes around him. The two officers opened fire in his general direction. Ducking behind a tree, Zenti wrapped the two invaders in his Gift. Only a Gifted could see the tendrils of his Talent of Life Sensing as it bathed the two invaders in red.

Every Gifted had a shade of the color spectrum that was a tale-tale sign of their Gift. Though some hues were similar, each was unique. The secret to understanding the color variation was the more potent the Voidal access, the richer the color shade. However, the invaders and non-Gifted could not see those Voidal energy streams if the Gifted did not want them to.

Zenti watched as one of the officers pulled on a pair of glasses. The glasses were resting on the front of the invader's helmet. They were nearly identical to the ones the white wolf had taken off other dead invaders. Zenti observed as the officer began to scan the bushes in the area where they just fired. The second officer began tapping at a wristwatch and suddenly vanished.

However, the invader's technology could not suppress Zenti's Gift's effects. The invisible invader was still visible to the silvery-white wolf. The Gifted Talent of

Life Sensing continued to outline the vanished officer in a blood-red glow. Peeking around the edge of the tree, Zenti saw the officer retreating across the empty field. The silvery-white wolf was still tired from the long, shared link between him and Mari. He needed rest and more high-quality food. The military rations just did not fuel his body as fresh food did. Every use of his Gift drained more and more of his rapidly waning strength. Zenti leaned back against the tree and searched within for a small reserve of energy while he examined the situation.

Standard tactics for the invaders, Zenti thought. The senior officer flees while the other stays. Zenti looked back around the tree and watched as the remaining officer scanned with a similar pair of glasses like those he had acquired. So the invaders suspected that he might be using captured technology. Zenti wondered if that was a universal concept or if it was just this officer's guess. Waiting for the sole remaining officer to scan in a different direction, Zenti watched the one that had engaged the PRISM device move about the area. Through the outline of his Talent of Life Sensing, he could see that the invisible officer was picking up a few of the papers. It took but a few seconds to gather the scattered documents before the officer headed down the road. He was moving away from Mari's camp. Zenti waited quietly until the fleeing one was out of sight.

Silently Zenti stepped out of the brush and deactivated the PRISM, becoming visible. Quickly he removed the glasses he was wearing. It took but a moment to shake the disorientated feeling he got when switching back to ordinary sight. The effect of the lenses was akin to a sense of vertigo if one was unprepared. Zenti focused on the table that the remaining invader was hiding behind. With a brief call on his Gift, Zenti telekinetically slammed the table into the officer hiding behind it. The Talent of Object Manipulation was new to the white wolf, and its use brought a moment of unsteadiness.

Zenti could not afford to hesitate and staggered a few steps before racing forward. Watching the table, Zenti leapt at the last moment and rolled when the invader pulled up over the edge and blindly shot. Zenti was exhausted, and he had not forced the table as hard as he would have liked. The table only knocked the officer down, not unconscious.

A shot rang out, and Zenti could almost feel the bullet moving the fur on his body. Pulling up in a crouch, flames erupted from his paws, engulfing the lone enemy, searing the flesh from the furless body. The table caught fire, and he could smell the burning of metal and rubber. Zenti staggered as the Void assaulted his body. The Gift naturally demanded a heavy price for accessing such power. In his weakened condition, the Gift was taking an exacting toll.

Blood dripped from his nose, gums, and eyes. Advancing on the table, he checked the burned body to make sure the invader was dead. The rush of rage subsided, and the silvery-white wolf sat down hard. He rested for a moment as a lightheaded feeling washed over him.

"Heavens and Hells," Zenti said, "I need to learn to focus faster and harder when trying to move something as heavy as that table. Moreover, I need to eat." Pulling a ration pack out, Zenti ate the only thing that sounded appealing. The sugary sweet treat was not enough to sustain him, but it did give him a boost.

Checking the body for useful items, he noticed that everything was melted and burned. Growling at the loss of potentially beneficial invader technology, Zenti resolved to exercise more control of his Gift. Moving to a large trunk, he began to pilfer the items, happily finding what he hoped to find. He took a satchel full of rations and began to eat as he searched the rest of the area. The invader's military rations were more nourishing than the standard rations the Mitdonian military carried. While hurriedly eating, Zenti reflected on the expansion of his Gift.

His ability to summon fire was getting stronger. Amongst many things, he needed to practice controlling that aspect of his Gift better. Some things required a more delicate touch. Zenti continued to search but found nothing of use. Deciding the more essential items must be in the fleeing invader's possession, Zenti dodged into the tree line. The fresh rush of sugar began to fuel his body. That was another benefit of the Gift; it radically accelerated the body's metabolism. The silvery-white wolf sprinted off after the lone retreating officer. Whatever the invader risked his life to pick up must have vital information, and he was not about to let that escape his grasp.

****

Mari groaned and flopped down on her cot once Hayden was gone. The vixen took a deep centering breath and let her body relax. It was not healthy to be this stressed all the time. That was something her mother tried to instill in her. However, the vixen had never learned to let go. Mari picked up the note again and wondered how Zenti could have been wrong about the situation. Had the thirteen months diminished his sharp military mind, the vixen wondered?

Deciding she had to know for her patron's safety, Mari decided to risk another contact with Zenti. The vixen hoped she had not forgotten how to do this. It had never failed in the past. Zenti explained he always maintained a connection with her. For a moment, Mari wondered if he had severed that connection in the past thirteen months. Brushing that thought aside, the vixen closed her eyes. Mari let her mind drift to Zenti, trying to reach him as she had done so many times in the past.

Mari felt like she was floating, as if in a dream. It was as if time stood still. This was the same feeling she had shared with Zenti all those years. When she had needed him, all the vixen had to do was close her eyes and think of him. For the sake of her patrons and species, Mari once again reached out for Zenti's help.

****

Taking all the collected papers from the dead officer he had finished tracking and killing, Zenti resisted the urge to read them. Instead, he cut across the forest to where the road would intersect ahead. The silvery-white wolf pulled up short when a series of lights began to sweep across the forest. He counted about thirty or so of the invader's soldiers. These were not the heavy combat troops but the average troops. Spread out in standard skirmish formation, the soldiers swung the flashlights about carelessly. The invaders were arrogant and overconfident. Surely, General Hayden must have informed the invaders that Summoner Semineu would be in the area.

However, there was no telling what the panther had running through that feline brain of his. General Hayden could be setting up the invaders and Mari at the same time, Zenti thought. He would not put it past Hayden to employ such a tactic. However, Zenti thought it was kind of the invaders to illuminate themselves. It would make for a much more convenient exercise of 'target practice' thought the silvery-white wolf. A contented grin grew across the white wolf's muzzle at the pun.

A warm feeling washed across Zenti. In a moment of calm, he remembered the soft, gentle touch of Mari when she was very far away from him. This felt so much better than the hammer-like contact she made when in closer proximity. It was like in their early years when she would just be thinking about him and find herself looking at the world through his eyes. Zenti always knew when she did that as she was usually very bullish in her telepathic contacts. He had spent years trying to teach her to be gentle. It was a skill she never fully developed.

That was a long time ago that he tried to teach Mari to be gentle with her thoughts. However, this brush felt like a gentle breeze passing over his skin. Zenti knew Mari was a few miles away. Therefore, she had not forgotten how to use his sight to see what he was seeing. Mari had not forgotten her way into his soul. Then Zenti remembered the bitter words and knew that she was looking through his eyes for the sake of their species, not for the sake of his heart. Summoner Zenti Semineu knew that the price he would pay for Jayden, for Mari, would be more than he wanted to pay. However, the silvery-white wolf also knew he had chosen to pay the price. Therefore he opened himself up to her mental touch and allowed her to see what he was seeing.

~   ~   ~   ~

Mari saw the lights sweeping back and forth. The vixen steadied herself and attempted to orient herself to Zenti's rapid side-to-side movements. Mari's head spun as she forgot what it was like for her body to be stationary, yet her mind thought she was moving. She had forgotten much in such a short time. It made her sick to her stomach for a few moments until she recalled how to block it. Mari's stomach settled, and the vixen could see clearly now.

Zenti had moved out of the way of the sweeping lights. Mari, through Zenti's sight, counted at least two platoons of invaders moving through the forest. It was evident that the soldiers were searching for something. Mari could see all this through Zenti's eyes. Zenti was hunting **THEM.** Mari's heart raced, but she was not moving. Mari saw one of the invaders aim a light at Zenti. The light crossed his body. A shot rang out when one invader shot at Zenti's shadow in the dark. Mari heard the gunfire and called out to Zenti in fear. At that moment, Mari Semineu realized for the first time in her mated life that not only could she see through her connection with Zenti, but she could also now hear. There was one other thing that the vixen discovered through her link to Summoner Zenti Semineu. Mari Semineu touched the Void.

~   ~   ~   ~

Zenti froze in his tracks when the shot rang out. He then doubled back and began to swing away from his last location. The direction Zenti was traveling lead away from Mari's Faction camp. The silvery-white wolf moved fast and expected the invaders to be hot on his heels. However, when Zenti stopped for a survey of the situation, he could only see the invader's soldier moving away again. The soldiers were heading back towards Mari's camp.

Zenti could feel Mari calling out to him as she had done when they were much closer. Strange, he thought. What was in Mari's heart that had not allowed her to crush their mental link to her? Did Mari still love him, or was this a Gift that she possessed? Zenti recalled her father's words the night he died. The lion said the invaders were searching for two Summoners.

The enemy quickened their pace towards Mari's Faction camp. This was all confusing. Zenti wondered if Mari was a Gifted Summoner? Was she still in love with him? Could this feeling be just a residual from their earlier link? Determining what he felt was the latter, Zenti dismissed his wishful thinking and let Mari continue to use the residual link for her own needs. Her fear was distracting, but he soon accepted the fact that the residual link would fade, and the contact would be lost.

~   ~   ~   ~

Mari could see *THEM* and knew that the soldiers were coming towards her camp. The vixen snapped out of the shared vision. Forcing herself up, she raced out of her tent on unsteady legs. She did not call her troops to follow her. Instead, Mari shouted commands to her patrons and soldier. However, she did not stop running. The vixen headed into the woods towards the area she saw through Zenti's shared link. Her ears and nose serving as her guide, Mari sniffed her way towards *THEM* and Zenti. Within a few steps, the vixen vanished into the tree line. She could hear the bustle of her Faction Camp trying to recover to its former heightened state of readiness. However, Mari had to reach Zenti before the invaders killed him.

****

Zenti felt the link break with the typical Mari hammer-like blow. Something was not right; the invaders should be chasing him. Why would the soldiers be headed towards Mari's Faction camp when he was right here? Hayden was there, and if invaders were in league with the panther, it would put his troops at risk as well. It made no sense. Curiosity overcame caution, and Zenti followed the invaders closely.

The silvery-white wolf watched as the invaders came upon the area where the communications camp lay in ruins. Climbing a tree, Zenti watched where the soldiers briefly stopped at that former camp and then moved on. The invaders barely gave it a cursory inspection.

He watched for another ten minutes. Making sure there was not a second wave of invaders before climbing down. Following the invaders at an accelerated speed, he made up some of the lost time. Zenti ignored the exhaustion creeping across his body. His muscles ached; he was hungry and needed sleep. However, this situation with General Hayden and the invaders was all too odd. The invaders did not seem on a heightened alert as they should be. The foreknowledge that a Summoner was in the area, especially one as hunted as he was, should have filled the soldiers with terror. However, the invaders were all too casual. Something was missing, and Zenti could not put a claw on it.

****

Mari's ears flattened to her head as **THEIR** scent wafted past her nose. Fear snaked its way into her thoughts. She had run about four miles away from her encampment when she encountered the soldiers. The vixen reached for her gun only to realize that it was not on her hip. She had taken it off when she had laid down earlier on her cot in between meetings with her camp's Elders. Oh, Heavens and Hells, Mari thought; how could she have been so stupid and careless? Just where was her head? First, there was Zenti, next came Hayden, and now the unpreparedness. This was all too reckless of her.

She backed away from the invader's soldiers, her heart pounding as they came ever closer. The totality of the past day's events kept her mind distracted, and she tripped over a fallen branch. Mari cringed at that loud cracking sound it made in the otherwise quiet forest. She could hear the voices and knew she was in trouble. After thirteen months of rejecting him, the vixen's first thoughts were her only action. Mari mentally cried out to Zenti.

****

"Did you hear that," one of the soldiers asked? The male invader whispered into his headset, and the soldier stopped, then spread further apart.

"Find out what it is," replied another invader.

Zenti had caught up to the invaders and stalked to within four miles of Mari's camp when a loud crack resonated through the woods. Moments later, two of the invaders at the far end of the skirmish line broke off. The two soldiers seemed to be searching for the source of the sound. It was then that he felt Mari calling him, not like before, but out of fear. He stopped and sniffed the slight breeze, and he could smell Mari's scent in the direction that the soldiers had moved towards. He was too far away to make an effective rescue attempt, so he did the only thing he could. Zenti knew his action would divert attention to himself. He called on his Gift.

Fire lit up the trees amongst the invader's ranks randomly. It seemed as if the forest was burning everywhere. Zenti just let loose with no control, no thought, and no fear of retaliation. His only desire to protect his mate, a passion that he found evoked an unprecedented surge of raw power.

As Zenti backed away from the fiery mess he started, his mind raced over those words again. His mate. Yes, he still was very much in love with Mari, and he would destroy this whole planet if it meant saving her. In that one thought, the fires he summoned blazed even hotter.

Mari's heart raced as she saw the forest erupt in flames. Without a doubt, before the question could even form in her mind, she knew their source was Zenti. The vixen darted around one of the many fires when the soldier turned away. Mari ran in the direction she suspected was the source of the fire. One area of the forest was not a raging inferno. Zenti must be there.

Mari heard soldiers coming from someplace behind her. Quickly, she pressed her back to a tree. It was one male invader, and she could see him, and if he looked hard, he would be able to see her as well.

Zenti found a low-branched tree and climbed up it. He crossed the limb from one tree to another, looking for what might be Mari, when he noticed a single invader stop and search the area. The soldier stood in a ready-to-fire stance and began to carefully sweep the trees with his light. Zenti moved in that direction, darting across the tree limbs. He was not careful, nor did the silvery-white wolf care what sounds he made. Zenti raced from tree to tree.

Calling on the Talent of Shadows, Zenti moved like a whisp of smoke, leaving only a trail of noise. Soldiers fired into the trees, but only as a reaction. Zenti moved until he was just a few feet away and above his target. The sound of gunfire masked his final approach. He then noticed what the invader was trying to locate.

He found the invader's target more by scenting Mari than sight at first. Once he saw Mari, Zenti knew the invader would eventually find her. All things considered, the invaders were not poor soldiers. However, they were over-confident in their superior technology, which made them careless and stupid. Stupid like right now, knowing full well there was a Summoner in the area, yet taking no precautions whatsoever.

Mari frozen. It was not really the prospect of facing **THEM** that scared her; it was facing Zenti with no way of protecting that part of her that was still attached to him. Behind her Faction Command, she could detach herself. Within the safety of commanding her Faction troops, the vixen could keep Zenti at arm's length. But without that support, there was nothing between them.

Mari pulled out her knife, holding it tightly in her grasp, ready for the soldier to try to capture her. Deep in her heart, she wanted Zenti to save her and to run into his arms for protection. The battle raged inside Mari's mind. The spoiled brat told her Zenti was still the enemy, the traitor. However, her heart remembered everything Zenti had sacrificed for her in the past. Everything he had done was simply in the name of love. Confusion dominated the vixen's thoughts as her mind and heart waged war.

Jumping out of the tree, Zenti made no sound as he landed on the back of the soldier, driving the male to the ground. He shoved his paw to the rear of the invader's helmet and focused. Zenti's paw glowed a bright red. He could hear the flesh burning and crackling under the flames of his Gift. The white wolf shoved the soldier's face further in the ground to muffle the screams.

Without looking at Mari, Zenti scanned the area to see if there were any more soldiers nearby. For whatever reason, the invaders had moved on; they must be under strict orders to assault the camp. Zenti could see none, but from the direction of Mari's camp, he heard gunfire. It was sporadic at first as the invaders must have engaged Mari's outlying patrols. The gunfire continued to increase and turned into an ongoing firefight. Zenti then looked back towards Mari.

Mari stood there for a moment, silently watching him as though she was trying to figure out if he was real or just a figment. Before Zenti could react, Mari pushed off the tree and ran to him. Throwing her arms around Zenti, the vixen buried her muzzle into his chest and held on for dear life.

Zenti felt her hit him full force, and he wrapped his paws around Mari, pulling her close. He held her, rubbing his muzzle against the side of her head and ears for what seemed hours, but the sound of the gunfire brought his attention quickly back to the present.

"Mari, something is wrong here. Is Hayden not in the camp? It does not sound like a company worth of firepower," Zenti said as he knelt to the ground. The silvery-white wolf pulled the vixen to her knees. Together they found concealment in the thick underbrush. Reaching out with his Gift, Zenti caused the underbrush to brightly illuminate the area around them. The blinding light rendered them undetectable. Drops of blood began to fall from the tip of his nose.

"Yes, Hayden is there," she quickly replied, "I did not want to let him into the camp. He is on the outskirts. Ricket was posted to escort him," Mari answered. The vixen thought for a moment about what Zenti was implying. She was trying desperately to ignore how close she was to him. Zenti felt warm and comfortably familiar. Mari jumped at her last statement.

"Ricket was Hayden's escort for the night, oh Heaven and Hells," Mari exclaimed. Immediately the vixen pushed herself up and scrambled away from where they were. Grabbing the invader's rifle, Mari sprinted back toward her camp.

"Somethings never change," said Zenti as he watched the vixen dodging his summoned flames. With a wide grin on his muzzle, the silvery-white wolf raced after the vixen. It was just as he had done many times before. Yes, some things gladly never do change.

Chapter 7

Wounded

Mari Semineu raced towards her Faction camp where the invaders were attacking. The vixen darted through the sparse woods at breakneck speed. Behind her, the forest flared like a multitude of bonfires. Mari could scarcely believe the magnitude of Zenti's Gift. He was affecting an area that had to be at least several miles wide.

Ahead, Mari noticed three Mitdonians in civilian clothing. However, they each had Crown Military-issued canvas backpacks. One male otter leaned on a staff as he moved towards her camp. The three were about a mile and a half away from her Faction camp and moving towards it. Because unarmed civilians were moving towards a battle zone, it gave Mari pause. The vixen slowed down. She was directly behind them when she came upon the body of one of her scouts, laying muzzle down in the underbrush.

The three had directly traveled this way as the vixen saw three sets of boot prints in the crushed scrubs. The three could not have missed the body and should have attempted to render aid. Kneeling by the body, Mari identified the male skunk as Scout First Rank Tevis. The dead male was nearly fully recovered and was due to return to his Faction in two weeks. She had assigned him scout duty to help return him to combat readiness.

Mari reached to turn him over when she paused. Something did not feel right about this scene. Instead of turning the dead male over, the vixen slid her paw under his chest and slowly moved it down his body. Finding his forearm, she followed it to his paw. That is when she felt the steel of the G12 grenade. Grasping the edge of the G12, Mari gripped it tightly and pulled it free of the dead male's paws. The vixen rolled the deceased male over and examined the male skunk for wounds. There was one single would to the chest. Mari looked at the grenade.

The G12 grenade was shaped like a disc. It was the preferred anti-personnel weapon of the Fouche Isle Faction troops. Gripping the edge of the disc and depressing a button in the center hub armed it. It could remain armed indefinitely until the edge of the disc was released. Once the edge was released, there was no disarming it. Shaped like a kit's toy, the disc could be thrown in several different ways. Throwing it over or under paw was the least preferred method as the distance it would travel was minimal. Blowback from the powerful explosive could harm the thrower.

However, a skilled soldier could make the disc travel a considerable distance, just like the distance a toy disc in the paws of a capable kit could achieve. Because the G12 did not need a high arc nor as much effort to throw, it was better than the oblong G6 or the G9 orb grenades. However, it was not easy to master. Scout Tevis was not from the Fouche Isle and, to her knowledge, had not learned how to throw the G12. Mari deactivated the G12 and then removed the central hub trigger.

Mari looked at the skunk's chest would and determined it was not from a small-caliber round. Nor was the wound from a larger caliber firearm as there was no exit wound. The entry hole in the male skunk's chest was nearly two digits wide. It could mean only a paw-held, piercing weapon killed him. That was consistent with the invader's shock rods.

Looking back up, the vixen noted that the three civilians had not slowed down. The sound of the firefight continued. Mari moved towards the three who were moving towards the sound of gunfire. No unarmed civilian would head into a firefight.

As the vixen drew closer to the three, it was apparent that these civilians were unphased by the sound of military gunfire. They were either deaf or seasoned combat veterans; Mari was betting on the latter. Gripping the pilfered rifle, she advanced on them cautiously. As Mari approached from behind, the vixen could hear them talking. Moving closer, she listened to the conversation, and her curiosity turned to rage.

"Do you think we brought enough shackles," asked one of the hooded civilians? Mari thought he was a feline; she only caught a glimpse of his muzzle when he turned his head.

"Damned if I know. The Barron wants captives, but it sounds like the camp is putting up a stiff defense," said a female. Mari could not see her muzzle.

"I just know this backpack is heavy. I can not wait to shed some of this weight," said another male.

Mari raised the rifle and took aim. These were slavers. There was never any legal slave trade in the history of Mitd. The Crown strictly forbade it. However, that did not stop some from attempting it. Mari wondered which Barron was stupid enough to risk the wrath of the Royal Assassin. That foul soul showed no mercy in carrying out the King's Command. As much as she detested the Crown's need for a Royal Assassin, Mari Semineu stood resolute with the King on this matter. Even though the Royal Assassin was a disgusting piece of work, slavers deserved no mercy.

****

Zenti slowed down when he saw Mari aiming at what appeared to be three civilians. However, he did not attempt to intervene. The vixen must suspect something as she was not a cold-blooded murderer. Neither was Mari a knee-jerk reactionary when it came to making life and death choices. The sound of gunfire began to wane. Screams came from the east, and Zenti moved off in that direction. When the cries of pups reached his ears, the white wolf raced faster to the east. Behind him, he heard two shots, but no more. Perhaps the third had surrendered.

****

"You complain too much, Wixer. The Barron is paying a premium price for the pre-gifting day kits and pups. How can you complain when you are being offered twenty-five hundred Bring per capture," asked the hooded female?

"Yeah, well, the backpack is still…" said Wixer. However, he never finished his retort. His head snapped forward when Mari's bullet impacted the back of his skull. Wixer was dead before he hit the ground.

Mari pulled the trigger and shifted to a new target before the kit slaver hit the ground. The female slaver crumpled to the ground just as fast as her compatriot. The third turned to see who was shooting at them. The feline froze when he saw the female vixen aiming at him. When the shot did not come, he ducked into the brush.

Mari cursed when she pulled the trigger, and nothing happened. Ducking behind a tree, the vixen noticed that the bolt was open. Popping out the magazine, Mari curse again when she saw it was empty. How stupid of her to grab a firearm but not spare magazines. Throwing the rifle aside, Mari looked around the corner and saw the feline slaver having trouble shedding the backpack. Mari noticed a long hunting knife was the only weapon the feline was carrying. It was strapped to the side of the pack.

Mari drew her combat knife and dashed at the slaver. The unexpected tactic startled the feline, who was halfway through shedding the heavy backpack. The male feline froze as the vixen charged through the underbrush brandishing a combat knife. He finally shed the gear when Mari was less than twenty feet away. The feline reached down and pulled the blade from the pack. In a blinding flash, the male slaver turned and slashed at the empty air. He never saw the vixen slide between his legs, nor did he feel the initial razor-sharp cut as the combat knife sliced through his inner thigh.

Mari did stop to deliver a second blow. The vixen rolled and continued to run towards her camp. She knew there was no need for a second thrust. The slash to the feline's inner thigh was deep and cut through the femoral artery. He would be dead in less than two minutes. That was too short a death for a slaver, but Mari Semineu had other concerns. On the vixen's way past the fallen male otter, she noticed that his staff was an invader's shock rod. Growling, Mari raced on towards her Faction camp.

Ahead was the rundown structure of a mine shaft elevator building. It was in poor condition, but it still stood. However, it but barely functioned. There were no soldiers of either force nearby. Mari scrambled up the rear service ladder. She watched from the outskirts of the camp, hiding on top of the building housing the mineshaft entrance. What the vixen witness broke her heart.

The few faction soldiers that remained in her camp were fighting, but the invaders had outnumbered her troops by nearly three to one. As a result, some of **THEIR** soldiers had advanced into her base and had started to attack the refugees. Most of her troops had fallen back into the tree line, though some remained in the camp. Mari's faction troops were fighting with a life-and-death ferocity. However, Mari could tell they were losing the battle. The dead were everywhere as Mari formed a plan of action.

Males, females, and pups did not matter to the invaders who they killed. There were bodies strewn about the entirety of her camp. The death toll was typical for the invaders, killing everyone they could find that was not of use. Three of her soldiers lay dead beneath an overturned cart to the left of the mine shaft tower. Looking at the cable spool overhead, Mari could tell that the elevator car was at the bottom. However, it did not look like the structure or cables had sustained direct damage. The vixen hoped that most of her patrons were down there.

Mari needed to get down to a gun below. Looking around to make sure it was clear, the vixen slid down a drainpipe on the front of the building. Her tear-filled green eyes came to rest on the body of the pup she had comforted only hours ago. He was skewered on one of the short spears that the invaders carried. The tip had been driven through the pup's body and stuck firm to the wooden shed wall. Mari wondered why the invaders were killing pups instead of leaving them for the slavers. Was it miscommunication, or was there something she was missing?

Typically the invader's spear was used as a prod. The shaft had a power source that delivered an electrical charge, much like a herd prod did. One end was blunt and used as a club. The other end had a sharp point that allowed it to penetrate a Jaydonian's fur. This setup allowed the electrical charge to reach the flesh more effectively.

Mari had to turn away from the sight of her dead patrons. Their bodies were everywhere, scattered about the camp. Rage began to flow through the vixen's body. However, sorrow soon overwhelmed her as another pup was found impaled, pinned to the bottom of the overturned cart. The three soldiers must have been trying to get the remaining patrons into the mines below.

Dropping to the ground, the vixen checked the three dead soldiers for any signs of life and then picked up one of the fallen rifles. Moving between crates and buildings, checking for the dead, she found no signs of life. Most were her civilian patrons who had taken up arms. Sounds of gunfire in the woods told her that the few troops she had remaining were still fighting. She noticed the invaders were moving to the far end of the camp where Hayden's troops were. However, the panther's troops were not firing at the invaders. Just as odd was the fact that the invaders were not firing at Hayden's troops.

****

Zenti came upon the source of the screams. Five pups and one post-Coming-of-Age female lay dead at the base of a tree. Their throats had been slit. Turning back towards the Faction Camp, Zenti raced to the edge of the tree line. Ever aware of Mari's presence, the silvery-white wolf scanned to her precise location. There was something terribly wrong with this attack. The invaders had not suffered enough casualties; Mari's troops and patrons were well trained.

Zenti watched Mari as she headed into the camp. The vixen began checking the wounded and dead. He could feel the sorrow start to creep into her. He wanted to go to her, comfort her, but something was not right here. Mari had about fifteen nearly healthy soldiers and maybe thirty wounded who could still fire a weapon from what the silvery-white wolf remembered. Hayden had about thirty from his blood memory he had taken from Jolet earlier. That was roughly equal numbers to the invaders. Unless poorly trained or positioned, a defending force equal to the attacking force should inflict higher casualties. However, Zenti noted this was not the case.

The fight should not have been so one-sided. This was just another battleground with the invaders involved. The dead should be about equal. The invaders never like to attack alone. It was standard tactics to send a wave of the Jaydonian species as the initial shock troops. This was not the case. Neither Mari nor Hayden's camp should have been caught unprepared.

Deaths of all ages were common. Over the past year, between Mari's rejection and the invader's surprise attacks leading to uncontested slaughters, the silvery-white wolf had become as cold as a lake of ice. Zenti looked among the dead. Most of the deceased were the recovering wound, civilians, and only a few of Hayden's soldiers. It appeared that Hayden's soldiers had been shot in the back. The question was, who attacked them? Was it the invaders, Mari's troops, or Hayden's own? Zenti stayed to the outskirts as he moved around the camp. The white wolf made his way towards Hayden's temporary base.

Scanning Hayden's camp, Zenti saw it was empty. It looked like there had been a minor skirmish, but it was not nearly a mess as Mari's camp. This looked staged for someone's benefit. A few of the invaders were moving out of Mari's camp, heading towards Hayden's. However, they moved at a leisurely pace. Zenti looked towards Mari.

The vixen was trying to chamber a round in a gun she must have recovered. Zenti watched as Mari fought with the bolt before throwing the rifle to the ground in frustration. Mari dashed to her tent. The white wolf felt the vixen's anger rising. In his mind's eye, fueled by the Gift, he watched as the vixen grabbed the gun that she had taken from the armory earlier. However, her pistol was not on the cot, and she did not bother to try to find it in the tent.

Zenti picked up one of the discarded assault rifles and pulled back the bolt. A spent casing ejected, and he chambered another round. Taking aim, the white wolf pulled the trigger; the gun fired, but it felt wrong. Pulling back, the bolt ejected another spent cartridge. Taking the magazine out of the lower receiver assembly, Zenti popped empty round after round out of the magazine. These were training blanks used by new recruits to familiarize them with the rifle's recoil. Someone had loaded the magazines with blanks. No wonder the battle was so one-sided, thought Zenti. Someone within Mari's Faction, besides Jolet, had betrayed her.

Racing out of her tent, Mari took aim at an enemy in the ruins of her camp. One shot, one dead, then a second. The shocked invaders fell back into a defensive posture. It was clear that they were not expecting Mari Semineu to be in camp. Three more invaders fell as she repeatedly shot until the clip was empty. The invaders were screaming her name in shocked surprise as they dove for cover. Mari Semineu was to be in Hayden's camp, not her own.

In the lull in her firing, one of the invaders located the vixen. The male invader rushed forward and brought his gun up to shoot. Mari saw him coming; he was her next target. However, she was out of ammunition. That inconvenience did not mean Mari Semineu was out of options. The vixen did something unexpected; she leapt at the invader. Mari swung the gun like a club as hard as she could before he could train his rifle on her leaping body. The strike hit the invader with such force that it fractured a vertebra and rendered him unconscious.

Pain shot through the vixen's left shoulder. Another invader attacked her from behind. The tip of his spear-like prod pierced clean through the vixen. The end protruded through Mari's shoulder just shy of the joint. The thrust had not been perfect, or it would have killed the vixen.

Simultaneously, the force of the vixen's swing propelled her forward, and she jerked clear of the spear-like prod. Ducking, rolling, and spinning, Mari follow through on the swing of the gun. The blow landed between the invader's legs, catching her attacker unprepared. *IT* crumpled to the ground, groaning in agony.

Three more invaders circled the vixen. One male thrust his spear-like prod at her from behind, barely grazing the vixen. However, the electrical shock from the spear dropped Mari to her knees.

The invaders were close enough that Mari could hear *THEIR* labored breathing when a sudden burning sensation began to overwhelm her senses. Fear raced through the vixen as another electrical charge drove her flat to the ground. Her skin felt hot yet numbingly cold, and for a moment, Mari thought that Zenti had come to her aid. However, something felt different. She did not feel the heat of Zenti's summoned flames but the burn of freezing. It felt like she was in the middle of a blizzard with nothing on and all her fur shaved off. That was not the feeling of Zenti's summoned fire.

Huddled on the ground, Mari tried to wrapped her arms around her chest and ball up. However, her body would not respond. The vixen's whole body felt as if she were holding on to a live electrical wire. Mari braced herself for a continued attack. She could not move, and mentally the vixen screamed. The invaders would kill her. Mari could not accept this was how her life was to end. Her body continued to feel electrified. She was numb, and her muscles would not respond.

However, inside, the vixen felt as if she was on fire. There was more work for her to do on Mitd. She needed to help save her species from the vile invaders. Mari Semineu willed her body to move, yet it failed to respond. This was the end, her mind screamed. Yet there was a raging storm within the vixen's heart that said otherwise. Again, her mind tried to crush her heart's optimism. **THEY** would kill her and all her species. This was the end, her mind said, but Mari's heart won the war. Somewhere within the vixen's heart, the burning cold erupted. This was the end her mind said in one final attempt to subjugate her heart.

However, the end never came. The air rapidly froze around Mari as she raged inside. She saw **IT** come up beside her as she huddled on the ground. The invader raised the stock of the rife, ready to bash her head in. At that moment, the titanic battle between Mari Semineu's heart and mind ended. With her heart victorious, the vixen cried out in a primal rage. The vixen's breed's[19] high-pitched cry pierced the air as it deepened into a primal growl of pure fury.

Zenti heard Mari scream and turned toward her just in time to see one of the invaders ready to strike her with the butt of a gun. Mari was balled up, screaming in a rage-filled fear. About to summon a globe of fire to surround and protect his mate, the silvery-white wolf abruptly stopped. Zenti watched in amazement as a wave of ice-blue fire and white lightning erupted from Mari's body. All four invaders surrounding Mari were engulfed in a massive azure glow. The vixen leaned back and flung her

---

[19] Each breed of Jaydonian has its own voice. Though the breeds fall into a specific family, a vulpine does not sound like a canine.

arms wide. Lightning lept from her paws and enveloped each of the invaders. Individually the four fell to the ground. The ice blue sphere held for a moment, and the white lightning danced around the four frozen in ice.

Zenti shifted his vision to that of the Gifted and looked at Mari. There was a wildness in her eyes and a raging power that coursed through the whole of her body. It was something the silvery-white wolf knew very well. Mari was touching the Void just as he had when he was five. Zenti knew the feeling as Mari was experiencing the first embrace of the Void. Zenti watched the vixen as she released her fury upon the invaders of Mitd. The azure sphere flashed out across the Faction camp.

Mari was now on her knees, arms splayed wide, claws outstretched, head back, chest out, and arching backward as she released a second raging scream. His suspicions were confirmed. Mari's father, General Haverick Waxton, was correct; there were two Summoners the invaders were hunting that night he passed to the stars. There could be no other conclusion. Orra's Prophecy of the Monster and Saviour had begun.

Mari felt her heart slowing down and wondered why had *THEY* not killed her? Slowly lowering her head, the vixen's gaze met the frozen bodies with surprise. She immediately scrambled away from the dead, her eyes wide, heart pounding once again. She stood in the center of her devastated Faction camp, stunned and confused at what just happened.

"Push the attack, advance, and take no prisoners. Use your sidearms," ordered Zenti. His Gift amplified his voice, and it thundered across the battlefield. A wave of fear pulsed out from the silvery-white wolf as he grabbed a pistol and fired on the invaders. The stunned invaders momentarily gawked at what the vixen had done. Fear struck the camp affecting only the invaders. Blood oozed from the pores of the silvery-white wolf as he tapped into the Voidal energy with reckless abandon. Zenti did not stop firing until he ran out of ammunition. The invaders were in full retreat. Howling in rage, Summoner Zenti Semineu lashed out at the fleeing invaders.

The remaining faction soldiers and armed patrons obeyed Zenti's command immediately without question. Pistol fire from the woods intensified, and invaders fell. Then the Faction soldiers burst from the woods, descending upon the camp. Screaming as they advanced across the base, they pressed the attack as Zenti raged. Mari's patrons and soldiers were too afraid to disobey the Monster that had ravaged Mitd for the past thirteen months. However, there was more that drove them to obey. The Monster that devastated the traitors of Mitd was there leading them.

Fires, summoned by Zenti, erupted from the now fleeing invaders. The Faction soldier and Mari's patrons pressed the attack. The Faction troops found the battle one-sided as the burning invaders did not attempt to fight but merely tried to flee while putting the flames out. A radio chirped to life on one of the dead invaders near Zenti. The white wolf understood the order given.

"Mari!" yelled Zenti as he pointed to the woods behind her. "Run east! NOW, FAST!" was all he said as he began to shout orders to the remaining Faction soldiers, who obeyed with precision and without question.

Mari obeyed the command of Zenti instantly. She ran towards the forest, scooping up a little cub from her camp along the way. With the petite pre-Coming-of-Age bear cub secure in her arms, Mari Seminue disappeared deep into the woods. The vixen now understood that Hayden had set up an ambush. Her Faction soldiers and patrons were paying for it with their very lifeblood. Those remaining in the camp rushed about, trying to run into the woods. The survivors scattered in all directions, still shooting as they retreated. The soldiers attempted to follow the silvery-white wolf's orders. The invaders were in full retreat. Hayden's forces were nowhere to be seen. Mari ran deep into the woods as Zenti commanded.

The cub in Mari's arms was crying, wailing for his mother. Finding a tall, thick-branched tree, Mari used her hunting knife to aid her in climbing as far up as she could. Driving the blade into the tree's bark, the vixen cuddled the cub close. The little male was scared. The Faction camp had never been attacked before, and the chaotic events traumatized the little bear cub. The vixen whispered softly into his ear.

"Aw, why does a brave little cub cry," Mari whispered? The vixen stroked his ears and nuzzled his neck. Watching as the cub slowly calmed down, Mari licked his tear-stained cheeks. He sniffed at her, watching her with his bright blue eyes. The little male bear recognized Miss Mari. He felt safe in her arms. "There we go, what a big male."

Her mind drifted back to Zenti. Part of her hoped that he would not get hurt, no matter how unlikely that was. If he was anything like the wolf of their past, he always put himself in harm's way when leading. That fact triggered a memory of her father's advice as a kit. When Mari was a pre-Gifting Day kit, she felt her father's old scars while lying in his lap. Her father's words would never leave the vixen. 'The mark of a great leader, sweet one, is their ability to lead from within the fire, though there are always great risks.'

"And there are always great rewards," Mari whispered, finishing her father's sage advice. The pre-Gifting Day cub looked up at her with bloodshot eyes. The vixen found herself looking at the cub in her arms, noticing how he looked up at her. It was much like her sister had looked at their father when she was young. She flinched just as a thunderous explosion shook the area from the direction of her camp. Mari looked back at the flash of light back with shock. Was that artillery?

The first of many artillery rounds landed in the camp. The explosions sent bodies and debris everywhere. Zenti hoped the invaders had not changed their firing pattern. The white wolf hit the ground when an artillery shell exploded. As the wreckage came raining down, the white wolf ran directly into the blast cloud of the last explosion.

Diving into the blast crater, Zenti saw the brilliant explosion as another round hit, blowing up what was left of the armory. That was a close call, thought the white wolf. He had just moved past the armory tent. Looking around, Zenti saw one of the invaders pointing in his direction and talking on a radio. Zenti pieced together what was transpiring. He dashed out of the crater. The invaders had planned on him being here and had a spotter directing artillery fire. The invader realized too late that he had been noticed by Summoner Zenti Semineu.

Racing toward the spotter, Zenti leapt at him. The white wolf summoned flames around the invader. The male spotter screamed as the summoned fire began to burn his uniform. The spotter attempted to run towards the woods. Zenti snatched up the discarded radio and dropped it in his belt pouch before racing towards the opposite woods. Calling on his Gift, Zenti intensified his summoned fire. The whole of Mari's Faction camp and Hayden's temporary camp erupted into massive bonfires. The panther's troops had not rendered assistance as the oath demanded; therefore, their life was forfeit by Crown law. The white wolf claimed the right to render punishment. With extreme prejudice, Summoner Zenti Sermineu met out justice. Everything burned as the silvery-white wolf enforced Crown law.

The invader continued screaming just as another barrage landed right where Zenti had previously been. The artillery round exploded close to the white wolf, and searing pain shot throughout his lower body. The explosion threw Zenti to the ground, stunning him. Years of battle instinct drove him to his paw pads, and Zenti staggered into the woods. More explosions rocked the camp, destroying what was left of the old mining structures. However, the mineshaft building remained standing.

As Zenti dodged deeper into the woods, he could not help wondering how deep this plot to kill him was. Jolet's blood memory was not fully complete. Details were missing, and fragments appeared to have been suppressed. Had a Shaman used the Talent of Obfuscation to hide the rabbit's memories? Zenti had a deep gut feeling this was all about him. This had been a trap set by Hayden and possibly more. The panther bringing his troops here, and the invaders conveniently showing up, was all too suspect. Add to the equation that Hayden's troops had not engaged in defending Mari's faction camp led to one conclusion. This entire ruse of Hayden's visit to Mari was all a pretext to kill him. The loss of Hayden's troops and all of Mari's encampment was of little consequence to the panther. To General Hayden, collateral damage was acceptable, and he had demonstrated that in numerous victorious battles. No, this was planned; there was no other explanation, Zenti thought as he raced through the trees.

For a moment, Zenti wondered if Mari was involved as well but quickly dismissed the thought. He would have detected it during the Talent of the Union. Mari still had not learned to hide her thoughts very well. If she were part of this betrayal, he would have been able to detect it. This had to be Hayden's plan. Zenti would have one of his associates delve deeper into this mystery.

The white wolf ran into the forest, twisting and turning in the direction opposite of where Mari ran. He listened for a fourth artillery barrage. However, no further explosions rocked the night. With a moment to catch his breath, Zenti knew those explosions were too small to be the invader's artillery. Those were Mitdonian made artillery. Hayden must have brought the small-bore, portable PA 75 batteries. Those artillery pieces were easy to assemble and disassemble. That made them easy to carry by a limited number of soldiers. The PA 75 had a greater range than the M50 Mortar.

The radio he had taken from the spotter filled with chatter. The invaders were ordering search parties. However, it seemed the more significant talk was concerning using loyal supporters as the main body to search for survivors. Zenti knew what was meant by 'loyal supporters.' They were traitors to his species and to Jayden. The search parties were being organized to look for him and Mari. This search could get excessively bloody, and Zenti knew he had to end this and end it fast.

Taking the recovered radio out of his belt pouch, Zenti took his personal radio out as well. Clicking both transmit buttons, he held them apart as not to generate feedback. Dropping low to the ground, pain searing through his lower back and legs from the shrapnel, Zenti growled deeply. Each movement was almost unbearable, and anger took control.

"Hayden, you worthless bastard. I know you are out there listening to this. Know this, cat; what I have done in the past will now pale compared to what I will do. The invaders and those who support them will be the full focus of my wrath now. However, you can count on this, you pathetic waste of seed. Your family, from your dead mate's parents to your remaining kits, will never be safe. Never!" the silvery-white spat into the captured radio. His personal radio echoed his words to all of Mitd that could receive his signal, which was vast.

Mari could not believe the anger in Zenti's voice as she heard it come over her radio. What was worse was the level of pain she was feeling from her back and legs. The pain was foreign, as the vixen had no wounds there. Her body rebelled against the pain, and her legs cramp up as she held onto the tree for dear life. She held tight to the cub in her arms for fear of dropping the little bear. Mari felt terrified, but she refused to show it.

The vixen held the cub close to her while holding on to the tree. It was in that instant, holding on to the tree for dear life, that the vixen realized she and Zenti were still sharing a telepathic link. Mari found she could not break the telepathic bond between her and Zenti. Mari tried to close the link as the echoes of Zenti's anger-filled voice rolled across the airwaves.

"You can't threaten me," Hayden snapped back through the radio, "she isn't yours anymore. You are the butcher of Mitd, and I will hunt you to the ends of the land. I am the Crown Champion, and you are a worthless blot. I have promised the Crown I will put you down like the cur you are."

"This is not about Mari, you pathetic foul excuse for a Jaydonian," growled Zenti. His voice embued the hate in his very being for the traitor Hayden. "It never was about Mari. This is about you selling out our species to the invaders. Whatever the invaders are offering you will never be worth what I will take from your family. That is right, cat, before I execute you, I am going to make your family pay," growled Zenti into the two radios. Pain shot through his body, but through the sheer force of will, Zenti continued.

"I am not the betrayer wolf. I am Mitd's Champion. I have done for Mitd what no other has done. You have betrayed Mari and Mitd," hissed the panther into the radio.

"Wrong, cat. This is about you setting up Mari's camp to be attacked and destroyed while you and your soldiers were doing nothing to help. I am not stupid, Hayden. I know your primary school tactics. I hope your loyal troops are listening to this, you betrayer of Mitd. Not only will I kill everyone that you hold dear, but I will also kill everyone precious to those who follow you. They are all traitors, and I will make their families pay for their crimes. If they turn themselves into Mari or another Faction Leader for execution, only then will I spare their families," growled Zenti.

For miles, the air filled with wave after wave of raw emotion as it poured out of Zenti. His Gift amplified the pure emotional hatred that flowed from the wounded white wolf. The fear his Gift exuded sent shock waves of terror into the hearts of the traitors and invaders. Zenti embraced the Void yet resisted the madness that it brought. This was not the time for him to lose control. With remarkable restraint, the white wolf continued.

"Nevertheless, rest assured, cat, your family is already forfeit. Also, for the record, yes, I still love Mari, but I do not own her. I will not beg her. If I am alone for the rest of my life, but she is happy, then it is a small price to pay for her safety. But the price for your crimes will be paid with the blood of your kin," growled Zenti. The rage in words continued to radiate throughout the airwaves.

Mari could feel the pure hatred in each word as it came across the radio and wondered if the others listening felt the same wave of fear that was gripping her. Oh, Heavens and Hells, the vixen could feel unadulterated rage in Zenti's voice. Mari felt terrified. Could he be so heartless as to kill the traitor's entire families? She found herself shaking as he began to speak again.

"Tell them to make peace with Orra because I have lost all my faith. Death is my closest friend, and I feel like personally introducing her to each and every member of your extended family," growled Zenti. The pain racked his body as he found another place to hide. Stopping, the blood-covered silvery-white wolf decided the pain must end if he was to continue.

Focusing his Gift on the multitude of metal artillery

fragments, Zenti ripped as many of them out with the pure force of the Void. A primal howl filled the evening air, rushing out like waves crashing onto the shore.

The cub started to cry the moment the roaring growl echoed through the forest. Grabbing the cub by the muzzle to quiet him, Mari shook with fear at that sound. Never in their past had the vixen felt or heard such rage or pain from Zenti. It was as if the whole of his existence was being poured out of his very being.

Oh, Orra above, Mari silently pleaded. The vixen could feel Zenti's pain as her body burned. Mari knew that Zenti was ripping shrapnel out of his body; she had seen him do it in the past. However, it was never like this. It was as if the phantom shrapnel was being ripped from her body. This was too much; she could not hold on any longer with the shared pain. Closing her eyes, she did everything she could to slam her mind closed to his.

Zenti felt Mari attempting to closing her mind to him. He thought this must be some lingering residual of such a long emotional connection from a few hours before. However, that was not the case, Zenti realized. This was not a residual effect; it was a Voidal connection. Mari was trying with such force to close off their connection that it broke his concentration. Mari slamming the telepathic connection shut caused the white wolf to lose concentration on his Gift. The results left many artillery shells fragments still in his body.

Zenti felt the exhaustion of the past days drain the

remaining stamina from his body. He did not have the strength to call on his Gift for another attempt to remove the remaining fragments. It was all the white wolf could do to control the pain. He knew it was bad enough that he would need a shaman or doctor. Assessing the situation, he accepted that he could not fight in his current condition.

Through the Gifted Talent of Unity, Zenti knew where every metal fragment rested in his body. None were near major arteries. The internal bleeding would be minimal. Maintaining the Talent of Unity was something every Gifted could do with minimal effort. Though he did not have the strength to rip the fragments from his body, Zenti knew he could at least move them around without inflicting more damage. However, he needed to rest first.

Sadness crept in, and Zenti felt sorry for allowing the lingering effects between him and Mari to continue. He could have closed the link long ago., but he wanted her to see the monster he had become. No, not the monster he became, but the monster he relished being, Zenti corrected himself. Mari deserved no less than to see the truth. Perhaps the truth was too much for Mari to see. That realization brought back a snippet of wisdom from Mari's father. 'Truth, son, cost the soul, but the soul is all you can take to the stars, so always speak it.' Zenti looked to the stars where the departed souls looked down upon the living. He missed the elder lion.

When Mari's mind had severed the link, her body stopped trembling. Something else happened that shocked the vixen. Her wounds healed, though not entirely.

However, the only thought that raced through her mind was Zenti's words. The vixen felt her heart speed up as she repeated the words that Zenti still loved her.

She looked at the cub in her arms and smiled. Mari knew that the little bear cub knew nothing of what was going on around him. The cub looked up into the vixen's face, and Mari could not help but grin at him. She was crying again, and the cub gently touched her cheek. Mari caressed his feather-soft ears.

Mari sighed. Just because Zenti still loved her did not mean that she wanted to openly admit that she loved him back. The battle still raged between heart and mind, and she continued to cry. Mari cried for those who were dead and for their families, who continued to survive. The vixen cried for the tragedy that was this war. Mari thought of all those who paid the price for freedom, including her family, past and present. Her tears continued to freely flow.

****

The radio went silent, as did the woods, leaving a peaceful wake as the lingering smell of explosives began to drift away. Zenti moved on from the battle area, hoping that his rage-filled message had given the attackers something to think about. In the past, it had, and because he kept his promises, those loyal to the invaders knew his words were not empty threats. Hoping the others in Mari's Faction camp had gotten away, Zenti moved on. He knew that his wounds would require a lot of attention, and he decided that he trusted a shaman more than he did a doctor right now. Doctors were good for aches and pain, but it took a shaman to heal the deep wounds, and Zenti knew just where he needed to go. However, it would take many more days than if he went to a doctor loyal to the Crown.

Hayden's men were still out there, as was an artillery battery. The battery had to be to the north-northwest of Mari's encampment and less than ten miles away, probably on those foothills just off Kings Road forty-six. He knew he was in no shape to deal with that situation. His Faction was twenty miles away, preparing for a strike on a supply convoy late tomorrow. However, a quick strike on the artillery emplacement would be more productive. It would also allow Mari and her patrons to escape. Carefully he found a hiding spot, pulled his radio out, and set it to his Faction's encoded channel. He pressed the record key, enabled the scramble code prefix, and began to talk.

"Malachi, a new target. An artillery battery is near KR forty-six, within ten miles of my original destination. This is not a recovery exercise. Send recovery aid to Mari, and beware Jolet, he is a spy," Zenti ordered while trying to bite back the pain in his voice. He hit the stop button, then pushed the transmit key and listened as the scrambled message chirped over the radio.

Moments later, a series of chirps told him Malachi acknowledged the message and that there was a voice reply. Zenti played the message.

"Saw the massive smoke, heard the battery engage, figured recovery was not an option, be finished before our midnight snack. Will send medical aid. Thanks for the warning; good hunting," replied a quiet male voice.

Malachi was Zenti's second in command and the fastest learner he knew. Though Zenti would have liked to enlisted his talents elsewhere, he knew Malachi was a professional soldier with a sense of honor. Though that was an admirable trait, it did not always serve the white wolf's primary purpose. Nonetheless, listening to the reply, Zenti beamed with a twisted delight, knowing that there was no escape for the artillery crew. Mari's Faction soldiers and her patrons would have aid shortly. Zenti put the radio back into its holster.

Quietly he slipped out of the forest and headed south. Zenti followed a game trail for ten or so miles. Stepping into a shallow stream, he made his way further down, leading to the southwest. The night was in full bloom and slowly becoming overcast. The cold water brought a welcomed comfort to his wounds, but it was not cold enough to deaden the pain. When using his Gift, Zenti did not count how many wounds there were, but soon they all started to burn. The pain made his movement slower. The water was rapidly losing any heat from the previous day, and the cold was welcomed.

Zenti journeyed on through the night, and by the pre-dawn hours, he had reached a small village along the now widening creek. The mist rolling off the water had settled over the one main street. It was still too early for activity and no lights burned in the windows of the few homes.

This was Myhre, a small communal farm that produced mainly vegetables. The Crown ceded land grants to major landowners with the understanding that they would use most of the land for production. The Crown paid for the upkeep and maintenance of the town's infrastructure in return for thirty percent of the harvest. Whether it was food crop, timber, mineral, or other goods, the Isle of Mitd had never gone without. That was until the invaders began their attacks in earnest. For centuries, the invaders only raided, and only on a small scale. All that changed two decades ago. Though the invaders were few in number, they created a loyal following that ravaged the land of Mitd. Fortunately, Myhre was still an unscathed farming village of little importance to the invaders.

Like all villages and small towns on the Isle of Mitd, the Crown engineers designed them. This practice was established almost five hundred years ago. Small villages and towns that were already established were razed to the ground and rebuilt at the Crown's expense. It was a bold stroke that King Taimus Corinth the Fourth had implemented in an ultimately successful attempt to unify the chain of islands. In taking this innovative initiative, it was hoped that as the citizens traveled or moved, they could feel that life was stable.

Mitd had a multitude of dialects of the Mitdonian

language. Though they shared the same root language, the vast number of dialects made it seem like many different languages. The King and all subsequent kings hoped that not feeling like a stranger in a strange land would promote unity. However, creating one language was more problematic than making towns look the same. The larger cities had rules they had to follow but had a lot more freedom only because of the complexity required to control their designs. This bold initiative was one of the many factors that help Mitd survive during the current escalating war. When you moved from town to town, the base layout was the same.

Slipping through the pre-dawn mist, Zenti entered a barn on the outskirts of town. There he found a mount and tack that would fit his needs. After saddling the horse and adjusting the tack, Zenti found feedbags. He left a note for the owner informing them who had taken the mount and equipment. In the message, Zenti told the owner to take the note to the bank in any city. They were to give it to the bank manager. The sum of Breng on the note equaled more than triple the sum of what it would cost to buy everything new. However, the signature on the note was of a Crown official, not Zenti Semineu.

On the way out of the barn, Zenti filled the bags of oats from a storeroom. Much to his luck, he found two bottles of liniment. It was not for the mount but for him. It would keep the pain of the wounds moderately in check and help keep the infections down. Quietly he led the horse out of town, right back to the broad stream. Painfully Zenti mounted the domestic horse and guided the mount into the middle of the shallow stream. The silvery-white wolf continued westward. It hurt to sit on the wounds, but he kept his pace only moderate for the next two hours before the sun rose. Zenti then exited the river and made his way to the main road.

Following the main road for a short while, Zenti turned into an age-ruined abandoned barn. After tying off the mount, Zenti began to smear the liniment on his wounds. Laying the black salve on thick, the initial sting actually felt better than the dull, continuous aching. Cutting strips of discarded vegetable sacks, Zenti wrapped the wounds comfortably tight. After pausing for a short while, he ate a tasteless military ration. Afterward, the white wolf redressed himself and left the age-ruined barn. He was tired but knew he could not stop just yet. Calling on his Gift, he allowed the soothing Talent of Negation to ease the pain. Zenti knew it was a temporary fix, one that would exhaust him faster, but he needed to move on. Returning to the stream, the white wolf continued his trek.

Riding for part of the first day, Zenti kept to the shallows of the stream. The stream widened and, he knew it would turn into a shallow river in a few miles. That shallow river eventually fed into the Jetton River. Exiting the stream, he moved inland for a few miles, found a secure spot, ate, and fell asleep. Zenti awoke to the sounds of the land awaiting dusk to evaporate into darkness.

Nightfall found the white wolf still tired and hungry. The pain began to grow as he moved about.

Continuing his trip, Zenti came upon a farmhouse. Making his way along the riverbank, Zenti dismounted. Dipping his paws in the river and then wiping them on the back of his trousers, Zenti smeared a little of the blood on his muzzle. Then he did the same around his eyes before he went up to the door and knocked.

A middle-aged boar gasped when he answered the door. A stuttering, meek, and timid Zenti apologized for interrupting the farmer's evening. The white wolf told a tale of being robbed and how he lost all but a few Breng he had tucked away in his saddlebags. When the farmer looked at the mount, Zenti added how it was fortunate that the horse bolted but did not go far. The middle-aged boar accepted the story when his mate fussed at him for being so cold to an injured Mitdonian.

The farmer invited him to come in and eat, but Zenti told the couple that he really wanted to get home. However, he would be more than willing to pay for some fresh water and a meal to go. The boar was more than happy to help and refused the Breng for the dinner of stew and bread. His mate insisted that the white wolf rest while he ate. The three sat at the bank of the river on the docks. This was the couple's favorite spot to relax after a hard day's work.

The farmer's mate, a happy doe, refilled Zenti's bowl twice, chiding the white wolf for even suggesting he had eaten enough. Zenti looked as bad as he felt. Between all the horse liniment, blood, and mud, the two did not recognize Summoner Zenti Semineu. The three of them talked for an hour while Zenti ate the hearty meal. Sitting still actually helped the white wolf control the pain more effectively.

Zenti listened to these two farmers explain how they and others benefited from all the local Faction's aid. In the past four months since Mari's Faction had established camp, the area became safer. Though they had never met the vixen, the two praised her kindness. Zenti inwardly smiled. Even when others did not personally know Mari Semineu, she touched lives, he thought. The doe begged him to rest the night. He thanked her but refused, saying he wanted to get back to his family. In true Mitdonian fashion, the farmer and his mate insisted on him taking several days' worth of food. The doe scolded Zenti when he politely refused. She warned the white wolf it might take more time to reach his home than he anticipated. It was hard to argue with the doe's logic. The couple said they were blessed by the generosity of Miss Mari and her Faction. How could they not bless another in need?

Zenti thanked the couple, and when they were not looking, the white wolf left a few large denominations of Breng on the pump handle after he filled a canteen. Zenti left the couple and rode all night long, heading southwest, following the river. He made good time, though all the while, he focused on controlling the ever-increasing pain. The food had indeed done him a world of good, and he was grateful that the doe had been so forceful in making him eat. Her logic was that of a simple farmer who knew the value of a full stomach. The doe told Zenti the meal would carry him through the night. She was correct.

As the midday sun hung high in the sky, the white wolf again slept in the thick of the woods. Resting during the day was his best protection against detection by those loyal to the invaders. Most were not actively involved in raiding full time. The randomness that Zenti's Northern Faction employed made risking daytime incursions unprofitable. Rumors circulated that Summoner Zenti Seminue preferred to 'hunt' during the day. To reinforce that rumor, the silvery-white wolf had done nothing but daylight raids for nearly two months. The ensuing result was short of stunning. Those who support the invaders stopped venturing an attack during the daylight hours. Though the invaders appeared during the day, Zenti knew the invaders preferred the cloak of darkness. That left Zenti an opportunity to remain restful during the day.

The white wolf awoke in darkness, and slowly he pushed on. He was exhausted. It was not physical or mental exhaustion but something deeper within. Zenti felt that he had a fever, and though he could not see the wounds, he knew from the way they reacted to his touch that they were infected. He would need to move faster if he were to make it to the buzzard's home and still be able to survive the Shaman's "delicate touch'. He chuckled at the word and even that hurt.

Stopping in the late-night hour, he walked into the river and let the coolness of the water soothe his wounds. As the water soaked his pants and shirt, his fur released its crusty hold on the tattered clothing. They peeled off with little effort. He felt scabs peel off his skin and fur, and the rush of cold water on the hot open wounds felt briefly divine.

It took almost half an hour for the fur to become completely un-matted, by which time the cool water had numbed the many tiny entry wounds. Zenti washed his clothes, wrung them out, and draped them over his shoulders. Wading ashore, the night air began to sting at the multitude of angry lacerations as he hung his clothing and cloth bandages on a branch.

Again, the white wolf packed as many of the wounds as he could reach with the liniment. Unfortunately, that used the last of it up. Zenti was able to treat most of the lacerations. Focusing his Gift on the cloth bandages hanging on the branch, Zenti watched as they began to steam and then dry thoroughly. His skill at controlling his Gift was growing stronger each day. Zenti started the laborious process of re-bandaging his wounds and then got dressed. It took him almost an hour to do that simple task, and it wore him out. He felt his temperature returning as the cool water dried. The evening air would not be able to keep him chilled. He knew he was losing the battle and decided to risk riding harder.

Zenti rode on for the rest of the evening through a thinning forest. This was a large, sparsely uninhabited area mainly used for grain farming. The evening air grew warmer, sapping his strength much faster than he had anticipated. He went back to the river and followed it, sometimes riding for a while on the shoreline, sometimes walking in the water to let it combat his rising temperature. Sunrise was coming. He decided to continue along the river, knowing he would need the water's cooling effects again before noon. Every movement now became labored, and Zenti found it taxed his mental state more and more. Heavens and Hells, he hated artillery.

Zenti calculated that he would run into an enemy patrol within four days. Like many of the Factions, those who supported the invaders attempted to avoid the major cities and thoroughfares. The vast empty interior of Mitd's main island was prime farmland. However, it was not exactly the type of place one would build a metropolis. The land was relatively flat, and rail lines and highways were the fastest way to cross Mitd. It was not much to look at, but it would cut weeks off anyone's travel.

Zenti was not far off on his calculated time. It was about an hour before noon on his third day when his peaceful journey was interrupted. Zenti stood in the river's cooling waters when his Gift heightened senses picked up the invaders' scent.

He left the river cautiously to avoid a heavily armed patrol of invader troops. He tied up his mount, securing it deep into the sparse clump of woods, and repositioned himself far away. For the first time in thirteen months of hunting the enemy, Zenti hid. The white wolf watched as twenty invaders march past. This marked the first time Summoner Zenti Semineu let the invader pass him by without lifting a claw. Frustration almost got the better part of him, and he prepared to attack the patrol. However, a series of movements in the distant tree line stayed his temper.

Pulling out a pair of binoculars, Zenti scanned the tree line. He counted nine, no ten, snipers positioning themselves to give excellent cover fire. Were they tracking him, or was this just a random patrol? He was just not sure. Again, Zenti wondered if the invaders had found a way to follow his use of the Gift? The silvery-white wolf watched as the heavy patrol moved on. Fifteen minutes later, the snipers moved out in groups of two, waiting five minutes between pairs, keeping to the tree line, or moving through the mid-spring crops.

No, the invaders were not tracking him but hunting him. Usually, trying to trick someone into giving themself away was a good tactic. However, Zenti wondered just who could have thought that he was so rash as to blindly attack. How stupid did the invaders believe he was? That question took a moment to sink in, and it made Zenti chuckled. He realized that if he were not so seriously wounded, he might have attacked. Perhaps not the heavy troops, but the snipers. The heavy forces wore sealed armor that offered limited protection to his summoned fire. With time, even the heavy armor could not protect the wearer. However, time was not always a luxury that battle afforded.

Zenti reminded himself that the key to victory was randomness, not dogmatic tradition. That was the one lesson that the late General Haverick Waxton had drilled into his thick skull. Be so random that even your allies do not know what to expect. It had not failed him in these past ten years. Ten years, Zenti thought to himself. He missed the guidance of the elder lion. In those ten years, the war had progressed from invader raids into roving bands of invader loyalists creating havoc across Mitd. No sooner than he could quell one fire than another one would spring to life on the far side of the Island chain.

Though it took him nearly seven years to piece together, the silvery-white wolf had figured that pattern out. For little more than a year, Zenti was able to predict the areas of conflict. He would be somewhere nearby to crush the traitors before they could inflict severe damage. Zenti had those who would obey his every command without fail or question to call upon. For a while, it looked like the invaders and their supports would be defeated. Then he was captured, escaped, and then rejected by Mari. In his absents, the tide of war shifted again. Those loyal to him were leaderless, and though they continued to act, it was without his guidance. When Mari rejected him, the tide of war once again shifted.

Not only did the invaders attack in the predicted patterns still, but the traitors also began attacking the main cities. With the help of the invaders, over twenty cities fell to the traitors. Zenti had a solution to that problem. It was effective yet earned him his current reputation. However, the silvery-white wolf cared little for what others thought of him. He was random in his acts. That was a significant weakness of the enemy.

The one weakness both Hayden and the invaders

shared was a significant lack of foresight concerning unconventional battles. Though they both were highly effective in their planning, neither were prepared for his unpredictability. Zenti watched the snipers move out, and he tracked the invader's movements as they continued moving away.

Pain shot up Zenti's legs as he changed position. That simple movement sent a wave of rage back to the forefront of his mind, and Zenti almost lost control and attacked. Forcing himself to be calm, Zenti surmised that someone used Mari's Faction camp to set a trap. That trap had not been to capture him or Mari but to kill them. Killing him, Zenti could understand. However, all his information indicated that Hayden wanted to capture Mari. The ploy was good, and perhaps the invaders were not as stupid as he first thought.

Someone had been feeding the invaders information on Summoners. It had to be Hayden, thought Zenti. That foul cat was teaching the invaders how to wage war like a Jaydonian. The invaders were beginning to learn more, and that concerned him. It was fortunate that Hayden did not like the anarchy and randomness that the white wolf thrived on.

Laying in the foliage, Zenti waited in silence for five hours. The length of time resting was more from his wounds than being overly cautious. Occasionally he would visually search the surrounding area for enemy signs. However, it did give him time to rest. His body needed it. A thought crossed his mind, and Zenti disliked it. What if someone suspected that Mari was Gifted like he did. What if someone had set up the attack on Mari's Faction camp to see if she would come into her Gift. Knowing the Orra Prophecy and his prominent part in it, perhaps someone suspected Mari's part. It made sense. It also made sense why someone tried to drive the two of them apart. Zenti pushed the thought aside. Mari was not strong enough to fulfill that part of the Orra Prophecy. Zenti knew that only time would tell if she would grow strong enough.

Scanning the area again, Zenti found no one near, and having rested a bit more, he made his way painfully back to the riverbed. The pain slowed his movement considerably. Soaking in the cold water again helped lowered his temperature to where he thought he could ride. Returning to the spot where he left the mount, he found a set of tracks leading it away. Someone had found the horse and thought it was abandoned. Deciding he was in no condition to follow them, Zenti turned back to the river.

The waters moved steadily but not rapidly. Grabbing onto a rather large section of a tree caught on the riverbank, Zenti pushed out into the water. Using his Gifted Talent of Repulsion, the silvery-white wolf maneuvered further towards the center of the slow-moving river. This beat walking. Zenti continued this way for the rest of the daylight hours and into the night. The cooling water did wonders for the fever and helped numb his body's aches.

With the occasional push from his Gift, five hours of drifting placed Zenti at the point where he would have to abandon the river. The river veered in a westerly direction, and he needed to continue south. Exiting the river, Zenti struggled along for half an hour. Deciding to rest, the silvery-white wolf tried to climb a tree for some sleep. However, the pain was intolerable as he climbed the first few limbs and almost blacking out with each step. Deciding on a more conventional course of action, he turned back to the river. Zenti remembered a small farm with a barn and corral a quarter-mile inland. He began the trek through the sparse woods and then across open fields to the barn.

The house was a simple single-story farmhouse that looked well maintained. The roof was a low pitch, shingled roof with a chimney on one end and one in the roof's center. The moonlight cast a pale glow on the two-story barn, and a shed roof overhang covered part of the corral. Had an artist been here on a night like this, they could have painted a masterpiece. It was tranquil and enchantingly beautiful. Zenti approached from the far side of the barn, placing it between the house and him.

Slipping inside the barn, he found two stalls, each occupied with plow animals, which repeatedly brayed until Zenti backed out the door he originally entered. Turning, he met muzzle to barrel with the business end of a shotgun-wielding weasel.

"Whatever you took, wolf, put it back, and I won't pull the trigger," said the weasel, keeping the gun trained at the wolf's chest. By the look on the weasel's muzzle, it was apparent that he was serious. There was no fear in his eyes.

Zenti looked at this middle-aged weasel. He was maybe six feet tall with brown and black fur that showed the early stages of aging. He looked physically fit for a male in his late forties or early fifties. However, the weasel's eyes were sharp, and he did not squint in the moonlight, Zenti noticed. Slowly the silvery-white wolf brought his paws out to the side, his palms outward, and showed that they were empty.

"I took nothing, friend. I simply wanted a place to bed down for a few hours, as I am exhausted. I just need to rest. I will give you what few coins I have for just a few hours of peaceful sleep," offered Zenti, as he eased the pouch out of his belt pocket and emptied the Breng into his open paw.

The weasel looked at the outstretched paw. A quick visual count told him there was enough Breng in large denominations to buy a season worth of seed, perhaps a new plow, and a few things for his family. Looking up at the wolf suspiciously, he decided if he wanted the risk of the stranger being in his barn or not.

A cute little otter stepped from behind the weasel. She was young, appearing to be a quarter of the weasel's age. Her fur was a ruddy brown with splotches of tan along the underside of her neck. The tan fur went down into her nightgown. Her hair was a dark reddish-brown and was a mess, having just gotten out of bed at such a late hour. She looked at Zenti for a moment as if she knew him, but with the dirt and exhausted look on his muzzle, she was not sure.

"So, what's the wolf want, stealing our plow animals?" she said and then noticed the outstretched paw filled with Breng. Looking between the two males, she finally settled her gaze on the weasel with a look that said, 'well, answer me.'

"He wants to bed down in the barn tonight and is willing to pay," said the weasel.

"Well, if he is offering that sum, don't just stand there, invite him in the house for some food and perhaps a bath as well," she said, tipping the wolf's paw and dumping the Breng into her paw. She looked at Zenti's onyx claws and smiled. Dropping the Breng into her front apron pocket, she put a free paw on the barrel and started to slowly push it downward.

Stepping back, the weasel lowered his gun the rest of the way and nodded towards the house. Zenti followed the otter, and the weasel followed the two of them. Zenti hobbled all the way over. His fever spiked, and his muscles hurt from the infection beginning to take root. As he approached the house, the front light was on, and he could see that it was painted a soft green with lavender trim work. Flower boxes lined the small stoop, and decorative baskets hung from the fascia. The sweet smell of the flowers tickled his nose, making him smile. Zenti followed the female otter into the house.

The home was warm and cozy with sparse but charming furnishings. The walls were a soft bone-white with a decorative border of a floral pattern along the top. The wood trim was stained a cherry red, as was the chair rail that ran around the whole of the house. The furnishings were well maintained, but Zenti could tell they were antiques, more than likely passed down from generation to generation.

On the east side of the house was the kitchen. It occupied a third of the main room, with cabinets lining the walls. A wood stove sat in the center of the kitchen with thick stone tile countertops, one on either side of the oven. A breakfast counter created a quasi barrier between the kitchen and the dining room.

A table, set with breakfast dishes, was the centerpiece of the main room. A small open-hearth fire divided the center main room and the final third of the room. That was a sitting room with two oversized chairs and an overstuffed couch. A large ceiling fan with five lights hung over the table, illuminating the whole area.

The back half of the house had two open bedrooms divided by what could only be the bathroom. This was an old but cozy house built by farmers. Obviously, it was still occupied by farmers- the simple people who fed the great kingdom of Mitd.

"I am Lari, and this is my mate, Adam. We share-crop this land in hopes of buying it someday," the young otter said, pointing at a chair in the center of the table for Zenti to sit at. Adam sat at one end, shotgun at his side.

Lari picked up a kettle on the stovetop and poured

three cups of hot water. Taking three tea bags, she dropped one into each cup. Turning, she placed one in front of Adam and one in front of Zenti. The otter then tapped a claw on the table and scowled at Zenti to sit. She then picked up her cup, began to sit, and growled lightly at him again to sit.

Zenti sighed, knowing that this would hurt, and sat for a moment only to dig his claws into the tabletop the moment his legs and back touched the chair. Standing back up immediately, a low growl rumbling from his throat. The weasel brought the shotgun back up, pointing it at his chest.

"Forgive me, I mean you no harm, I am just injured, and the pain is unbearable if I move wrong," said Zenti as he leaned on the table.

The otter moved behind him and, in the light, noticed the blood-encrusted pants and vest. The back of his clothing was fairly shredded from the shrapnel. She placed a paw on Zenti's forehead, then on his neck, and finally on his chest.

"You are burning up. You have a massive infection. Here, take this for now, but you will need to see a doctor soon," she said as she returned from the kitchen area. Lari handed him a level spoon of white powder she had dipped out of a glass jar from a kitchen cabinet.

"Thank you," Zenti said, taking the spoon and put it under his tongue. He made a sour face at the very bitter taste. She handed him the cup of hot tea, shaking her head, and rolling her eyes at the way he took the powder. It was the same way Adam did. The smile on the elder weasel's muzzle said he had seen that look before.

"Well, since we have established your hurt, take your shirt and pants off and let me take a look at those wounds," Lari ordered as she stood Zenti upright. She began to unbutton the vest, to which she slapped the white wolf's paws when he tried to protest.

"Best not argue with her. We have been mated for eleven months. I have already learned that to argue with her is a time-consuming waste," said Adam as he eased back into the chair. Zenti noticed that Lari smiled a cocky grin.

He decided not to test her as she unbuckled his pants and began to remove them, to which he again growled in pain as the wounds had caked to his fur.

"Oh, quit being such a pup," she chided as she reached for a pair of scissors and began cutting the pants away, and when they finally hit the wood floor, he heard her gasp loudly.

"That bad," asked Zenti? The silvery-white wolf, covered in blood, looked down over his shoulder at her kneeling at his paw pads, and the look on the otter's muzzle said it all. Something tickled his memory about this scene.

"Many of these are too deep for me to get to, but I can get a few out, although it will not be painless. I can give you an herb that will render you unconscious for a while," Lari said. She went to a kitchen cabinet where she had gotten the white powder. The otter opened a small ceramic jar and scooped out a level spoon of a green herb. Mixing the green herb in the new cup, she poured a tablespoon of hot water into it and crushed the leaves until it was a paste.

"I will deal with the pain. I am sorry; it is not that I do not appreciate your offer. However, I have enemies, and being unresponsive now is not really an option," Zenti said as the otter got a few essential medical tools.

Laying the tools on the table, she cut away the remainder of clothing and bandages with scissors, trimming fur when needed.

"What is your name, friend, that you would have so many enemies?" asked the weasel as he eyed the blood-soaked wolf. There were many scars, and Zenti's white fur was blood red with angry wounds that had puss oozing from them. It was hard to tell if Zenti's fur was brown with white or gray streaks with red splotches.

"Friend will do nicely," replied Zenti, to which Adam gave him a wary look. Lari finished cutting away the rest of the bandages, then started trimming up fur around the more infected wounds.

"You ready for this," she asked, to which Zenti nodded yes? Lari proceeded to probe and then dig out each piece of shrapnel that she found. When he growled deeply at one, she could not get out; Lari would put a pat of the green paste on it and move on to the next. Lari repeated the process some twenty times as she talked.

"Adam, remember where you bought me at?" Lari asked, to which Zenti gave the weasel a distasteful frown.

Purchased mates were outlawed nearly two hundred years ago. However, just because there was a law did not mean that everyone complied, and the practice continued in secret circles. Many poor families sought to ensure their pups' success in life. The war had caused many families into hardship or left them broken. Those hardships forced the family to enter into indentured servitude contracts.

Occasionally males were sold into indentured servitude. However, indentured servitude never lasted past their Coming-of-Age date. Females were never sold into indentured servitude for fear of them becoming sex slaves. However, should the female agree, she could arrange to become a purchased mate within six months of her Coming-of-Age date. Many females understood that this was a chance to improve their lot in life. Their family received compensation for the arranged mating, which helped them survive. It was not looked upon with respect.

Zenti sighed deeply and turned back to Lari as she poured a bluish-green thick liquid into a cup. Over the past two decades, the war had brought the practice back to life in the more war-ravaged parts of Mitd. Stirring the liquid, the otter measured a level spoon of the white powder into it and then remixed it.

"Yes, I remember. It was Dotharian almost sixteen months ago. You were five months from your Coming-of-Age party when your father and I came to an agreement.

When Dotharian was destroyed, I thought I had lost you. What of it?" said Adam, not having missed the distasteful frown on the wolf's muzzle as the weasel sipped his tea.

"Afraid you had lost your investment," Lari teased, smiling at him coyly? The otter gave Zenti the glass of liquid she had just finished stirring. The weasel snorted and rolled his eyes at her comment. It must have been a cute game between the two, Zenti surmised by the otter's playful grin. The white wolf sat the undrunk glass back on the table. He smiled apologetically at the otter while shaking his head no. She kneeled down to check a few more wounds.

"I really do need my wits about me. I appreciate that you are as gentle as possible. I know you are doing your best, and I really do thank you. I just cannot be unconscious," Zenti said as he patted her on the top of the head gently as if she were a pup, not a mated female.

"My dear mate," began Lari, "*friend* would be a less than an appropriate name for this wolf." The otter looked up at Zenti as he patted her.

Zenti looked at her muzzle closely, and memories from Dotharian came back to him. He remembered this otter, and his ears lowered. His shoulders slumped as he rolled his eyes. It was almost the same stance that had occurred some thirteen months ago in a zoo-like jail cell. There, she had kneeled before him, begging for his help. Lari looked at Zenti and could almost see the memory expressed on his muzzle. The expression said he knew that she knew.

This was not what Zenti had planned at all. Almost thirteen months after Dotharian, of all places, would he have expected to run into a survivor, this remote farm was not it. Damn his luck, these were friendly folk, and he hoped it would not get out of paw. Many feared and hate him at the mere mention of his name. To be in the presence of someone from the destroyed city of Dotharian could present issues.

Lari said nothing but motioned for him to turn around. Zenti complied, and she picked out another piece of shrapnel and then another. She looked up to Zenti, and he looked over his shoulder to her, both deciding what should happen next.

"Well, are you going to tell me why *'friend'* is less than appropriate," asked a slightly perturbed and suspicious weasel? Lari stood and moved over to her mate and put her paw on his shoulder. Kissing his forehead, she gently stroked the fur around his ears.

"Adam, you know I am here because Dotharian was saved from **THEM.** I would like to introduce you to the savior of Dotharian. This is Summoner, Zenti Semineu," Lari said as she kissed her mate on the tip of the ear.

****

The noonday sun warmed the fur on Zenti's back as he traveled toward the Shaman Torit's home. The pain had subsided overnight, thanks to a little otter. He had to laugh at it now because it was absurdly funny. Zenti replayed the events in his mind as he traveled on. Lari had insisted he get into a tub of hot water and soak. That in itself was not funny; it was how she made him get into the tub that was absurdly funny.

****

Neither he nor Adam was thrilled that the post-Coming-of-Age female otter made him strip to bare fur. Zenti had even growled at her in refusal when she had escorted him to the bathroom. Much to his surprise, Lari grabbed the white wolf by his sack[20] with her right paw and the back of his head with her left so fast he could not react. She then bit him hard on the bottom jaw and growled through bared fangs that if he did not do as she said, he would have new pain, and it would not be his jaw that would be hurting. He felt her claws starting to dig into the tender skin beneath the fur of his sack.

Shocked at her tenacity, Zenti allowed the otter to undress him fully, and then he eased into a tub of hot water. For the next hour, Lari kept the water hot as Adam sat on

---

[20] Though technically called a Scrotum, the Jaydonian word translates into 'a sack to house testicles'.

493

the toilet. The three talked to Zenti about his exploits and the whimsical escapades of their mutual friend Torit. Zenti was shocked to find that these two were close friends of the elder Shaman. Torit was reclusive.

Torit, a powerful Shaman, did not share his list of friends with the silvery-white wolf. Adam and Zenti had not met each other before meeting in the barn. However, they shared crazy stories of the old buzzard, both laughing at the other's memories. For the first time in seventeen months, Zenti laughed amongst friends. Adam warned Zenti about disregarding Lari because of her age, stating the young otter's tenacity was that of a much older female.

When Lari felt Zenti was good and waterlogged, she told him to get up, and he started to protest that the wet fur would not hide certain parts of his body. She laughed and told him she had five brothers and a mate, nothing he had would shock her. The otter snapped her claws and motioned for Zenti to stand. Both males laughed at the young otter commanding the most dangerous Summoner on Mitd around as if he was a pre-Gifting pup.

As he got out of the tub, Lari deftly clipped fur around a few of the worst wounds with scissors, exposing them more to make it easier to work the silvery-white wolf. Handing him a towel, Zenti smiled as he used his Gift to dry the fur without touching the wounds instead. He told Lari it would be less painful for him this way.

Lari made Zenti drink the liquid she prepared earlier. The otter laughed at the silvery-white wolf's grimace at the taste. She told him it was much better tasting warm and then took Zenti to the root cellar. In the basement, Adam revealed a secret passage into a room that his great-grandfather had built. When Zenti questioned the need for it, Adam explained. His great-grandfather used the hidden room to hide a whisky still when homebrewing was illegal. Homebrewed alcohol avoided paying the Crown alcohol tax. Since the change in the alcohol laws, it was no longer needed for that purpose.

It had been converted into Adam's hobby room now. However, because of the stout and integrated construction, they had never removed the secret door. Laying a thick quilt on the floor, Lari made Zenti finished drinking the concoction she had prepared for him earlier. Ordering Zenti to lay down, she told the white wolf to relax the best he could. To Zenti's surprise, the thick quilt felt wonderful to his tired body. The numbing effects of the drink helped deaden the wounds, and when he relaxed, Lari began her work. The young otter pulled a few more shards out and then bound up the wounds as best she could.

****

Yes, the sun felt good on his exposed back, and he smiled. For a short time, the monster had lost a battle to a yearling[21] otter. Zenti was still hungry as the early morning

---

[21] For the first year after their Coming-of-Age date, a Jaydonian is

meal, though temporarily satisfying, left him with an empty feeling that he needed more. He opened the small sack of food that Lari and Adam had so kindly given him. The stuffed meat pie dripped a succulent, flavorful gravy, and with its thick flowery shell, the white wolf savored every bite.

The pie was just as delicious as the meal he had been served the evening before. Lari finished removing as many of the shrapnel pieces that Zenti could tolerate. She then made a midnight meal. The young otter forced Zenti to eat. She had listened to the conversations between Adam and Torit. The young otter concluded that the Gift took a toll on the body. Lari made Zenti eat until he felt like bursting.

However, Zenti knew his body needed the food. He had been exceedingly reckless with his Gift and was paying for it. One day he thought he would have to learn a modicum of self-restraint. The three talked a little more before the effects of a full belly, combined with exhaustion, forced Zenti to retire.

However, in the conversations, Zenti learned several surprising bits of information. The Savior of Dotharian is what they were calling him in whispered circles. Those were words he thought he would never have heard associated with his name. As brutal as the white wolf had been in the past, tonight Zenti sat with a unique couple

---

known affectionately as a yearling. However, in some circles, it can be considered an insult. Most refrain from using the archaic term, though it is correct.

that had treated him as if he were family. Lari and Adam thought he had fallen asleep while she was checking the binding on his wounds after the big dinner. But, for a while, Zenti simply listened. She and Adam whispered about what they knew about him.

Their home had no television. Adam had only heard tales of Zenti's exploits by word of the muzzle but had never seen the silvery-white wolf. Adam told Lari most of the news came from the radio, and papers talked about Zenti almost all the time. Some articles vilified him, while others praised him. However, all had agreed that Summoner Zenti Semineu was a vile sort and that no one would ever open their doors to him. Lari had a different opinion of the silvery-white wolf than all others. She knew of his kindness first paw. Zenti listened to them for a little while until the medicine she had brewed overtook his senses, and he slept.

****

Zenti thought the young otter and the middle-aged weasel made a lovely couple. Cresting a small hill in the late afternoon, the white wolf laughed a little as he reached into his belt pouch. While getting his binoculars, Zenti found a pawkerchief filled with the Breng Lari had put in her apron in the barn. She must have known who he was all along and was just fishing for truth or knowledge. Again, Zenti chuckled, knowing that Adam was in for the adventure of his life with that little otter. He would never forget her pleading eyes in that filthy zoo jail in Dotharian, nor would he regret fighting for her future with Adam. That was the very reason Orra raised him. Summoner Zenti Semineu accepted what he was to the Orra Prophecy thanks to that young otter and her mate.

Letting the Breng fall back into his pouch, Zenti looked below to the open fields. Surrounded by gently rolling hills sat the home he had traveled the past five days to reach. Inside he had hoped he would find the Shaman Torit. There were times he traveled here only to find the Shaman gone. Zenti casually searched the area looking for signs of cnemics. However, as expected, he found none. The enemy had at least enough sense not to come to Torit's home.

The elder buzzard was rumored to be over six hundred years old. Zenti knew that not all rumors were true. However, the Shaman's Gift was without peer. Torit touched the Void with such ease that it amazed Zenti. However, after his capture by the Invaders, Torit's lesson and medical attention had become quite intense. It was as if the old buzzard knew something, though getting him to share that information was worse than finding lost treasure.

Smiling, Zenti looked down at the modest mustard-yellow stucco home with graying wood-shake shingles. The house sat in a hollow surrounded by fields. Thinking back to the conversation with Adam and Lari last night brought back more memories of the Shaman. In Zenti's opinion, the old buzzard could raise the dead. Over the

past thirteen months, Zenti felt like he had needed the
Shaman's Gift more and more. Today would be no
exception. The silvery-white wolf knew that shortly the
pain from the wounds would overwhelm his self-control.

Sitting on the plow horse loaned to him by Adam
and Lari, Zenti looked around the fields. He sat at the top
of the hollow and looked around the area once again. This
time without the aid of the binoculars, taking in the
landscape as he had done many times before. This was not
the best of places for defending. With wide-open spaces, a
decided lack of trees, no significant hills, with only several
shallow hollows was a dream for a mechanized assault.
Yet this place was safer than any fortress or steel-plated
battle cruiser.

The old buzzard was the oldest living Shaman
known, and his Gifted access to the Void was legendary.
Zenti took a deep breath and steeled his nerves. Lessons
Torit taught usually involved a lot of pain. The Shaman
never thoroughly numbed Zenti's wounds. Pain teaches
lessons, Torit would say. It was time for another class,
thought Zenti as he spurred the mount on.

Riding down into the shallow hollow, Zenti
gingerly dismounted. Pain shot through his body at the
action. He let the mount drink from the water in the
decorative fountain before he tied it up. Making a mental
note, he reminded himself he would need to get the mount
back to Adam and Lari somehow. Turning to remove the
saddlebags, Zenti noticed that the mount's saddle and
flanks were covered in blood. The ride had opened his

wounds, and he had not even felt it. Taking a deep breath, Zenti knew he could not forestall the lesson awaiting him.

Knocking on the ochre-colored wooden door, Zenti waited as a few moments passed. Torit's house was not large but comfortably small. Raising a paw to knock, the door opened. The old buzzard seemingly appeared, looking just the same as he had a few months ago. Torit looked as if he had been sleeping; the feather-like hair around his forehead and neck were ruffled. His eyes were saggy and glazed. Zenti smiled because Torit appeared just the way he had a few months ago. Some things never change, he thought.

"Well, look what the wind blew in. Zenti Semineu, it's been a long time. What, two months have passed since I last had to patch your sorry tail up," Torit asked sarcastically? His cracked, old, beak-like nose moving lightly, and his feather-like hair ruffled in the gentle breeze. Looking the wolf over, Torit stepped out of the way and waved Zenti into his small but comfortably modern home.

Zenti looked around the home, noting that it had a fresh coat of paint, new window dressings, and maybe even a new rug. The elder buzzard always surprised him at the changes he made to his house. For a male as old as he was rumored to be, he was ever-changing.

"I see you got some ambition and remodeled," Zenti said as the old buzzard closed the door.

"Remember Mer'eit," Torit asked?

"The widow whose husband owned the old mechanic shop a day or so away from here," replied the wolf?

"That's the one. Mer'eit comes by once in a while, being all nice and sweet. She brings her family over 'to help improve my dull life,'" said the buzzard, rolling his eyes as he poured himself another cup of tea.

"More than likely, she is trying to get her claws into you, old bird. Or are you so old that you don't know when you're being sniffed after," laughed the wolf, who then cringed in pain?

"That old goat scares me something fierce, pup. How Mer'eit's late mate lived with that nagging windbag, I will never know. But he went to the stars five years ago, and time has not changed her muzzle one bit. She is still a windbag, but she continues to stop by every three or four months and always has little surprises," chuckled Torit.

"Well, at least you got a few niceties from her visits," said Zenti, pointing at the new curtains and paint.

"And a few good things to eat too. The old goat was always a great cook. But her youngest daughter has a real talent for it. She brings me a basket of food every time she goes to see her intended mate. She reaches her Coming-of-Age date soon. The young feline's intended lives a day from here, and she brings him food. I let her spend the night inside so she does not have to camp out when the weather turns bad. It's a good arrangement. Though I dare say my waistline is going to force me to buy new clothing," Torit laughed as he patted his belly. Zenti noted the old male was just as skinny as ever.

"What does Mer'eit do now that her mate has passed to the stars? Did she sell that shop of his? They had no sons to carry on the work," asked Zenti. The wolf tried to sit down on a dining room chair only to growl in pain.

"Get those pants off, pup, and lie down on the table and let me have a look at what you have done to yourself," Torit said, pointing at the table. Zenti moved over and struggled to remove his pants. Torit sighed at the pathetic attempt. However, he continued to talk to the injured wolf as if this were a lunch conversation.

"Mer'eit manages that little farm they always had. All but one of her daughters is mated. They all live in that big house she made her late mate build. As a family, they work the land together and the mechanic shop," answered the buzzard, moving to help Zenti get to the examining table.

"What killed her mate," asked Zenti? The white wolf tried to peel the pants off his blood-soaked legs with aid from the buzzard.

"The lift failed in his garage and crushed him under a truck he was working on. Though I'm betting, he got tired of the old goats nagging and dropped the truck on himself to get away from the old windbag," replied Torit. The two males looked at each other and laughed. Torit could tell even that hurt when Zenti laughed. Torit rolled his eyes at the blood-covered wolf's condition.

"It also appears that time does not always change things or endow you with half a brain, pup," Torit said. The elder male shook his head at the multitude of lacerations on Zenti's legs and lower back. The elder buzzard made the wolf lay stomach-down on the table. Blood had caked Zenti's fur, matting it down to the scar-covered skin beneath. "Last time you were here, you were in pretty much the same shape, all cut up and hurt. Wait, don't tell me, let me guess, you were in the center of that firefight at Mari's camp?"

Zenti snapped around to face the old buzzard; furling his eyebrows, he spoke in a low growl. "What and how do you know of that ambush?" Zenti realized who he was talking to when Torit gave him a reprimanding gaze. The silvery-white wolf's tone softened. "Forgive me, old friend; these days, I push myself harder than ever. I have found that trusting someone will get me and others hurt. The weight of this war falls heavy on these shoulders and the freedom of our species in these paws. I fear that I may not be strong enough," he said, laying his head back down.

The old buzzard laughed as he dismissed Zenti's growl like he was a pup. Moving to a wall table, he went to get a set of surgical tools. Zenti tried to relax as he put his muzzle in the hole cut into the table. He rested his face on the thick, soft-cushioned ring designed to support a prostate patient.

"Do you think that word of that battle has not traveled through the Gifted Talent of Union or that it must be reported on in the news broadcasts to be known about,"

Torit inquired?

Zenti sighed and rubbed his temples slightly. Even that movement was painful. The white wolf attempted to crack his neck; that always brought a measure of relief. However, Zenti could not as pain shot through his body. Torit removed the white wolf's paws away from his head and gave Zenti a little warning growl. Torit called on the Gifted Talent of Life Sensing. He could see the pain in Zenti's legs was becoming intense enough to take the silvery-white wolf's control away.

Torit began the procedure by giving the wolf something extremely nasty to sip on. Zenti balked at the bitter taste of the drink. The tall glass with the long straw sat on a low table below the wolf's muzzle. Torit growled at Zenti to drink the damn medicine and stop whining like a pup about the taste. Zenti grumbled something about adding sugar wouldn't hurt, which only brought another growl from the elder buzzard. Zenti sipped at the drink reluctantly, but soon the old buzzard was cutting away at each of the wounds without the wolf flinching.

"Are you going to tell me what happened, pup, before you finish that concoction? Or have you decided that it is not important enough to share? Also, do not forget to include which Shaman got most of that shrapnel out of you. I highly doubt you found a surgeon who would work on you. There have been no reports of you near any cities," Torit said. The elder buzzard put a thick syrup-like liquid on the wounds without shrapnel in them.

Zenti did not look back at Torit but knew the Shaman was using his Gift to guide his search for the deeply embedded metal fragments. Over the past thirteen months, Zenti had learned when a Gifted used their Gift or one of the Gifted Talents. Though he did not understand how, nor did he trust asking anyone, the white wolf could feel the ripples in the Void when another Gifted touched it. The range was limited, but Zenti had tested it by using the captured PRISM device and standing near a Gifted. However, his understanding of the Gift grew every day.

"Lari got a lot out last night, but I ripped most of them out with my Gift the day it happened," said Zenti, to which Torit slapped him in the back of the head. Thankfully the white wolf could not feel the sting of the slap.

"You're an idiot. Never rip them out. There is an easier way. I will show you how one day when your wounds are only slight. If that day ever comes. Adam's Lari? Well ain't she the brave little pup," laughed the old bird?

"Yes, Adam's Lari, and let me tell you that weasel had better stay sharp, or he is going to find himself on an extremely short leash. She is a tenacious one," laughed Zenti. Surprisingly laughing only caused a dull pain. Zenti thought Torit must be in a generous mood and using his Gift to numb the pain. Though he could tell what other Talents a lessor Gifted was using, Torit's Gift was beyond his current level of comprehension.

"I think it's already too late from what he has told me," snickered Torit, "Now get on tellin' me what happened."

"Mari had sent word for me to meet with her. Most of her troops are on loan to General Breymore, leaving her with little in the way of offensive or defensive capability. I requested that my second in command, Malachi, shift down to near Mari's camp and conduct covert operations. I wanted him to keep a watchful eye on her. That is why I stayed to the north and west so long," said Zenti.

"When did you make him second in command? I thought he was a little too timid for your taste," said the old bird as he tugged at a deeply embedded piece of metal? Though Zenti could feel his body being manipulated, it did not hurt.

"He was until about six months ago. I assigned him as a watcher of a farming community. The invader's raids' pattern indicated that this was one of three villages that might be attacked. The Northern Faction is not strong enough to defend more than two such villages. I made a mistake and had the bulk of the Northern Faction guarding the other two villages. Malachi had to watch as every villager was executed. He snapped that day, and ever since, he has become as bloodthirsty as I for revenge. He is a good solid leader, just lacking in tactical training. I'm glad the troops like him and follow him, which they won't directly me anymore," Zenti explained. Even the deep aching pain no longer hurt.

"So, he is the one teaching them to be bloodthirsty, eh? And are you sure it was a mistake you made" asked the Shaman?

"Yes, he is teaching them. They saw the video he recorded as the Watcher. Soldiers can accept the killing of soldiers; that is the nature of war. Malachi's troops even accept the brutality that comes with purging the traitors when they will not surrender. However, few can stomach what I do. You know very well what the King has commanded of me. You also know my hatred of traitors. I don't know, but now that I think about it," began Zenti. He let his mind drift back to the unguarded village the invaders slaughtered. "I suspect that at the time, we had a traitor in our midst. You remember what shape I was in seven months ago," asked the wolf?

"Yeah, I do. You ended up pretty much just as you are now, prostrate on this table with pieces of shrapnel in your backside. As I remember, you told me you had a recon party with you, and out of nowhere, an artillery barrage struck," Torit said.

"That's right," said Zenti, recalling the event that ended him up in the same predicament.

"You and one other lived if I remember our conversation correctly. Whatever happened to that dingo," asked the buzzard?

"He left the Faction and returned to his family in the northwest. He was pretty beat up and had trouble walking. You should remember, you tended to his wounds," said the wolf.

"I sure did, and I healed those wounds. They were far less severe than yours, yet you say the dingo had trouble walking," asked Torit?

"Yes, about two weeks ago, he said he was done. I remember Malachi telling me that he had just gotten up one morning and said he had enough. The dingo wanted nothing more than to try and live out a peaceful life with his family," replied Zenti.

"Let me guess, he said this just the day after you suggested Malachi move his even troops closer to Mari's camp. Did you inform him that you were meeting with her," asked Torit? The Shaman cut open a section of the wolf's back and pulled a large metal piece out. Again, Zenti did not flinch.

"In fact, it was the following day. The Northern Faction had just taken a vote to no longer follow me into combat, or they would disband. I respect their courage and made it clear to Malachi that I would no longer operate with any Faction units," explained Zenti. The pieces of the mystery were coming together. He would have to have the dingo questioned soon.

"Damn lucky thing, pup, that those idiot scientists wove all this metal into your muscle and bone. I doubt they knew it then, but it is keeping your vital organs well-protected," quipped the old buzzard.

"Silver linings," retorted a bitter Zenti.

"Kredomis actually, not silver. Pup, you're still alive because of it, aren't you?" snorted the old bird. "Besides, use that brain of yours for more than planning destruction. Now get back to tellin' me what happened at Mari's encampment," demanded Torit, and obediently Zenti continued.

"I met with Mari a few hours from her camp, and of course, it did not go well between her and me. However, that is secondary to the fact that we were attacked by Royal Soldiers. I lost my temper, and Mari witnessed first paw a few of my changes. A second squad arrived after Mari left, and I learned that something was not copacetic. I decided to continue the discussion with Mari and went to her camp after few hours of, um, cleaning up," Zenti said. He did not like talking about the number of those he killed. He and Torit had an understanding of the meaning of 'cleaning up.'

"Did you find anything interesting during the cleanup," the old bird asked? Torit used his Gift while trying to locate the remaining more embedded metal fragments. However, the elder buzzard masked precisely what he was doing. He knew Zenti could sense when a Gifted accessed the Void. However, Zenti was not prepared to better access and manipulate the Void at this juncture of his learning. The white wolf was just too reckless.

"I found that there was going to be some type of action. I decided to visit Mari's camp and sat down with her. She wanted to see why I abandoned her as well as what I had become," Zenti said when Torit cut him short.

"Oh, Heavens and Hells, pup. Don't tell me you let her see what happened to you," the bird said. When Zenti said yes, Torit slapped him in the back of the head again.

"Mari deserves to know just what I have become and why. And I needed a few questions answered myself," Zenti replied. Fortunately, he felt the impact of the slap, but there was no corresponding pain.

"So, you showed her everything then," asked Torit? He pulled what he hoped was the final piece of metal out of Zenti's lower legs.

"Yes, she saw everything. I think it pushed her further away. However, when I left her before the attack, I was followed by a spy in her camp. After the attack began, I knew that Hayden was involved with the invaders when his troops did nothing to help. As a matter of fact, I think they staged their own attack and then retreated. I found out something then about Mari that I have suspected for a long time. She is Gifted, but you knew that I am sure. However, before I could speak to her, the artillery barrage began. I confirmed Hayden was behind this attack, and I believe that someone in the Crown is aiding him. I just don't know who," finished Zenti.

"Finish your drink and don't whine that it is bitter," said the old buzzard. Torit purposely redirected the conversation away from Mari being Gifted.

The white wolf had hoped Torit would confirm that he knew Mari was Gifted. Obediently Zenti finished the last of the drink. His thoughts flashed back to Mari and the attack on her encampment. Her abilities were the exact opposite of his. Could it possibly be that it was not just a coincidence?

"Torit, do you believe in fate," Zenti asked in a very drowsy voice. He thought perhaps the drink was playing tricks on his mind; maybe he just imagined the connection.

"I've lived so long, how I could believe in anything else," laughed the old buzzard? Torit began to prepare a paste to smear on the lacerations after stitching them up. However, the unconscious Zenti did not answer. Torit looked at the silvery-white wolf and smiled.

"So, you have become aware of Mari's Gift, eh, pup. Well, *fate*, it seems, has found you once again and is about to kick you in the tail one more time. Be assured, pup, it will not be the last time *fate* kicks you in the tail," said the old buzzard as he patted the unconscious wolf on the back of the head.

With the compassion of a father tending a son's wounds, the elder buzzard continued to sew up the multitude of lacerations on Zenti's body. A deep sigh escaped the small lips of the buzzard. Though he could use his Gift to close the wounds, Zenti needed a constant reminder that he needed to grow beyond the warrior rushing into battle.

"Well, pup, the Prophecy has begun. I pray that you and that vixen of yours are stronger than the previous two who failed to fulfill the Prophecy," said Torit before leaving Zenti to a much-needed sleep.

Chapter 8

Aftermath

Mari woke to the sound of the cub whimpering in her arms. It was still very dark, and her first instinct was to hush the little male. **THEY** could always be near, and she did not want to endanger him with being forced to fight. The vixen nuzzled the little cub's ears gently, murmuring words of calming comfort. Mari's mother would whisper those identical words to the little vixen when she was scared. Mari remembered her mother and realized she was very much her mother's kit. Mari Semineu was the mother to her Faction and to all those who loved her. The vixen also realized one other thing; she missed her parents immensely. The cub quieted, and soon Mari coaxed him back to sleep. Once the little bear cub drifted off to sleep, Mari sat in the crook of the tree wide awake. The vixen listened for anything that might come toward her.

The night had gone silent. Looking at her watch, Mari realized she had been asleep for about four hours. She listened again for any sound of **THEM** but heard none. As a matter of fact, the vixen heard nothing. Mari's fur stood on end, and her senses sharpened, she sniffed the air for anything out of place, but the smell of gunpowder on her fur kept her from getting a clean scent. Her ears twitched as she strained to listen; a distant sound could be heard but was the faint noise from machinery or something else?

According to the Watcher's video reports, the invaders were never quiet after winning a battle. Mari decided to let the night go by and see what daylight would bring. Her mind was a fog of events, and quickly exhaustion overcame the vixen's will to stay awake. The vixen fell asleep again with the cub cradled in her arms. Sleeping in the stout branches of trees had become a standard way of hiding from an enemy from Mitdonians. Though her own species had a better chance of detecting someone in a tree by tracking their scent, the invaders could not.

The most common tree in the central and southern regions of Mitd had thick, stout branches that forked often. The dense growth of the broad leaves provided a superior visual cover. After years of war, sleeping up in the tree branches was second nature to most Mitdonians. One of the remarkable oddities about the trees on Mitd is they shed heat. Why this occurred was still conjecture. Scientists had studied the phenomenon for centuries with no reasonable explanation. Thankfully it confused both Mitdonian and invader heat sensing technology.

Snuggled in the fork of a tree branch with the young cub's warmth reminded Mari Semineu of the times she held her little sister, Rini. When her mother and father were not available, Mari would help by holding the troubled lioness until she reached a peaceful sleep. Snuggling with the cub also brought back memories of how Zenti would comfort her when she was exhausted. With those pleasant memories, Mari fell back to sleep.

Mari woke again to the cub in her arms, crying. Sunlight shone through the leaves of the canopy, and the cub obviously wanted out of her arms. Holding him close to her, the vixen climbed down. The silence still surrounded her, unbroken from the night before. The bear cub must be hungry, the vixen thought and probably needed to relieve himself.

Mari nodded to a tree, turned her back, and reached into her pocket. As the little cub relieved himself, the vixen pulled out a rations bar after waiting for the pre-Gifting bear cub to urinate. Mari thought the military ration bar was not the best-tasting food on the planet, but it was edible. It took her a moment before she could recall this cub's name. Malyx was what his mother called him. Looking down at him as he stepped up beside her, Mari handed him the ration bar. The cub reached for the food, and Mari spoke in a soft, soothing voice.

"Malyx hun," she began drying the tears from his eyes, "eat this and be very quiet. *THEY* may still be out there. I don't want them to find you, do you understand?" Mari asked. He nodded, yes. Mari led him to a safe spot and told him to stay hidden and answer no one except her. Again, he nodded yes. Mari turned and headed off toward the camp. The cub and his mother were relatively new to her Faction camp. Mari did not know either of them as well as she should.

The vixen's steps were light and quick, her heart pounding as she anticipated what she would find. Mari did not know if she could face the hellish nightmare that the invaders had inflicted upon the camp last night. Mari chided herself for sleeping for such a long time when her patrons needed her, even though she was still tired. However, the vixen could not believe what she did last night; it was inconceivable.

Was it an effect of the lingering connection to Zenti that she was able to summon the ice and lightning? It had to be that. The Gifted showed signs of the Gift at their Gifting Day, or thereabouts. That is why it was named The Gifting Day. However, only a slim few possessed the Gift. It was not hereditary, nor could it be cultivated. Either you had it, or you did not. Mari was now twenty-one years old. The Gift never waited to reveal itself that many years. That fact was recorded history.

The only way she could have summoned the ice and electricity was because of the connection to Zenti. However, Mari had never heard of a non-Gifted ever using the Gift. It was too much to think about, yet it lingered in her thoughts. Though plagued by the previous evening events, Mari bravely pressed on, finally reaching the camp.

The vixen felt her heart both sink and rise simultaneously as she surveyed the battle-ravaged Faction camp. Most of the tents had been demolished. Shrapnel had also ripped through several of the wooden structures. Debris was everywhere. So were the bodies of those that had fallen. There were patrons still in the camp, primarily females and kits. The uninjured were tending to the injured, and the young were silently holding to their mother's skirts and watching.

Mari's view came upon Ricket. The young parrot

was severely injured and reclining in a wooden lawn chair. Someone was stitching up one of the small male's legs. Mari could not tell who was tending to Ricket. However, the vixen could not miss the fact Ricket's other leg was gone.

The vixen had seen death before, and she had seen the maimed. However, the thought of someone as devoted and young as Ricket being so gravely injured evoked strong emotions. Mari made her way into camp and moved straight for the young parrot. She stopped by his side and took his paw. It was then Mari realized that he was strapped to the chair and heavily sedated. She looked at the medic with an inquisitive look. The male cheetah shook his head. Mari nodded her head in understanding and started to move on to other survivors.

However, Mari stopped. She did not recognize the muzzle of the medic. He was not one of her Faction medics. She wanted to look for Malyx's mother, but not knowing everyone in her Faction camp was an issue. Mari was about to ask the male cheetah who he was, but Jolet interrupted her. The rabbit's ears were folded in submission, his head was bowed, and his voice quivered. At the sound of Jolet's voice, Mari snapped around. The first thing she noticed was his shoulder wound had been bound.

"Ma'am, all of the soldiers are dead," Jolet said, but the words came out choked. The rabbit was trying to hold back the tears.

Mari's heart stopped, and she shook her head; no, they could not all be dead. Looking around, she noticed only her civilian patrons. There were none of her soldiers around, though she thought she saw soldiers at Hayden's temporary camp. It was also destroyed. The dead were being moved to an area where they could be burned. It was her Faction's standing policy to burn their dead. That prevented the invaders from experimenting on the bodies. Her patrons smiled at the vixen. They were happy to see Mari, but more work needed to be done, and they continued. When things were more secure, there would be time for condolences and well wishes. These were her friends, her family, the only family Mari had anymore. It broke her heart to see such devastation. The vixen looked at the rabbit standing in front of her.

Slamming a fist into the rabbit's injured shoulder, the vixen drove the Jolet to the ground. Grabbing him by the injured shoulder, Mari dug her claws into the wound and turned him by his shoulder. Mari forced Jolet to look around the camp at the destruction through his teary blue eyes.

"Your fault, traitor," was all Mari spat at the rabbit.

She wanted to slit his throat, but Zenti had spared him for a reason. She knew her Zenti well; he never spared a traitor. Mari forgot about the unknown medic and continued her search for Malyx's mother. Leaving Jolet on his knees, the vixen walked past him as she searched through mockery after a mockery of medic stations. She found that same sad shake of the head at all of them. Her patrons were caring for the dying, where just a day ago, they laughed with them. Mari stopped and collected her thoughts.

Turning, she found that Jolet had followed her. The vixen wanted to shoot him, but the look on his face told her all she needed to know. For a long moment, the vixen contemplated what to do to him when a question broke her train of thought as a female patron spoke in a shaky voice. The ewe was in her early thirties and had lost her mate and their young ones a few months ago.

"Please, Miss Mari, what do we do now? Hayden and his troops did nothing to help us. Hayden is gone. We no longer have our soldiers to protect us. Why would Hayden not help? Why," the eve begged? She began crying again, and Mari noticed her eyes were already red from crying all night.

"Because Hayden is a coward," Mari snapped. "We're big females. I am sure we can do what we need to survive." Giving the ewe a gentle pat on the back of the paw, the vixen continued. "Go tend to what supplies we have left. We will be moving as soon as we can," directed Mari. The ewe nodded and hurried off. Again, the vixen pushed around Jolet, this time walking on, listening to him following her. Mari knew her frustration with the rabbit would soon make her snap. She tried to remain calm and focused.

Mari scanned Hayden's camp and noticed a male fox and a female cougar coming from that general area.

She did not recognize the two, but both had a military air about them. They were still several hundred yards away and heading towards her. Mari stopped short, and Jolet plowed into her from behind. Mari spun around and growled at the traitor.

"Alright, Jolet, where is Hayden" the vixen demanded as she moved away from her camp? Mari waited for an answer after walking a dozen yards or so towards the approaching two unknown soldiers. When Jolet did not answer, she turned around and growled. "You will tell me."

Jolet fidgeted, which instantly angered Mari.

"Now!" Mari's ears folded flat to the side as she hissed the command. The rabbit jumped at her raised voice and laid his long ears flat.

"I don't know. I never knew where Hayden was, but I knew he would be close. But I don't have a radio anymore; I can't contact him," stammered Jolet. Mari Semineu was frightening when she bared her teeth.

For a moment, Jolet thought that Mari would lose her temper. She was dangerous without losing her temper. When she did lose it, she was terrifying. The vixen had that look on her muzzle, one he had seen many times during a battle. *Oh, Heavens and Hells,* he thought*; I am so dead.* Quick he continued to speak, hoping that she would not kill him by redirecting her anger into finding a solution to their current predicament.

"What do we do now, Ma'am," Jolet asked? "Where do we go from here? We can no longer fight, our supplies are gone, and our troops are dead." The rabbit's voice trailed off as he realized exactly what his traitorous actions had brought about. Orra above thought the rabbit, I have welcomed death into the camp. Through tear-filled eyes, the rabbit looked at the vixen for guidance.

Mari groaned. She hated it when subordinates made a valid point; it made things so much harder for her. Groaning again, the vixen reached down to her thigh and expected to find her knife to fiddle with. It was a habit that Mari had developed when she was deep in thought. However, the knife was not in the sheath. She froze; it was still in the tree! Suddenly she was agitated at herself for leaving little Malyx for so long. Mari started fidgeting with the empty sheath. Holding the handle of her knife seemed to help her focus. Mari knew it was a silly habit. However, it did bring her clarity to fidget, and in a flash of clarity, Mari decided.

"We join Zenti," Mari said as her mood darkened. The vixen knew that to save the remaining patrons of her Faction, she would need his protection. Zenti was what Jayden needed. Deep inside, she needed the safety that Zenti offered. She also needed one more thing. Mari Semineu wanted to win back his heart.

Jolet's eyes grew wide, and his jaw quivered. "You can't be serious. He is a mad wolf. He kills his own, destroys everything, he, he, he will be our deaths," the rabbit blurted out.

Mari remembered young Malyx and that she had not found his mother. The poor cub must be scared. Turning, Mari grabbed Jolet then and glared at the trembling rabbit. The vixen drove her claws into the open wound again, causing him to scream loudly, drawing the whole camp's attention.

"I will not take no for an answer," Mari growled. "Now would you please do what we all know is very difficult for you and make yourself useful! I do not have time to wet nurse you around. So get off your pathetic ass, and start atoning. I need to find Malyx's mother."

She let go, and Jolet crumpled to the ground in pain. Mari scowled at him, and quickly the rabbit, with his free paw, pulled out a journal and rushed through his papers as the vixen turned to leave. The whole Faction camp was watching intently.

"Malyx? His mother was Ameiya; she joined us just a few months ago," began Jolet. Mari stopped as he spoke again. However, she detected a hint of trepidations in the rabbit's voice. Mari gave him a glare that said, get on with it.

"Ameiya is dead," said Jolet, looking up with a graven expression on his muzzle, trying to determine if she was about to cause him more pain. Mari stopped just long enough to look at the rabbit; her eyes met his. Her next words were spoken with clarity and purpose. The entire camp gave Miss Mari their full undivided attention.

"We find Zenti. Gather up all those that remain,

have them ready to move out in two hours. Those that are wounded will need to be cared for and moved with caution. They are to be given the best of what we have, and we are to move out to Zenti. I have a cub to recover and a certain knife that still has your blood on it. I want you to look at each one of our family here. I want you to burn their muzzles into your memory. I want you to know everyone here and everyone who will join my family. I want you to be their servant," Mari growled as she moved closer to Jolet's face.

Mari eased her muzzle at his ears, and she growled a whisper. "I hold you personally responsible for this atrocity Hayden has brought upon us. It was you who spied for him, and I want you to see what you have cost *my* family."

She turned and moved a few steps away, then looked back over her shoulder. Mari glared at Jolet with a burning pair of eyes and spoke directly to the rabbit only but was loud enough for the entire camp to hear.

"I want you to be able to tell Zenti muzzle to muzzle just why you betrayed our family. Because rabbit, it was Zenti that knocked you on your head," growled Mari and pulled a slip of paper from her pocket. "It was Zenti who gave you this note for me. His Gifted Talent of Blood Memories still lingers in this little spot of blood. He knew all along that you were a spy for Hayden. He let you live for a reason. Think on that rabbit. Zenti let you live. You best be able to prove your worth to my family before you meet him again. Zenti's memory is long, and his conscience is short. He has never been the forgiving type. Best hope you can reverse that tendency in him."

Slowly Mari looked at her patron. The vixen saw they understood. She turned and walked off, leaving the rabbit kneeling there. The vixen thought she could smell piss in the air as she walked away. She paid no heed to the two approaching soldiers, who were still one hundred yards away. She had a cub to recover. He was a good little male and would remain where she left him. It was not far, but she quickened her pace.

Walking back, Mari veered off into the woods, hurrying to retrieve the knife that she had left in the tree. It was between the Faction camp and where she hid the little male bear cub. Mari scampered up the tree, and when at last the vixen had the knife Zenti gave her, Mari breathed easier. As she held it in her grasp, she felt a small wave of relief wash over her. Mari looked at the engraved letters *For Ever And a Day*. Reading them made the vixen feel like she had always felt. Whether it was when her father comforted her when she was small or when Zenti held her, Mari felt loved. *For Ever And a Day*. Mari took a deep breath and took control of her emotions that she has suppressed for 13 months.

Malyx was waiting for her just where she had left him. How was she going to do this? How could you tell a cub that its mother was dead? Was there even a proper way to do it? Sighing, Mari crouched down and ran her claws through her hair in frustration before speaking. Malyx sat quietly, hiding safely.

"Malyx," Mari said softly. Malyx looked up at Mari. He was a brave cub, the vixen thought. He had sat there all this time being quiet, holding the ration bar's wrapper in his paws. It dawned on Mari that those bars were salty. They make you thirsty, and this cub had not gone looking for water. Smiling, she handed him the canteen, and he drank sloppily. When he gave her back the canteen, he flattened his ears, waiting for a rebuke for being so messy. Water ran down his muzzle, but Mari just wiped the excess gently away without a word. The poor little bear cub just sat there looking up at Mari. His eyes began to tear. Mari gave him the canteen again, and he took another drink of water, and more ran down his muzzle. The canteen was too big for his little paws, but he did not hesitate to grasp it when the vixen offered. He was trying to be a big male, Mari thought.

Smiling gently, Mari waited until he was done, then wiped the water away with her sleeve this time. Taking the canteen once he was finished, the vixen pulled Malyx into her arms. The vixen smiled and cooed to him gently. Opening her paw, she waited as he placed the ration bar wrapper into it. It was breaking her heart. How was she going to tell this little male he was now without a family? Malyx began to tear up again.

"Oh, why is such a brave little male crying," Mari asked? Gently stroking his fur, the vixen smiled at the little bear cub sweetly. Kissing his forehead once, Mari wiped his tears away. She started to put him down, but he shook his head and clung to her. Mari lovingly stroked his fur.

The vixen had a feeling that the little cub already knew what had happened to his mother.

Malyx said nothing but simply cried. Mari started back to the camp and held Malyx close. Something of this whole situation tugged at a memory of her mother holding Rini when their dad had gone off to battle. Lillian Waxton let her youngest kit cry without trying to silence her. When Rini finally stopped crying, Lillian Waxton kissed her daughter and shared words of comfort. Those words came back to Mari, and she whispered them to Malyx

"Life has but one goal, Pumpkin, and that is to stop living," began Mari. Life was hard on Jayden, and it was not the Mitdonian's way to sugarcoat the facts. "All things must die, Pumpkin. We each have our time to travel to the stars. Sometimes it is long, sometimes it is short, but we must all go to the stars when the time comes. Do not cry because it is not an end but the beginning of a change. See, Pumpkin, when we die, it is only our body, like a fallen tree or a cut blade of grass. But the thing that makes you who you are keeps living. My little Star Spirit, we all follow that spiral that winds us up towards the stars. Orra does not give us a choice." Mari found herself repeating her mother's words to this young cub.

Mari remembered her mother's voice and the calm, firmness that it had. Lillian Waxton had a way that imparted an incredible feeling of love with just the sound of her voice. Mari felt tears well up in her eyes, and she shook them away. She needed to be tough for her patron and especially one little bear cub. The vixen gave Malyx a gentle kiss on the tip of his nose. It was as much to console herself as the young male. Malyx held onto Mari like he would have his own mother. Mari knew that she was not and would never be his mother. However, the vixen did not have the heart to let him go. Mari Semineu held him closer, nuzzling him gently. Today, Mari became even more of a mother to a little bear cub and to her patrons.

"We're all going to go on a little trip, okay, Malyx? We are going to find someone who can help us, someone who I know can protect us. I need you to be a good little cub and ride in the cart with the rest of the kits. Is that okay," Mari asked? Malyx nodded against her neck as she re-entered the camp.

Mari stood at the edge of the remnants of her Faction camp. Her patrons were working incredibly hard to pack up what was left of their possessions. It was heartbreaking, but this was war, and Mari had to face the fact that it would not be a gentlemale's war. Jolet came to Mari as she stood at the edge of the camp, taking a visual inventory. Mari noted the rabbit had changed his clothing. An elder puma came when Mari beckoned her over and took Malyx from Mari, leaving the vixen alone with the traitor Jolet.

"Ma'am, there is someone to see you," said the rabbit in a quivering voice as the black and gray fox walked up behind Jolet.

This was the soldier that was approaching from the remnants of Hayden's camp. She vaguely remembered this male's muzzle from the past. However, she could not recall who he was or where she saw him. He was tall for the fox breed. However, there was no mistaking his commanding presence.

"Greetings Miss Mari, I am Malachi, Sub-Commander of the Northern Faction. Zenti has asked us to assist you in whatever way we can. I brought two medics and a truck full of supplies and food. I regret we cannot be more helpful. I have a hunt planned for tonight," said the male fox, offering a kind but sorrow-filled smile. Mari shared a smile with the fox that only those in command could give. It was a sad smile that said duty called. However, to Jolet, it seemed that Mari Semineu scowled.

"Your help is most welcomed, and the supplies are needed," Mari replied, shaking Malachi's paw in gratitude.

"Jolet," Mari said, turning to face the rabbit. The vixen was about to give him an order when Malachi drove a fist into the rabbit's muzzle. The blow knocked Jolet on his ass. In a fluid motion, the male fox drew his saber to strike. Mari stayed his paw.

"Zenti informed me he was a spy, and we have only one sentence for spies in the Northern Faction," Malachi said with a look of confusion on his muzzle.

Jolet scooted back in an attempt to flee when Mari growled at the rabbit. Her swift boot to the rabbit's chest pinned him to the ground. Jolet froze in place when Mari barred her fangs.

"Zenti informed me as much. However, he chose to let Jolet live for whatever reason. We will be joining Zenti soon. I have decided to give this rabbit a chance to redeem himself in my eyes before that meeting. If he fails, I am sure Zenti will deal with him," she said. Jolet gulped hard, not missing Mari's point.

"As you command, Miss Mari, it is my pleasure to serve both you and Zenti," said Malachi as he put away the saber.

"Jolet, get someone to assist our guests. NOW!" Mari growled when the rabbit hesitated a moment too long. The frightened rabbit scrambled away. "Zenti may not have to deal with the traitor if he keeps pissing me off," said Mari to Malachi. Both vulpines smiled.

A young ewe came, listened to Mari's command, and led the fox away. Moving to what was left of her tent, the vixen rummaged through the remains. Gathering all the salvageable items, which were very few, Mari decided she needed to limit her personal items even further. Looking at her smashed desk, the vixen's spirit sank as it had not survived. It had been her father's desk he used when he traveled from the Hasha training camp.

Mari sighed. Years ago, in a moment of reminiscing, the vixen had mentioned to Zenti how she would sit behind that desk and pretend she was her father. A few days later, Zenti went off to 'hunt.' Two weeks later, the small desk arrived with a bow and a note. The note was long lost, but Zenti's words were not.

"Because you deserve fond memories," recited Mari. Those were the words of that reckless white wolf of hers.

Mari touched the splintered surface of the last remnant of her father's possessions. No, Mari thought, there are two things of her Mom and Dad's left alive. Mari sighed again at the distance that had grown between her and her sister, Rini. Mari looked at the shattered desk with profound sadness. The desk looked as if it had been blown apart. She rummaged through the splintered materials hoping to find the two mating rings. However, they, along with most everything else, were destroyed or missing.

Sitting on the ground in the ruins of her tent, the vixen looked at the wreckage and sighed. What more could go wrong, she thought, when a little voice clearing its throat caught her attention? Turning, Mari saw Rochet standing quietly, trying not to be intrusive but still wanting her attention. Mari smiled that the little parrot was unharmed.

"Yes, Rochet, how can I help you," Mari asked?

"I have the video of last night, Miss Mari. I hope it is not too shaky; I was terrified," the little parrot said as she held out the camera.

"Keep the camera; that is now your official job. Do you want it," Mari asked? Much to the vixen's surprise, her words sounded like the matronly kind that really did not give Rochet a choice but allowed her to say no.

"Yes, Ma'am," said the little parrot with pride.

"See that fox over there," Mari asked, pointing out the non-existent door? "That is Sub Commander Malachi; please take the recording to him for safekeeping," Mari said and gave the young female a wink. Rochet started to turn away and then stopped.

"Miss Mari, are you looking for these?" Rochet asked. Her tiny paw held out the silver and gold mating bands, "I came to your tent looking for you this morning and found them. I thought I would keep them safe for you."

"That was very kind of you, Rochet," Mari replied while taking the rings from the little parrot.

"Did Mister Zenti live, Ma'am," the young parrot asked in an unsure voice?

"Yes, hun, I'm sure he did," replied Mari with a quizzical look on her face.

"Is he coming back," Rochet asked with a quiver in her tiny voice?

"No, Rochet, we are going to him. Does that scare you," Mari asked as she took the little parrot in her arms?

Rochet shook her head no and then hugged Mari tight, whispering into her ear. Mari sent her on her way as the little parrot's words echoing in her mind, 'He kills **THEM**, which makes him good.' Mari saw Jolet approach. He was shaking as he came to the vixen.   Mari was not in a sympathetic mood, and the rabbit had reached her tolerable limits.

"How is Ricket," Mari asked before Jolet could say a word?

"I don't know," Jolet stuttered, and he flinched when she growled at him, "But I will find out," he hastily said. The rabbit hesitated for a moment before continuing. "Ma'am, which way are we to head? How will we find Zenti? Do you know where he went," asked the shaking rabbit?

"Keep Rochet busy and away from her brother. Better yet, go ask Malachi to instruct her on how to take better recording," order Mari. The vixen's tone was sharp enough to cut fur and flesh.

"Ma'am," said Jolet. The rabbit cringed, not sure if he wanted to be near Malachi.

The vixen looked at him with such a hateful stare that he shrank away and went to find the little parrot. However, Mari had to admit Jolet had a point. Zenti did not come back after the explosions. Mari knew he was alive. She also knew Zenti had been gravely injured; the vixen felt it last night before she severed the bond between them. However, Mari did not know where he had gone to. If he did not come back, it meant he was trying to lead **THEM** away, hopefully.

Mari sighed heavily, and she softly cursed herself for putting such a vast distance between them. She was not fully ready to forgive him for not coming forward with the truth sooner. Zenti could have shared those memories months ago. However, that little voice in the back of her head reminded her that she was the one who rebuked him. Deep inside that rebuke, the vixen knew that the hard-headed, angry wolf was doing what was best for Mitd. Mari also reluctantly admitted Zenti was doing what was best for herself as well.

Haverick Waxton's words came back to the vixen about having someone to take care of her. Mari remembered how angry she was at her father for making an arranged mating. She could hear her father's deep, determined voice, and for a moment, Mari recalled all that Zenti had done for her. The vixen thought she understood her father's words more clearly as she looked out over the destroyed camp. Without Zenti, all those survivors would be dead.

Looking at her paws, she remembered how they were ice blue last night. Mari recalled Zenti's paw that afternoon in the forest clearing less than two days ago. She had just finished rebuking Zenti harshly. His paws glowed a brilliant red in anger. Yet, he had not hesitated to defend her. The vixen had thought Zenti was merely protecting her, when in fact, it may have been so much more.

A mated pair thought Mari as she looked at the two rings; one of Kredomis and one of Garamite. She sighed and shook her head in disbelief. Was she a Summoner? Was she part of a mated pair of Gifted? Had her father known nearly ten years ago that the arranged mating was her destiny? Mari chuckled as she thought that the arranged mating was only in the traditional sense. Jolet had returned, and she realized the rabbit had been standing there for some time, he started to address her, and she cut him off.

"We head West for now," was all Mari ordered. The vixen whistled loudly, garnering the attention of her patrons.

If Zenti was hurt, he needed a healer. The vixen knew of only one healer who had repeatedly tended his wounds, or so the stories went. There was a particular Shaman who did not care what Zenti had done. It seemed that all the mysterious Shaman cared about was that Zenti was doing something to save Mitd. The Shaman Torit lived to the Southwest of their current position. West took them along the Jetton River, which offered plenty of fresh water and food. To begin this trek, West it was. Again, Mari looked at her paws as she thought about being Gifted. At the thought, the vixen's paws glowed a faint blue. No one in her fractured camp missed Mari's glowing paws. Their spirits instantly lifted. Their beloved Miss Mari was Gifted.

"We head West," Mari called to the patrons of her camp. In short order, the remaining patrons prepared to move out.

"Commander Mari, we have done all we can," began Malachi, "however, your wounded are unlikely to survive. I am sorry we could not do more. That little

Rochet took a good recording last night. She wanted to see her brother, but I told her he was asleep. He will not survive Miss Mari. The wounds are just too extensive," said Malachi as he shook the vixen's paw.

The vixen nodded in understanding. War claims its share of life. She watched as the tall fox made his way over to the old farm truck. He talked to his two medics, and they left a considerable number of medical supplies. The male fox looked back to Mari, and the two vulpines shared an expression unique to their breed. The look was one of warry hope. However, both knew the cost of hope would be high.

Both knew that Zenti had declared open warfare on every member of Crown Champion Hayden's family. There was no turning back now. Summoner Zenti Semineu had cast the die of fate, and where the pips ended up was unknown. However, there was one certainty. Vzdoch would have her paws full, escorting the dead to the stars. Both knew the silvery-white wolf well enough to know he was as good as his word. The two gave each other a nod. Malachi and his companions drove off down the rugged dirt road, disappearing into the woods.

Mari moved to the lead wagon and started to climb aboard. Jolet waited at her side as a messenger. The messenger would walk at the side of the wagon. His duty was typically delegated to a pre-Coming-of-Age kit who would run commands back to the various carts and wagons. Military radios were in limited supply, and civilian radios could not be encrypted. Runners were the most effective means of communication between the caravan wagons. It was primitive but very effective.

Stopping, the vixen decided to walk back to her patrons and check on each group individually. The caravan was small, barely a tenth of her standard wagons. There were no motor vehicles left in working order. Mari put on a smile that bolstered her patron. However, the vixen knew this was a rag-tag group of survivors. Some would not make it to Torit's home. The vixen looked over at a pile of debris. Piled within the trash, there were many of the supplies that her Faction camp would have carried. They were being left behind because the few draft animals she had to pull the box and canvas wagons could not haul all that additional weight. In that pile of debris were the remnants of her patron's former lives. Mari continued her inspection, knowing war brings change.

Stopping beside the wagon that carried the young, the vixen smiled. Mari played with them, trying to lift their spirits. The pups and kits could not tell that her mind ghosted away towards Zenti. What the tired, dirt-covered youth saw was the bright face of Miss Mari. While the vixen tried to reach out and touch Zenti's mind, she found her concentration repeatedly broken by the youth's playful hugs and kisses. Mari wanted to focus on what Zenti could do to help her patrons, but his declaration of love the night before clouded her thoughts.

Had Zenti honestly meant it; did he really love her still? Mari could not believe Zenti could continue to love her after all that she had put him through. The bitter words that she was no longer his mate and never would be again came crashing to the forefront of the vixen's thoughts? Mari wondered what drove a male to have such devotion to another. The vixen thought back to the only source she had of learning. Her father loved her mother in the very same way. Mari thought of how her wounded dad went to town for a bit of candy for his mate. Could Zenti be as devoted to her as Haverick Waxton was to Lillian Waxton?

Mari continued to wonder how Zenti still loved her enough to protect her after everything she had put him through? Did he love her enough to destroy the world to keep her from being a slave to the invaders? Holding the little cub's paw, Mari continued to absentmindedly rub Malyx's fur. The little bear cub did not mind, and he nuzzled her paw in return.

The more pressing question that Mari's mind kept asking her heart: *are you ready to admit once more that you love Zenti?* The vixen could not answer that question. She did not dare to because that meant exposing her heart once more to him. To admit she loved Zenti meant letting him in to see the many scars that that remained since their parting. She did not dare to let him know what she had become. She had been such a hateful vixen to him. Her bitter words were not reserved for her alone. The battle between Mari's heart and mind raged on.

Malyx tugging on her sleeve brought Mari back from her internal struggles. Looking around, Mari realized that she had been walking for hours, lost in thought of her predicament. The sun was midway through the afternoon

sky, and Mari wondered when they had started the journey.
Jolet walked by the vixen's side and slightly behind her.
The rabbit held a clipboard, ears lowered, looking up at her
waiting as if for an answer.

The cub's eyes looked haggard and red as if he had
still been crying. Picking Malyx up from the wagon, Mari
held him on her hip. Malyx curled up against her shoulder
and nuzzled her cheek. Looking at her watch, Mari
realized that it had been almost six hours since they had
started their westward trek. Where had her mind wandered
for all those hours, she wondered?

"You must be hungry," Mari said with a smile, and
the little bear nodded.

Turning her head towards Jolet, she ordered a halt
and temporary rest, including a light midday meal. The
group stopped and prepared for a brief repast without
breaking the train of wagons and carts. Mari moved to the
lead wagon and climbed in the back. Sorting through a
stack of papers collected from the remains of the desk in
her tent, she pulled out a well-worn map. Stepping down,
the vixen called for one of the small, folding card tables to
be unloaded from a cart.

Unfolding the warn map, Mari spread it out on the
card table. Mari began to mark their original camp's
position when Kaper, a yearling otter, handed her a cup of
water. Mari thanked her, then returned to the quick
calculations of the distance they had traveled.

"Eighteen miles, oh so little," Mari muttered.

However, the days were long this time of year, which would help their travels.

No, they needed to make about five miles an hour to reach the Shaman's land, which she had circled just to the West and south of her original camp. Quickly calculating that, if they could make five miles an hour for twelve hours a day, it should only take them six days to reach the Shaman's place. How it would have been nice to have a few vehicles, but they were with the rest of her troops with General Breymore or destroyed in the attack. However, she had made do with less, and now would be no different.

Mari recalled the elder Shaman Torit. Her mother would visit the elder buzzard a few times a year when she was just a little kit. Mari recalled how she would sit all afraid of the buzzard as he would share tidbits of information on this plant or that herb with her mother. Remembering her mother's gentle words about the old buzzard's kind nature, the vixen smiled at the memory.

"Good memories, Ma'am," asked Kaper? The otter refilled Mari's cup and smiled at the vixen.

"Yes, thank you. Jolet!" Mari shouted the rabbit's name. Jolet jumped; he was patiently standing, not two feet behind Mari.

"Kaper here is going to be your personal assistant. You are to spend every moment making this wagon train move faster. We are to move sixty miles a day. She will be here to inspire you. You, rabbit, are to personally motivate and move things forward. You report to her. She is to report to me. I do not want to see your muzzle until the end of the day. We will be here for one hour, then we will move on again," ordered Mari, then added. "One more thing. Do not ever stand behind me again, or so help me I will gut you where you stand. Now go," the vixen snapped at the shaking rabbit. Jolet bolted off to implement her orders.

"Kaper, I want you to do nothing but keep a boot in his ass. I do not want him to have a moment's rest," Mari said. Putting both paws on the young otter's shoulder, Mari looked at Kaper with a big grin. "Do you think you can handle him?"

"How far up his ass do you want that boot," Kaper asked? The otter beamed a wicked grin at the vixen and sauntered off after Jolet. The brash young otter, who had always taken charge of a situation, left Mari with her first happy chuckle in quite a while. The vixen considered Kaper, a capable coordinator. It was good to see the otter willing to rise to a new challenge. Repeatedly Kaper had proven that she could handle both soldier and Council Elder alike.

Looking at the map again, Mari marked a few backroads and planned their evening camping spots. A young doe brought her a sandwich. Smiling, the vixen thanked the doe with a nod of her head as she took a bite. Mari looked at Malyx, who was happily picking away at a large, shared platter of food with the other young. Quietly the vixen slipped away from the young male cub.

Walking amongst her patrons, Mari counted six open carts, four enclosed carts, four canvassed wagons, one boxed wagon, and five open wagons. Three months ago, Mari's Faction camp consisted of two hundred civilians patrons and four hundred troops. Three hundred seventy-five of her Faction soldiers were on loan to General Breymore. The remaining troops were unfit for frontline duty and had remained in camp as personal guards for Mari's patrons. The vixen had taken in some thirty wounded soldiers for medical treatment two months ago and an additional forty-five civilians who needed refuge.

Before the attack last night, the vixen's camp consisted of three hundred. Less than a day later, as Mari walked among her patrons, she counted no more than fifty, most females and kits. There were only two soldiers in her entourage. Mari stopped by to visit them. However, they were unconscious. Those attending them smiled the weak smile that said they were not expected to survive through the day. The sad reality of the attack, and the death toll, brought Mari's no-nonsense attitude back to the forefront. The vixen returned to the map table and motioned for Kaper to come over. The young female otter said something to Jolet, and the rabbit's ears folded back.

"Kaper, it is time we move out. Have that traitor of a rabbit get us moving. Station the cart with the two soldiers at the rear of the wagon train. Have a group assigned to burn their bodies when they pass to the stars. Instruct them to use a twelve-hour delay timer to start their pyres. I will be in the lead wagon," said Mari as she folded up the map. The table was placed back into the cart.

The otter began giving orders to clean up and prepare to move out as Mari climbed into the seat by a middle-aged female badger. Mari started explaining the route and speed she wanted to achieve. The female badger, a farmer's mate, nodded and checked the two domestic draft horse tack. Soon they were ready to be on the way. Dismounting, Mari moved along to the rest of the wagon train.

Stopping by the cart with the pups, she looked at Rochet, who was currently helping take care of the younger ones. The young parrot looked tired and as if she, too, had been crying. Mari reached out a paw and beckoned the young female to come with her.

"Rochet, your brother is hurt badly. He will not make this journey much longer. You have seen too much death for one so young. Stay with me, and we will sing your brother to the stars tonight," Mari said, wiping the tear away from Rochet's eyes. The young pre-Gifting Day female shook her head and hugged Mari before heading to the cart where her brother was.

Mari nodded and raised a paw to dismiss the cart driver's unvoiced question when the little parrot climbed in the back. Both Mari and the elder female ferret understood the young parrot's need to be with her only kin.

Mari returned to the wagon train's head, climbed up onto the bench seat, and patted the badger on the paw. When the female badger looked at Mari, the vixen nodded to go ahead and move out.

The remainder of the day went peacefully. The first evening had the paw full of Council Elders sitting around Mari's fire pit, quietly listening to her plans for the following days of travel. They usually would feel inclined to interject their opinions. However, the meeting went by without so much as a discussion. Mari soon found herself eating alone that evening when the cart that carried the two wounded soldiers made its way into camp. She began to get up from her meal when Kaper, shaking her head no, waved Mari off with a dejected look on her muzzle. The otter hugged Rochet and led her to a group of mothers who took her in. The little parrot's bother, Ricket, was dead.

Forty-eight out of three hundred of her patrons survived all because Zenti acted. No, Mari corrected herself. Two hundred fifty-two were dead because of Hayden. The panther was the real villain, and she could not even reconcile the fact that there was even a glimmer in her eye from him. How could she have even considered him? Her thoughts were interrupted when Jolet cleared his throat.

"Ma'am, all has been done as per your orders. What else shall I do before the night grows old," asked a dejected and exhausted rabbit?

She looked at him with disgust for his cowardly actions. Perhaps it would have been better to let Malachi kill him. However, Zenti let him live; therefore, there must be a purpose to the rabbit's miserable existence.

"Assign a standard watch for the night and scouts for the roads we will take. Send the scouts out tonight after they have had a few hours of sleep," Mari said without really acknowledging him.

"Ma'am, we have neither soldiers nor scouts," he began when she cut him short with a quick, searing look.

"Then you will appoint guards and scouts. Don't fail me in your choices," Mari snapped at him. Jolet backed away, quickly heading back into the evening camp.

The evening fires burned low when sleep finally came to Mari. The vixen's dreams drifted to Zenti as the heavy sleep caused by the stress of the past two days weighed on her like a millstone, drowning her in nightmares. The vixen found restless sleep, but sleep, nonetheless.

By the third day, Jolet had the group moving at almost seven miles an hour by scheduling no-stop food breaks. The rabbit had organized the daily meal preparation in the previous evening. Scouting and foraging parties were hard at work as well. The rabbit's keen sense of organization kept the remaining camp Elders away from pestering Mari with petty questions.

The tired group of Mari's patrons listened to the radio on that third evening. Their spirits lightened as the news reported of one convoy and two traitor camps had been destroyed by elements of the Northern Faction. Mari explained that the attacks would undoubtedly divert the invader's troops, and their Mitdonian supporters, further to the north. Kaper explained to the younger patrons that those attacks by Summoner Zenti Semineu's Faction had bought them a lot of extra time to escape. The atmosphere of the whole wagon train of rag-tag survivors lightened considerably.

By noon of the fifth day, they came upon a small farm where a young female otter was outside scrubbing laundry. Stepping down from the wagon, Mari saw in the corral an older weasel mending the railing. Mari turned to him and approached.

"Good day sir, can we impose upon you for some fresh well water for our horses and my patrons?" Mari asked as she extended her paw to the weasel, who shook it firmly.

"Help yourself, I need to mend this railing, so I won't be able to assist," said the weasel, pointing to the well pump at the side of the house.

Turning away, Mari snapped a claw at Jolet, pointing at the pump. Mari noticed a young post-Coming-of-Age otter looking at her while doing the laundry.

"Hi, I am Lari," said the young otter as Mari approached, her paws were covered in soap, still half-buried in the washtub.

"Hello, I am Mari. Your father has graciously allowed us the use of the well. We can get it ourselves, so please don't stop your wash day chores," Mari said, smiling at the young otter. Lari laughed loudly, to which Mari just raised an eyebrow in total confusion as the otter shook the soap from her paws.

"Adam is my mate. It was an arranged matting," answered Lari. Mari hid a slight grin when she noted the twinkle in the otter's eye. Mari could tell that the yearling was in love with the older male.

"As was my matting," Mari said, with a smile which soon turned to a distant look as she remembered that fateful night her father introduced her to Zenti.

"Mine has turned out good so far, though I dare say yours has been not what you expected," said Lari, looking at a distant Mari, to which the vixen looked back at the otter in shocked.

"I am sorry, have we met before? I do not remember your muzzle," said Mari with a confused look of shock.

"Miss Mari Semineu, do you think you are not so well known by many? Though I doubt that a few have ever had the pleasure of sharing food with your former mate," replied Lari as she shook some of the soap off her paws and looked at a stunned Mari.

"Explain yourself," said Mari as she looked at Lari with suspicion. After what the vixen had heard of Zenti's exploits, who would want to spend an evening with him? The rumors of his actions and the rage-filled anger the vixen felt a few nights ago did not suggest anyone would like to spend dinner with Zenti.

"Your former mate was here a few days ago, in pretty bad shape, I might add. I had the pleasure of taking care of a few of his wounds as well as sharing a meal. It was the least I could do to repay him," said Lari. The yearling otter took Mari by the paw and lead her over to Adam. The male weasel stood up from mending the railings and smiled lovingly at his young mate. The otter was quite the sight standing next to Miss Mari Semineu. Adam could not help but chuckle at the soapy water still dripping off his mate's paws.

"Adam, Orra blesses our house once again. Can we not allow these travelers an afternoon's rest and use of our bath? If I am right, they are on their way to the Shaman Torit's home," Lari said with a smile.

"They are welcome to stay the night if that is what your heart desires, love, but tell me, how we are blessed again?" he replied.

Mari could tell this older weasel was in love with this yearling, only by the way he looked at her. There was unconditional love in his eyes, and he was lost in Lari's pretty smile. "Adam, this is-" but Lari did not get to finish the introduction.

"I know who Miss Mari is, though I doubt she remembers me," said Adam, softly smiling while wiping soap off the otter's cheek.

"I am afraid that I don't," Mari said apologetically, her ears folded back slightly. This was more and more confusing. The vixen did not remember this weasel or otter, but they knew more about her than she cared them to.

"This has been my family's share-crop farm for almost two hundred years. Your father, Haverick, that crazy Shaman Torit, and I used to hunt these lands; I am sorry for your loss," he said, patting Mari on the paw in condolence.

"Adam," questioned Lari. This was news to her.

"I am at a loss," said Mari.

"You and your mother would stay in this same home when you were but a tiny kit. Your last visit was when you were four years old, just after the invasions began in earnest. I am sad to say I only got to see your father a few more times after that," Adam said, hugging Mari over the fence railing when she started to tear up.

"I'm sorry, I don't remember you, though I remember my mom coming to Torit's to learn about herbs. Was the house blue before," Mari asked as snippets of memories eased into her thoughts? The vixen wiped tears from the corner of her eyes. Something was vaguely familiar about this farm. Hearing that her father and mother knew of this place brought a depth of sorrow the vixen had long suppressed. Mari looked around.

This was all very real now. The faded memories came back, but they were nothing more than a whirl of colors blending with no defined pattern. They were youthful memories and blurred dreams, but nothing more.

"Yes, it was blue, and I would not expect you to

remember, Mari. I am sorry things between you and Zenti failed. I am not sure exactly what happened, and it is none of my business, but I owe him far more than a meal and a bed for saving my Lari from Dotharian. However, the least I can do for my late friend's kit is to offer you a warm bed, a hot bath, and one of Lari's delicious dinners. Though I do not think she can feed everyone," Adam said with a smile.

"Let me tell my patrons of your kindness, and then I would love to hear some stories of my father," Mari said, fighting back more tears, which soon became a losing battle as she stood there.

Mari motioned for Jolet, who came running at the summon, then listened intently at every word and every instruction and hurried off. Turning, she noted the confusion on Adam and Lari's muzzles.

"He is trying to impress Zenti by obeying me to save his sorry ass," Mari said and let the conversation drop.

"Lari has been simmering a stew all day, and it will just melt in your muzzle. I have some more work to do around the barn. You can set up over there by the silo for the night," said Adam as he went back to mending the railing. Lari held up her soapy paws and nodded at the washtub. Mari smiled in understanding and left the two to their daily chores.

****

The stars shone brightly that evening as Mari, Adam, and Lari sat on the back porch drinking hot-spiced tea and sharing memories of the past. There was nothing more comfortable than sitting in a rocking chair with a full belly on a cool spring evening. Listening to new friends share old family tales soothed over the horrors of war. It was a rare comfort Mari Semineu missed.

Though Mari did share, mostly the vixen listened to Adam tell her stories about her father. Between laughing herself silly and crying a soul emptying cry, Mari found that she really grieved her father's death for the first time. The vixen only remembered General Haverick Waxton as a strong military commander who was very loving to his family. However, her father never showed the ridiculously fun-loving side that Adam was sharing with her now. Though her young home life was happy, the stories Adam share made her miss her father even more.

The hours passed with laughter drowned in tears as Adam told story after story about this adventure or that. Some of the stories Mari could remember her father talking about. But she never knew whom her father was talking about. Mari could now put a muzzle to some of her father's happiest memories of his life outside the family. Adam bought Mari a cigar box from the cellar filled with little trinkets. These were toys of her youth, relics of a time long lost.

Mari laughed at the little toys, and each one brought

a flood of new memories. The toys brought more tears as Mari thanked Adam for saving them. The vixen was sure that the pups of her Faction camp would love these to play with. Closing the box, Mari kissed Adam on the tip of his nose. It was something she now remembered doing as a young pre-Gifting Day kit when she visited this home.

The talk eventually turned to Zenti's visit with Adam and Lari. Mari explained that it did not bother her to talk about Zenti. Mari admitted that she knew mistakes had been made concerning their relationship. The vixen found herself laughing at how easily Lari had convinced the hard-headed wolf that he needed to get in the tub, sans his underwear. Mari laughed at the story so hard the vixen found herself crying at the thought of Zenti being gravely injured.

Flashbacks of the shared memory of Zenti lying on a metal table, sliced up like some dissected animal, haunted the vixen. Mari listened to Lari tell her how badly hurt Zenti was. Lari became silent and remorseful. When Mari asked what was wrong, the yearling otter explained. Lari said the small amount of medical assistance she performed for Zenti made a tiny dent in the debt she felt she owed him. Lari went on to explain how Zenti had saved her from Dotharian. Mari found herself wondering how many more felt they owed Zenti. How many wounds had the white wolf suffered, how much blood had he spilt for the safety of their species?

"If I know that hard-headed wolf, he would say that a good meal was all that was needed in payment," said

Mari trying to lighten the mood.

"Sounds like something Adam would say," teased Lari, to which both females laughed when Adam rolled his eyes.

"Come sleep inside tonight, Mari," said Lari.

Mari smiled but shook her head, stating that she liked to be with her patrons though she really appreciated the offer. Lari poured another round of spiced tea. The three laughed a little more as the night grew old.

Bidding Adam and Lari good night, Mari made her way to the tent that Jolet had erected for her. A small fire burned just outside the tent flap a few feet away. Patiently waiting for the vixen was the traitorous rabbit.

"Is your report important," Mari asked as she approached? When Jolet shook his head, the vixen motioned for him to leave. The rabbit turned away without seeing that Mari had been crying.

Jolet had worked with Hayden, who had betrayed her to **THEM.** It was the invaders who had killed her father. Jolet was the reason Zenti had been wounded so severely, Mari told herself. However, deep inside, the vixen knew the real enemy was Hayden and not this cowardly rabbit. Sighing deeply, Mari called Jolet's name, and he stopped.

"Be prepared to move us out in the morning early, and don't bother me from breakfast, I am tired," stated Mari and waved the rabbit off before entering her tent for the night.

****

Mari was thankful when the wagon crested the modest rise. The vixen looked down on the slight depression that the Shaman Torit called his home. The morning had gone as smooth as any of the others. Breakfast was served, cleaned up, and the carts were packed. With happy goodbyes, the remaining Faction survivors left Adam and Lari's farm and moved on. They were only a daylight ride from the Shaman's home. That day-long journey had been peaceful and passed quickly.

Looking down at Shaman Torit's house, Mari took in the surroundings. The home was situated in the middle of the depression, with a small pond just outside the front entrance. The whole area was landscaped with colorful blooming flowers that gave it a homey look and feel. Various stones from each of the Mitdonian islands formed the central water fountain. Glistening water trickled over the top of a birdbath bowl.

The second wagon reached the clearing in sight of their destination and pulled up beside Mari's wagon. Kaper looked down at the peaceful settings and then over to Mari in the first wagon. There was a light breeze, but the day was cloudless. It was the kind of day that picnics were made for.

"Do we move them all down to the house," Kaper asked? Mari replied she would go alone to talk to the old healer as she dismounted the lead wagon. The vixen looked back to her patrons. They seemed at peace for the first time in many days.

"Have that rabbit get everyone ready to move down to the clearing. Set up camp so that it will be less likely that they would be ambushed like before. Keep the tents separated in case **THEY** bring artillery again," said Mari as she started to head down to the Shaman's home. Stopping, the vixen turned to Kaper and smiled.

"Thank you, my dear, you have done a wonderful job of moving this Faction forward. Do you like feel like you could continue doing this job," Mari asked?

"It would be a pleasure to take some weight off your shoulders," Kaper said with a smile.

"I will make it official shortly. Consider yourself my second in command," Mari said.

"Are you not giving that position back to Zenti? I thought perhaps," the otter let her voice trail off.

"Zenti has more important things to do than be the second in command. His Gift has grown. After what I recently learned, I am afraid that the monster we have heard of is winning the battle within him," Mari replied, then abruptly stopped. Tears began to well up at the recall of Zenti's shared memories. Mari looked at the young otter. Kaper looked back at the vixen with knowing eyes that held an understanding far beyond the otter's age.

****

Zenti pushed himself up from lying on the surgical bed. His body was still sore. Several of his wounds were still bleeding after being freshly opened to pull more of the shrapnel out. Several pieces of the metal had been missed. This was his second full day in Torit's care. The old buzzard had been pulling out more and more shrapnel shards every few hours. Some of the metal shards Torit removed surgically. However, others, the elder buzzard, used his Gift to withdraw.

"Heavens and Hells pup, I thought I got all of this out two days ago. With all that damn Kredomis metal in your body, I cannot seem to find every piece with my Gift," said the old bird as he gave Zenti a revolting thick liquid to drink. "The artillery shell fragments must also be made of Kredomis."

"Scrap Kredomis is very common these days. When the invaders attacked the Port City of KerGavda five years ago, most of the Mitdonian Navy was destroyed. For years the Crown has been scrapping those submerged hulks for metal. The few ships that survived were not in port at the time of the attack and are in hiding," offered Zenti between sips of the foul liquid.

"That would explain it. On the older warships, the

internal armor plating protecting the vital command area was made from Summoner forged Kredomis. Though you can not reforge the metal, it does make effective shrapnel. I think I have it all out," replied Torit. The elder buzzard hoped he was now finished removing the last piece of shrapnel.

"Summoner forged Kredomis is exceptionally rare. I never knew the King commissioned Summoners to heat Kredomis for a warship," said Zenti.

"A Summoner forged the internal armor plating for the command and control center on each of the battlecruisers," said Torit. The elder buzzard did not offer any further explanation when Zenti gave him a questioning look. There was a lesson in that statement. However, Zenti's mind was not able to focus on the implication in Torit's words.

As the silvery-white wolf lay on the surgical bed for a moment longer, he thought about the past few days of pain. Zenti corrected himself. The pain of surgery meant extreme discomfort but nothing like what the invaders had done to him. However, Torit had not been gentle, nor had he been over gracious when the white wolf complained.

In all, Torit was his usual 'charming' self. For all the lack of the elder buzzard's bedside manner, and his gruff, harsh exterior, it was amazing what Torit could sometimes do. His Gifts were unmatched, and his skill as a healer unparalleled. Now, if he could make a better tasting medicinal brew, Zenti thought as he tried to choke down more of the foul substance that Torit had shoved in his paw.

"You missed a few pieces. I can still feel them. However, I want it all out now, so if you will bear with me and stitch a few more wounds, I am going to get the remaining metal out of me," Zenti said.

Before Torit could object, Zenti howled in pain as he used his Gift to rip the remaining shards of metal from his body. He promptly passed out from the act.

"Feeling better, pup," the old vulture asked? He was sitting in his oversized chair in the corner of the room. Zenti noticed Torit briefly glanced over the book that he was reading. Zenti wondered how long he had been unconscious.

"I think so," the wolf said, noting that the buzzard did not look back up to his answer.

"You should be after that damn fool stunt you just pulled. You have been out for over four hours. If I thought it would do you some good, I would smack you in the back of the head again," said the old bird as he continued to read.

"Some things never change. However, those pieces of Kredomis were embedded in those metal fibers," said Zenti. Torit just snorted and rolled his eyes, "I guess I should get up now."

"Well, pup, that's a good thing 'cause we have company. *She's* on her way to us this very moment," said Torit.

Zenti did not have to ask who *she* was; he had felt Mari's presence for about three hours now in his dreams. He stood, and his legs rebelled at the forced movement. Grabbing one of the roof posts, Zenti steadied himself. He paused and reflected a moment at the scope of the damage done to his body. Heavens and Hells how I hated artillery, thought Zenti. He hated Hayden even more for using it on his own species.

"Hells, I hate artillery," Zenti moaned. Passing by a full-length mirror, the silver-white wolf looked at his reflection. His back and the back of his legs were a patchwork of skin and fur. There were stitches everywhere, and he quit counting past thirty. He looked at the old bird who had stopped reading to watch the wolf's expression. Again, Zenti nodded his thanks as he started to put on a shirt, howling in pain as the cloth touched the wounds. Torit went back to reading.

"Told you pup, best be going around with not much more than that loincloth there. You're still bleedin' and pussin' and if you rip them wounds open, I ain't gonna stitch them up again," Torit said without looking up from his reading.

Zenti pulled the shirt off carefully and dropped it to the floor. Giving Torit a frustrated look, Zenti saw the elder buzzard was reading a book about something boring. The old bird sure put on a damn good show, but Zenti could tell Torit was deeply concerned. However, the white wolf was not precisely sure what Torit was more concerned with. Zenti wondered if the old buzzard worried about his health or that he was abusing his Gift too much. Torit was decidedly hard to read.

"Do you really think I want her to see me like this," Zenti asked? The seemingly inattentive buzzard burst out laughing.

"You're already mated to her. Who do you think you're going to impress by tearing open those wounds while trying to be modest," asked the old buzzard? Torit watched as Zenti slowly regained his composure and forced the pain away.

Zenti shook his head. Mated to her? She hated him still. But those were the bones cast in his life, thought Zenti. He must live with them. The white wolf walked to the door and opened it up. The sunlight blinded him for a moment, and it took Zenti a short time to gather his bearings. He saw a blurry, shifting shape walking toward him, but even in the shadowy blur, the silvery-white wolf knew that vixen form. His heart raced when he saw her clearly. In the distance, Zenti noticed the small train of carts and survivors of Mari's Faction. However, Zenti did not see any active soldiers and shook his head at the senseless losses.

He did not know if she had seen him, but the light was starting to bother his eyes. He tried to shield the sun, but the light continued to hurt them. Zenti was rapidly developing a headache, and the headache was starting to hurt everything else on his body. Closing the door, Zenti sat on the cot. Torit walked to the door, slapping the wolf on the back of the head as he passed by. Zenti looked up, and Torit gave him a disappointed look at having closed the door on Mari. Torit opened the door.

Mari raised her paw to knock and jumped as the door opened before she did. The old buzzard that stood there was not an unkind face, but he was a frighting sight, nonetheless. Torit was considered one of the two most powerful Gifted on Jayden and potentially the oldest.

"I came to speak to Zenti," Mari said in subdued tones. She knew that Zenti could not have been there more than a few days. However, Zenti had just closed the door on her.

"I know you have, vixen. Come on in, sit down and talk. The medicine has made Zenti's eyes overly sensitive to the light. The effects won't last long. I will be outside seeing what I can do for your patrons," said the old bird as he walked past her after giving the vixen a tight hug. Torit smiled and patted Mari on the head like she was still a kit. Mari blushed. She remembered that is what Torit did three years ago when they had last seen each other.

Mari entered the house as a warm wave of comfort ran across her body. That, too, was the same feeling as the last time she saw Torit. Turning back to the Shaman, she smiled as he was walking away. Drawing a shallow breath, Mari turned and entered the cozy home. Her first sight was of Zenti sitting on the cot, dressed in only a loincloth. She did not know what to say or do. There were just too many things to address. Mari, unsure where to being, just stood there as the door closed behind her. She had not shut it, so it must have been Torit.

"Come, Mari, sit down, have something cool to drink. Tell me of the evacuation and the survivors," said Zenti. The white wolf moved deliberately slow as he stood, reaching for the pitcher of water. He poured Mari a glass.

The vixen could tell Zenti was in obvious pain but never lost his air of command. He was professional, and Mari felt the distance between them grow. She did not want to cry but could feel the tears welling up in her eyes. Biting her lip, Mari's ears lay flat to the side of her head as she tried to fight away the burning droplets of tears. Zenti's words came out cold, uncaring and detached. However, Mari felt a slight undertone of sorrow to them. She did not want to be angry with him for his military demeanor. However, anger was a crutch that had served her well in the past. Mari Semineu's kit-like attitude crept out when she spoke.

"They were my friends, Zenti. Do not stand there and act smug because you do not care. They were all that mattered to me," Mari yelled at him. However, deep inside, she was not angry at Zenti. She was mad at *THEM*. However, Zenti was a convenient target of her anger, as he had always been.

Mari was furious that *THEY* had come to her camp. Moreover, she was incensed that her judgment had failed her in a critical moment. She should never have distrusted Zenti. Mari Semineu was furious at Hayden for not helping. The whole series of events was all so confusing and frustrating. Deep inside, Mari knew the only one responsible for the death of her patrons was herself. That wave of self-realization crashed down upon the vixen.

"It was all my fault," the vixen screamed. Tears ran down her cheeks, wetting the soft red fur. Mari turned to the door to leave. Once again, the conversation that needed to occur with Zenti was getting out of control. It was because the vixen was getting out of control. At least she saw it this time and had enough sense to walk away.

"You have it all wrong, Mari. The fact is I do care. I care very much, and it was not your fault. The fault lies with Hayden. He wanted to talk, wanted to convince you to join in his machinations. The foul cat has an insidious plan, and he wanted you to join his cause," Zenti said, slowly walking over to her. His motions were stiff as he tried to avoid overtaxing his damaged muscles. Mari stopped and looked up at Zenti.

The white wolf reached out with the back of his paw and rubbed the tears off her wet fur. He wanted to hug her so badly, but he refrained. Mari was not his anymore.

Handing Mari the glass, Zenti slowly walked over to the table and pointed to a map and some notes he had recovered from the dead invader's senior officer. Motioning Mari over, he showed them to her. The vixen composed herself while walking over to him. Zenti was not to be underestimated when it came to military secrets and tactics. She would never underestimate his ability to win. Battle after battle gave credence to his prowess. If he had something for her to see, she would review it. Only after she had reached the table did Mari realize Zenti had brought a measure of calm to her tormented spirit. He had not done it with his Gift but by wiping away her tears.

Mari looked at the map and notes, but she did not fully understand **THEIR** writing and symbols. However, the vixen could make some of the basics when there were Mitdonian words next to them. When she looked at Zenti with a quizzical expression, he began again.

"Hayden made a pact with the invaders to get all of the factions under his command," Zenti began. The white wolf pointed at a document. It was primarily in the invader's language, Mari noted. However, the vixen did not put together that Zenti might be able to comprehend more of the invader's language than he let on. He did know some as he practiced her father's teaching of 'know your enemy.' The white wolf continued.

"In a mock battle, Hayden would 'drive' the invaders out of key infrastructure regions," explained Zenti pointing to various locations on the map. Mari noted those were essential food and necessary commodities production hubs. However, none of them would aid the war effort. She looked up at Zenti, who just cocked his head knowingly.

"Hayden would then be seen as the greatest military leader in Mitd's history. The panther would be able to claim leadership of all military and civilian manufacturing.

In the name of safety, of course," said Zenti sarcastically as he pointed to a paw written note in Mitdonian. Mari read the brief but informative missive between Hayden and his daughter. However, Mari did not know which daughter, as Hayden had three. Mari touched the paw written, note as if making sure it was real. This was treason. She looked up at Zenti with eyes that questioned how he got this information. However, the silvery-white wolf did not acknowledge her inquisitive look before continuing.

"Then, in secret, Hayden would begin reforms that would work for the benefit of the invader's plans. Not too complicated a scheme when you think about it. However, I do not think that he expected you to be the force that you were. That is the reason for the artillery attack on your Faction camp. I may have been a target of opportunity. Though I do believe that Hayden planned the events to unfold the way they did," explained Zenti. Before Mari could comment, Zenti finished his thoughts.

"I am sorry that I could not fully warn you before the attack. I did not know if Jolet would meet with someone before returning. That is why my note to you was so vague. Your troops fought valiantly and with honor. Your patrons are well trained. I can truly see why they flock to your camp. Your father would be proud of your achievements," offered Zenti. Mari realized that his words sounded both apologetic and regretful that he had again failed her. However, her patrons died, and she had to withdraw from battle. How would her father be proud of that?

"What force was I?" Mari asked pitifully, "I was inadequate and powerless. I made the mistake of counting on Hayden's help. Why would he do this? Was it because I refused to be his mate? Is that what this is about? Is that why he did this? I knew Hayden did not like the fact that my heart belongs not to him but to someone else." Giving a sigh, she stepped closer to Zenti. The vixen's heart soared at having admitted her heart belonged to someone else. Mari knew there was only one male she loved. The vixen took another small step towards Zenti while examining the map and notes. If even tiny, moving closer to him took away a little of that ever-pressing distance between the two. Mari picked up the papers and continued before she lost her courage to be close to him. The emotional wounds she inflicted upon Zenti were many and profound.

"It *was* my fault, Zenti. It was my judgment that failed us, not yours. You have nothing to apologize for," Mari said, lowering her ears and head.

"No, you did not fail, Mari. Hayden, as seen by many Mitdonians, is a hero. He has won battle after battle. What they do not know is that those were 'empty' battles, and we have the proof now," Zenti said. He tapped on the papers in her paws, "That and those who survived this assault will bear witness to the fact that he did nothing to help, and he was right there with his soldiers just outside the camp. No, Mari, it has nothing to do with you not giving him your heart. It has everything to do with control and power. I think he knows that you are a Summoner, and

I know that invaders fear us greatly. Hayden thought he could control that power if you were on his side. On the other paw, if you were not on his side, then you and I were better off dead. Therefore, Hayden did not render aid, just as he planned all along," Zenti said. The white wolf staggered slightly when he shifted his weight. Quickly he steadied himself against a roof support post.

He looked down at Mari, and for the first time, the words 'my heart belongs to someone else' sank in. Zenti took a deep breath and accepted the fact that she no longer loved him. Stealing himself for the eventual letdown, he became distant again.

Reaching up, Mari ran her paw over the soft fur of his cheeks and muzzle, her eyes calmly watching his as he leaned against a post. She knew he was hurting. There were more knots of scars that she had not felt a few nights ago.

"I think Hayden knows that he can't kill you," Mari said softly, "I think the panther knew from the beginning that he couldn't, and he was counting on me to kill you." The vixen smiled apologetically, her claws tracing down his muzzle. Mari drew a deep breath and looked Zenti in the eyes.

"And when I did not kill you, I think Hayden realized something that I think I knew all along. No matter how angry I am at you, and no matter how long that anger lasts," Mari paused, not knowing if she dared to admit it.

She loved Zenti. The vixen knew that she did. If

she did not, their link would have been long since broken. But it was still there, still very much alive, and it connected them to each other. When she needed him, all she had to do was call him, and he was right there.

Zenti said nothing; he dared not. He had never stopped loving Mari. It was she that stopped loving him. For the first time in over a year, he opened his soul to her. Like a condemned male, he waited for the dagger to his heart.

"I love you," Mari whispered, "Even when I told you that I didn't, inside, I knew that I was lying."

She ran her paw down, tracing the contours of his neck, feeling every scar. Mari removed both physically and mentally a little more of the distance between them by taking another step closer.

"I never stopped, even though I wanted to so badly sometimes. Even though it hurt so much, I never really stopped," Mari's words trailed off, and the vixen dared to look up at Zenti.

He stood there, not saying a word as tears streamed down his fur. He reached out a paw to Mari, and it glowed red-hot.

"This is who I am. My heart has always been yours and always will be," Zenti said. "However, this is who Jayden needs me to be. Orra blessed me with the Gift and tasked me with what I need to be."

Mari looked at her paw again, and it was glowing

ice blue. Slowly, she reached and took his paw in hers. It was an odd sensation, but it was not unpleasant.

"I don't care what you have done. I don't care what you become. You are the same wolf to me. I have been so kit-like, and it has cost you so much," Mari replied. Reaching, she took his muzzle in her paws. The vixen ran her tongue up his muzzle, gathering tear after tear. It was a gesture of personal consolation, and she did not stop until his face was clean of the salty drops.

"If you two are done talking, we have a few wounded here that I would appreciate a little help with. I am also sure that Mari was followed by a scout. I think that the scout is half a day behind. I would suggest that you do something about your tracker," said Torit as he quietly stood in the doorway. Zenti understood Torit's knew his lands better than any other. The elder buzzard's Gift kept him in constant contact with anything for scores of miles. The old buzzard started to leave, then turned back to them when Zenti cleared his throat.

"Do I need to go to Adam and Lari," asked Zenti? They were friends of Torit's; therefore, they demanded protection.

"Naw, I got them covered," replied Torit, then continued. "Two things. First, put those damn rings back on your paws. There are three Gifted that I would call friends and do anything for. Two are standing in this room now. All of Mitd need to see the unity that you present. They love you, Mari, and they fear you, Zenti. Those are two of the most powerful emotions I know of. Second, there is a rabbit out here crapping his pants because he thinks Zenti will kill him. I think a little mercy is what these folks need to see right now. If he must die for his crimes, let it be later, in the dark of night, alone, out of the sight of the others," said the old buzzard.

Torit looked sternly at Zenti to make sure his point was not missed, then turned and walked away, leaving the two alone. Mari understood Torit's last statement. However, the vixen could not comprehend Torit's true meaning. She would not understand for many years to come.

Reaching into her pocket, Mari took out the small gold ring and wondered just how that old bird knew she had them? She would have to thank Rochet again for finding them from the wreckage of her tent. The vixen looked up at Zenti before slipping the gold ring onto her paw. Mari hoped to see in his eyes that he still wanted her. The vixen needed to know that Zenti was not just obeying Torit's command. Looking up into those onyx-colored eyes, Mari thought she found what she was looking for.

Pulling the second ring from the same pocket, she looked at the wide silver band. It was scared and battered, pitted with pockmark, which was not unlike Zenti's body.

"I never understood why you insisted that our rings not match in metals," she said quietly as she slid the ring onto his paw, and even there, she felt scar after scar. Taking her muzzle in his grasp, he looked her in the eyes.

"Because I knew that you were more precious than me. At least in my eyes, and the difference in our rings would reflect the difference that you and I are. You will always be more precious than I," Zenti whispered to her.

Leaning up, Mari nuzzled her muzzle against his, not daring to hug him. It was more because he was still seriously injured, and she knew that she would hurt him if she wrapped her arms around him.

"I suppose we should go," the vixen softly whispered.

"I suppose we should," the white wolf replied. Gingerly he moved over to the door and opened it for Mari.

The light again assaulting his eyes, squinting, slowly letting his vision adjust to the midday sun. Zenti stood in the doorway for a short while. His headache was returning, but he knew it would go away eventually.

Outside, there had been a lot of activity in setting up a temporary camp. The wounded were being cared for as best as possible. Preparations were being made to move on in a few days. Jolet, with ears folded, head bowed, and eyes lowered, slowly started to approach the vixen and the wolf. All eyes in the camp turned to the open door as the two stepped out. The entire group of survivors, adults, and pups alike, stopped and watch with anticipation what happened next.

Crossing the front yard, Zenti stepped up to the rabbit and leaned down to his ear, placing a paw on the back of his neck and head, pulling him close. Mothers covered the eyes of the young as others turned away.

"For now, rabbit, you have been given a second chance. You can thank Mari for sparing your life. I hope that you should never fall from her graces again," Zenti whispered in the rabbit's folded ears. There was no growl, no hatred, nor menacing vocal inflections, just soft, calm words.

Jolet nodded without saying a word. What was there to say? He was guilty, and by the grace of Miss Mari, he lived.

"We need to leave you for a while. There is a small matter to take care of. We will be back after I finish hunting. Do everything Torit says, and you might live to see another day," Zenti said to the rabbit. Zenti walked away from the shaking rabbit and up to the old buzzard.

"Old friend, I need to be able to travel and fight. What can you give me that will numb the pain without numbing my mind," asked Zenti.

The silvery-white wolf expected a sharp rebuke. Instead, the old buzzard grumbled something and shook his head in exasperation. Torit knew that to save Jayden, the wolf would come to further harm. Torit knew Zenti was still coming into his Gift.

It takes centuries for a Gifted to truly comprehend the Gift without risking Voidal Madness. Jayden did not have centuries. Most Gifted did not live that long anyway, and that was the beauty of the Gift. Age rendered the Gifted from becoming too powerful, with one exception. Thankfully that one exception was not accessible but to a very select few. Still, Zenti would need help, and the old buzzard dug into his robe-like overcoat and found a small vial of greenish liquid.

"This should do the trick," he said, peering at the vial over his cracked old beak-like nose.

Zenti took it with a word of thanks and a look of suspicion at the color. The silvery-white wolf thought it looked remarkably similar to the vile-tasting stuff he had been taking for the past two days. He looked at Torit suspiciously, but the elder male buzzard was already tending to the wounded.

Mari had hurried off to find Malyx. He was sitting in the wagon where she had left him. The young bear cub had not gotten out with the other young because Mari was not there. The moment he saw her, he ran on stubby legs, jumped out of the wagon, and launched himself into the vixen's arms. Malyx threw his arms around her neck and held tight. Mari smiled, petting his fur as she nuzzled his nose. She had seen her mother do it to Rini a hundred times before. Holding him and stroking the fur around his ears, Mari headed for Torit and Zenti.

Zenti drank the greenish liquid and almost puked. The white wolf swore he thought he saw the old buzzard laughing at him. However, he felt the concoction begin to work as he headed to the house to get dressed. Torit moved over to a wagon with an injured male badger and began examining his wounds.

****

"Torit," Mari said. The buzzard looked up from the wound he was dressing when Mari called out to him. The vixen was coming back with a young cub in her arms; he raised one furrowed brow at her.

"Did you need something, my dear," Torit asked curiously? The vixen smiled and whispered for the cub to look at the Shaman. Malyx obeyed and turned to watch the old buzzard with a fearful look in his eyes. Malyx quickly huddled against Mari like the scared cub that he was.

"This is Malyx," the vixen said softly, "his mother is dead, and I need someone to take care of him while I am gone." Mari gave the Shaman a wink. The old buzzard looked at the cub, then looked to Mari and smiled like a father might have.

"I would consider it the highest of honors," he said gently, taking the cub from the vixen and holding him up. The cub started to cry. Mari smiled sternly at Malyx and clicked her tongue at him.

"Now, why does such a brave little cub cry," Mari asked playfully? "Are you really that scared of this scraggly old buzzard?"

The cub laughed and reached for Mari again, and both she and the old Shaman laughed. However, Mari did not take the bear cub; instead, he nuzzled him.

"Come now, cub, I'm not going to hurt you. I am just going to watch you until Mari comes back," said Torit. Mari thought the old buzzards voice had grown softer when he spoke. The cub tipped his head, and the vixen leaned to kiss it.

"I will be back soon, but until then, stay here with Torit and do as he tells you to," stated Mari. Begrudgingly the cub nodded, and Mari found it in her heart to give him another soft kiss.

****

It took Zenti a long time, but he managed to get dressed. The liquid dulled his pain receptors. By the time Zenti stepped outside, Mari was over by Torit with a small bear cub discussing something.

Zenti watched Mari's patrons and admired the way they worked. They showed a dedication that many commanders would envy. Mari was much more of a leader of civilians than he was. He felt the cold of the ring on his paw, and it embraced him as he headed over to Mari.

****

Mari kissed Malyx again before turning to leave a few final instructions to her patrons. The vixen jumped when she found Zenti silently standing right behind her. Malyx gave a little giggle when Mari yipped in surprise.

"Your mother was right," was all Zenti said as he looked at the cub and then moved off to the crest of the hill.

Mari looked over her shoulder at Zenti, who had a light shirt and short pants on with a wide belt and a pouch. Looking closer, she could see that there were many spots on the back of the shirt that was a darker color and wondered if he was bleeding again.

Looking at Zenti's profile as he stared off to the east, the vixen became puzzled. The silvery-white wolf moved out across the fields following the wagon cart tracks. Mari watched as Zenti's features seemed to change. His expression grew dark, and she noticed her patrons began to whisper. Puzzled, she moved a little to better see more of his face. For her first time since their meeting in the clearing, Mari took in a small gasp in fear. Zenti, that frustrating wolf she reluctantly loved, seemed to be a distant shadow. Mari heard the whispers of her patrons. Mari realized at the edge of the field stood the monster of the many rumors. Zenti appeared as a ghastly apparition, a phantom of death.

Liri, an elderly otter who had tended Mari's troops, as well as the common folk, touched the vixen's paw. Mari jumped at the sudden interruption.

"Miss Mari, dear," began the old otter, "remember the tales they told of Zenti over the past year?"

Mari, still in shock at what she saw of Zenti, nodded her head yes. The vixen could hardly believe her eyes at Zenti's visage.

"That is the wolf that stands here now. Look at your patron's, Hun. They fear that wolf more than they fear **THEM.** I know you loved Zenti, no matter how angry with him you were. There was always a touch of love in your voice when you spoke of him. But what stands in front of you now is what we all need. Yes, your wolf is in there, crushed beneath the monster you now see," said the old otter.

Mari looked at the old otter perplexingly. Zenti moved towards the edge of the old buzzard's cleared patch. Taking her paw, the otter wrapped her free arm around the vixen.

"I have seen what Zenti does to foes, Mari, our kind, and **THEIRS.** He is what we need, but my dear, we also need you. You are the true leader between the two of you. However, do not chain him up with your shock at what he has become. Instead, be strong, even if it turns your stomach. Because dearie, if you are not strong, he will falter to shield you from what he is," said Liri.

"How can you know this of him with just a look?" asked Mari. When the elderly otter spoke, the answer shocked the vixen.

"I knew your father, kit, and I knew that wolf pup's grandmother. I cleaned him when he was little; I was there at your mating. I am sure you won't remember it, but I sewed his clothing for him the night before your mating. Zenti had ripped his pants, trying to make it back in time with that ring you wear. I know that he loves Jayden. I also know that he loves you more than all of Jayden. I know that he harbors nothing but anger and hate right now. I saw it twenty years ago when his parents were killed. I was one of the first to arrive at Zenti's desert home after the five-year-old lashed out at **THEM** with his newly discovered Gift. I have quietly followed him all his life. His mom and I were the best of friends. The night before you were mated, Zenti told me he feared he would never be the leader your father wanted him to be. I told him he was never meant to be Jayden's Saviour," explained the elder otter. Liri patted Mari's paw the way the elderly does, patronizing like, but her look was gravely stern. Mari looked perplexed.

"The citizens will look to you because you are the better leader. If they see fear from you, then they will unjustly fear. They will become more like those who follow and serve **THEM** or even that coward, Hayden. Mitdonians see Zenti as death. However, you are life to them. There cannot be one without the other. Show them you are not afraid to walk at his side. Fight with him, and even kill with him. And for all our sakes, kit, never show the fear I just saw. We need you as much as we need him," the old otter sternly said. Liri kissed Mari's muzzle and returned to help the others, leaving the vixen to her thoughts.

Mari looked at Zenti, watching him silently. Slowly, Mari summoned the commander within and grew used to the sight of the white wolf. Mari realized that he was a fearsome force to be reckoned with. However, not once in these thirteen months had she ever heard that he was cross with her. His rage seemed directed towards the invaders and to those who aided **THEM.** Mari looked at Zenti with the eyes of a mate.

The fearsome monster faded in the vixen's eyes, and the memory of a rain-soaked young white wolf with ivory claws reaching down into a hollowed-out stump filled her memories. Mari walked towards the clearing's edge with unwavering confidence, where Zenti stood surveying the distant forest.

"Well, don't you look handsome," Mari teased as she proudly walked up the embankment. The vixen gave the wolf a pretty smile as she looked up at him.

"I can still remember you on the day of our mating," Mari said wistfully as she reached to touch him. Her paw ran up the fur and scarred flesh of his arm. She stepped closer to him.

All eyes were on her. Mari could feel it, and every patron of her camp was watching her talk to the monster from their nightmares. Mari was the bravest in their eyes. However, it was a pity that those patrons could not see they had nothing left to fear from the monster. Granted, Mari had jumped and had shown fear. However, only Liri had seen that. What the patrons of Miss Mari Semineu's Faction saw was a fearless leader they could follow.

Mari went on looking at Zenti, and the more she did, the less of a monster she saw. This was her mate, even as frustratingly hard-headed as he was. Zenti was different. Yes, time and pain had hardened him much more so than she remembered. But even so, Mari could see he was still the same wolf.

"You were so handsome; I thought I might've died and gone to the stars," Mari giggled slightly and moved ever closer to Zenti. She wanted to reach him, to make him smile at her as he had before. The vixen wished Zenti would look at her as he had on the night of their mating. She wanted him to look at her with those same eyes, the same fire, the same hungry need, and the unconditional love that he had before. All Mari could see were the onyx eyes of a hunter focused on some unseen prey. The vixen knew ever so well that all those feelings were still inside Zenti. However, the kit-like vixen wanted to be able to see them.

His focus was on the invaders when Mari came up beside him. For a moment, the white wolf paid the vixen no attention. Zenti's mind on nothing but the invader's destruction. However, somewhere within her words, he heard her plea, and for a moment, the pain, hatred, and burning fire for destruction faded away. Looking down at her, Zenti licked Mari's nose as he had done on their mating day and smiled with all the hate gone.

Zenti leaned down to her ear and whispered, "Vixen, see your wolf, for he is only here for a heartbeat. The monster that rages within can only be chained so long, and right now, the fire of revenge burns within me like the noonday sun. Come hunt with me; see what I have become. See what our enemies fear, and do not rebuke me when I am done. For this is what I have become for our species-" Zenti's voice wavered, "-for you."

The vixen nodded briefly, her eyes never leaving the silvery-white wolf as he spoke. To show that she was not afraid to accept his request, Mari extended her paw for him to take.

"If what you do is for Jayden, and me, then there is no reason for me to rebuke you," Mari replied firmly. "I am not afraid, even if you are the rumored Monster of the Orra Prophecy. Especially not of someone who gives selflessly," Mari let her words trail off.

A hush had fallen over the crowd of patrons as they watched their beloved leader speak and offer herself to the monster that haunted them. Zenti, like on their mating day, simply kneeled and bowed his head for a moment. Then, like on their mating day, Zenti looked to the sky, bearing his throat to Mari. It was a primal act, once considered base in a civil society. However, the meaning of his action was not missed on those watching.

Mari smiled at the gesture. Instead of placing her teeth on Zenti's exposed throat, a sign of dominance, Mari leaned down and pressed her nose against his. The vixen folded her ears flat back, a visual symbol for all her patrons to see. Mari was asking Zenti's forgiveness.

"Please forgive me for the wrongs I have done to you," Mari whispered.

Beyond knowing that she needed him, Mari wanted him to see that she loved him, that she was willing to walk through the fires of Heavens and Hells if it meant to be at his side. Bringing her paws up to cup his face, she felt her touch chill, just a cool touch against his fur and flesh. For a moment longer, his eyes reflected the wolf that she remembered. They then returned to the darkness of the monster that all feared. However, in that brief moment, Mari again saw what she needed.

"We must hunt now," was all Zenti said as he stood.

The sun was slipping behind afternoon clouds, and a soft wind had picked up. There would be a spring storm arriving within the day. Zenti looked out over the camp without emotion, and with no fanfare, he turned and trotted off towards the distant woods.

Mari looked down at the ground and found within herself the steel that she needed to hunt with Summoner Zenti Semineu. She was not sure what to expect beyond the extremes she had already seen from him. Perhaps that is what truly made him what Jayden needed. Maybe it was his willingness to go to the extreme. It was time for her to find that willingness to go to the extreme as well. Without a word, Mari nodded to her patrons, and the vixen headed after the monster. In that first step, the kit Mari Semineu was, began the journey to oblivion.

Epilogue

Royal Oracle Rini Waxton stood on the balcony looking out over the Crown City. A soft glow of radiant sunlight caressed the young lioness's cream-colored golden fur as she waited for her paw servant to return. The warmth of the sun did little to subdue the chills running through the sixteen-year-old Oracle. Rini was five years past her Coming-of-Age date and still unmated. Though that was not unusual, having no suiters was uncommonly rare for someone as important as she was. However, there was a reason Royal Oracle Rini Waxton was not pursued by suiters. Her Gift was potent, and that made the lioness extremely emotionally unstable. Three days had passed since the Crown Champion's announcement, and the morning found her screaming from a nightmarish Gifted Vision.

Rini stood trembling on the balcony as her paw servant Ellsinore Brendma place a cup of hot-spiced tea in the lioness's paws. The tea was laced with strong liquor, and a particular herb the King's Royal Shaman prescribed for the young Oracle. The orange and white-furred manx guided Rini a step away from the edge and turned the trembling lioness to face her. Lifting the cup, Elli helped the shaken Oracle sip the tea until the cup was empty. When Oracle Rini Waxton was like this, the lioness was all but helpless.

Wrapping a shawl around her mistress's shoulders, Elli pulled a chair closer to the railing. The manx sat and then gently pulled her mistress into her lap. For two hours, Elli held the young lioness as the elixir worked its soothing magic. The shaking subsided, and the young lioness slipped off into a restful sleep.

However, the position was not comfortable for the young lioness. In the end, Elli helped Rini to her paw pads. Rini leaned on Elli as the manx took the lioness back into the Royal Observatory's anti-chamber. Other than Royal Astronomers, very few visited the Royal Observatory, making it a quiet hiding place. However, Rini was not hiding from the Crown but from herself. The Oracles Gift was as much a curse as it was a blessing. Today, the curse far outweighed the blessing.

Elli supported her mistress as she hobbled around the outside of the large room. Simultaneously, some of the younger astronomers helped clear the way of chairs and stacks of papers. The astronomers were not the Crowns Scientist's neatest, but as only a few of them were in the room, it made little difference. Rini's movement became more manageable. The need for support became less as the stiffness began to work itself out of the lioness's hip. The wounds received as a young kit never healed correctly, leaving Rini Waxton to struggle with even walking.

The manx guided Rini to the lioness's chambers. Elli undressed and then undressed her mistress. With years of practice, the manx helped the lioness into the bathtub. It was nicely warm, and it pleased the manx that Rini Waxton's servants were obedient. Elli had instructed the servants how her mistress like everything kept. The servants had performed their duties to the letter. In this case, they kept the bath perfectly warm. Making her mistress comfortable, Elli began to gently massage the lioness's wounded hip until the manx could feel the knots working their way out. Finishing Rini's daily mid-morning therapeutic bath, Elli helped her mistress dress for the day.

A knock came at the chamber's door. A messenger informed the room attendant that the Queen requested the Royal Oracles presence. Upon reporting to the manx, the room attendant returned to her station, leaving the two female felines alone in the dressing room. Elli dressed the young lioness in a loose-fitting skirt and blouse. When she finished dressing the lioness, Elli began brushing Rini's fur. Carefully the manx groomed the young lioness.

"Do you feel you can stomach any food, Mistress?" asked Elli, to which Rini shook her head. The lost, painful look on Oracle Rini Waxton's muzzle was heartbreaking. Elli smiled at the lioness before the young Oracle headed out of her dressing room. Exiting her chamber, Rini left the manx to finish drying herself and then to get dressed.

Elli made her way to the kitchen and fixed herself a light breakfast from the left-over morning food. The manx was tired from watching her mistress since the late hours of the night. A room guard had awaked her when Rini started screaming from the nightmares. That had been ten o'clock in the evening, and it was now almost noon. Sitting in the chair, Elli propped her paw pads up on the ottoman after setting her plate on the adjacent stand. Picking at her food, Elli was just about to doze off when a knock came at the door. Getting up, the manx opened it to find a messenger bearing a note.

Thanking him, she opened the note as the door closed and began to read. Looking back at her bed longingly, Elli tossed the paper into the fireplace and headed out of the room. Sighing in tired frustration, Ellsinore Brendma knew that this day was only going to get longer as she quietly walked down the hall to her designation.

****

Sitting in the Queen's private meeting room, Oracle Rini Waxton relaxed as the Queen sat across from her. The elder kangaroo was stirring her cup of tea slowly. The scowl on the Queen's muzzle plainly showed the disgust that they both were feeling.

"Tell me our Crown Champion did not die in the fiasco that occurred last night," stated the Queen before taking a sip. The middle-aged kangaroo had a pretty muzzle but was considerably overweight. However, she wore the weight like the royalty she was.

"No, my Queen, he did not," replied Rini.

"Have you seen where that bastard wolf has gone," asked the Queen?

"I have not seen him alone. I have only seen shadows of him with my sister, and I fear my Queen, that she has had her eyes opened," said the young Oracle as she accepted the second cup of tea from the Queen. "Please forgive me as I cannot see him clearly."

"Does your sister know everything," growled the kangaroo? The Queen's frustration was directed at the situation, not at the young lioness. Royal Oracle Rini Waxton was her pride and joy. The lioness was a pet project growing nicely into maturity.

"She does not, or at least I do not think she does. I still see confusion in her mind, a lingering doubt, and a lot of hatred," answered Rini. "Again, my Queen, where that cur wolf is concerned, I cannot see Visions clearly." Rini's voice was weak and filled with exhaustion. However, there was no trepidation in her tone. The Queen smiled warmly at the young lioness.

The Queen sat back in her chair, cup in paw, and pondered the situation as she slowly drank the warm tea. Hayden had failed in his plan to kill that bastard wolf or to bring Mari back into the fold. For a moment, the Queen wondered if someone had betrayed the panther within his ranks. She would have to start a little investigation into this disturbing matter. How difficult could it be to kill this one Summoner? How many would die at the white wolf's paws, she wondered? No, the kangaroo needed to formulate a strategy to stop this wild card before he destroyed the other plans that were carefully laid and implemented.

"Perhaps we should ask the His Majesty to discuss this matter with the Crown's Royal Assassin. Has he not shared the identity of the Left Paw with you? Why does the King continue to keep it such a secret" asked Rini?

"He tells me it is for my own protection, though I do not understand his intentions fully. I do understand that the Royal Assassin is not to be employed lightly. The rumors abound about him, yet no Oracle has been able to see who the Royal Assassins has ever been throughout the Crown's history. The Royal Assassin Corps is so afraid of retribution that they have refused to reveal their master's identity even upon the pain of death. However, I will ask His Majesty to speak with the Royal Assassin," replied the Queen. Taking a sip, the kangaroo pondered that conversation but for a moment, then continued.

"That consideration notwithstanding, I have a new task for you, my dear Royal Oracle. I need you to divine where your sister will be and then personally go collect her. Whatever her part is in the future of our species, I want her in our care and control," smiled the Queen as she offered another cup of tea, to which Rini refused.

"As you command Majesty," said Rini as she stood. The lioness curtsied before leaving the Queen's chamber. Oracle Rini Waxton did not miss the fact that the Queen had not stopped her from curtsying. The elder kangaroo knew how much it hurt the young lioness. 'Pain makes you stronger' was the kangaroo's mantra. Rini Waxton needed all the strength she could summon to deal with that cur white wolf.

****

Elli stood in the market, watching the crown patrons go about their daily business. It had been a frustrating two hours attempting to find the hiding place of the message left for her. The original note was exceptionally cryptic in nature, much more so than in the past. She purchased a sweet fruit tart and a cup of wine from the last café vendor she checked. According to the original cryptic note, this was possibly where the authentic message had been hidden. However, this was not the only place that fit the original notes description. The purchase helped to distract the vendor and create a plausible trail should anyone be watching her. It was Elli's third café. However, it was not unusual for her to visit multiple cafés when out in the market. Her mistress occasionally enjoyed the treats the ordinary Mitdonian ate. Though the Crown chefs were masters at their trade, something was missing in the food preparation. It was something that reminded the young lioness of her humble origins. Elli was grateful that her mistress allowed her so much time to spend away from the castle. Elli was the daughter of a teacher and an accountant. Neither of them was well paid. The income earned in service to the Crown helped her family survive.

Strolling in the marketplace, the manx looked at the new wares, including some gorgeous dresses. All the manx's personal clothing was utilitarian. Not one of the manx's gowns was simply for pleasure. Elli longed for a lovely dress, much like that of the court females. However, those dresses were exceedingly expensive. Though the manx was well cared for, all her Breng went home to help her poor family survive. The war had caused them much hardship.

Elli strolled into the gardens near the marketplace cafe. This was one of her favorite spots to escape. Finishing her treats, Elli lifted the wine cup to drink. The oversized cups used by that particular café held a considerable volume of liquid. However, it was not the volume of fluid that the cups were ultimately used for. The bottoms were false, though Elli was sure the café owner was completely unaware of that fact.

Elli wiped the cup's bottom after acting as if she had been careless and spilled a little of the warm content. However, that too was a ruse. The cloth the manx used had a particular chemical that caused the false bottom to open. Elli palmed the folded note before setting the cup on the table. With practiced slight of paw, Elli 'produced' the message from within a skirt pocket. She began to read as she sipped her spiced tea and rested in the tranquil gardens. The mid-day sun felt warm on her fur, soaking deep into her tired body. Elli was enjoying a moment of tranquility.

It has come to the Crown's attention that your mistress is being misled and used for purposes that she is not aware of. This is most disturbing as she is considered one of the Crown's greatest assets. A time will come when she will be pushed to the breaking point, and the Crown cannot allow that to happen to someone so vital to our species' survival.

You have served the Crown faithfully as well as caring for your mistress with loving devotion. Your time of service will end in two months as you have reached the term of your contract. The Crown has decided to renegotiate that contract but rest assured that your family will be well compensated for your service.

The Crown considers your original contract fulfilled. All you were promised shall be paid in full upon your contract termination date. However, the amount will not be the original as promised. To reflect the extent of your devotion and service, the amount will now be ten-fold.

However, the Crown now asks you to carefully consider this new offer over the next two months, as the negative ramifications of failure are severe. The Crown asks you to continue to serve and now protect our Royal Oracle's sanity. This will not be an easy task, but the Crown has faith in your abilities to care for our treasured Oracle.

As before, the Crown does not wish to deceive you on the penalties for failing to perform this task, so weigh your choice carefully, as the punishment is extreme. The

Crowns Royal Assassin is occupied. It would be ashamed to interrupt that occupation simply to administer that punishment should our Royal Oracle come to any harm.

In just compensation, the Crown offers you this.

Your family will receive the north Isle Kingdom of Fouche, and your parents will be granted the title of Duke and Duchess. They will receive all the rank, benefits, aid, and respect due to such nobility and lands.

The cup trembled in Elli's paws as she slowly sat it down. This was an incredible offer until she remembered who the Crown's Royal Assassin was. Elli now understood that the slip of the King's tongue had not been a slip at all in one of their private conversations a short month ago. The King was preparing her for this moment by telling her a secret so great that it would cost her family everything.

"Oh, Heavens and Hells, what am I about to get into," whispered Ellsinore Brendma?

Continued in:

The Chronicles of Jayden Volume II

Monster and Saviour

A Chronicler of Deeds Novel

Chapter Epilogue

Acknowledgments

About the Author

"I am a gray muzzle, but I refuse to grow old or up! Neither should you!"

Born in Louisiana in 1962, Wolf has been a furry as long as his fuzzy mind can recall. Bugs Bunny was one of his favorite cartoon characters growing up as he knew no limits. A long-time storyteller of role-playing games, Wolf has been playing all forms of games since the mid-'70s. Later, he turned that into live-action storytelling at conventions. In April of 2009, Wolf responded to Courtney Grigg's ad on a popular furry art forum for a story collaboration. For the next year, he and his collaborator wrote the first 300 pages. Real-life interrupted their collaborative writing, and Wolf continued alone. Over the next decade, through the darkest period in Wolf's life, he finished writing the Chronicle of Jayden. (Read Land of the Sleaze and Home of the Slave for all the truth-fill facts. It is available at Amazon) (Land of the Sleaze and Home of the Slave: Government Criminals in the American System of Justice - Kindle edition by Wolf. Professional & Technical Kindle eBooks @ Amazon.com. https://www.amazon.com/dp/B08QTZCRS9)

What began as 300 pages is now a Dekalogy. Ten books, filled with the most beautiful story ever told, now span well over 2.5 million words. Wolf was already writing what is now book four (Two Hearts) before he and

Courtney started The Gifted collaboration. Book four played heavily in the development of the first three books involving the story of Jayden. (Which were to be a later release.)

The Chronicles of Jayden are part of a broader family of books known as The Chronicler of Deeds Novels. Book One of The Brotherhood Chronicles is complete. However, that series is on hold until the remaining Chronicles of Jayden are published.

Wolf temporarily lives in Montana now and continues to expose the corruption in the justice system. However, all of the Chronicler of Deeds Novels' manuscripts are in safekeeping to be published should life interrupt Wolf's writing again.

About the Collaborator

Courtney Grigg is an aspiring author and comic artist from the State of Michigan. The Chronicles of Jayden Volume I, The Gifted, is her first published work as a collaborator. She hopes to have many more. She lives with her sister and their pets. She spends her time exploring her numerous hobbies that inspire much of her work.

About the Awesome Artists

Cover Art:

Hello! My name is Evgenia, and I am from Russia. I draw different things, plots, and characters. Still, most of all, I like to illustrate military and post-apocalyptic themes. You can always find me under the nickname Conofid or Kanadakano on various resources!

But the more famous of them are Furaffinity gallery and my public venue on the Russian social network VK.

https://www.furaffinity.net/user/kanadakano/

https://vk.com/arwigin

Chapter 6 Art: (Page 356 Print Copy)

Hello! I'm Dinara, and I live in Russia. My endless love is mysterious stories and cats.

You can find me as purrofa or sgrech.

https://vk.com/purrofa1

https://www.furaffinity.net/user/sgrech/

Printed in Great Britain
by Amazon

78142657R00345